THE FLAWED GOOD MAN

Sanskriti Singh

Leadstart
INKSTATE

ISBN 978-93-90463-37-4

First published in India 2020 by Inkstate Books
An imprint of Leadstart Publishing Pvt Ltd

Sales Office:
Unit No.25/26, Building No.A/1,
Near Wadala RTO,
Wadala (East), Mumbai – 400037 India
Phone: +91 969933000
Email: info@leadstartcorp.com
www.leadstartcorp.com

Disclaimer: The views expressed in this book are those of the Author and do not pertain to be held by the Publisher.

Editor: Vaibhav Pathare
Cover: R. Maharajan
Layouts: Victor Patali

To Shiva

नमः शिवाय च शिवतराय च।।

I bow to Shiva, the one who accepts everyone and everything
in the universe.

ABOUT THE AUTHOR

SANSKRITI SINGH is a self-published author of a book called "Ram's Sister; True Scion of Raghu" and an avid reader. She is eighteen and has grown up reading and listening to the stories of Smrities, Shruties, Itihas, and Shastras. She writes articles in the regional daily "The Shillong Times". she has won many national level essay writing competitions and her work has been admired by prominent mythologists of India. You can find some of her articles on Google with titles like "Kshatriya Princess" "History not Myth" "Reading the Dictators Mind" "Learn To Live Like A Child" and many more. She is deeply interested in the subjects that can be explained not only through spirituality but also by logic and sciences, mythology being one of the subjects that can have logical and spiritual explanations if looked for with dedication and is her favourite.

She is a lover of art, mythology, and history. You can connect to with her through social media platforms like Instagram (im_sanskritisingh) or through twitter(@Sanskriti2390) or go to her page which is in her name i.e. Sanskriti Singh.

ACKNOWLEDGMENT

First, I would like to show my gratitude to the protagonist of this book and that is Karna. The man who is an epitome of sacrifice and grace, writing about his struggles, has given me the treasure of a lifetime.

I take this opportunity to thank Maa Shakti, who gave me the strength to understand the complex character of Karna. And I can never be less grateful to India, the country that has such powerful stories to tell. Everything here is beautiful that I thank my stars to have been born in this country.

I thank my mother Mrs. Mamta Kumari Singh who is my spine always. Every time I am doubtful about my interpretations of the Vedas. And my father Dr Sanjeev Kumar Singh for all the technical help, which I constantly need as I am not at all good with computers.

I would also like to thank Professor Sudhanshu Kumar Mishraji (retd.) whom I have bothered every time I was stuck while doing my research. I had tons of questions while reading the epics, and he was always there to answer. I cannot be less thankful to all those people in my life who have been a support throughout. My family, friends, and teachers, everyone made this journey beautiful.

I thank my editor, for guiding me and helping me in making my writing better and also suffering my draft manuscript with so much patience. The book would never look the same without the endless effort put into it while editing the work.

To my publisher, for showing confidence in me by publishing my book and accepting my script. It must have been difficult to believe in an eighteen year old with mythology and I am so thankful that they believed in me and took up my work. It would not be possible to bring Karna to the world without the Leadstart team.

To Vedavyasa, the man behind the greatest epic of all times.

And last but not least, thank you to all the readers who have always given their amazing responses to my articles and my essays. Without the readers, the writer is nothing and I am grateful I had such readers who accepted my ideas.

Every book had a reason to be written. And this book has a very strong one, which I may not be able to tell you, but I want to say this that Karna is a beautiful character, and is that not enough to make it worth reading and writing? Karna was a very emotional character; strong and weak both. The emotional turmoil he went through to his passionate love for Dharma make up the most formidable warrior and a very sensitive man worth admiring, and I thank all the people who supported me while sketching the emotional side of Karna. Ideas always play a very important role when a book is written.

Karna is a complex character and I want to thank all those people who had said that "You cannot do it." Thanks to them, they made me do this. Every time I sat down with this book, I ended up crying, wondering, "Can it be any more difficult for someone?" Karna's character is worth all the tears shed while writing about his life, and such is the momentum of his character that no one can hate this man.

CONTENTS

PROLOGUE

The fragrance!

The first rain of the season brought about the sweet fragrance in the air. The sweet-smelling flowers diffused their smell in the surrounding. The soil was moist, and it felt soft. The sun had risen in the eastern horizon, long back but looked dull. The small drops of rainwater that rested upon the leaves sparkled a few moments ago in the blazing sun, but now were left limp and still. The sun was gone. The day looked grey, and the sun peeped from behind the clouds. The lustre and grandeur were all lost. The river flowed swiftly, making its way and breaking the silence of the quiet morning. It was melancholy that enveloped the bank of the flowing river. The breeze cool and soft provided peace in the ever-growing heat of the surrounding.

A man at a distance struggled to stand straight with no support. He could barely walk. He dragged himself towards his chariot. With all the fragrance infused around him, he could get a pungent smell.

Blood!

It was an unmistakable smell as the blood was flowing from his torso; his chest ripped out of his skin, the layer beneath his skin was exposed and painfully numb. Blood dripping from his earlobes, his naked chest covered with blood, and a nerve wreaking pain left him shivering. The soft muslin, his white dhoti was slowly turning red soaking all the blood that slowly moved down his body. Tall and well built, a man with broad shoulders was right there in a state of immense pain.

"Water, water, wat..."

He could utter no more! His words sunk before it could escape his lips. He shivered because of the pain. This pain was ripping out all the energy that he could gather to move forward. He desperately needed water!

He kept walking back to his chariot. Slowly, trying to maintain his balance, he took the help of the Ashoka tree within reach.

It was becoming difficult now.

Fall!

He fell on his knees, trying to remain steady while resting his weight on his knees. His head burrowed down. Eyes full of water, he looked at the soil. With one finger, he digs out the ground, which quickly came out. He felt-light headed, unable to think of his next move. After staring at it for a long time, his vision was blurred, unable to see anything around him. He collapsed, falling on the ground, unconscious and murmuring the words "Water..." Darkness took over him.

1   Kunti calls Suryadev

The dawn broke several colours dripping from the movement of the rising sun in the sky. They changed slowly. Breaking the darkness and making it look red. As the sun moved up further up the horizon, the redness became prominent. The clouds that drifted in the sky even appeared red. Kunti stood on the bank of the river that flowed in the beautiful city of Kuntibhoj; her foster father. In her hand, she held a Kalash full of holy water.

Along with her surrounding, her skin glowed in the colour of the rising sun. Her hair looked various shades lighter, almost brown. She stepped in the moving water of the river; her steps disturbed the reflection of the sun, mountains, and trees that reflected the surface like a painting. The colour's penetrated her soul. She began her puja.

Slowly holding the Kalash high to the level of her forehead and offering the water. Suddenly an idea triggered in her sixteen-year-old brain, still childlike and immature. It was some time back that rishi Durvasa had visited the palace of King Kuntibhoj, her father. The awe-inspiring Maharishi stayed for about a year. During this stay, Kunti attended to the sage's requirements. Without thinking of her comfort, she served him each day. He would vanish suddenly and return to the palace at odd hours. The world knew well that the sage had a considerable entourage of disciples. They travelled along with him. The other issue was to take responsibility for initializing all the yajnas he conducted while he was in his sessions of worshipping his aradhya. Yajnas needed to undertake as per traditional methods, and he was obsessed with the customs revolving around the pujas. It was somewhat of a sensitive issue to tackle as Durvasa was not an easy man. They had to remember that one could not annoy the temperamental Durvasa. He was well known for how he cursed people who annoyed him. The slightest provocation he was known for giving pronouncing curses. The next problem was that he never gave notice of his movement in and out of Kuntibhoj's palace. Much to his astonishment, he always found Kunti rising to these occasions and ready to serve him with a happy face. At all odd times, he found her happily serving him. He then slowly began testing Kunti to see if he could encounter even one flaw in her service. But all into vain. There was not one time that Kunti would give him a chance to complain about the arrangements of yajnas or any of his necessities; the quality of her service always left him in awe. Kunti's selfless service and the Maharishi's antics and tests continued, till he finally decided to go after a year's stay at the palace.

Before his departure, Durvasa sent for Kuntibhoj and addressed him saying: "Rajan I have been here for almost a year now and it is time for me to leave and move on, and thus I summoned you today". Hearing these words, the King turned pale. He feared that some lapse in hospitality had annoyed the finicky sage. Even the thought of any such breach in service made him tense. He walked to the sage, trembling in fear. The Rishi smiled and consoled him. He then sent for Kunti. He called the princess and asked her to sit before him. Kunti glanced towards her father, who stood nearby with a happy face. The Rishi spoke "In these many years, I have never been so satisfied and happy with anyone's service. You have served me with a lot of dedication. Today I grant you a boon, ask for anything you want."

"I feel privileged that I could attain the chance to serve you. I do not need any boon Rishi Var," Kunti said to the sage.

The Rishi was stunned! He was impressed by her selflessness. Her patience, love, care, and thoughtful nature made him adamant about giving her the boon. Without asking her about her choice, which he was sure she would not choose, he granted her the boon of begetting a son from any God she wants.

Standing there, Kunti thought about the boon Durvasa Rishi had granted her. Every word was embedded in her mind. "When you chant the mantra, whichever god you will call will give you a child." Really? Was it even real?

Kunti, being a curious person, kept questioning her father about the sage's boon to which her father had simply replied "Kunti! You must not question the great sage. He has performed Tapasya all his life and possesses great powers. They might sometimes be larger than life, but they are true. When the time comes, you will yourself realize how true his words are?"

Kunti was then a child. She failed to understand what her curiosity would cause. She extracted out the doubts from her mind and kept aside the puja thali. She walked back to the riverbank. Standing there she began thinking of some God she could call. Which god would she call using the mantra? She looked around her. Her surrounding was full of greenery. The flowing water added up to the beauty of the forest: tall deodar trees, bare rocks, and a clear sky. By then the sun risen, eradicating other colours and filling it with its brightness.

The birds filled the river bank with its beautiful chirps, but even amidst all the noise that the animals and birds created in the region, there was an unusual silence that enveloped the forest. That silence made Kunti uneasy suddenly. Was this right? Was it wise to do so? Her beautiful face was laced with a fear that was unknown to her.

Kunti looked up! Sharp and intense rays of the sun glared towards her. Harsh rays that instantly made her close her eyes. She again got an idea.

"Why not call Surya dev himself? Yes, I should call him." thought Kunti.

She again began with the small vandana that she would usually say before she began her prayer every morning. Her whisper was soft enough to blend with the soft chirping of the birds.

Om Suryay Namah! Om bhanve namah! Om Khagay Namah!

She went on speaking her mantra. She did, with all her dedication and sincerity. Soft, cool, and calm, she ended the mantra. Kunti's hands were in a namaste in salutation, and eyes closed in prayer. Now her lips went still. She remained in that position for some time, and then slowly opened her eyes.

What she saw was a clear blue sky and the same green trees along with the scenery around. She had chanted the mantra, but there was no one to be seen in that part of the city, she stood alone. There was no one around! She giggled and spoke, "I knew this could never happen. How could a mantra even attain a child to a person that too from a God? Why would God even come? I am no yogini."

She turned around to leave. Walked a few steps, picked up her aarti thal which she had kept there some time back. She was nearly on her way to leave her usual place for puja when someone called her name. She paused; eyes wide open in shock and dismay. She slowly gathered her courage and turned around to see who was there as she saw him there before her in his entire splendour. Broad shoulders, beautiful eyes, his crown complementing his position of the life-giver, his attire yellow, and the beautiful lotus flowers adorning his neck, Surya stood before her. She had no words to describe how beautiful the sight was.

Blunder! She thought. Guilt took over her; she had made a significant mistake by calling Surya. She looked towards him in despair. Surya glanced towards Kunti and began, "You have called me with the help of the mantra that rishi Durvasa had granted you! Do you know what the sign significance of this mantra is? Do you know what have you done to yourself, Kunti?" Kunti now made a feeble attempt to ward off this ill fate. She looked at Surya and spoke in a soft tone, nearly ready to break down again.

"Yes! I only called you to test the mantra lord. Please go back, lord. Please forgive me for doing so! Please do!" Kunti pleaded to Surya.

"I am bound, Kunti! I cannot leave from here before providing you with the boon you are bound to attain! You have chanted the mantra. And you remember that the effect of the mantra you have chanted is irreversible. "

The moment she realized what was to happen next, a feeling of anxiety struck her. Kunti gasped for air. She had no way that she could use to undo her mistakes. The words to Surya echoed in her ears. She had brought this upon herself. She could suddenly understand what people meant when they said: "sometimes curiosity kills". What could she do now? There was no way to undo this whole situation.

With tears in her eyes, she looked again towards Surya. He could sense the gloom in her eyes. She had worshipped him since she was a child. Every morning, without fail, she had performed her puja. How he wished she did not chant the mantra. He gave out a sigh. Closed his eyes, mumbled few words and the river water shone with the light that spread around. The light shone for some time and vanished away, leaving no trace of Surya. He left, and the silence descended back. The little birds that were singing in the silence were quiet now, making the silence even more dreadful. Kunti wanted to hear someone speak, but it seemed like even the wind was not ready to blow around making noise that could give him a little solace.

Kunti spoke nothing. Sitting on a rock flat and straight, she stared into nothingness. Dressed in blue silk, she sat there. Kunti was beautiful. The daughter of King Prithu was named Pritha. Her father then gave her in adoption to his childless friend Kuntibhoj, after which she was named

Kunti. She was a woman who had admired knowledge. Leaving her home, she would spend long hours reading the endless books stacked in the library of the beautiful palace. Large brown eyes, moderately full lips, a sharp and small nose, and her jet black curly hair that reached till her waist complimented her long face. She was fair and tall.

Kunti went back to the palace. Suddenly, that day, her father discovered a sudden change in her behaviour. That night she did not talk to anyone. Remaining confined to her room, she kept to herself. When a dasi went in, she felt a new fragrance filling the room. It was sweet and enchanting. She tried to recognize it but could not. She looked towards Kunti; she looked beautiful! Bashfully beautiful! She never looked that beautiful. Her beauty was more elaborate and more graceful. She was seated on the couch in her room. Eyes full of tears; she kept staring out of the window towards the river. It was as though that one day had changed the bubbly and chirpy princess of Kuntibhoj. The dasi tried to persuade her to have food, but she asked her to leave. As days passed by, she gradually became an introvert and kept quiet. She stopped talking to her friends, her dasi's, her father as well. Kuntibhoj was tensed; his daughter remained confined to her room, spending her time alone. People at the palace saw her less frequently, and after few days, she even stopped going out of her room.

One day Kuntibhoj walked down to her room with a motive to talk to his daughter. He found her worshipping the idol of Narayan. As he interrupted her, she stood up and welcomed him in. He looked at her daughter, the playfulness in her eyes had ended, she looked more mature, and her beauty extended. He tried beating around the bush for some time, but realized that he would never extract the truth that way. Kunti understood what her father was trying to do, and hence she spoke in her usual manner "Father I am fine! I am. You do not require to be so tense about me. I do not talk much these days; that is what worries you? The reason for this is: as I served Maharishi, I have come up to a conclusion that it is essential to know oneself from within. That is possible only through meditation. Hence I would like to continue this penance for some time. I would not be able to meet you much during this period. Please do not feel apprehensive about me. Priyamvada is there to look after me. If needed, I will send word through her."

Listening to her, Kuntibhoj felt assured. He was now sure that his daughter was fine. He assured her that no one including him would disturb her during this period of penance. He left, he sent for Priyamvada and asked her to take good care of her. Priyamvada was surprised, as Kunti had been avoiding her as well. Kuntibhoj left for his quarters. Kunti, on the other hand, was blaming herself for having lied to her father. She was awkwardly silent; her inner self was going through a period of turmoil. She had no other option other than to lie in the prevailing circumstances. She had thought a lot about it and derived the conclusion that only Priyamvada could help her through this, and it was essential to take her in confidence. Priyamvada had served her since childhood; hence a friendship developed between them, which would be beneficial for Kunti now that she was in trouble. She felt incredibly selfish, but this was what the need of the hour was. She could do nothing else. Kunti invited Priyamvada to sit near her, which she accepted happily. She sat there, and after a moment, Kunti began narrating all that had happened. Priyamvada, being a keen observer, could notice the fear in Kunti's eyes. She was scared that everyone would find out about her little secret, which was not little at all.

On hearing Kunti's words, Priyamvada burst into uncontrolled sobbing. She could not accept how Kunti's childish mistake had resulted in such a dramatic change in events. She was crestfallen. Priyamvada had served Kunti to the best of her ability. She was even more distressed thinking Kunti was unable to believe in her friendship and confine the biggest secret of her life. Kunti hugged her and held her there for some time. She consoled her and said, "Priyamvada I should have believed you when you advised me not to doubt the words of the sages. What baffled me was that even the gods were susceptible to the rishis mantra; they could not reverse it either! The strange assertion cried out to my doubting mind. I truly felt I needed to test and validate the mantra. Such a fool, I was Priyamvada! I guess Maharishi's words were true. Whatever is happening today is all compiled by destiny that I can never change."

"I am paying a heavy price for my doubts, and this will continue until I live. I feel ashamed that I committed this sin, today I shudder to think of the future and the implications of destiny for my family and myself.

Kunti rolled on the bed in a fit of sobbing. She could not handle facing the past and also the present at that moment. "Priyamvada I do not know of anything right now other than this one fact that we require tackling this problem and do it without any loss of time."

Kunti got up saying this. Priyamvada knew now that Kunti had already devised the plan of what she would do. "Listen carefully! I do not know which divine power guided me when I lied to my father about the penance. But now whatever we do has to be done around this one lie of mine. My lie about the penance would assure both of us with complete privacy. No interference. But I do not know what do we do of the upcoming childbirth? How do we hide it from the world?"

Priyamvada whispered, "Don't worry princess, and I know what to do with that and how to tackle that situation."

Months passed by as she spent all her time alone in her chambers. She only had Priyamvada who visited her during this period. That morning Priyamvada came to Kunti and spoke to her about leaving the palace for some time. She had to go to a far-off village to get a midwife who could deliver the child safely. The midwife had to come from a very far away town where there could be no rumours or any silly talks. Nobody noticed her absence as it was still early in the morning when she left. Kunti spent a tense day in her room. Priyamvada came back early, as promised. She came back with a woman of about forty to forty-five years. After preliminary introductions, the two women left, and Kunti was alone again. Kunti in recent days woke up and slept without a particular timing. It changed from time to time. She would even fall asleep suddenly as she sat down to read books she had once read, staying awake all day and night.

For the next one and a half months, she saw the midwife a couple of times, but not frequently. And Priyamvada was always there. Even if there was a slight movement in the room she would come in and ask Kunti of her wellbeing, this continued day and night till one day early in the morning when the sun was not yet up in the sky which lay a very light colour of blue, Kunti developed labour pains. Priyamvada managed everything with clockwork precision. Kunti finally gave birth to a radiantly beautiful male baby almost coinciding with the sunrise outside. The midwife was of great help. She assisted Kunti during labour, constantly rubbing her head and whispering softly the mantras of the vedas. Priyamvada ran errands for the midwife which included bringing the hot water, soft mulmuls and other such requirements. They all tried their best to do everything silently and without causing much commotion in the corridors. After hours of labour the child was born happy, healthy, beautiful, and sweet. Kunti looked out of the window, and she felt as though the sun had come up today, thrilled to welcome the beautiful child.

❊ ❊ ❊

2 Child and Fate

That morning, the surrounding was full of illustrious light of the sun. It gave an impression as though the birth of his child had made him shine brighter with happiness. A similar glow illuminated the beautiful face of the princess, the mother of the beautiful child. The three women in the room forgot that the event that had taken place in that room was something that needed to remain a secret. It was fraught with basically bizarre repercussions for Kunti and her child. Kunti's eyes were full of tears. Tears of happiness kept flowing down her blazing red cheeks, caused possibly due to the exhaustion of labour she had just gone through. Her new born lay next to her, in deep slumber. Even in sleep, he was exceptionally calm. He would sometimes smile, even while asleep. Those were reflex smiles that new born usually gives. Kunti's gaze directed toward her son. The little small thing slept peacefully alongside his mother.

Never have I ever seen a creature so beautiful and calm before!

The child was delicate and fair and frail. His body was languid as a newly planted sapling. Everything about him looked wonderfully dainty and soft — his movements were faded, his hair curly, his eyes small but beautiful, covered with a soft muslin cloth around his miniature form. His chest shone as the sun rays fell upon it. The armour he was born with was the reason. It clung to his skin; it was a part of him. It was a protective shield provided to him by Surya. His fist clenched because of the palmar grasp reflex. Usually, the cause is an immature neurological system or a first remnant for holding on to their mothers. He lay on his back most carefully, the safest way for a new born to sleep. It looked as though the child gained assurance by just curling up his small fists. Out of nowhere, he would open his eyes, alert and then again close them falling into a deep slumber. Those eyes were the most striking, sharp, small, and pacified—the most beautiful part of his face just like his mother. Kunti's beauty enhanced even more than before. She radiated a goddess-like shine. Having her hair open, she looked wonderful as though the girl had suddenly become a woman.

Kunti was marvelling over her beautiful son. The sun rays that had illuminated the room were slowly leaving it. Noon was approaching. Priyamvada first regained her composure. She sought Kunti's permission to take away the midwife. Kunti hardly heard what Priyamvada spoke, the only thought that surrounded her was that of her child. Considering the intensity of Kunti's affection for her son, it was more important to get rid of the midwife before bringing Kunti back to reality.

She left Kunti with the child, while the midwife accompanied her. Kunti now alone with her son happily cuddled her child, carrying him, she kept basking in the beauty of the newly found bliss. The bliss of becoming a mother.

Mother!

She was now a mother. A mother of a celestial child. The son of Surya. But she was not married. She was back to reality again. It was staring right into her face. Raw and rotten truth! She did not want to face it. No! She did not. Kunti was in a dilemma. What would she do? The child, where would he go? How would she leave him, the one whom she had given birth? Who brought her happiness? Who made her a mother? Kunti held her son close to her bosom, shedding silent tears. The young boy cringed. Kunti was distracted by all her thoughts. His need drifted her away from the approaching situation; she was living in the present. Her son was her present.

Priyamvada had a perfect plan of how would she get rid of the midwife. In the first place, she knew she had to pay off the woman thoroughly enough to keep her mouth shut. She walked the midwife to her room where a generous amount of gold, jewels, and many other items kept around. The midwife's eyes glittered. She went up to the edge of the bed and touched the gold coins held in various small pouches.

"5000 gold coins! That's something I can never think. It is wonderful." the midwife spoke with glee.

"This is the price of keeping your mouth shut. Never gossip about anything that happened here. Remember; you came here to serve the royal family in the absence of the head maid, happy with your service you received these rewards. No gossip should escape your mouth" Priyamvada strictly cautioned the midwife.

The glow on her face made it clear that she would not utter a word before anyone. Priyamvada then asked her to get ready to leave; she had to pack everything given and leave for her village hastily. Priyamvada went to get Kunti's permission to leave the palace. The midwife was to remain in the confines of her room until Priyamvada sent for her.

Priyamvada hurried towards the room of the princess. Kunti was engrossed with her son as she had been when Priyamvada had left the room. She could see that Kunti had drifted away from reality. She was in her world of happiness. Whoever would look at her during those hours would witness her excitement. The son had filled the heart of the princess with joy. The women who had barely smiled during her nine months of pregnancy now were fussing over her child.

Kunti's happiness ripped Priyamvada of her courage. She did not want to break her heart, at least not then. She had to face reality how Priyamvada wished that the son was Kunti's firstborn after her marriage. Such a beautiful child was the boy; he threw no tantrums. Lovely and calm was what he was. Priyamvada silently observed the mother and son; she spoke nothing to Kunti. She just couldn't. She left the two together. She knew he deserved her love; every child has the right to attain that love. She let Kunti shower all her affection over her son. The reality was to strike her later.

Priyamvada left the room without speaking a word she called for the midwife. The night was silent. The two walked on the lonely path which was full of the hustle and bustle during the day but the nights were equally silent. Every home belonging to the commoners of the city was quiet. Sleep had consumed all; the only voice heard around was that of the crickets and some few insects. The scent of the night queen filled the night. No one needed to see them going.

The two women passed the streak which was the home of the citizens of the Kunti kingdom. When they arrived at the riverbank, the midwife noticed a boat, empty, left there for use. But who would row the boat? She surveyed the area, tall standing mountains of stones, hard and cruel. The river flowed violently, everything to her eyes felt "not Normal". She felt something not right; something very wrong was to happen.

Priyamvada hastily got into the boat, called the midwife in, and unleashed the anchor. They began rowing across, difficult? No, but challenging it was for her to move forward. A lot of her energy went in the get the boat move on; she struggled for what felt a whole long prahar. The sun was now to rise. Priyamvada could now see that everything was taking longer than it should have. The child had to live with Kunti one more day. They got out of the boat, and Priyamvada rushed the midwife to her house. She left her there with one last warning that she would not utter even one word about anything that happened in the palace in the previous months. She went to the midwife's village with her face covered through the forest route, back to the banks, and then to the castle. Till she came back to the palace, it was already daylight. She walked indirectly to Kunti's chamber only to find her nursing her child. She welcomed Priyamvada with a pained expression. The dasi now could witness acceptance in the beautiful eyes of the princess. But there was something that she wanted to say, some resolution. Kunti somehow looked calm.

"Such a lovely child, he is Priyamvada! He did not trouble me even a bit in your absence." Kunti began.

"But princess, are you ready? You have to abandon him. If you don't your father wi...."

Even before Priyamvada could finish the sentence, Kunti interrupted. "I will abandon him! I will have to, but not for my father or myself Priyamvada. For him, only for him."

"For him." Priyamvada said. Kunti could not make out weather she was surprised or confused but the princess continued to speak.

"Yes, for him. So that when he grows up, he would not be called the son of a princess with a flawed character so he does not need to face insults that no child would ever want to hear in their entire life. I will do this to save him. Only for him."

Priyamvada could not speak. Priyamvada knew well that the calmer Kunti looked on the exterior, the stronger was the turbulence within.

Kunti held her child in her arms and brought him close to his bosom. His face divine. "Go to get a boat like structure made, through any boatman, provide him with so much money that he won't open his mouth before anyone. The boat should be small enough for a child, and that can handle the waves of the river with no harm done to him. Make it safe and soft enough in the inside for him to not get hurt by any piece of wood. Arrange as many lotuses as you can and also get the holy thread from the temple, for my son."

That night Kunti was ready! She had to part ways with her son so that the society does not hurl him with insults. Kunti was sitting at the same cliff where it all began, where she had called for Surya. The event played in her mind like a picturesque. She that day had made a mistake, and it was today taking away the rights of a child who was not any way at fault.

She held her child close to herself as though someone would snatch him away from her. The small boat like looking basket was kept next to her, lined up with a layer of soft cotton and linen to prevent any injury. Kunti gathered all her courage, gathered lotus flowers, and spread it over the soft linen, she slowly placed her child on the flowers. She stared at the small sleeping figure with profound love. The fear of separation was tearing her heart apart. She was unable to imagine him going away from herself and the night now beginning to leave its darkness, the chill in the air reducing slowly. The current of the water was strong, and the sound of the flowing river induced music in the air. Kunti flinched as she saw him move uneasily in the small boat was in the shape of a lotus. It had a cover as well made using bamboo strips, split of young bamboo, then strapping them till a very smooth texture came up. The bamboo strips are then woven together in the desired design. She trembled, her right hand resting on the edge of the boat-shaped basket and the other hand on the cover towards the left. Making up your mind is easy, but making up your heart is the most challenging thing one can do. Kunti was facing a similar conflict between her mind and soul. The decision boils down to one last thing that even though she knew where she should be and where she wanted to be. Everything that was happening with her was breaking her internally. She wanted to go back to that day and change the course of events. She knew she couldn't.

Your choices entirely depend on you, but the consequences are not what you control! Your destiny defines outcomes.

Not anymore! I cannot look at him. I won't be able to send him away from me. But he has to go away.

She took the lid and covered the small boat. The clouds that hovered above the mountains parted to reveal the cold crescent-shaped moon peeping through the mountain ranges. Kunti pushed down the basket into the water. It trembled but was swiftly carried away by the current. Kunti tried holding it back, but it had moved forward down. Kunti gave a loud cry: something inside her died that day at that moment. Dejected, with the last scene etched in her memory forever, Kunti walked back to the palace. Her child was gone- away from her, unknown of his destiny and truth. He would never know her, ignorant about the existence of a mother who left him. He would hate Kunti for the rest of his life if he ever comes to know about her and while trying to know his mother and understand his crime she hoped he would understand that it was his destiny to be left. Kunti at that moment became silent, and her face was like that of a dead body: drained of energy and blood. She had nothing to speak that day. Priyamvada placing her hands on her shoulders tried talking to her, but Kunti stopped her by ordering her to leave the place. When people lose directions, the ones with intellect look within, this is what Kunti wanted to do- find purpose in solitude!

❉ ❉ ❉

3   Radha and Adhirath

Meanwhile, the small boat carried its tiny passenger along with the strong currents of river Ashwa. The tiny boat structured basket drifted along with the strong winds. The boat structure gave a reasonable amount of balance to go about in the water quickly. It maintained its speed as it joined the Chamranvati. As it moved forward, various small stones that stood in the shallow part interrupted its movement. The basket would get stuck because of the hindering rocks in the river. As the basket entered the Chamranvati river, it got stuck for some time again, till the current pushed it forward. After the stretch of River Chamranvati ceased, the basket reached the mighty Ganga via the Yamuna where it faced the least obstacle. By the time it reached the clean and pure flow of Bhagirathi, it was the time for the sun to rise. The forlorn basket moved forward, but its pace slowed down as it moved to a clearing and then began drifting away towards the bank of the river. The bank was a ghat built for serving the purpose to allow people to pray to Devi Ganga, the goddess. As luck would have it, the boat slowly moved towards the right bank, dotted with a small populated area in contrast to the left side which was covered with dense forest hardly having any habitation, or any trace of human touch. The Ghats had stopped the basket as it specially built to slow down the current; the jetty construction enabled the population living there to perform their daily obeisance.

On the eastern horizon, the sun had come up, while showing the small traces of the scattered lights that followed it always. It was the time when the ghat welcomed its new visitor along with its long known devotees who visited the bank every morning. The few first visitors that arrived did not pay much attention to the small basket; their haste showed their need to go for their work. Amongst the first group came the last man. His movements were slow, and his body language showed no sign of haste: Adhirath, the charioteer of Prince Dhritrashtra of Hastinapur. The basket caught his attention because of its distinct shape and a cover over it. He saw it just in time before the current could carry it further again. He brought it to the ghat and opened the lid covering the basket. His surprise knew no bounds when he found a new born baby cooing inside. The face of the child mesmerized him; in the first instance itself, he could make out that the child belonged to some Kshatriya royal family. The manner the boy slept in the basket also helped him guess the fact, the many lotus petals, the soft muslin cloth spelt royalty. The design of the small basket and the earrings in his ears. Too large for his small size, the earring jingled in the child's ear; at times he would begin playing with it and then again become static as sleep took over his small frame. Adhirath, while shouting to attract his wife's attention, scooped the baby into his arms. The baby opened his eyes for once to examine the disturbance in his sleeping position and then again drifted back to sleep. Radha walked, no she ran towards her husband as she noticed from a distance the baby in his arms. When she came near, her instincts told her that the baby was hungry; if not fed, he would starve and die for once. Everything else could wait, but the child was more important than anything else.

Radha and Adhirath being childless were extremely happy to have the child. They craved for a child always and here out of nowhere, they found the little bundle of joy. Inside their humble home, they fed him with goat milk, which was a better supplement to replace the need of the mother's milk to the child. In a bowl full of milk, they used a thick cotton wick, as thick as one's index finger. The wick helped the baby slowly suck the milk, as he did not know the manner of drinking it from a tumbler yet.

Adhirath was not a very tall man; he had a lean frame but a considerably well-built body. He was dark in complexion and maintained a thin moustache. His hair reached his mane and was getting black. The soft brown shade of his eye twinkled at that moment as he watched the little child cooing in his wife's arm. He stood leaning to a wall of the small front room of the kutcha house; the walls plastered using mud, cow dung, and hay mixed into a paste. He wore a white dhoti and a cream angavastra which was fluttering slightly because of the early morning breeze entering the home through the open door. Radha, on the other hand, was tall as her husband. She was fairer than her husband. The one expression that she always held was a smile. Warmth and love everpresent, but the hidden pain of not having a child to shower all that love on was visible in her small eyes. Her saffron colour saree complimented her natural happy-go-lucky personality. The only piece of jewellery she wore was a pair of earrings and a thin silver necklace.

Radha was delighted to find the baby. Her eyes were wet with tears when she said to her husband, "Swami, it seems our desire of having a child has come true. Lord listened to our prayers! Let him be with us as our son."

He replied while he straightened up "I agree to what you say. We will bring him up as our child."

Adhirath had noticed the earrings that were in his ears. "Gold! He is a child of some rich Kshatriya family, I feel. He looks to be one of them!" The moment these thoughts clouded Adhirath's mind, he dismissed it. It was nearly evening when Adhirath went to a Vishnu temple nearby and requested the priest to give the baby a name. The old pundit looking at the baby was amazed. "Your son looks celestial!" was the remark made by him. "I see him having divine earrings on; hence I would suggest the name, Karna."

"Karna! Karna! Karna! Kar......." Adhirath kept repeating the name. As he walked back home with the little boy, the name was playing like music in his mind. Karna was not only a boon but the ray of hope that lightened the couple's life; they were now no more incomplete. All because of Karna!

4 Blessed Childhood

With Karna's arrival, the lives of Adhirath and Radha had witnessed significant changes. The child had filled their time and home with the light of hope and happiness. Radha's otherwise dull days were now full of events, Karna was the centre of attraction for all neighbours. The beauty of the adopted child amused them. His smiling face, his activities all filled his parents with joy. His antics would fill them with enormous pleasure and happiness; he was the very centre of their universe. Life was never good enough without Karna. He grew to look bigger than his age. His face gained a sharp look with beautiful features.

Radha had a second son called Shom. Shom was a loveable child full of life. Yet this did not affect the love she harboured for Karna. He was still the most beautiful possession she nurtured and loved more than anything else. Shom differed greatly from what Karna was. As time passed Adhirath noticed a change in Karna. Radha fussed over the beauty of Karna and performing rituals to ward off the evil eye was a common ritual, but she could hardly notice the difference in Karna's character. Adhirath was the one who could see that slowly he started talking less and was unable to mix up with other children of the village. He spent most of his time playing alone or sitting for long hours on the river bank. He sat in the most desolate part of the bank where hardly people came. Everyone could quickly notice his outstanding qualities. Karna's skill and strength in any kind of game, no one tried to mess up with him, and he became a natural leader amongst the children in the village. At a very young age, he would come up with solutions to village problems. He had a mind beyond his age! His brother would feel protected in his presence. But even in play, Karna was different; different from all other boys in the village. He quickly lost interest in the games and would leave the games incomplete in between. He shaped beautiful clay toys and outside his significant interests were wrestling, races, or martial arts. He would snap branches from trees and shape them into swords, bows, and arrows. He would try aiming with the bow and arrow he made and practice wielding the sword. Other children soon lost interest in his antiques, could not relate to his part, and resumed playing their regular games. Because of his peculiar interests, he avoided the other children's company, and he played all alone. Whenever there were fistfights amongst children, he would emerge a victor, but he left as soon as the fights were over. Parents would complain to Radha about Karna, and Radha would punish him for all his mischief. The only child who looked up to him was his younger brother Shom, who hero-worshipped his elder brother. Shom was often made fun of by his friends with the name "tail" implying to how Shom would walk around following Karna. Though he did not understand Karna and his interests, he found great joy witnessing his brother grow each day as a warrior. Shom would stand amazed when Karna gracefully hit a target without much difficulty.

Radhey was outgrowing every other boy of his age group. His strong personality and handsome face attracted everyone's attention, especially girls. Anyone could easily distinguish that he did not belong to the category of the village lads. He intimidated the children in the village owing to his strong muscular frame, the result of intense practice and exercise. Slowly, as Shom grew up, he became detached to his brother, even though he still worshipped Karna he began playing with boys of his age, and Karna was deprived of his brothers' company too. Not that it made much of a difference to Karna, he became a loner. Most of the time he wandered outside the village aimlessly, walking by the river bank and practising his archery. The only kids who loved his company for some time were the juniors for whom he carved beautiful clay toys. The little kids amused him, and those were the rare times when he smiled. Not all could get access to that affectionate, infectious smile. The news about the political circumstances of Hastinapur filled him with interest, and he would spend long hours deriving conclusions about the same. The oath of Bhishma was something he loved analyzing, and what he did was write the consequences of it shortly. He would spend hours thinking about the blind king Dhritrashtra and his inability to become a king, the excellent and knowledgeable Vidur, and the righteous and kind Pandu who was becoming a popular figure amongst the people for his soft and kind deeds for his countrymen. His world was actually different from those around him.

When finally, Radha noticed his detachment, she began showering him with more motherly love, which only made him feel lonelier. He was treated differently by all. And this feeling made him an introvert. When inquired by his mother about his ways, he cut short the discussion with the same sentence all the time "Maa, you are a perfect mother, and there is nothing that bothers me." He always left after saying this.

One constant thought that bothered him was that he did not feel the connection with anyone in the family. He felt like an outsider. After sitting on the river bank, he would mutter under his breath that "I do not belong here, there is something that does not let me be who I am. I do not belong here". A teardrop would escape his eyes.

It was in the time of one of his visits home, and he noticed the prolonged absence of Karna from the house. In response to his inquiry, Shom told him that Karna was on the bank of the river. Adhirath was surprised that Karna no longer plays with the village children and keeps his thoughts within his periphery. Adhirath was now concerned about Karna and headed towards the riverbank in search of Karna. It was now that his assumptions gained meaning and importance. His fear that

Karna was no typical child but a son of an elite or Khatriya stood barely staring at him. It pierced him and also filled him with concern for his son. On the way, he only thought about Karna and his childhood. His distinguished interests and difficulty to fit in opened the possibility of him sinking deep into some kind of mental trauma because of loneliness.

❉ ❉ ❉

5 Mother's Pain

Days were passing by, but Kunti's situation did not get better! She was living with the trauma of losing her son. Her state was that of a lost woman with no direction. She could not understand what she wanted to do. She would spend long hours on the river bank where she abandoned her son. She would weep for long hours. No matter what she did, Karna was always on her mind. Her words were that of mothers, and her feelings were now more rational and thoughtful. She would fear her actions. Things were never the same after that one day.

She had all her life secretly loathed her father for giving her away to the Yadav king in adoption without her consent. After her adoption, she had to give up her name, her family, and her motherland. Her desire for a mother's love remained a dream, Pritha the name she loved was changed to Kunti. Also, she left her home and came to a new place where she had to begin a new life and grow up in an area that she would call home in a few years. Though King Kuntibhoj was a father whom Kunti looked up to and still, she did not forgive her parents, who left her with Kuntibhoj. Whenever she thought about her childhood, tears welled up in her eyes. Her mind would cloud with questions about Karna. His situation would be much worse than hers. She had abandoned him when he needed her the most. She had left him alone, leaving him to his faith. Trying to separate a child from its mother is considered the worst deed. She had committed this deed. She had taken away her son's right to call her his mother, his right to have her back, and receive her guidance and love.

Alone and friendless, she always longed for Karna! Then her father announced a swayamvar for Kunti, sending the invitations to all the kingdoms. Kunti dreaded the day of her swayamvar. The thought that bothered her the most was that of telling the truth about Karna. She knew well that a relationship could never last forever if its foundation does not have validity and honour along with mutual respect. Kunti was ready to speak the truth to her suitor, but the real question was that who will accept her with her flaws.

✳ ✳ ✳

6   Son of a Kshatriya

Karna did not fit in! He knew it himself, his looks, his armour, his earrings were meant to be a boon but were becoming a chain that strangled him. He felt choked living around people whom he once called family. Excess of everything is never suitable for anyone. So was Karna's situation with his family. His mother Radha would shower him with lots of love so much that it was suffocating. He longed for the scolding filled with affection that an average child would expect from his mother. Her undying sugar-coated love would make him feel an outsider every time he went home. His mistakes were ignored, he never knew why his mother treated him that way, but he knew that he did not like it at all, though he was a well-mannered child who felt that it was his moral within that guided him. As the days went by, he felt distant from family, playmates, people, and life. It was like he was breathing just for the sake of it, not because he wanted to live. It was like he carved for some affection that was real. Though he knew that Radha and Adhirath loved him more than their life, but he felt something amiss. With each passing day, his search for that something intensified, and at the end of the day, he felt empty, lost all hope to find his true self. He wanted fulfilment. He was searching for everything around. He just did not know what that everything was! Karna felt defeated, frustrated, and the best way to get rid of it was to indulge in tiring activities. He practised shooting arrows, wielding a wooden sword, and exercising.

Like any other day, Karna kept on punching a large sack full of sand. His fists bruised, his knuckles protesting in pain, yet it did not stop him. Unlike the other days, Karna today felt extremely frustrated. His heart wanted to control, but his mind would not let him. The reason was dominating nature. The heat of the sun grew more potent, and sweat was dripping from his body. His dhoti was clinging to his skin and his skin colour darkened. His tanned body looked much more attractive as the sun rays fell on it, making his skin glow a little. His handsome face was flushed. His eyed red with anger and crying, the two beautiful eyes were puffed and swollen. Tears still streaming down his eyes as at the time, his vision blurred and the punching bag of a sack fell as the branch it was hanging from which had broken due to excessive friction.

Karna backed and fell on his knees; he could no more bear this frustration. He felt weak. The pain that was in his heart was now becoming a physical one. It was hurting him physically. No one could understand how it felt to be friendless and lonely even though he was with his family.

Karna stood up; his eight-year-old brain was much older. Life had already taught him so much in such a short time! It can never be fair for an eight-year old to grow beyond his age. When kids of his age were playing around he was dealing with the difficulty to have friends and inability to match the other kids of his age. Maturity before time always makes life difficult for a child. His mental age did not match his chronological age. He could see through people, and there was always something that he saw in the people's eyes that told him he was not one of them. His brother's put him on a pedestal, expecting him to live up to their expectations.

Karna stood up and walked towards the bow and arrows he had made for his practice using the branches of trees. His long, well-crafted figures were brushing the thin arrows. A teardrop slipped from his already puffed eyes, speaking of his longing and desire to become a warrior. He wanted to learn to gain knowledge; he wanted to know every mystery of archery. Who would teach him? He was a Suta Putra. A lowly son of a charioteer. The society he existed in did not even accept him as an equal, forget considering his abilities. He unconsciously shot an arrow, it flew with the friction and slit straight through a ripe fruit hanging on the tree. He saw the fruit fall with the arrow in it. He blankly stared at the fallen mango with the arrow; he felt the same. Daggers of pain slit through his heart, exhausted he closed his eyes which were not burning due to excessive crying, and let out a deep sigh. He again opened his eyes and looked around. No one, not even his family, could ever see Karna as weak. He would let no one see his state.

"This pain is mine, my only possession. The tears I shed are a treasure, the treasure that strengthens me each day and gives me the strength to survive." He would always say this whenever he cried, a young child who was unconsciously bearing the pain of a mistake that would later cost him his entire life.

After ensuring that no one was there, Karna went down to the river and walked towards the water. He dipped in the water several times and remained standing there. The cold water comforted him; he looked up towards the sun. No one could stare at the sun, but Karna could. This connection made him a devotee of Surya. He would worship him every day. The only god he prayed!

"*Om, Suryae Namah*" The world bows down to you, I bow down to you, Lord.

Away from where Karna was, Adirath stood hidden behind the foliage. He witnessed everything. Everything! He could not gather the courage to face his son. He knew now that Karna would ask questions, not literally, but yes, his eyes, those piercing eyes that could look through you would ask him silent questions. He could not answer them. He was sure now that Karna was a Kshatriya. Adhirath saw Karna's anger, his pain, his frustration. He knew very well that he needed to live with those who were of his kind. Yet who would accept him? He was called his son, a Suta.

Disappointment filled Adirath. He wanted to free Karna of his agony that was burning his beloved son from within, but he had no path. Yet he knew that he had to do something that could relieve him. Give him what he wanted. The only way was to take him to the city of Hastinapur.

Little did Adhirath know that Hastinapur was Karna's beginning and eventually become his doom.

❈ ❈ ❈

7   Leaving Home

Karna walked back home alone, nothing new to that, though. He hid his not so unique looking wooden arms in the bushes and left the place. No one could find those from where he hid it. The part of the riverbank stood deserted, and hence he did not have any fear of being caught. He knew the consequences he and his family had to face if he ever defied the rules of the caste system. Lord Surya forbid, he did not want to be caught ever, just to face the wrath of the elites.

It was evening and time for the prayers to begin. The streets were now becoming empty as the people headed towards the temples for their evening prayers. He was one of those who were not allowed inside the temple. Karna had already finished his evening prayers. By the time he reached home, it was already dark. His eyes now went back to normal, and the swelling had gone down. His fingers were still bruised, at certain intervals the pain would make him shiver, he flinched. But one thing he never did was complain about his problem.

He found his father sitting on the steps of the verandah in deep thought. Karna briskly walked towards him and stopped just in front of him. He looked at his father with curiosity. Adhirath looked up at his son, and their eyes met. Karna sensed something wrong, something that he could not put his finger on. Pain, unhappiness, and grief - it was a mix of all, something felt amiss. His father usually would wrap him in a warm embrace the moment he saw Karna, but today he did not do that. He kept on looking at Karna, trying to speak, but the words did not come out. After a moment of brief silence, his father stood up and embraced Karna. Karna stood there in silence. By reflex, he wrapped his arms around Adhirath. Karna spoke in a hushed tone, "What is wrong, father?"

"Nothing, I just was tired after the long journey. Also, it is sweltering, so I felt a little down." Adhirath spoke almost immediately, trying to cover up.

Karna just looked at him, and he knew there was something he was hiding. Something he was unable to speak about.

"Let us go inside, father." was what he said after a long silence. He knew his father wouldn't speak.

Reaching inside the hut, he saw Radha packing his belongings. He was puzzled and asked about it.

"Why are you packing my clothes, mother? Where am I going?"

"You are going to Hastinapur with your father tomorrow Karna. I am packing for your journey. You will leave tomorrow morning." Radha's voice shivered as she spoke.

"Why am I going there?" He looked at Adhirath and Radha trying to gain answers.

Adhirath was the one who spoke "The day after tomorrow King Pandu is coming to Hastinapur with his new bride Princess or from now on Queen Kunti the new Maharani of Hastinapur. You can see the procession for their welcome and then we will talk to some gurus for your education. I have heard about a teacher Drona. We will request him if he can teach you or else, we can even go to Guru Kripa."

Karna looked at Adhirath for one long time and then left the place. He had to go away from Champanagri. Not that he was in love with the area, but his family lived here. His brothers and his mother. He did not spend much time with them, but yes, Karna had some attachment towards them. Shom was the closest of all he was the eldest after Karna and a very loving brother. Shom looked up to Karna and admired him. He worshipped Karna like a devotee.

Amongst these thoughts, one more thing caught his attention. The name that he just heard from his father. The word that he had never heard before, but something attracted him to it. He knew nothing about "Kunti", but something drew him about her. Karna who should have been excited about his education was excited to look at Kunti.

It was unnatural how his mind needlessly kept on going back to Kunti. His thoughts kept on wavering. Even when Radha served food to everyone, Karna was lost. He felt irritated about how he just could not stop thinking about the new queen of Hastinapur.

That night he did not sleep well, though he was excessively tired and needed sleep, he kept on waking up because of dreams. His dreams felt meaningless, and he saw a child cradled in the arms of a young woman. She looked like a princess. She then put the child in a basket and pushed the basket in the flowing river. The woman was crying uncontrollably. He wanted to reach out to her, hold her and console her, but he couldn't. He became restless seeing her cry, and in his dream, he called out "Maa". He woke up, sweating profoundly, panting. He looked around and saw himself on the verandah where he slept in the summer. The cool breeze felt nice. Karna sat there alone, trying to figure out what that dream meant. The entire night he kept on changing sides in sleep, he couldn't drift back to sleep. In the morning, Karna woke up early and went back to the same place, his sanctuary; the river bank. He took a bath and prayed to Lord Surya. The dream did not leave his mind yet.

He walked back home and paid his salutations to his mother and his brothers. No one wanted him to leave, but something called him, something was attracting him to Hastinapur. Adhirath pulled the reins of his chariot, and they left for Hastinapur.

Adhirath dreaded the moment he would talk to brahmins for his son's education. Karna, on the other hand, was lost in his dream of last night. He had never called Radha "Maa" it was always "Mata". Karna could not bring himself to say that word to her. He felt that he was deceiving someone, he felt like someone else deserved to be called "maa". He felt like he was cheating his soul. But how easily Karna had called out Maa to the lady in her dream. He felt distressed now. That beautiful face. He kept on recalling it. Those eyes, just like his, were full of tears, and it filled him with grief. The last thing he thought was, "How could a dream affect me this way? Why am I so caught up with it?"

Karna sat distracted that he did not notice that they already entered the borders of Hastinapur. The imperial city was a subject of discussion amongst the masses. Adirath just could not understand Karna. For him, his adopted son was the greatest mystery ever. He loved him, but he was beyond his understanding. Quiet yet confident, loving yet withdrawn. He did not fit in the society he was living. His manners were that of a nobleman, his speech calculated and measured, his thoughts comprising war and politics, and he looked like a beautiful divine prince right out of a la-la land of Gods. "Karna is not meant to be my son." Adirath thought sometimes.

❅ ❅ ❅

8   Kunti's Swayamvar

Kunti stood behind the translucent curtain in the Darbar of Kuntibhoj. She watched the princes coming in and taking their respective seats in the court where the swayamvar was to take place. The princes and kings from all kingdoms had assembled today. The princes looked confident; they knew that they were powerful and held influence over thousands in their periphery of lands.

Amongst all the arrogant faces she noticed a man, he was no doubt a member of an aristocratic family. He had a calm demure yet a powerful aura. Soft eyes and a playful smile made him look more like a young, naive prince, but his clothes and the crown proved him to be a king. A powerful king! His lean muscular physique emitted power, and his postures were graceful. He looked around the court with curiosity, and at last, his eyes rested on the woman peeped from behind the translucent curtains. He was sure that someone was watching him. His smile widened when he saw her nervously pull back behind the blinds.

Kunti pulled back and nervously looked around her. No one saw her peeping, but that man did. She called out for Priyamvada and asked her who he was.

Priyamvada glanced towards the man Kunti pointed at and spoke. "He is the new king of Hastinapur. He is young, and his name is Pandu."

Kunti knew the entire story of how Pandu had become the king, and his brother had not been allowed to sit on the throne as the per dharma which said that a man born blind cannot inherit the throne.

Pandu was to become the Senapati, but because of the turn in events, he became king. Vidur whereas remained the Prime Minister of Hastinapur. She very well knew that according to the rules, the eldest son inherits the throne. But her guru had once said that when it comes to inheritance of the throne, one must be fair. When all sons of the king have similar qualities and are equally able, then the eldest son must be king. But if the eldest son is flawed, then the choice must be made by considering all the sons, and the one who is the ablest must become king.

Kunti had then questioned that "If none of the sons are capable of becoming king, what can be done?"

"One must adopt a suitable heir," the guru said.

"But will the adopted one be accepted by all? And does he hold rights over the kingdom?"

"It is a pity that the kings today consider the kingdom their property, but the truth is that the king is only the one serving his people. His supreme duty and dharma are to save his people, give them assured protection, do justice, and work for the betterment of their kingdom. Goddess Sita, the daughter of King Janak, had said that no human could establish his ownership on the kingdom because this earth is nobody's possession. No one owns the earth, nor does he have the right to control it. You cannot rule upon your motherland; she is sacred, like one's own mother. These words apply at all times. A king is there to serve, and anyone can be the one serving."

Only Kunti knew how much she admired Sita, the princess of Mithila. She could read the connection Sita had with Janak, which she never had with her father, but lately, she realized that not every father is Janak, and not every daughter is Sita. She worshipped Ram, but she adored Sita. A perfect lady. She was going to question the suitors about Ramayan. Few read Ramayan because either they were ignorant or they were not bothered. Kunti came out of her daze when she heard her father call out her name. She stood up and walked near the curtained partition she did not come out though. Kunti was a well-educated princess and taught well. She looked around once again, the court that she had been inside many times looked beautiful today. Flowers adorned the pillars; carpets laid on the floor, curtains adorned the windows. The throne where her father sat was the same but looked better in contrast with the colourful surrounding.

Kunti spoke after a moment, making sure everyone heard her. Kunti looked straight at Pandu from behind the curtains as he could feel her eyes on him; something about her was unusual for him. He did not know what, but realized it.

Kunti with the grace of a princess spoke, "Lord Ram left Maa Sita because his subjects did not want her as queen. She had to live in the forest, was insulted by the subjects of Ayodhya; they deprived her of her rights. Yet Sita did not oppose it. Do you think she was right when she did so? Do you think what Ram did was justified?"

An uncomfortable silence fell on the court. No one spoke for a moment. Then one of the many princes said, "Ram was right. He did his duties as a king. He listened to his subjects."

"Then what about correcting his subjects? It is one of the duties of a king. And what about his duties as a husband and a father?" The speaker hushed when Kunti reasoned back. He should have known whom he was talking with—a well-read princess.

"Sita was right; she followed the orders of her husband. That is her duty!" another speaker stood up.

"Vedas speak that when you keep mum upon being wronged, you are a bigger sinner than the one who wronged you. So, are you considering goddess a sinner?" he did not learn his lesson. Kunti spoke in a calculated tone, but it was enough for the prince to gain few glares. Though few read the Ramayan, they worshipped Lord Ram and Maa Sita.

Kunti's breath hitched when she saw Pandu stand up. His answer was something she was waiting to listen to.

"I pay my salutations to the respected king Kuntibhoj. I ask for the approval of the princess to answer her question." He spoke to her, but not directly addressing her. She hissed a soft "Yes" after which Pandu began. "Yes, it is true that as a husband and a father Lord Rama failed himself at a certain point in time, but there is another truth that if he favoured his family, he would forget his ancestors. He was bound to perform his kingly duties. He had to do it because he was there to serve his people. He was chained and tied, there was no way for him to free himself, but he knew that he could free his queen from all the taunts she would hear from his subjects. He pushed her away from himself. Ram has clearly stated that he left his queen, but Maa Sita will always remain his only wife till the end of eternity.

Sita, on the other hand, is Lakshmi, the nurturing mother who fulfils the lives of people. She is Jagat Janani, she never abandons anyone, nor can anyone leave her. Sita could feel Ram's pain and could understand him more than anyone else could. Ram left Sita, and this was his loss, she let him perform his dharma, this was Sita's greatness. And again we cannot judge the two individuals because we never knew them. Situation matters, decisions are just a part of the deal. We cannot characterize anyone just because we want to. There is always a hidden aspect of every story."

Kunti was struck basically because of the last few lines. There was hope flickering in her heart. She could feel that if he ever comes to know about Karna, Pandu will understand and accept the truth. He won't judge her because of her past. And then she knew that she found the right man. Pandu was that man.

❊ ❊ ❊

9 Mother and Queen

Karna had arrived at Hastinapur in the evening. He admired his surroundings. It looked beautiful! The lined-up shops, homes with beautiful designs were lined up on both sides of the road, leaving a good eighteen feet of road in the middle. From a distance, one could see the dome of the imperial palace with a flag fluttering in its glory on the highest flag post. Temples adorned the city, yogis, and brahmins walking around in their saffron and white attires. Then the chariot suddenly turned into a much smaller road that after a few minutes revealed the hidden picture of the splendour that covered the city. He could see the poverty in its worst form in Hastinapur. Children wailing for food, they looked malnourished. Their ribcage was popping out of their chests and eyes looked huge as if they were ready to pop out of its sockets. Karna unintentionally shut his eyes; he had seen poverty but never like this. The homes here were small little huts with little space that could hardly stand if a thunderstorm was going to come. The chariot stopped in front of one such small house. He got down and stood in front of the little hut. He wondered how his father ignored the miserable state of the people around him. His father saw Karna's concerned eyes scanning the people and the surroundings and spoke, "They are the Shudras of Hastinapur Karna. They have no option but to live in misery and deal with hunger."

Karna suppressed the anger raging within and followed his father inside the little hut. The tiny house was only meant for two people to live. It was just one small room actually with a small kitchen for cooking food. On the other corner, there was a folded set of bedding that his father used when he stayed there most of the time. There was a small opening to the small backyard attached to the hut. Adhirath had said that this was the big hut amongst all the others in the colony designated for the ones serving the upper casts. The backyard had a small pond like structure in it. It was so little that it looked more like a ditch with water filled in it. Few vegetables were growing on the other end. He knew that his father had the "biggest" hut because he was the charioteer of Bhishma, the old son of Devi Ganga. Bhishma's father Shantanu, who was once the king of Hastinapur had married Ganga, who was also known as the purest river in the world. She was worshipped by one and all. Bhishma was a fine warrior, and his devotion to his father was beyond comparison. He was born as Devvrat, but name Bhishma because he vowed to celibacy for his entire life and he also promised never to ascend the throne. His father's love for Satyavati, the daughter of a fisherman known for her beauty, had deprived Hastinapur of a great leader and a king.

Karna was lost in thoughts when Adhirath called him inside to have dinner that he had prepared. Karna sighed, thinking about the past politics of Hastinapur. He went inside and found his father waiting. Karna sat down after washing his hands to eat. Karna did not feel any difference because even if he was in Champanagri, he was always very distant and distracted to notice the people around him.

Adhirath broke the silence first and asked Karna, "Will you come tomorrow to see the king and queen coming to Hastinapur?"

Karna cursed under his breath, Kunti the queen had occupied his mind for so long that he now felt irritated as to why he could not forget a stranger. He had finally forgotten, but not for long. Karna knew that his father was telling him to come and not asking him. "Do I have any other option, father?"

Adhirath always got annoyed as to why he would always answer a question with a question. He could simply not answer straight sometimes. Karna understood his father's annoyance and spoke again, "If you want me to come, I will come along."

Adhirath sighed and let the matter go and smiled at his son.

The next morning came faster than Karna had expected it to come. He again had the same dream where he called out the woman "maa". His sleep was also disturbed, and his mind kept on going back to Kunti. She was there in his brain. Karna sighed and went back to the river bank to perform his morning puja after his bath. He paid his homage to lord Surya and came back with Adhirath, who had joined him some time ago at the river bank.

Adhirath asked him to follow as the Royals were coming in a short time. Karna walked behind Adhirath and only stopped at the pavement where the crowd was beginning to gather. People, for sure, loved the present king and were happy to have a queen coming along. Karna just then thought of something as he saw the pond behind him. He slowly walked out of the crowd and moved towards the pond. He went to the tree nearby and broke a thin branch in one swift motion. His long hours of exercise had made him strong enough. He looked for a strong enough thread. He then took out the knife that he always carried and pushed the branch smooth, revealing the clean wood beneath it. He then tied the line on two ends to get the desired structure. He looked at the bow he had made. It was lovely to look. He then got a thin bamboo and got a small piece of wood that could act like the arrowhead.

It did not take him much time to finish his work as he was an expert after all those times he spent making them for practice back at Champanagri. In the background, the crowd went crazy as Pandu and Kunti's chariot entered the city. Pandu motioned the chariot to be stopped right in front of the place adjacent to the pond. That's when Karna positioned his arrow to shoot. After some time, there was a shower of flowers on Kunti. Karna aimed the arrow at the lotuses that had blossomed in the pond. The arrow hit the stem and the flower flew upwards only to descend on Kunti, the new queen of Hastinapur. Karna smiled with satisfaction. He had never done something like this for Radha ever, but the moment he saw the lotuses in the pond, he was instantly reminded of Kunti again.

He walked back to the pavement again, leaving the bow near the tree and stood next to Adhirath. The people around were excited and looking around, searching for the person who showered the flowers. Pandu curiously looked back, his playful smile on his lips and soft eyes alert with happiness. Karna then looked at Kunti, and she was searching amidst the people for that one person who gave her this warm welcome. But what caught his eyes was that Kunti looked alarmed, and her eyes were like that of a frightened doe trying to save her life. Kunti was looking around when her eyes fell on Karna. The beautiful boy who was the part of the crowd. He stood out because of his outstanding features. His handsome face reminded Kunti of the son she left long ago. Their eyes met, and a teardrop unknowingly escaped their eyes, Karna nor Kunti realized it. Tears kept on streaming down and made their faces wet. Just then the chariot started moving, Kunti was pulled out of her daze so was Karna. But their eyes never left each other until the chariot turned and descended towards the royal highway.

Karna touched his cheeks; the tears dried long back. His face was wet with dry tears—his heart felt heavy. Kunti's eyes gave him solace. He felt a different kind of affection and the motherly love that he never felt in Radha's eyes. Radha adored Karna, Kunti's eyes reminded him of the word "maa" the word that never came out for Radha. She never noticed it, but Karna did, he knew the difference between "maa" and "mata". He felt ashamed that he never could call his own mother "maa" but a woman whom he had just known for a few days reminded him of that same word. But Karna did not know one thing that the woman he felt he knew only for a few days had a connection with him that can never break. He was born from her womb and shared her blood. He was her child, her first son.

And far away in the palace as the night descended, Kunti wandered in her room anxious and unable to sleep. She could not think about anything but the little boy in the crown. Tears welled up in her eyes when she thought about him. Oh! What a beautiful kid he was, different from everyone. He only reminded her of her Karna. His eyes caught her attention. They were just like Kunti's. She was anxious; this one fact made her nervous. Was he the child she had left years ago? Was he the son she longed to keep even today? Was he Karna? Her firstborn.

10   Pursuit of Knowledge

For a few days, Karna lived around at the hut Adhirath had at Hastinapur. His days there were as routined as it was in Champanagri. Karna never changed his routine. He had a rigorous way of life. Even though he would quickly get sometimes frustrated yet, he never changed his performance. Every morning he woke up before sunrise, he then went to the riverbank, performed his morning bath and prayers. He then practised archery and wielded his sword. There were times when he would forget that he needed to go home for food, and he would drown himself in his practice. When it came to archery, he often lost track of time. And when he was famished, he would eat the fruit's growing near the river bank.

Hunger does not matter when you are passionate about your goal. Nothing can waver a determined man. Even though Karna had his fair share of struggles with emotions and life, he did not let anything matter when it came to his passion- archery. He wanted his art to become better day after day, and he even invested in working to achieve that perfection, but he needed a guru. A guru who can lead him to complete the model he so wanted to gain. He wanted to learn. He tried to understand what the dharma said, what the Vedas spoke about, and what the world failed to know.

On the other hand, Adhirath wanted to introduce Karna to Bhishma; he was the only man who could help Karna gain an education. But he knew that Bhishma was an efficient man; he can never stake his image on a person who is not worth it. Adhirath wanted Karna to meet

Bhishma, but he had to show him that his son was capable of achieving something. The simplest way was through the competition that was to be organized by the Raj Parishad. Bhishma was to remain witness to the game. It was a competition for the charioteers and archers. He would only be allowed to take part as a charioteer; he could somehow show his skills to Bhishma.

Adhirath walked towards the hut that evening after the day's rounds around the city were over with Bhishma. He had left his chariot in the Palace itself because there was no place anywhere near his hut to keep the chariot. He was sure that his son would not like the idea to join the contest as a charioteer, but he also knew well that he would oblige to his request. He was a dutiful son. He's found a treasure. Adhirath walked inside his hut and found Karna getting food ready for two. He never failed to fulfil his duties as a son, but there was always something missing in his eyes. His gestures made Adhirath feel like he was working because he was following his mind. Yes, Karna did everything from the heart for his parents, but the feeling was more of duty and dharma. Karna respected his parents, but the respect came up as though he was indebted. He never showed any rights over his family because he never felt it. He did not scold his brothers for annoying him because he did not feel the right over them that an older brother felt. He would just quietly walk away or gave them a small smile or else indulge in a few games that they played. Karna never understood it, but he knew that these feelings were odd and unfamiliar.

Adhirath was the silent spectator of all this, Radha was too ignorant to notice. She was too much obsessed with his son and his beauty ever to see his state of mind. Only Adhirath knew how he contained himself to tell Karna about his adoption and take him out of his pain. Adhirath just felt scared that he might lose the already distant son. Adhirath knew why Karna did not feel that belonging. Water is never that strong.

Adhirath sat down with Karna to eat the simple food of Rice and pulses his son had cooked. Karna glanced towards his father and spoke in his usual gentleman's grace, "If I am not wrong, I guess that you want to speak to me about something."

Adhirath did not understand whether it was a question or a statement, but he thought it to be a reminder to speak. Adirath began, "Son there is a contest organized in the city. I think you should participate. You have to participate as a charioteer, though." he glanced at Karna while his son flinched when he heard the last few words. Adhirath paused as he thought that his son would not agree. He resumed eating and spoke nothing. After a long silence, Karna said, "I will participate in the contest father."

After he said it, Karna walked out to the pond taking his plate and his father's plate along with him. Adhirath did not understand as to why he had agreed so quickly. He did not want to ask, as well.

On the other hand, Karna knew everything about the contest beforehand. He knew it very well that it was difficult for him to enter as an archer. But when Adhirath told him to go in a charioteer, a sudden idea flicked in his mind. He thought that if he could impress Bhishma, he might as well have the luck to be recommended as a student to Drona. The old sage, who was well known for his skills.

Drona was a great teacher known to many people. He was trained by Parshuram the great sage known to be the sixth form of lord Vishnu himself. But Drona was also known for his rigid rules and his firm belief in the caste system. He was going through suffering right now. He was not flexible at all. Yet Karna thought that he might consider him as he was good at his art. He might just take him in, considering his talent. But what Karna did not know was that he was playing with fire. He was too good to know that the world he was living in did not believe in the principles of talents.

❋ ❋ ❋

11   The Competition

Karna was ready the next morning after his prayers. He was waiting for his father to come to him and take him to the contest arena. Karna was confident that he was capable of winning this contest. It was not overconfidence; he just knew his strength and his weaknesses. He was aware of his abilities and where he lacks.

Adhirath saw Karna was waiting for him outside the hut. He knew that his son was no commoner and deserved something extraordinary.

They together walked towards the arena; there were various chariots lined up. The one that caught Karna's eyes was with two white horses. The chariot was beautiful, and hence he couldn't take his eyes off it! To his surprise, he had to control the same chariot. He was younger than any other charioteer who was a part of the contest, but Karna's height did not make him look an eight-year-old. He looked like a fifteen-year-old child; also, he had a well-built body. If he did not tell the truth, he would quickly get in as an archer, but he never lied. He could not deceive himself or his father. He was never ashamed of being a Suta, but he did feel unfortunate at times as he was not able to learn what others could.

The man taking part as an archer was a gentleman. He had a soft voice and soft eyes. He looked at Karna and said, "Child, I am surprised that you are not participating as an archer but as a charioteer! You do not look to be a charioteer, though."

"Looks can deceive people! What looks good from afar might not be a reality." Karna spoke in his usual soft tone.

The archer was stunned by listening to Karna's words. He did not expect an eight-year-old to say those words he just said, and that he had been given no severe education as well. Indeed, God Has his mysterious plans. He certainly was going to become something in life.

Karna was ready when the archer climbed up into the chariot. Karna surveyed his surrounding; the field had a boundary with low bamboo fences. Flags were fluttering in the soft breeze and were placed after one another with a gap of six feet. He then saw the target prepared for the archers. It was far away but could easily be examined by Karna. The small earthen pot was placed in the centre of the setup, but the trick here was that the pot was being circled by walls of shining metal all around it. There were three metal walls in total. Each metal wall was placed on a wooden frame that was rotating, making the large pieces of metal go round the earthen pot. The earthen pot was the primary target. The metal walls had a ten-inch consecutive gap, Karna saw that the speed of the wooden frame did not change; hence the pace of the metal pieces remained the same as it revolved in the circular motion. Arrows needed to hit the target straight from the ten-inch gap, judging the time as well as the speed of the revolving metal pieces. First, there had to be a chariot race so that the charioteers could help archers reach closer to their target. There were a total of ten participants. All stood at their designated places. Karna was second in a row. He eyed the man who was to show the signal to begin. The commander stood towards the right on a tall wooden stage. He held a red cloth high up in the air—the moment he let it go, all the participants stout to reach their target. Karna used the reins to control the horses well. The horsed pulled the chariot behind as the one holding it handled it well. The archers began shooting in the direction of the earthen pot but in vain. No one could understand the science behind this setup. Just then the wheel of Karna's chariot was caught in a small ditch in the field which was left uncared. Karna out of reflex jumped down from his seat and tried taking out the wheel of the chariot. He held two opposite spikes of the wheel and applied all his might to pull it off the ditch. It was then that something unusual happened that was noticed by many. Suddenly a golden layer of metal began appearing on Karna's body. It soon covered his chest and back, making a beautiful breastplate. As the afternoon sun hit the armour, it glittered. It looked splendid. The wheel came out, but an arrow hit the archer on the shoulder. One of the men trying to target had unintentionally hit the archer in Karna's chariot, and he had collapsed. Karna then took his place and picked up the bow and arrow. The horses began pulling the chariot on Karna's command. Karna aimed and remained in the same position for some time before he shot the arrow. He was waiting for the metal wall to change its position. Karna's breath hitched when the arrow entered through the ten-inch gap between the metal wall and hit the earthen pot, shattering it into small pieces. A small smile appeared on his face, and he stopped the chariot by pulling the reins of the horses.

Karna was so involved in the competition that he did not notice the grand regent's eyes on him. He intently was examining Karna's movements. He was unable to take his eyes off the boy. What surprised him more was the armour that appeared on his chest magically. The golden shining breastplate made him look god-like, and his skills were surprisingly extraordinary. He shot the arrow skillfully, understanding the science behind the target that was setup. Anyone could figure out that his perfection came from long practice and perseverance. Not everyone could do it, but Karna did it, and he hit the target.

Bhishma glanced towards his charioteer standing next to him, alarmed, scared. He ignored it and questioned him about Karna. He spoke in his deep husky voice, dripping with authority and power.

"Who is this child? Find out and let me know Adhirath." Bhishma ordered.

"Sir, there is no need to find out who he is. I know him. He is my s-son." Adhirath stuttered while he spoke the last word. He dreaded what would happen next. He knew how Hastinapur worked. Karna had dared to pick up the bow and arrow being a Suta.

Bhishma could barely believe Adirath. He was surprised because he knew for sure that Karna was born with some special boons like the armour. Adhirath seemed to be trying to say something. Bhishma was intently looking at him and searched for answers. There was something in Bhishma that people could never hide anything from him. His piercing eyes were enough to get someone speaking.

"He is adopted, years back I saw a basket floating on the banks of Ganga. It had a child in it, and the child was Karna. Sir, I haven't said this to Karna too. Please do not let him know." Adhirath was already pleading.

Bhishma took a deep breath. He knew that the child before him was capable of becoming the best archer that the world has ever known, but he was called the son of a Suta. His father did not want him to know that he was adopted. Bhishma wanted him to know that he was holding his son back. The son he so loved; his love was going to take away something precious from society.

Then he noticed Karna walking towards him, with all his beautiful natural aura. Oh! What a delicate young child he was. He so wanted to take him and teach him whatever he had learned himself. Lord, what a shame that society would lose such a talent. Karna respectfully bowed before the grand regent. He had so much respect in his eyes for Bhishma. Bhishma knew that this respect would soon fade away when he does not receive the education, he so wanted.

Bhishma spoke again, looking at Karna "You are a fine archer child. Also, you are an outstanding charioteer. Since you won the contest, you gain a hundred gold coins, fifty for being a charioteer, and fifty for hitting the target."

Karna was crestfallen when he realized that Bhishma was not at all going to help him with his education. All his hope was shattered into pieces. He kept his eyes low and spoke, "Sir, I do not want the money you are giving me! I came here for a path for knowledge. I have learned that this is not happening, anyway. The archer who is hurt there needs the money. Please give the fifty coins to him. I respect you a lot, and I expect to have your blessings for my future. I request you to allow me to touch your feet and gain your blessings."

Bhishma felt a sting in his heart; he knew it well that Karna had sweetly abused him of his partiality and inability to support the truth. He did not say it but made him feel that his conservative ideas did not change even a bit. His old traditional ways of casteism and irrationality were still a part of his mind. He was not ready to bring about change. He was a great man, but his greatness was of no use if it did not bring about change. Karna squatted and touched his feet; Bhishma looked at him for a while and placed his right hand on his head. Karna instantly stood up and walked away. Bhishma looked at his retreating figure and thought about a long-forgotten shloka he had heard his mother say.

"Gauravam Praptyate Danan Tu Vittasaya Sanchayat.

Stithiruchiye payodanam Payodhinamadh sthiti."

You become significant only when you work for the betterment of others and help everyone. You are powerless when your power cannot help someone. Bhishma was powerful and considered a great man, but today his strength had failed to help a child. He felt weak for the first time! He had never felt so helpless. He had to go to the banks of Ganga today. To his mother, the place where he felt protected. He knew Karna would one day emerge, but Bhishma had failed today.

Karna, on the other hand, felt nothing! Emotions had vanished, and hope ended. He finally came to know what people say when they say that when expectations shatter, people become helpless and hopeless.

12   Drona – The Conceited Guru

After the contest was over, Karna got the gold coins he won. Fifty gold coins, money that was never important for him. His priority was to attain knowledge, and he loved to learn. When he was at Champanagri, he would hide behind the bushes sometimes and hear the little Brahmin kids study the hymns. He would listen in rapt attention as the teachers recited the tributes and stories from the Vedas and Upanishads. From the few times that he visited the place, he learned various shloka's that only a few were allowed to know. It was then that he came to know about what Dharma meant. Though he did not understand it, he did get the core meaning of the word. The principles of Dharma made a strong mark in his innocent brain.

Karna kept the prize money amongst his clothes and forgot about it. For him, the value of the prize was nothing before the knowledge he craved. He was well aware that there was nothing that Bhishma would do for him. The older adult was stuck with the old school of thoughts that dominated the entire society. He knew that things needed to change, but he did not have enough of the will power to challenge society. Karna did respect Bhishma, but only the warrior he was not the person he was- a man with fixed intentions about tradition. Karna now decided to go back to Drona himself. He had full faith in his ability, and he felt that Drona would accept him if he watched him shoot the arrows.

Beliefs come up so that they could shatter one day to bring about change. With all the courage that Karna could muster, he walked towards the little ashram of Drona. Drona lived in a small cottage on the bank of a tributary of Yamuna.

Karna reached the little cottage where Drona lived with his wife Kripi, the sister of Kripacharya the Kulguru of Hastinapur. Rumours had made its way to various cities that Drona and Kripa did not get along very well. People said that Drona belonged to the old school of thought, where Kripa was a man who supported the new school of ideas. He believed in educating everyone equally, but the only fault he had was he was said to be a man who valued money a lot. His guru Dakshina was difficult to pay, and hence he remained the Kul guru of Hastinapur.

Karna wanted to walk in the entrance of the cottage, but he stopped, knowing Drona might get angry. Kripi was the first one who noticed Karna standing on the other side of her threshold. She walked towards Karna and spoke in her usual low voice, "What have you come here for child?"

Karna did not look up at Kripi out of respect, looking at an unknown woman direct in the eyes was wrong, and Karna did mind doing wrong to people. He did not like being the reason for someone's pain.

With his head lowered Karna with folded hands and began speaking "Mata, I am Vasusen Karna, the son of a charioteer. I have come here to meet Guru Drona. I want to learn the art of warfare from the great sage. May I request to let me meet him?"

Kripi was impressed with the boy's manners. She liked it how he was respectful and had distinct manners. Only she knew how eagerly she wanted to let him meet Drona her husband "How dare you even dream of learning warfare Suta? Have you lost your mind?!"

Drona's voice boomed from behind Kripi, who stiffened hearing his voice. Karna now instinctively knew what was coming. He had already imagined this before coming to ask Drona. He was ready to face the Brahmin's wrath. Yet Karna had some belief in the sage, thinking he might consider the saying of the Vedas that a guru must be selfless in giving his knowledge irrespective of the rank of the student intending to learn. Drona walked towards Karna silently, he was wearing a red dhoti, and an angavastram was draped around his shoulder. He had a long beard, and his shoulder-length hair was open. He looked like any other yogi indulged in a long-time penance, yet his age was not much. He was in his late twenties; his age was what made him special. Gaining the knowledge, he had at a young age was something special. Karna's heart almost stopped beating when he saw the guru stop in front of him. His fists clenched.

He did not speak for a long time. The silence was scary for Karna.

"I only train the Kshatriya's in warfare!" Drona spoke finally.

"Sir, please do accept my salutations. I am aware that you only teach the Kshatriya's, but sir is knowledge not the right of every human being. Karma can be governed with knowledge. I..."

"Suta, I have to reiterate that I do not want to break the rules that are governed by the society. You are supposed to learn how to serve not to fight." Drona looked away, crossing his hands over his chest.

"You cannot do this, Swami! He is a child who wants to learn. Your dharma is to teach, and you must fulfil your karma as a Brahmin." Kripi spoke, trying to resist her husbands' harsh manners with people.

"Honorable wife, I do not wish to say this, but alas, you force the words from my mouth. Do you not remember what caste he belongs to?" Drona spoke to Kripi sarcastically.

"But how does it matter?"

"It might not matter in the home you come from, but here it does matter! You might share the ides that your foolish brother holds, but here you must remember that you must follow the rules I follow. And sadly wife, I do not accept these so-called liberal ideas of your father's home."

Kripi's face flushed with anger and embarrassment. In the court hierarchy, her brother was far above Drona. Drona had no place in the court of Hastinapur, yet she had to keep mum when her husband spoke such things about her maternal home. Karna did not want to hear any further argument; he knew it was over. Karna could not control his tears.

Drona turned to Kripi defiantly, "Do you think you can convince me into taking a low-caste boy as my student. Do not think me to be like your foolish brother, Kripa. He can do whatever he wants to but do not think Kripi that you can instil those stupid values of your family in my home. Keep what you learned from your father and brother at bay when you are at my house. You can never force me to act against my faith. Starvation is better than teaching a Shudra."

Karna felt great pain for Kripi than for himself; he was mentally prepared for Drona's words, but Kripi! She did not deserve such treatment. No wife was supposed to bear such taunts from her husband. As a husband, he must have respectfully talked to his wife, but Drona did not. He was too arrogant even to address the way he spoke to his wife. Karna could see that Kripi was trying to control her anger, just then a teardrop escaped her eyes.

Kripi then ignored the tears blurring her vision and bowed to Drona, emphasizing the salute. "Your command will be followed by me, Swami."

The courtesy and sarcasm hit Drona hard. The mocking was more substantial than the words she could have spoken. Without any comment, Kripi left the place, and Karna also turned around to go with folded hands. His head bowed, and with his heart heavy as he left. Tears were streaming down his face.

Drona could not face Karna, nor could he meet his gaze. When he heard him speak, he was enraged, but the moment he looked into Karna's eyes, he was moved. He had never seen such beautiful eyes with so much depth and some long-hidden pain. He had never seen so much respect in anyone's eyes for him. He knew Karna did want to learn from him, but he did not want to break the rule that he grew up following. When the contest had taken place in Hastinapur, he had seen Karna shoot the arrow. He knew the boy had the making of a great warrior. "Unfortunately, he was from the wrong cast," he thought.

Drona was unlike his brother-in-law, Kripacharya, who was a more extraordinary scholar. Drona detested and feared him. Kripa was a much better teacher in warfare than Drona. But the only problem was that he was an unreliable maverick. Kripa deliberately broke the rules and happily did it. He was not at all sorry! He feared no one, but yes, he was despised by many not so intelligent Brahmins on Hastinapur. These were the ones who could never compete with him. Men tend to hate people who are more significant than them. The mind is all that matters in the end for them. Fear always comes forth as hate. The low-key feeling of fear is what becomes high-key hate. Intelligence is a costly commodity. God does not distribute it with abundance. But the irony of this world is that the people who have intelligence are either stingy or arrogant, and only a few are selfless. Kripa made Drona feel inadequate and unfortunately, he was married to his sister with a similar mind. He could not stand his wife when she spoke like her brother.

Drona had to look for a way to get an equal or nearly an equivalent position in the court of Hastinapur. At last, he was a man, and he could not handle being lower than his relative.

But Karna, he hurt the child deeply, and he knew it. He felt frustrated because he knew that if he wanted to, he could contribute to the making of a great warrior. His rigidity was confining him to do so. He was missing a chance that God had directed towards him. Yet he was a man who had a hidden fear of breaking the rules. In the end, not everyone is Kripa or Karna!

* * *

13   Kripa - The Maverick

The incident at Drona's ashram had hurt Karna a lot, but not enough to lose hope. When you mentally prepare yourself for the worst, it does not hurt much because there are the least expectations there. You are ready to face the worst that comes your way. Mental readiness makes you strong! Karna felt bad for some time, but he did not let himself lose hope, such was his passion for knowledge. He had noticed how Drona had spoken about Kripa. He knew that Kripa was a man of unorthodox thoughts and did not fear breaking the rules of society.

Karna never spoke about the incident with Drona, but Adhirath knew that he must have been turned down by the Guru. He knew why it happened, yet he could not bear the courage to tell him about his adoption. He felt that he might lose his beloved son. Adhirath had readily decided to go with the little boy to Kripa the Rajguru. Adhirath had the experience of a few encounters with the Brahmin. He feared most of the Brahmins of the city, but he respected Kripa. Whenever he came face to face with Kripa, he never felt the sting of being a low- caste. Kripa, without hesitation, would touch him and never passed insulting comments against the people of his group. Yet Kripa was well known for his mischievous taunts and sarcasm. Well, there was something else he was famous for - gambling. He loved playing chausar! But most of the time lost the games.

Adirath agreed to accompany Karna to Kripa. He knew Kripa would accept his son because he was an actual liberal man. It was afternoon when the son and father approached Kripa. Kripa was sitting beneath a banyan tree talking to his friend Charvaka. Charvaka was one of Kripa's types, an unorthodox and man of independent thoughts. They were good friends as their ideas bonded them together. Men with similar beliefs tend to find each other easily. The tree had an elevated platform around it, and the two friends were sitting on it. They were in between a serious discussion! It was a surprise that they were not playing their favourite game of dice today.

Adhirath stood meters away from the Acharya, and his eyes fixed on the ground. his hands folded in a namaste. That was the differential manner of a Suta who wished to talk to a Brahmin. Karna was anxiously waiting behind his father. Kripa stopped talking and looked at Adhirath in surprise. Why did Bhishma's charioteer here?

"Dev, I have come here with a request….."

"I have no money to lend you Adhirath. Even if I had, I would have enjoyed a few rounds of Chausar." The two men broke into boisterous laughter.

Karna knew that Kripa did not care for ethical norms. There were murmurs all around that now that Drona had come near Hastinapur, he was trying to take Kripa's place in the palace. Kripa had no care in the world. He would be seen in a tavern, laughing and having a great time with his fellow mates while other caste Brahmins were busy performing yajnas and pujas and performing priestly duties in and around the city. The conservatives considered him a threat to their cloistered existence. Second, he was a much more intelligent man when it came to scriptures and education. Of course, he was a student of a great teacher. No one dared to challenge the Acharya, and he would quickly shut them up with his logical arguments. It is better to stay put than get insulted and let everyone know how much "knowledge" you have. No one had answers to his questions about the scriptures, and he deliberately mocks them for not knowing what they must have learned. Karna knew that his father nursed the hope that Kripa would help.

"Sir, I do not seek anything. He is my son, Karna. he dreams of learning from you and becoming a warrior."

"Hmm, so he wants to be a warrior." Kripa walked slowly and deliberately towards Karna. His eyes were examining the boy from head to toe. He had seen him before! Forget it. He stopped a few inches away from Karna's face and looked straight into his eyes. Karna retreated, fearing to break the caste rules. But the moment he did this Kripa with his palm grabbed Karna from his nape and pulled him closer. Kripa had now broken the caste rule by coming so near to him, nothing new in it though. People were now used to seeing him break taboos. Now the passerby's stopped at a distance to witness what was happening there. Kripa was always a subject of interest and people wanted to know what rule he would break next. Kripa did the unthinkable. He lifted Karna with his one hand that held Karna's nape, and with his left hand, he punched Karna in the stomach numerous times. Then he slapped Karna across his face. Karna felt unbearable pain that made him shiver throughout his body. His fair skin was becoming blue-black in places Kripa had hit him.

"Please stop, Acharya, please do not hit him..."

"Stop fool; I am just testing your son. You think the blows are beating! It is a test to check whether he is good enough to even dream of becoming a warrior." Kripa withdrew, and Karna's feet finally touched the ground. Kripa gave a sideways glance towards Karna. Not even for a mini second did Karna flinch or let pain overtake his posture. His body had marks of the "Test", yet he stood there with his head held high. "Excellent for a warrior!" Kripa thought. He turned his gaze back to Adhirath and spoke in a relaxed tone. "Your son is courageous. With proper directions, he will be a great warrior; he can become the greatest warrior." Adhirath knew Kripa did not sugar coat his speech. If he said Karna could become the greatest warrior, he would indeed become one. Adhirath's face flooded with joy.

"So do you agree to teach my son, Acharya?" Adhirath tears in his eyes.

"Yes, he deserves an education. He deserves the knowledge."

"But we are the lower caste. We are Shudras!" Adhirath spoke, this time his voice shaking.

"That is not my concern, charioteer. I just know I teach and gain my Dakshina! Your caste is none of my business," Kripa said, caressing his long beard.

"When will you accept him as your student, Acharya?"

"As soon as you can arrange my Dakshina, that is 1000 gold coins!" Kripa said with no emotions in his eyes.

The colour drained from the father's son's face. They were shocked. The hope that flickered in Karna's heart instantly died. Where was his poor father going to bring that much money!

He had never even thought about how would a thousand gold coins look like together.

"I... I Acharya..." Adhirath's words did not leave his throat. His eyes are wide, with shock clear in them. Even if he sold himself as a slave to a Mlecha, he would not get a thousand gold coins. "I am not that rich, Acharya... I can never even dream of earning that much, I just...."

"Adhirath, not everyone dares to dream. And the strata of society you come from will take a long time to gain the courage to speak up against the injustice you have been enduring. Let's not talk about your courage to dream as that also will come when you speak and since you are not going to speak now, so let us talk about the fees. You do not have the money, that is not my problem. I do not care which caste you belong; I will teach your child. I care about my fees. I am not one of those you see standing there" Kripa pointed towards the priests standing at a distance watching the event. "They will ask their students for a Dakshina, which is service. You will have to serve them as a slave, and that too will happen only if they accept your son as their student, which is not happening anytime in this yuga! So why not be rational and pay me my fee and gain the knowledge you want? I will make your son the warrior he can be. Otherwise, you can teach your son to be a charioteer like you."

"Acharya I...."

"You fool! Decide what you want to do and tell me when you are done. I do not have a whole day for your pleadings. I am getting impatient. Come with the money or never come back." Kripa turned around and began his discussion with Charvaka.

Karna just stood there in silence. He spoke nothing at all. He just kept on looking at the maverick talking to his father and then to his friend. He had so much hope that Kripa would give him the chance to gain an education. The onlookers now just gave evil smiles and left the place. The priests were talking and laughing, looking at the father and son. Adhirath had his head low and could not even face anyone around, not even his son. And elsewhere Karna zoned out and stopped thinking about what was happening around him. He just did not want to look at his father. He felt ashamed that he had to endure such insults because of his education. His body was shivering because of the pain of the blows he had received. He for one moment thought it would be better than Kripa just refused like Drona. This was more painful than what happened at Drona's Ashram. He had been sure that Kripa will accept him as his student and let him gain knowledge. He had his expectations high. This rejection did hurt, and it gave him a wound, a lifelong injury.

Adhirath turned around and looked at Karna, who stood there like a stone. His face looked void of all emotions. Karna's face suddenly changed when he looked at Adhirath. He felt ashamed of seeing his father shedding tears. He looked down.

"We will try Karna. He will accept you as a student. I will ask for help from Maharaj Bhishma. He will help you and..."

"No! I do not ask his help, father. You will not be able to pay the debt ever even if you work for the Rajparishad even if you work there for your entire life. This investment will just be stupidity, father. Don't do it. I do not want to become an archer. I was just foolish. Just stupid." Karna spoke, his voice shaking.

Just then, Kripa and Charvaka turned around to look back at Karna. Karna's eyes met Kripa's and a slight moment of recognition flashed in Kripa's eyes, and it left as soon as it had come. Karna looked away and sighed heavily. He wanted to cry his heart out, but this was not the place and time to do so. He never wanted to let anyone see him weak and venerable.

As Karna left with his father, he heard the commotion around the temple and realized that it was nearly time for the sun to set and the worshipers to assemble in the temple courtyards to pray, actually beg for what they did not have. Karna parted from Adhirath as his father had to go to the palace, as Bhishma had to leave for some important official matter concerning the court. Bhishma had been very busy now as Pandu had given up the throne because he had killed a Rishi's wife who was n the form of a deer. The rishi had died and cursed Pandu that he will never be able to establish any relationship with his wife ever. Pandu had shot the arrow because he was provoked by Madri, his new wife, whom he married after becoming victorious in the war with Madra Desh. Pandu had left on the same day he came back with Kunti, the elder wife. Dhritrashtra was now the king of Hastinapur. The blind king! People were not very happy with the turn of events. They loved Pandu as he was a very loving man and cared well for his people.

On the other hand, the perception that people had about Dhritrashtra was that he only wanted to become the king. He was too ambitious and less caring. There were murmurs that he did not even care for his wife, who had herself blindfolded so she could fulfil her dharma as his wife.

Karna walked forlornly through the narrow streets, which were now becoming empty as half of the people must have finished running errands, and a half must be in the temple. Karna did not go to pray today. He did not want to go to the river bank today. He felt empty on the inside. He just did not like how he wanted to cry a few moments back, and now his tears refused to come out. You can empty your heart after crying; it relieves your wounds. When you stop shedding tears, remember you have lost something valuable from your heart. Karna walked straight to the pond in the small backyard. He sat there looking at his reflection in the water as the day was fading away, and the night was falling dark and deep. Today his father was not coming back. He had enough time to compose himself. He wanted to die there and then, but he had a duty; duty towards his parents and his family. He knew they had enough troubles, and he had no desire to add up to those. After sitting there for what felt like hours, he started hearing children squealing and playing in their homes. They were all making a lot of noise. Karna felt agitated. He stood up and left the hut to go to the riverbank because that was the only place, he will find no one around.

14 Dharma Vyadh and Kaushik

Karna descended, walked towards the river but again came across the same banyan tree where the Acharya had hit him earlier. He just looked at the place silently; he was breathing heavily. His search for a guru was just frustrating. Who else could teach him? Who else would he plead before? Bhishma had said nothing, but still, his silence told him he would not help. Drona had not even considered his words, and Kripa had just shattered him. Was it so difficult to impart knowledge? Was it so difficult to consider a man's talent and not his caste?

Until Karna had not come to Hastinapur, he had lived a life of servitude and reconciled himself to a life of accepting his frustration. Karna had just lived with his fate; he did not try to fight his destiny. He did not even dare to speak to his father about his dream. It was Adhirath who had brought him here and filled in hope in his innocent brain. The tiny shoot of hope was burned today with the acid-like words by Kripa. He knew Kripa was just practical and straightforward. He was helping to get Karna free of the Guru Rin. Yet such a huge price for that! A thousand gold coins were too much for him even to think. Karna just sighed and left the place and ran towards the river bank.

He surveyed the part of the riverbank that was bustling with people every day when he came down for the morning ablutions. Now, at this hour of the night, he could hardly find any human figure around him. There was a faint light that came from the mashals lit on the bank. The river flowed down, making a fuzzy noise as it flowed by. The breeze carried the fragrance of the night queen flowers. And a faint voice of the few pujaris left in the temple cleaning and getting it ready for the next morning could be heard. The night was dark though, and the Amavasya had no trace of the beautiful moon.

Now Karna wanted to do what he always did when he was angry or sad; practice shooting arrows. But he now had to make a bow for himself as well as the arrows. He did not mind the idea. He had a lot of time the entire night. He broke a branch from a nearby tree that could help him carve the bow and got the tender bamboo stems for the arrows. Within no time, he was able to finish his work. After he was done, he picked up an arrow and began shooting in the direction of a tree that had been the witness of his shattered hope the same day. He stood near the river bank itself and aimed. Several arrows were shot, and they all hit the target. He would finish all his arrows and then go back to collect them from the tree. He kept on doing this until his anger subsided. But frustration, that was something that had been a part of his heart now for years.

After a long time, he placed the arrows and bows on the ghat and walked in the river. The water was cold, colder than he had expected, but it was no concern for Karna. He kept on walking until he was entirely in the water. He gasped as he was engulfed in the dark womb of its depth with a million palms pulling him with the current. No trace of him around. He was just not coming out.

At a distance, someone was alarmed when Karna did not come out. Kripa was examining the water that went still. He could see no movement. He was frightened and ran towards the river bank. Was that idiot trying to drown himself and die? Why could he not choose some other means to study instead of suicide? By the grace of Lord Shiva, why would he not pick some other time to kill himself, maybe when he was not around? "Wait! Even if he died at any other time of the day, I was the only one to be blamed. I refused to teach him." Kripa thought and dived in the river. The moment Karna heard the splash in the river, he came up. He could see a head bobbing up and down and moving towards him. Karna was confused for some time and thought that maybe someone trying to drown himself. Karna started swimming towards the unknown person. But before he could help the person, whoever he was, he was himself pulled with force towards the shore.

While he was pulling Karna towards the shore with him, he realized the young chap was not unconscious. He was not dragging Karna, but he was swimming back with him without any protest. When they both were out of the water, Karna was startled when he saw Kripa all soaked. He instantly folded his hands in a namaste, fixed his gaze on the ground, and opened his mouth to speak something but stopped when Kripa began.

"You stupid small rascal, have you lost your stupid mind up there!?" Kripa spoke panting. He wanted to scream and slap the boy standing in front of him like he had hit him earlier.

"I ask for your forgiveness."

Kripa was surprised as the voice did not break; that means he was not at all trying to drown himself. Kripa felt terrible for the handsome figure before him. He looked at his face and felt sorry, "How much unhappiness must the little boy have endured that his eyes spoke million painful stories of life?"

"Why were you there in the river for such a long time? How did you stay there for so long without dying?" Kripa's eyes softened.

"Acharya, I was not trying to kill myself! I was just there with my breath held. I had learned this in Champanagri; a teacher was teaching his students a samadhi in yoga; it was how to remain inside the water with one's breadth held for a long time. I found solace in that water. No one accepts me as their student, but I am sure that I will not anytime soon kill myself. My responsibilities don't give the freedom to do so."

Karna spoke in a soft voice. He was scared about what the teacher would do.

Kripa recalled the events of the day. He remembered how he had treated the boy. "I should have made amends! I should have accepted the boy when he had looked at me later." Kripa was filled with regret as he knew he had behaved like a rogue! He did the same to him what everyone else did to him. The only difference was, he had discriminated him based on his economic condition and caste. "Both are painful" Kripa's subconscious mind spoke up to him.

No argument could have justified his actions. He looked back at Karna, and suddenly he was reminded of the time he had first seen Karna. The boy who had showered flowered lotus flowers on Kunti to welcome her. Ah! How much he had admired the skills of the little boy while he was standing at a distance looking at him, making the bow and shooting the arrow. "I do not remember your name child, but I remember you came to me today. I am Kripa."

"Why do I have to introduce myself? He knows me." Kripa thought.

"Yes, after what you did to him, he will never forget you!" His subconscious brain spoke again.

"I know you, Acharya. My name is Karna. Sir, why did you risk your life for me, a worthless Shudra?"

"Karna, you are a fool! Intelligent, but a stupid child. Why do you need to keep repeating that you belong to a low-caste and why do you think you are trash? No one in this world is low or high. You Karma makes you great, and your karma itself pulls you down. If you feel you are lower than anyone around you, the world will happily concede that to you."

"But this is the fact. I do belong to the Shudra jati."

"As I told you before, you are simply stupid. Can you not just listen and shut up? That will help you throughout your life. Now this advice was free of cost. Don't expect me to repeat it. Remember it. Now that you reminded me of how I was behaving like a rogue and I regret it, I will amend my mistake and teach you. Also, that you are thinking about how you would pay me, so now you can give me my Dakshina as much as you can arrange. Whatever you have. Now tell me, why are you here at this hour?"

Kripa had been walking towards the banyan tree whine he was speaking to Karna. And Karna just followed him. Kripa sat down on the raised platform. He asked Karna to sit next to him. Karna was hesitant but followed the teachers' orders. He sat down and looked towards the river that had so much inside it but hardly did anyone notice.

"I am sure that you are here because you are angry about how no one was ready to teach you. You feel I have not understood your expectations and turned you down. You feel I am the same arrogant Brahmin you think Drona is. You must be lamenting the fact that you were born in the lower caste and everyone rejects you. You must be contemplating the lord for not making you rich. You must be frustrated that your talent is becoming just a waste."

"Sir, I am not thinking about...." Karna was about to speak when Kripa cut him in between.

"You are not wrong in thinking those thoughts, boy. You have not committed a crime by wanting to gain things that you do not have. Yes, if this society would have given you your rights and treated you equally, you wouldn't mind being who you are. These thoughts will always motivate you in life. It will give you the strength to thrive so that those can be a part of your life one day. It will help you and motivate you to struggle. You have frustration and anger, and those thoughts will channel it in the right direction. Yes, never let it become greed."

"Life has its ways, Karna. It is uncertain as to the game of dice. You never know who will hit the winning number and change the entire scenario of the gamble. The only vivacious here is that when you have the dice fallen, you can think which way your life should turn. It depends on you what you decide to become. Either leave yourself on the mercy of others and become what they want you to be or lead your path. You are lucky that you are a Suta. Imagine being born a Nishad or a Dom. You would be living in a much worse condition. You would struggle for food. Have you seen the Nishads? They envy Sutas; they feel your homes are as good as palaces. The die of your life has already been cast, and you have no choice but to live with it. But it is up to you to decide what you want to be; a brahmin, a kshatriya, or a nishad.

"But I am a....." Kripa looked at the confused expression on Karna's face. Of course, he was used to listening to the people of this country.

"You know people in this country are fools because it is so easy to tell them all kinds of rubbish and gain their trust. You are not different from them. This society has made fools, as you believe in the existence of sacred and impurity. The opportunists sitting in the temple have taught you that you can become a Brahmin only if you are born in the caste. If you are a Suta, you are bound to be a Suta all our life."

"But the Vedas speak about the existence of caste. How can someone become a brahmin when he is not one from the caste? I....."

"The Vedas state no such nonsense. Have you read the Vedas? Have you read about the topics they speak upon? If you do think what everyone says is true, then tell me what do you mean by a Brahmin?"

"Brahmins are the highest in the caste hierarchy. They originated from the forehead of Lord Brahma. You are a Brahmin Acharya, I,"

"That is the explanation given to you by the priests. If you want to follow the rules of the Vedas, then a Brahmin is who goes in search of the eternal truth and finds Brahma. A Brahmin is he who finds God within and does not need to look for him in statues and idols placed in the temples. A Brahmin is he who attains spiritual truth in his thoughts, his heart, and all this he does when he attains supreme knowledge. Do I look like a person who has found God? Or do you think Drona in any form found God himself? If he did, he wouldn't refuse to teach you. He would do his duty to impart the knowledge he has. A Kshatriya is someone who must find God in his duties and actions. His duty is his god; his ability for humankind's security must be his eternal worship and his god. A Vaishya is the one who finds God in his work and trade. He who will find God in his business is a Vaishya. And a Shudra is someone who finds God in service, by serving the society by quietly helping in the flow of the society. Let me tell you the story of Dharma Vyadh and sage Kaushik. Kaushik had learned a great truth from this man. Dharma Vyadh was truthful, devoted to his parents, and had controlled his senses. He knew the subtle truths of religion."

"But Dharma Vyadh is not a Brahmin name."

"Yes, he was not a Brahmin. Kaushik reached Mithila, where Dharma Vyadh lived. Kaushik first noticed the clean streets that were artistically laid out and were clean; the ponds were maintained nicely. The citizens looked happy and healthy. Mithila's fame as an ideal city was because of Raj Rishi Janak. When Kaushik inquired about Dharma Vyadh, the residents directed him to a butcher shop. He was confused at first, but soon realized that the butcher inside was Dharma Vyadh."

"Did the sage meet him or did he leave the place, Acharya?" Karna asked.

"Dharma Vyadh stood up and received the sage. "O great sage! you have come to me; I am humbled."

Kaushik was astonished as to how much the man knew. He identified Kaushik without an introduction. At the request of the meat seller, Kaushik went to his home. He spoke freely to his host. Kaushik said, "You are a learned man, yet I did not like how you make your living."

"The work belongs to my caste. My forefathers did this same job. I don't share your disgust. I only perform my karma. I serve my parents, and I'm truthful. I bear malice towards none. I donate and entertain guests as best as I can. I do my work with devotion and also worship God with all the love I have for him. I do not eat meat, but selling it is the job of my caste men. I also don't kill animals; I buy them from the hunters and sell it to the people. Never give them rotten meat even if I have to bear the loss sometimes, I work with the truthfulness the scriptures tell me, and hence I attained my spirituality and knowledge I have. The sole is eternal, and hence where my body is born does not matter. I am a Shudra by birth but a Brahmin by karma. Like the king, Raj Rishi Janak is born Kshatriya, performs the duty of a king, yet his soul is that of Brahmin. He attained his knowledge from his work."

"So here you see Karna, this is what I am trying to explain to you. Your birth does not matter, yes you are a Suta by birth and the son of a charioteer. Hence you have to learn the art that your family carries. But since your aatma is that of a Kshatriya and you find satisfaction and spirituality in becoming a warrior, so be it. Become a warrior, but do not be ashamed of the caste to which you belong. Because your eternal aatma is a Kshatriya because you will find god in your bow and arrow."

"So according to you I can be born a Suta, but I can become a Kshatriya by karma! Like King Janak and Dharma Vyadh?"

"Yes, Karna, that is what I meant. Whatever the pandits tell you, is nowhere written in our scriptures. Karma is the ultimate truth in our scriptures. Our scriptures do not specify which way you will find God. He is eternal, and all the paths that lead you to him are right. The Vedas wonder with the mysteries of creation and the universe, it does not bind you to a caste just because you are born in it."

"But society does not say this! They do not accept it." Karna said.

"If the society says that the sun rises from the west, will you believe it?" asked Kripa irritated.

"No, because that is not true."

"So, remember, that even if thousands of people agree with what is wrong, it does not mean that the wrong becomes right. The Vedas clearly state that all four varnas are important for the maintenance of society. Love, law, knowledge, war, art, trade, service- all are important for society to function. There is a reason why we say that the four varnas originated from Brahma. Brahma is the embodiment of society. The Brahmins come from the head as they have to work as the mind of society and guide the people in times of crisis. Then come Kshatriyas, the warriors or so to say the protectors. They come from the arms showing that their job is to protect the other castes living in the society, in the same way as our arms help us protect ourselves from hurt and pain. Vaishyas come from the thigh of Brahma as they work as the traders who sustain the economy of the country. They are the traders." Kripa stopped and looked back at Karna "And Shudras..."

"Shudras the worthless ones like me are born from the feet of Brahma," Karna spoke in a low voice.

"Feeling ashamed about it, are we Karna? Do you think without the feet the body is of any use? Can you function without your feet? No, right? Similarly, the society also cannot function without the Shudras in it. Service is their job, but remember if the Shudras do not function then the other three casts can never function. Like your body needs all parts of your body to function similarly, the society needs all to function. Do you know what is happening today? The head is producing some useless philosophies without reading the Vedas, which is useless for anyone around. The head is saying they do not need the feet! God knows how are they thinking they will walk. Or maybe they are too lazy to walk and want to end the structure of society."

"But as you said earlier, our society had great thinkers like King Janak and Dharma Vyadh and....."

"Stop living in the past, Karna! You dwell too much in the past. And yes, even if the country had great thinkers, they have all gone now. What is left now are dumb men who are consumed by power and authority? If we keep doing what we are right now, mark my words that someday the westerners will rule us. The westerners are progressing fast and if we do not want them to rule over us, we have to come out of this stupid circle of caste. Remember how we are depriving talented people of education; we are going to lose our culture in the hands of the westerns. The people whom we contemptuously call Malechs will rule us. The people whom we despise for their uncivilized behaviour will take away our culture and the greatness of this land." Kripa looked towards the river in silence.

"So, if you are determined and ready to face the challenges that come your way, you will achieve your goal. Perseverance is needed Karna to gain what you are aiming for. If you feel that you can find happiness by becoming an archer, then strive for it. But yes, your way to success will be difficult and painful. You will have to remain strong and determined. You shouldn't have an iota of doubt in your heart about your goal. It is not at all wrong to dream big. Your dreams are meant to be big and expectations low. Never expect to find an easy road to success because I am sure you will never have an easy life."

"I know Acharya that it will not be easy for me to achieve anything. But to begin with, who will even teach me? No one is accepting me as their student." Karna spoke in a softly fearing to offend the Brahmin.

"Do I take that as an accusation, Karna? I did not refuse to teach you because you are a Suta. I asked you to pay me my fees, and you did not have the money to pay for it. Though I can teach you for free, I will not do so. There is nothing in this world you can get for free. Only a mother is so selfless to give away anything she has to her child for free. And if anyone is giving you something for free, remember there is foul play. Everything comes with a price."

"So, the price for teaching me is 1000 gold coins, which I can never have!" Karna sighed.

Kripa smiled and thought, "Talks straight! Is he even one of them? Not that there cannot be talent where he comes from, but his ways make me wonder. Does he have it in him, they become the best?"

"OK! I will teach you. Bring me whatever you can afford. I will still teach you. But not to become a warrior, but to be a brahmin."

"To be a Brahmin! I want to become a warrior, not a brahmin." Karna said bewildered. What was the Acharya even thinking?

"Yes, Karna, you want to become a warrior, but I have witnessed your skills. You must have a much better teacher that exists today. And that is neither Drona nor me. It is someone else." Kripa spoke, his eyes twinkling.

"Who will teach me, if not you?"

"Guru Parshuram! The man whom I learned from, the man who taught Drona. He is not only any common man Karna. He is an incarnation of Vishnu. But the problem with him is that he only teaches Brahmin's. Hence, I will teach you to become a Brahmin by action, and you can go back to him and ask him to teach you to become a warrior."

"Now comes the test. If Karna does not object, he will be nothing in the future." Kripa thought.

"But I cannot lie to the man whom I ask to be my teacher. Acharya, I cannot lie at all. Please do not make me do this!" Karna said.

Kripa smiled when Karna objected to the mere idea of lying. Kripa was now sure that this boy deserves the best. "Sometimes, when the guru is not Performing his duties, then what else can a student do, Karna? You have to do this, Karna. If you want to learn, then learn from the best guru that exists today. And there is no one better than Bhagavan Parshuram. I will teach you the Vedas and the scriptures. I will teach you how to behave like a Brahmin. And you can then take the trip to the land where Parshuram resides. But remember, the price you pay to him might not be good. He won't ask for money, but the price will be a heavy one, Karna.

But I am not concerned about that at all, that will come later. You deserve the best education, so you must go get it."

"But a lie, Acharya!" Karna was not convinced.

"What Parshuram is doing is nothing better, Karna! He is not following his dharma as a Guru, just like Drona." Kripa was happy that he was thinking about his actions.

"Come in the morning, Karna. It will take time to make a Brahmin out of you! Give me a few years of your life and then go to Guru Parshuram to learn archery. Yes, do not forget to practice your art while I teach you."

Karna stood up and bowed before Kripa. But Karna was troubled as conflicting emotions were filling his heart. Was this all right? But he brushed away everything and ran back home. It was a few hours left before the sun came up on the eastern horizon. He went home and slept with a smile on his face. After so long, he was having a peaceful sleep. Kripa's words had given him hope. He would now be what he desires to be—just a little bit of patience and a lot of hard work. The words of Kripa made an impression in his heart, and he could witness his possibilities.

Somewhere near the riverbank, the Acharya feared what Karna's fate was. There was an unusual restlessness when he saw the little boy's eyes. Something profound was hiding there in those calm eyes. Kripa closed his eyes and drifted off to sleep.

15 The Marriage

Eight years had passed since that fateful day at the river bank. Karna had been receiving his education from Kripa. Karna had informed his father that Kripa was willing to teach him. Still, a few years later he had to leave Hastinapur and go to Parshuram for his training in archery Adirath was at first not convinced about the idea of Karna leaving. Still, he eventually agreed when Karna said that this was what Kripa had asked him to do.

Karna was finally relieved that he would achieve his goal. And the fees, Karna now felt happy that he participated in the contest years back. The fifty gold coins that he had received were the ones he took to Kripa the next day as the fees. Kripa was astonished that Karna did not keep even one cash from the entire sum of money he had. He brought it and placed the cash in Kripa's feet. Kripa was impressed by his devotion as he had asked him to take out ten gold coins from the bag and take it back. Karna was puzzled and wanted to ask Kripa why, but the Guru has simply said that he should not spend even one coin that Kripa had refused. Kripa had ordered him not to use the money until he allowed him to.

Karna had bowed and followed his order. Kripa began teaching Karna. He started with the Gayatri Mantra and followed by all the Vedas, Upanishads, and scriptures he had known. Karna was a fast learner, and he had picked up the verses fast. Kripa taught him Yoga and told him all the stories of God's. Then came the time to say to him about Ram.

Maryada Purshottam, the man who was worshipped and loved by all, and the story of Sita, the ideal woman. Karna had listened to the recital of Ramayan with rapt attention. The first question Karna posed before Kripa was "What wrong did Ram do to live a difficult life of a sanyasi and why was Mata Sita punished for following her dharma?"

"When society is facing the worst crisis, there must be one person who can fulfil the responsibility to present an example before all Karna. Do not think that Ram was lord Vishnu and hence he could change everything that happened to him. Ram and Sita were born to put forth an example of an ideal society and the importance of Dharma. Stop considering Ram and Sita as God; they were mere human beings on this earth. The reason why their story was written and came down with the Shruties is that their life is a teaching of how one must let the society take form. The structure of an ideal society is what is being represented through Ram Rajya. Every character in a story comes for a reason, Karna. Even a rock can be a cursed Ahilya. It is not important to know the story and worship Sita and Ram, and it is important to learn what their life symbolizes."

Kripa was not a man who would be impressed with anyone easily. He was a man who considered the Aatma as the highest spiritual truth. And he knew Karna was a good child. After teaching him for eight years, he could see through his heart. Kripa admired the person he was becoming. He was happy that he could lead the boy. He would wonder at times that Karna was not an ordinary child. He had witnessed how he could look straight at the sun without feeling its glare. It was like no big deal for Karna to look directly at the Sun, but for Kripa it was! Anyone would find it peculiar. After years of Tapasya people could not do it and the young boy, did it every day.

And then talking about the looks, no one could take his eyes off Karna. The passers-by would stop and look at the boy and wonder if he was some prince. Kripa beamed when he looked at his student. His friend Charvaka would often tell him how lucky he was to teach a boy like Karna.

Karna was now sixteen, and his mother was fussing over how he must get married. Karna was back to Champanagri for a break he would get every summer. Kripa would let him go to meet his mother on these days. Yet even when Karna was in Champanagri, he would go to his favourite spot; the private river bank where he practised his archery. He loved the place because of its peaceful surrounding. When he had come back to Champanagri after a year, he found his bow and arrow still there, it was precisely in the same place he had left them. Karna carried it back to Hastinapur and kept it safe in his little hut. But today after eight years he was here for a different reason. He was not practising, but stressed about what his mother had told him.

When Karna had returned, his brothers ran towards him. He was their distant, quiet, and weird brother, but they loved him. Karna was happier now every time he came back. Not as glum as the time he spent in Champanagri. But the family was delighted for a different reason. Adhirath also noticed the change in Radha. She was merrily going around the house. Karna looked at Adhirath with a questioning look. Then, finally, Adhirath questioned Shom.

"Why is your mother so happy, Shom? This is some unusual happiness." Adhirath inquired.

Shom was hesitant but answered, not looking at Karna even once. He said, "Maa, has given the word for bhaiyas marriage."

Karna and Adhirath both were shocked, Karna more than Adhirath. This was not the time to do so. He had to finish his education with Kripa and then go to Parshuram. A wedding will be a restriction for him, and he instantly knew what Radha was doing. She was always adamant about how he should stay in Champanagri now and remain closer to his family, and the wedding was the simplest way to make him do so. He came out of his thoughts and called for Radha, who was out in the backyard of their cottage. Radha came in humming and asked his husband if he wanted something.

"Did you just fix Karna's wedding without letting the two of us know about it! Do you know what marriage will do to your son's education?" Adhirath spoke sharply.

"What will he gain with so much education, Swami? Our society will never change its ways, and he will be left with no other choice but to forget his talent. So, what we know will happen in the future, should be accepted and he should get married. I have already promised, and you cannot break that." Radha started quickly but did not realize how bad Karna felt.

"She is a suitable girl for Karna..." Radha continued "Her name is Varushali, and she is the daughter of another saarthi and is a nice girl. She is good at managing the household. She is a suitable match for Karna."

Karna closed his eyes for a second and opened it again. He glanced towards his mother, who had stopped speaking and looking at him with hopeful eyes. He was in no mood to argue with Radha; she will not listen. You can never convince a determined woman. Karna knew she would persuade him with her usual cries and a sad face. What was the use of resisting what was inevitable? Besides, his mother had promised the marriage, and him saying no would bring great disgrace to the poor girl. No one else would ever marry her after he says no to the wedding.

"When have you fixed the marriage?" Karna asked softly, suppressing his temper. Adhirath noticed it, Radha didn't.

"In the coming week. The preparations are halfway done." Radha squealed. Adhirath was surprised how she had managed to do this without even letting him ever know. Karna just nodded and left the hut.

Karna was not looking at the river. He just sighed and felt irritated. He hated it when he was helpless. And right now, he was, the marriage would be a burden for him—a difficult one. Karna was just not happy, and he knew Radha was adamant about it, and it was inevitable. "Women! They can just do anything when they are taken over by an idea. Lord, save me now." Karna thought. He knew he must make it clear to Varushali about his dreams and ask for her forgiveness if he was unable to be the husband every girl dreams of having.

The next week, the preparations for the marriage intensified with Karna being occupied with the rituals that were being performed. Karna was at times irritated by the number of pujas he had to do in a day. He just wanted everything to finish as fast as possible and then he could return to Hastinapur. The only thing Karna paid attention to where the shlokas were being read. They were all known to him. Kripa had explained each word to Karna. He had said how the mantras were so crucial in a marriage.

"Marriages are sacred!" Karna whispered to Shom, who was there sitting nearby. Both the brothers suppressed their laughter.

"And difficult to keep up with it," Shoma added referring to the numerous rituals, but the statement meant a lot more than that. This was the best thing about Shom. He was an excellent friend to Karna. He was less a worshipping slave to Karna now and had become more of a younger brother, more open to him than before. Time indeed changes things. Even Shom noticed how his big brother had become a happier person after he started studying. Karna would teach Shoma some of the things he learned from Kripa sometimes.

Soon the day for the wedding arrived. Karna was dressed in a red dhoti that reached his ankles and a golden angavastra. The clothes were the finest amongst what the family could afford. Karna looked amazing. The people who saw him couldn't stop looking at him. The girls were drooling over the young boy who would be a dream husband of any other girl. Karna was sitting on the mandap when the priest called Varushali. She was a girl with decided features; neither sharp nor blur.

She looked like a timid girl who would speak only when needed and here, speech was rare. She did not look up at Karna even once.

Karna also did not look towards her at all. He had never seen her father, he never had time to see who was around in the village. He had spent most of his time on the river bank perusing his passion. His work always consumed him. The wedding ended, and it was already evening when the pair came home. They were welcomed with the simple Geh Pravesh puja. Karna then left with his brother and Varushali was left with the woman and Karna's mother.

Leaving Karna's ignorance, it was Varushali who had seen Karna years back when she was young. She was a child then and had been playing around when she accidentally lost track of the direction while playing the game of hide and seek with her friends. When she realized where she was, she decided to go back to the central riverbank, just then she heard a sharp voice of a branch breaking from a tree. She was scared, but she gathered her wits and peeped from behind a tree. That was when she had seen Karna; he was busy carving something out of the branch. She had looked at him for a long time. After that, she had seen him several times while he was walking with his brother or sometimes coming back from the riverbank in the evening. Her cheeks would go red, and then she would go back to her house and sit in her little backyard for a long time, calming down her throbbing heart. She knew that Karna did not even know about her existence. When he left for Hastinapur, she would wait impatiently for the month he would come back. And when her parents promised her in marriage to Karna, she could not stop feeling anxious. She was excited, but a deep fear resided in her heart whether he would ever accept her. It was an arranged marriage, after all.

Varushali's thoughts were disturbed when the woman around her began laughing at a joke someone cracked. She gave a small smile so that no one was offended. Radha was the first one who said she should go rest in her room. "Karna will come later..." a woman said. Vaishali went red. Her entire face was full of colour as Radha smiled and took

Varushali to the separate room that belonged to Karna but was left unused as he preferred sleeping on the verandah. Varushali was left alone by her mother-in-law and then she began fearing what would she say to her husband. Even though she had loved him for all these years, she never dared even to face him. She could not even stand in front of him without having her face as red as a tomato. She was trying to list her entire speech that she would speak once Karna was there when she heard a knock and Karna came in. He entered, and she was red, nothing new. She was nervous and scared, had she not felt this forever now? For years she had looked at him from far away, never did she see him smile at anyone. He was that one boy whom the notorious boys feared. Never did he leave anyone who tried to hurt his brothers. No one dared to touch them because Karna was the one who kept an eye on them. His unsmiling face was beautiful. Varushali was trying to speak, but not even one word did come out of her mouth. Her throat was dry, and her eyes were wide open. She looked like a frightened deer. Karna looked at her for some time and then burst out laughing. He had never seen anyone so scared of him before. He just couldn't stop, she looked like a bullied child he had scared only by being there in front of her. Varushali was just staring at him, surprised, and then tears began streaming down her eyes. Karna noticed her tears and stopped. He realized he had offended her, but the care was something else. Varushali was crying, for she was unable to speak in front of Karna. She felt helpless about how easily he could intimidate her and shut her up. She was the chatterbox of her home, always talking, making everyone laugh. But here she was unable to speak. Karna came near her and placed his hand on her shoulder, Varushali flinched. Karna realized it and removed his hand. "Am I that scary!?" he thought.

"I am sorry if you felt offended because of me. I was laughing because you looked like...." Karna's eyes were twinkling again, as if he was suppressing another laugh.

Varushali looked up at Karna with her eyes wide open, expecting a nasty remark. Karna finally spoke.

"Have you seen the little children who go to learn in the gurukuls in the village." She nodded, and he continued.

"You know when they don't know the answer to a question, their face becomes red, they are unable to speak, and their eyes are wide open, and they look just like you do right now when they stand in front of their teacher!" And with that, Karna again began laughing. Varushali had now calmed down. She gave Karna a weak smile, which Karna returned with a grin.

"So Varushali, are you going to speak?" Karna said, sitting next to her. She wiped her tears while Karna kept looking at her, amused.

"I...I thought you don't like me." Varushali spoke for the first time, and Karna smiled hearing her voice which highlighted her childlike innocence.

"I do not know you enough not to like you Varushali! But yes, I do want to tell you something. I am not sure if you will agree, but I have to tell you," Karna said grimly, his smile vanishing. Varushali looked at him intently, not saying anything, which Karna took as an opportunity to speak further.

"Varushali I know you are my wife and hence you are my responsibility. I have to look after you but I... I just want to tell you that I still haven't completed my education and hence I will have to go back to Hastinapur to Guru Kripa. And even after that, I will not be able to come back to Champanagri; I have to go to Rishi Parshuram for my further training. I did dream of becoming the best archer in this country, and this is my only chance. Varushali, you can come along with me to Hastinapur and then to the rishi's ashram, and I promise I will fulfil my duties and try my best to keep you happy. Will you allow me to leave alone or would you like to come along? Or will to allow me to fulfil my dream of becoming an archer?"

"Why are you asking me, Arya? I am your wife, and your wish must be my command." Varushali said as this was what she had grown up hearing and learning from everyone around her. Women did not have the luxury to have this choice.

"I have to take your permission because you are my wife, and I am answerable to you about all my deeds. You have the right to question what I do, and I am responsible for you. So, tell me Varushali, what is your decision?"

Varushali thought for a moment and spoke, "I will allow you to go alone, Swami. You have a dream, and you should fulfil it! I will stay back here and fulfil my duties. I will be a happy person here itself. This is the place I have grown up, and I would love to live here."

"You are sure about it?" It was a relief for Karna because he knew he would never be able to give her the time she deserves in Hastinapur. The one month at home will be the maximum he can think of giving her. She knew it well too. Even though he was not impressed by the idea of marriage at first, he was happy to have Varushali who accepted him.

In the coming days, Karna noticed Varushali was a nice chirpy girl. She would go around the house, helping his mother with household chores. Her presence made the home lively. She was respectful of his Parents and loving towards his brothers. There was always something she found amusing, and at the end of the day, she would tell Karna about it continuously babbling. Karna just smiled and listened to her. She was the hyper one in the marriage, and he was the calmer one. He would have to tell her to stop talking and sometimes sleep as she loved to tell him little things that happened in the day. She would sometimes laugh witnessing her small antiques and her animated storytelling. Radha was beyond happy that she found Varushali for Karna.

Life had fallen in a predictable pattern for Karna. He would leave for Hastinapur after one month and return after a year and sometimes in between the year as he was on the final stage of his education and he had more time now by himself. It was always sad to leave Varushali behind as she would go quite a few days before his departure. She spoke very little in those days. Karna somehow liked her babbling.

Those were times when he did not like leaving seeing her sad face, yet his passion for archery could never waver his mind. Kripa was not bothered by the sudden marriage because he saw no change in Karna. He was as bright as ever and also smiled a little.

But soon his predictable life was going to end, and he had to leave and travel to the southern coast because now according to Kripa he was nearly ready to go to Parshuram.

Karna was sitting in his small room in the hut of Champanagri. It had been three years since he was married to Varushali, and Karna had come back and informed the family about it. His mother was not very happy because she had thought he would go back after learning from Kripa. She was more disappointed when he told her that he would not come back until his education was complete, which would take years for sure.

Varushali kept a smile plastered on her face, trying not to show her disappointment. He knew she was not happy, but for him, she could do anything. Karna was so lost that he did not even notice when his wife entered the room. He knew she was smiling just for the sake of it. He called her and asked her to sit next to him. Karna did not want to leave her behind, but he had no other choice. Why will she suffer and live in a forest just because he had a dream to fulfil?

16   Kunti and Pandav

Karna was back to Hastinapur to meet Kripa for one last time. The three years had passed soon, and he was going to Parshuram now. Kripa had been a fantastic teacher, and Karna admired him for all his ideas and knowledge. While learning from Kripa Karna had the good fortune to meet Charvaka numerous times Charvaka would explain to him all he knew about Kul Dharma and the importance of Karma. Karna would often think, "What was wrong with my Karma that I had to face rejection all the time."

Karna sighed and prepared to go to Kripa and take his gurus blessings one last time. Karna did not have any substantial connection with Hastinapur. He did not appreciate it as much. In the years that had passed, he had witnessed the change that happened in the country. The situation of the people had gone from good to bad. The king was oblivious to the changes. Karna thought that the blind king was mentally blind as well. Karna was told by Kripa how Vidur the half-brother of Dhritrashtra and Pandu had stopped the coronation of Dhritrashtra and suggested Pandu be the king. Though Pandu's reign over Hastinapur did not last long, the people were happy with him being the king. The way they welcomed Queen Kunti was the evidence of the love they had for their King.

All had changed in all these years. Dhritrashtra was a man with low will power and lower confidence. Any could easily manipulate him and his brother-in-law was said to be doing an excellent job in that matter.

Kripa had once said to Karna, "A king must hear everyone, but he must listen to his mind." Dhritrashtra seemed to be ignoring the entire idea of the Shastras. The present burning news of the city was that Pandu had died in the forest and Madri had taken a samadhi, Kunti was left with the five sons. And she was soon returning to Hastinapur after all these years. Karna this time was again bothered with the entire idea of her coming. He wanted to see her once again. There was this connection that he felt coming up again after all these years. He still could not figure out why he could not hold back his tears when their eyes met. His dreams had also begun where he would get up, calling out "Maa". Karna brushed away his thoughts and reached where Kripa was with his friend Charvaka. Kripa had his playful smirk on his face, and Charvaka was just looking at Karna with a small smile. Charvaka was not a complicated man, but his friend Kripa was. He could easily intimidate you anytime. He had his way of testing people.

Karna walked towards them with folded hands and bowed down. Kripa knew that his student genuinely respected him. His respect was genuine. He smiled, actually smiled instead of giving him a smirk. It was a genuine smile. He asked Karna to sit beside him. Karna obliged but he sat on the floor, as he knew that he could not sit on the same level as his Guru was seated. Kripa caressed Karna's head and spoke in an affectionate tone, probably for the first time in all those years of training. Kripa said after a few minutes of silence.

"Karna now that you have understood the secrets of Vedas, and also learned all that a Brahmin must know, you are ready to leave Hastinapur and go to the man who can make you the best warrior in this country. Karna the last thing I am going to tell you is that the knowledge I have given you will help you determine dharma. You will never have a simple life because you know you are going against the rules of this society. You must never compete with anyone but yourself. Karna remembers that the knowledge you gain should be for your salvation.

"You have found your God in being a Kshatriya, and you have worshipped archery. Till date whatever you have learned and whatever you will learn in the coming years must always serve a purpose. If you have decided to be a Kshatriya, then remember the Kshatriya dharma; protecting those facing injustice, fighting for good, and eradicating evil, your weapons must always come up to protect the weak and never to harm them. As a Kshatriya, you must never use fraudulent means in your life. Never harm an unarmed warrior and give out alms. Remember when you decide to be a Kshatriya your weapons are your God and the dharma is the simplest way to worship your God."

When Kripa ended his speech, Karna bowed down once again and touched Kripa's feet. He had listened to all he said a lot of times. Karna had always promised himself that he would ever do all he could to protect his dharma. He had sworn before lord Surya that he would forever follow his Dharma and perform his duties as a warrior. Kripa was well aware that Karna had a conviction that no one could break but his quest for being recognized as a strain for the Guru. He had this deep-rooted feeling that one day this very want for recognition will lead to Karna's downfall. And all Kripa could do was sit there and watch. Who was he to interfere in the designs of destiny?

"Use the five coins I had given you to travel towards the ashram of Parshuram and the other five while coming back Karna," Kripa said and at last dismissed Karna. He had to now figure out his aim and its difficulties on his own. There will be no one to help, and no one to lead. Karna bowed before Charvaka as well and left quietly. He did not even speak in monosyllables.

He was lost in his thoughts, walking out of the city with his meagre belongings to leave Hastinapur. He came out of a narrow passage towards the main Royal highway. The road that he had travelled from for the first time since he had come to the city. Every time he left the town was to go back soon, but this time he had to leave for a long time.

This time he had to become a warrior and then come back to prove his potential.

He was pulled out of his thoughts when he ended up in a massive crowd of people. They were all gathered on the road to watch someone coming back. He could see some of them shedding tears and some smiling with hope.

Hope!

Hope was something unusual in the hopeless city Hastinapur was beginning to become. It looked like day after day governing it was becoming a challenge for the Royals. Karna was suddenly pushed from behind him, and he landed straight on his knees, touching someone's feet.

"Lotuses..." Karna muttered under her breath. And then felt a palm caress his head. There was so much affection in that touch! Karna just closed his eyes, and for one minute he felt comfort, the comfort he had never felt in his entire life. He slowly opened his eyes, looked up, and his eyes met with a similar set of eyes that he had. What he saw perplexed him, "Queen Kunti!" He said in a hushed tone. Only he could hear himself say it. Karna stood up slowly, not breaking the eye contact, and unintentionally tears were streaming down his cheeks. He saw Kunti's eyes wet as well. Both were crying, "Why?" no one knew.

They kept on looking at each other for a long time then a voice came "Maa, let us go Vidur Kaka is waiting for us."

Karna broke the gaze first. He looked towards Vidur and then towards the five boys standing nearby. There was this sudden affection that flooded his heart. Kunti was still looking at him and muttered, "Lotuses...". Karna was surprised to hear what she said but did not ask her anything. He again looked at her and bowed before her. Kunti spoke, "Aayushman bhava.

Karna felt joy when he heard Kunti's voice. There was so much affection he felt for the Queen. She reminded him of the woman he frequently saw in his dreams and who he called Maa. This connection felt pure, so true. It was like something he would die and live for all his life.

Karna turned around, so did Kunti. They walked in opposite directions. Kunti towards the palace where Shakuni had sown the seeds of a deep rivalry walked towards the Guru who was about to give him everything and also take away everything.

Both did not know how close they were yet so far away from each other. However, Kunti kept turning back and looking at the retreating figure of the only person who reminded of Lotuses. He reminded her of her son, Karna! Every time she had come back to Hastinapur, those eyes had captivated her. He had cried with her; that connection was real. "But why?" Kunti thought. Karna was out of sight, and she felt great pain. Couldn't she look at that face for some more time? More tears filled her eyes on the thought of Karna.

❊ ❊ ❊

17   Guru Parshuram

Parshuram was said to be the sixth avatar of Vishnu and a Chiranjeevi. He would live for eternity. Born as a Brahmin, he had the traits of a Kshatriya; hence he was usually regarded as the Brahman warrior. Like any other incarnation of Vishnu, he was foretold to appear in human form when overwhelming evil prevailed and the human society was towards its downfall. When the Kshatriya clan had begun to misuse their power, and tyrannize people, Parshuram came up to correct the cosmic equilibrium by destroying those Kshatriyas. Parshuram was the son of the great sage Jamadagini and his Kshatriya wife, Renuka. While he killed all the Kshatriyas who were being difficult, he had vowed only to stop when he meets someone from the same varna who was capable enough to live and rule. He had found that capability in Ram, the son of Dashratrh. He had then retired to the mountains of Mahendra Giri living there worshipping Shiva, his guru. Parshuram, even though had retired, refused to take Kshatriyas as his students. He only taught the Brahmins and talking about the other castes; no one ever dared to offend the oppressing elites.

As directed by Kripa, Karna walked through the towering and massive mountain ranges of Mahendragiri. He walked in the morning and rested at night. After travelling for about a month, Karna was near to his destination. The place where he was supposed to go, the goal that would decide his life. When he had left Hastinapur, he changed himself into a white dhoti and a white angavastra. He shaved his head and wore the rudraksha mala signifying his devotion to Lord Shiva. When he was satisfied that he looked more like a brahmin boy now, he had begun walking. Karna would stop wherever he found little villages to have a little food, rest, and a bath. He was determined to learn from Parshuram and become the best warrior the world ever had. He was not ready to accept anything less this time. There is a limit as to how much a person can compromise. He was done with the society's rules of holding back those who deserved to fly and learn.

His thoughts were interrupted when he heard the chanting to mantras. The time for the sun to set was coming closer, and he knew the yagyas for the evening prayers must have begun everywhere. He was sure that he was somewhere near the ashram of Parshuram, or in the worst case, he lost his way to reach somewhere else. As Karna walked, he could hear the chanting getting louder. The mountains were echoing with the chants, and he could feel goose bumps on his skin. He neared the place and stopped at a distance of the ashram. He remained hidden in the foliage, watching the proceedings of the Yagya. He saw that in the middle of the ashram was a Yagya Kund where the fire was ablaze.

The fragrance of dhoop mixed with ghee was soothing. Numerous brahmin, possibly students, were sitting around in well-defined rows and columns. They were dressed in white dhotis, and white angavastras draped around their shoulder. There were saffron-clad brahmins as well, probably were the other teachers assisting Parshuram. And then Karna noticed the man performing the Yagya sitting before the sacrificial fire. He kept on chanting mantras, followed by his students. His hair was white and grey, symbolizing his age, it reached below his shoulders. He had a thick long beard and moustaches, which was also the same colour as his hair. He was wearing a white dhoti and a saffron angavastra with one end straight on his left shoulder, and the other end came around and again went back draped on the same side. The other end covered his chest and body. He wore numerous strands of rudraksha around his neck, Karna noticed an axe lying on his right-hand side. The famous axe that he was famous for and the reason his name was Parshuram in which Parshu meant axe in Sanskrit. The axe clarified Karna's doubt of reaching the wrong place. No one other than Parshuram can have an axe always with him.

Everyone in the ashram chanted the mantras in chorus. Instruments were being used as well. It was just divine; the surrounding the ashram, everything about it was sacred for Karna. After the Yagya was over, Karna noticed the ashram. It had small huts that were in a well-arranged row. In, the middle behind the Yagya Kund stood a massive shiva linga. It was gigantic; it was adorned by bhasma, and the three lines of Chandan decorated the linga. A large brass pot hung just above the linga. Milk and water kept dripping on the linga from the small hole in the pot for all twenty-four hours.

Karna took a deep breath and prepared himself to go to Pashuram. He closed his eyes and thought about Kripa and then about Lord Surya. He never wanted to lie, but there was no other way he could gain knowledge. He slowly opened his eyes and walked towards the ashram. The place was just about a few meters away. He stopped in front of the entrance to the ashram. He eyed the now walking around students when one of the saffron-clad Brahmin noticed Karna. He examined the boy from head to toe and then back. Their eyes met then the teacher came up to him and inquired about his whereabouts. Karna bowed respectfully. He spoke in his usual manner, calm and composed.

"Dev, I am here to meet Bhagavan Parshuram. I am sent here by Guru Kripa; he asked me to meet the great sage and plead him to grace me by accepting me his student."

The Brahmin again examined Karna for some time and then asked him to enter the ashram. Karna quietly followed the acharya; it seemed that his age might be about forty to fifty. He had a long tuft and small soft eyes. He directed Karna to a cave. The brahmin stood outside and asked Karna to enter the cave. When Karna entered, Parshuram glanced towards him with keen eyes, anyone could notice the sharp and intense gaze he had. Karna found him a little intimidating. Parashurama's gaze did not waver, not even for a split second. Karna went down on his knees and folded his hands in a namaste.

Parshuram did not speak, so Karna decided to begin. "I bow before you O great sage, Lord, accept by salutation and bless me."

"Manners..."Parshuram thought and smiled to himself while Karna's head was still bowed before him.

"Who are you, a young boy?" Parshuram spoke in his deep husky voice.

"Karna, I am called Karna Lord."

"Hmm, can you tell me why are you called Karna, Karna?" Parshuram questioned him.

"I was born with divine earrings and an armour. It was a part of me, an inseparable one. They stick to my body like my second skin, and that is why I was called Karna."

"And why do you come here to me?" asked Parshuram.

"I want to learn the art of archery from you, Lord. I want to be trained by you. I have come from Hastinapur to see you." Karna reasoned.

"You said you came from Hastinapur. My students Kripa and Drona are much easier to reach out, why come to Mahendragiri?" Parshuram said, questioned.

When Parshuram mentioned Drona, Karna flinched. The memory from years ago flooded his mind, and his eyes filled to the brim. Parshuram then clicked his tongue, looking at the boy before him. "Oh! Drona refuses to teach anyone except Kshatriyas. But why did you not go to Kripa, he is a Maverick he would have surely taught you?" Those words came as a statement from Parshuram.

Karna instantly composed himself and spoke again "I did go to Guru Kripa, he taught me the Shastras, the Vedas, Upanishads and talked to me about the shruties and smrities. But when it came to archery, he asked me to come to you if I want to become the best warrior in the country," While speaking the last line, Karna's voice was filled with determination.

Parshuram just smiled and shook his head. He stood up from his seat and asked Karna to follow him. Karna instinctively walked behind Parshuram. Though unaware where the man was taking him, Karna did not dare question the rishi. Parshuram was intimidating, and Karna soon realized that he was in the company with not only the best teachers or a fierce warrior, but he was also with Vishnu himself. The God who was well known for his antiques and tricks.

Parshuram stopped in a clearing of the forest in between the mountain ranges. On the way, he had asked the acharya who was waiting on the gate to get a bow arranged immediately along with some arrows. The Bow and arrows had been delivered almost instantly. Parshuram ordered Karna to pick them up and pointed towards the sky and said, "Do you see the plume of smoke there at a distance. That is arising because of a forest fire. Now use your weapons and stop the fire. How you do it is up to you, but yes, you cannot move from here even an inch."

Karna smiled towards Parshuram and turned to look towards the forest that was ablaze far away. He then glanced towards the sky, which was full of clouds. Karna smirked and aimed towards the clouds. He chanted the mantra Kripa had taught him, and he shot the arrow. Within minutes, it was raining in the area where the fire had been a while ago.

Karna turned back to Parshuram and folded his hands again, smiling at his accomplishment. Parshuram smiled back and said, "I do not know Karna why Kripa sent you to me, but I am sure your talent speaks for itself. You can become something one day, and since you have the determination and talent, I accept you as my student."

Parshuram turned around to leave but stopped in his tracks and said, "One more thing young boy, stop calling me Lord. If you keep doing that you will never question me and it's not good to accept everything everyone says. You must know this well enough that you come here as a student and leave to test all you have learned. Address me as your Guru. And yes, even a teacher can be wrong sometimes, mistakes are meant to be made, so the future generation learns from it."

"Yes, Guru dev..." were the only words Karna could speak. He was in a daze; he was now going to learn for what he had been working forever. The numerous sleepless nights and days of hard work had finally led him to the biggest dream of his life. Karna was pulled out of his daze when a student from the ashram asked him to accompany him to the residential part of the ashram, meant for the students. Karna walked along smiling to himself, happily walking, waiting for the next day to begin.

❋ ❋ ❋

18 Karna and The Dream

The air was hot and humid, but that did not take away anything from the beautiful surrounding of Mahendragiri. The night sky was illuminated with stars, and the moon shone brightly. The majestic mountains kissed the horizon, and the tall trees slept in silence. The gentle breeze played its little games in the shade of those gigantic trees. The moonlight entered into the forest through the canopies, making the otherwise dark forest shine. The night was quiet, and the ashram of Parshuram even more silent. The ashes of the Agni Kund had died down, but the mashals were lit all around. The students of the ashram had all retired into their huts a long time ago. The teachers were also nowhere to be seen anymore. But the man of the ashram, Parshuram, was still awake, coming back from where no one knew. He strolled towards the cave that was his residence for years now. He had his axe with him, nothing new; it was always there. It was like an inseparable part of him. Parshuram walked through the students' residence area but stopped when he saw someone sitting on the verandah of the last hut in the row of the student's residence. Parshuram came closer to the house and saw that Karna sat there, looking towards the ground in deep thought. He usually was a reticent boy. He spoke less and did not have many friends around in the Gurukul. Parshuram came and stood before Karna, who did not notice his Guru standing there. When some time passed, Parshuram cleared his throat after which Karna looked up towards him. He instantly stood up. Parshuram smiled.

Parshuram was a brilliant teacher, Karna noticed soon that his fame was for real. But Karna was also a devoted student; he was Parshuram's favourite. Karna would often think "favoritism is the beginning of destruction." But he brushed away these thoughts as soon as it entered his mind. Karna was the one constant student of the Guru; he would organize yagyas and pujas with such ease that Parshuram never got any chance to question his student. He was the perfect "Brahmin" student Parshuram ever had. The truth was that Karna had followed what Kripa had told him. He had thought of it every moment he breathed. "You are what you want to become!" Parshuram did notice how Karna was a perfectionist; he would practice for hours even after the classes were over, while others rested, he kept working.

Parshuram was fond of this student of his, and could quickly notice that he was troubled about something. Parshuram asked him to come to his cave. Karna followed his instruction.

Karna had noticed in the years he had lived in the ashram that Parshuram had never been angry, he sometimes even thought that was this man, the one who beheaded Kings who did not fall in line. Was this the man who had made hundreds of Kshatriyas face the tyranny of brutal murders. This man in front of him was calm, composed, and forgiving. But Karna knew well that the day Parshuram comes to understand who Karna was, he would never forgive him. Hence, he tried his best not to let his "true" identity be revealed to his Guru. The irony of this situation was that Karna himself did not know who he was, so even if Karna said to Parshuram that he was a Suta, he would lie to him.

Parshuram was sitting on the raised platform in the cave. It had a flat surface and hence served as a bed as well. Karna sat on the floor near the venue. It was Parshuram who spoke first.

"What is troubling you, Karna?" Parshuram spoke in a low voice.

"A dream Guru, a dream is what troubles me! For years now, I have seen this dream, and it is frustrating how I always see the same dream every time. I see this woman who cradles a child in her arms and frantically cries. After some time, she puts the child in a basket and pushes the basket in the river. But what's more frustrating is that I all the time wake up calling out, "maa". I call her, but she is not there, and then my dream ends." Karna did not realize that he was already crying. Parshuram could see he was unhappy with the same vision that kept disturbing him for so long. After he saw that Karna had calmed down a little, he spoke again.

"What pains you Karna? The child being pushed away in the water or the mother who is crying or you calling out to her saying, "Maa"? What is most painful for you?"

"Everything Guru, everything in this dream is painful. How can a mother be so heartless to push away her child in a brimming river even after crying for it? And me calling her, "maa"! Even though it is a dream, it is confusing. I have never called my mother, "maa". I just couldn't bring myself to do so. I call her Mata, but not, "Maa"." Karna ended his monologue.

Parshuram took a deep breath remained quiet for a short time before he spoke further. "Karna, do you know the difference between the two words "Maa" and "Mata"?"

"Humans are the most confusing yet astonishing creation of God. Humans are smart, very smart, and to compliment this smartness God graced them with feelings. Your heart is the strongest medium of communication. Not even words do what the heart does. The irony of human life is that we try to fool everyone around us. And a person can easily fool the person in front of him, but he forgets that you can never fool the soul that lives within. The soul knows the truth that you think you can hide from people. The soul knows what kind of soul is speaking to him." Karna suddenly felt bad as guilt took over his conscience. Was he not fooling the person before him? This was not the first time Karna wondered whether Parshuram somehow knew he was not a Brahmin?

Did Parshuram's soul know the truth Karna was hiding? Parshuram spoke further

"Karna your mind will tell you dozens of words, but your soul knows the truth. When you listen to your heart, you will know what you feel. You could never call your mother, "Maa". There must be a reason. You might not know it today, but someday you will. And when you do, you can decide, "what next". Talking about the dream, you must understand that whatever we dream about is somehow connected to our subconscious, unconscious mind, or the experiences of our life. Those experiences are termed as Turiya. Thousands of experiences from each birth we take are compiled together in this Turiya. And when your mind is continuously thinking about a particular event that is connected to some other experience, your conscious mind does not remember you see it as a dream."

"Guru, so you say that the dream I am agitated with can be one of my previous births or something related to my past?"

"Yes, exactly my point Karna, infantile and youthful reminiscences can easily enter into our dreams. What we cease to think about, or have forgotten, can be easily recalled by the dream because all of what is forgotten is also present in the Turiya. In your waking state, you might not think about anything that you see in your dream, but somewhere in the back of your mind, you have it stored which comes back because of one reason or the other. You might meet someone connected to the dream, or you are doing something connected to it. That something can be your name, a person, a place, or you."

"So, should that dream have any importance in my life? Should I try to search for answers?" Karna said grasping all that his guru had told him.

"I would say, stop bothering yourself. But the question is; do you want to get entangled in a mere dream or move forward and let time do its business?"

Karna nodded, no emotion playing in his eyes. They were blank and empty. Even though he had a blank look on his face, his mind was racing at the thought that had just entered in. Kunti! When he first time heard about Kunti, he had that dream. Was she connected to him, some way?

"No, what am I thinking? She is a queen, and I am a commoner." Karna thought. "But her name brought it to me. I had those dreams..." Karna shut his eyes to get rid of all the wild scenarios his brain was building. The next second he stood up, bowed to Parshuram and left the cave, and went inside the small hut that he shared with a fellow student. He took a set of fresh clothes for himself and left to go to the river bank. The day was about to begin, and whatever time was left, he would spend there on the river bank. Sleep had already deprived him.

For Karna, it was always great to hear what Parshuram had to say. Other than war arts he taught the students, laws of governance, mathematics, various sciences like Astronomy, Astrology, Philosophy, Ayurveda, and the manifold. In all his classes, Karna excelled. He was intelligent, and that gained him a lot of praises. When there is something good happening to you, there are numerous behind you looking for your mistakes. The students studying at his level were always waiting for Karna to make a mistake, but he didn't. As time passed by, Karna became a better student and the best warrior. Parshuram beamed looking at his student. The student he was teaching for years was on his way to become the best amongst all the pupils he ever taught.

It felt like archery was something God had gifted him, but little did Parshuram know how much he had endured for the knowledge he gained. A trail of self-denial failed attempts, insults, hard taunts and tears had brought him where he was today. He had given up everything he had for the knowledge he was gaining.

That same morning before the classes began, Parshuram called for Karna. He was waiting for him near the temple devoted to Lord Shiva.

When Karna went to Parshuram, he smiled. He asked Karna to take a seat opposite him, which he did. It was Parshuram who spoke first, actually asked a question.

"Why did you want to become an archer, Karna?"

"Because this is what my passion is Guru, I have worshipped this art like I have worshipped God himself. Guru Kripa had once said to me that one could only find God when he worships his Karma. I haven't only dreamed about becoming an archer, but I have worked for it each second." Karna said as his eyes were shining while he spoke about his passion.

"What is your dharma as an archer?" Parshuram asked him.

"Saving those who are weaker and in pain. Helping those who need my protection and protecting those who have been oppressed for ages!" Karna answers.

"How I wish those Kshatriya's spoke and did what you said just now Karna. But you are a Brahmin; hence your job is to help people learn this art. Good that you think about society. And my next question is, what will you do if you gain the Brahmastra?"

Karna had stiffened when Parshuram said he was a Brahmin. The weight of the lie was becoming heavier on his heart. He did strongly believe in Kripa's words, but he had worshipped Kshatriya dharma of war and protection. Even if he was a Kshatriya by Karma, he was still lying to his Guru. After the silence, Karna spoke to answer Parshuram's question.

On the other hand, Parshuram was praying that Karna would answer what he expects him to. He could not risk handing the Brahmastra to anyone who is not good enough to know the risk of using it. The only question in his mind was "Does he have it in him, does he have the quality to handle what I wish to give him?"

"It would be the last weapon I will use in my entire life. The world knows that the Brahmastra is the most destructive weapon on earth, and its effect will harm generations to come. No one has the right to cripple the future and ruin the present of this planet. Nature is not a meek bystander, Guru. It might be generous, but not weak. No. When we take it for granted, it will show its worst side. And that will not be plesant at all, not for us and not for the future generations as well. Hence, it will be that weapon which will be for use only for the worst situation."

Parshuram smiles as Karna ended his answer. He was satisfied, and he was thrilled at the same time. He now knew that his decision was not wrong at all. Parshuram asked Karna to recite after him the mantra. Karna at first kept staring at Parshuram, shock visible on his face. And then a small smile creeping on his face spoke of how he had finally succeeded after all the hard work he had put in he had gained the highest knowledge any archer can dream of. The secret mantra of Brahmastra. The deadliest weapon, his Guru trusted him enough to give it to him. And that trust was the most precious gift he was receiving. The gun did not count; in the end, the confidence that he had gained after this long was more precious than any riches of the world. Finally, his hard work was paying. Karna was overwhelmed with happiness. Parshuram too was thrilled. He was happy to find someone he can trust enough to give away something so dangerous yet so precious.

Parshuram began reciting the mantra of Brahmastra, and Karna followed him. Numerous times they repeated the mantra, and when Parshuram was assured that Karna knew the mantra well, he began speaking.

"Karna, now that I have already given you the Brahmastra, you must remember what you said. Your resolve must never break, and you must use this weapon wisely. Do not pass it on further because now that the Dwapar Yug in near to its end, and Kali Yug is to begin passing this Astra further will prove to be fetal. Do not think that anyone who follows the dharma can have it, power and greed corrupts the most honourable men in this world. Think a thousand times before using it, so that you do not regret it later in life."

"I'll remember that, Dev. But Guru, can any usual bow stand the power of this divine weapon? It is so powerful that I doubt that a normal bow can hold it up."

"You are right Karna; not all bows can stand the power of this divine weapon. There must always be a balance between the arrow and the bow being used. This balance signifies the formation of the entire universe. Balance is the key to sustain. Hence now I will give you something that can balance the power of this weapon. I will give you my bow, the Vijaya bow."

Karna was surprised and thrilled, and then he felt a knot in his stomach. Suddenly he felt unable to smile. Why? He did not know. For like the last few minutes that he had been grinning now he couldn't bring himself there for even a small smile on his face. He did not understand the sudden change in his own emotion, and the happiness that had flooded his heart was all gone now. He wanted to be happy, yet suddenly his gut told him there was something now right here. He was trying to figure out what was happening and what were these sudden rushes of emotions when Parshurams voice pulled him out of his trance. He did not hear the beginning, but whatever he did, he realized that the sage was speaking about the Vijaya bow.

"..... This bow was sculpted by lord Vishvakarma on the instruction of Lord Shiva. He had given the bow for safekeeping to Indra the king of the Gods. Indra had used this bow various times to defeat Asuras in numerous wars. It was Lord Shiva who instructed Indra to give the bow to me for combating the evil prevailing amongst the Kshatriyas of the world. The name of this bow comes from a Sanskrit word meaning Victory."

"What makes it so special, Dev, that makes victory inevitable for the possessor?" Karna asked by now his mind was already diverted because of the story Parshuram had been telling him about the Vijaya.

"If it was sculpted by Vishvakarma, it had to be special, Karna. Any weapon cannot break its string. Every time you will release an arrow from the Vijya Dhanush, it's twang produces reverberations similar to that of the rumbling of clouds during a mighty thunderstorm, causing nerve wreaking fear in the enemy. It also produces strong flashes of lights, as brilliant as the lightning in the sky, which blinds the enemy. This bow is so heavy that everyone cannot lift it, and also it cannot be broken. No weapon other than the Pashupatastra or Vaishnavastra can harm the warrior who carries the Vijya bow. Also, when you shoot an arrow, its energy is amplified by multiple times as this bow I charged and induced with sacred mantras. The energy that you will require Karna, to launch an Astra will be reduced by two times." Parshuram spoke of the Vijya with pride as his eyes twinkled.

"But you said, not everyone can carry that bow! Will I be able to lift it?" Doubt was visible in Karna's eyes.

"Doubting your talent and my teaching, Karna? Are we doing this?" Parshuram taunted a little hurt.

"No Dev, I can never doubt your teaching, nor do I doubt my talent. I am just unsure if I am worthy enough to have the mighty bow. "Karna spoke almost instantly, trying to clarify his point.

Parshuram spoke nothing. He stood up from his place and went into the temple. After some time, he came out with a bow. A bow that looked brilliant and its shape and size spoke for its greatness. It was a dark-coloured bow having bluish hues. It reached till Parshuram's shoulder. Karna was a little taller than Parshuram, hence he was sure that it might get somewhere near his chest when placed vertically upright on the ground like Parshuram had placed it right now in front of himself. Karna stood up his eyes, not leaving the bow even for a split second. He was in awe as to how beautiful the bow looked. It was like every archer's dream.

Parshuram called Karna to lift the bow and see if he was "worth it". Karna followed his orders and looked at the bow in his Guru's hand. He at first caressed it's a top limb and went down to the arrow rest with his right palm when he reached the grip, he tightened his hold. As his palm encircled around the grip, the veins in his lower arm were visible through his milk-white skin. His muscles tensed, revealing his well-built arms. Parshuram left the top limb of the bow, and then Karna pulled it from the ground and held it in the air like it was any usual bow that he used for practices. "Shoot" ordered Parshuram, which Karna did almost instantly. The arrow went straight in the direction of the sun. Karna did not care as to where the arrow went. He turned around towards his guru and said, "I did it, Guru! I actually can lift the bow and aim and shoot. And I don't have words to describe as to how beautiful it is and...." Karna kept on blabbering like a happy little child whose demand had just been met. Karna could look fantastic and have many throwing their heart in his feet if he decided to smile more. Alas, he did not get reasons to smile as much as he needed it. Parshuram stood there looking at his antiques and listening to all he had to say. When Karna finally decided to go back to the little cocoon, he had built around him, Parshuram spoke with a smile.

"I know you are happy, but never forget what bad this can do to you Karna if not used wisely. And I know you will think before you do anything."

Parshuram began walking back towards the ashram followed by Karna when he abruptly stopped. He turned around to look at Karna, who had been walking behind him. He placed his palm on Karna's shoulder and said with a smile.

"I think you need to learn how to look for happiness Karna. Smile more; it will help you set things straight. Life has a lot of miseries amongst those a smile won't do any harm. Don't dwell on things that happened to you in your past, son. Life is too short; well it is a different thing if you are immortal like me." Karna smiled. He knew his Guru did not like the fact that he had to live until eternity.

"Now that's somewhat better!" Parshuram said, looking at Karna's smiling face. Both of them chuckled and resumed walking.

❈ ❈ ❈

19   Parshuram's Curse

Years had passed after Parshuram had handed the Vijya bow to Karna. All of Parshuram's hopes were pinned on the handsome young man being groomed by him for years. He knew the threat that the nation was walking towards. They divided into janpadas and mahajanpadas. These divisions were making the country weaker day after day. He did not yet know if the next Vishnu had risen to work it out. And since he was unsure of the next Vishnu, he was building a warrior who could help him while he tried to step towards the unification of the entire nation. Parshuram internally lamented that the kings were busy fighting against each other, the Brahmin's were busy suppressing others and fulfilling their greed. Different casts feared the elites, knowing they were not allowed to speak much. The Maleches were becoming more assertive, and he feared that one day they would come and rule over the country. He did not want to lose everything the great leaders of these countries had fought passionately to build. He did not want to hand over his beloved country to leaders like Bhishma and Drona who were not ready to help unify the country. They were busy following the Dharma they had outlined for themselves.

Yes, he vowed to teach brahmins only, but that was because he knew how this group worked as the consultants and prime ministers for Kshatriya kings. They were the ones who imparted knowledge. But then he had not realized that one day his vow would become a threat to his mother-land. At this point, he was ready to forget the vow and take a student irrespective of his caste so that he could somehow bring in a game-changer. But just when he was losing hope, Karna came in. The moment he had stepped inside the cave, Parshuram knew that he finally got the person he was looking for who had the wisdom to behold the dharma he was trying to enforce amongst the people of the country the change that had to be brought soon.

Parshuram's eyes scanned the handsome young man standing before him. His reasonable frame, tall structure, broad shoulders, and glistering earrings and the shining breastplate he wore made him look like some magnificent God. He had a well-built torso and well-defined muscles, his face was handsome, deep eyes which could speak a million stories a sharp nose, and well-defined jawline. He wore a tilak which represented half of the sun. His jet-black hair reached till his shoulders perfectly combed in place. Even though he wore the assigned dress in the Gurukul, his looks distinguished him from all others. He walked with his head high. He spoke to anyone and everyone looking straight into the eyes.

Parshuram had trained hundreds, even students like Drona and Kripa, yet nobody could ever impress him as Karna did. Whenever Parshuram looked at Karna, his heart swelled with pride, wasn't he the best!? Everyone in the Ashram was well aware of how much Parshuram admired his student. "How could a poor Brahmin boy from Hastinapur look so much like a warrior?" He would think sometimes. The Young man looks every inch a warrior and no Brahmin. His height, body structure, everything, not even near to that of a person belonging to a Brahmin community. "Those idiots will be shocked when they see this epitome of grace and bravery, who is my student. I swear they are going to question their craft after he goes back to that wreaked city with an indifferent king!" Parshuram spoke to himself with a broad smile reserved for the stones of the cave he lived in. "Never will they speak of themselves to be the best. You all have a strong competitor coming your way." He spoke to himself, thinking about the warriors of Hastinapur.

He still remembered the time Parshuram tested him in his knowledge about the Vedas, mantras, smritis, and Upanishads along with the Puranas. He was impressed by the depth of his experience, and that way, he had taught his education into his soul. The boy did have skills as well, and with time he became better each day that he spent in the Gurukul. Karna's courage again made him question whether he was a brahmin.

He recalled how once an eight-year-old had slipped off of a cliff in some part of the Mahendragiri while practising, all of Parshuram's students stood there like meek spectators whereas Karna jumped off the cliff without a second thought. And that was when he had seen his armour magically appear on his chest. It made him look all the more warrior-like. He did save the boy; Karna had landed straight on his back yet he was unharmed. When asked, he had said that he never got permanent wounds; the power of the armour always healed them all.

He had imparted Karna the best training he could. The old form of martial arts incorporated with the very new methods of war that were scientifically developed. He taught him everything that made Parshuram himself the most feared and formidable warrior in the entire world.

He made sure that he imparted the same education to all, but every student inevitably takes it indifferently. Some do not pay heed whereas some like Karna took it extra seriously. You cannot make someone gain knowledge; it is to come from within; the desire to learn something. Not all students in a class become great scholars, one or two do, because in a group of thousands only a few listen.

Parshuram was lost in his thoughts when the bells were rung, signifying the end of the day at the Gurukul. After the first bell every day, Parshuram spoke to the students if necessary, conducted prayers, and then discharged them to have their days rest and some self-study time. He walked down to the centre of the Gurukul where the Yagyas were usually conducted. He reached where the students had already lined up in rows and columns. He scanned the students standing before him from the raised podium and stopped at Karna. He was the tallest, hence standing behind, in the row of the graduating students. He smiled and then the prayers began. He had nothing to talk about today. The afternoon sun was blazing hot, and the rocks were untouchable. The sun's heat made them extremely hot.

Later, when the prayers were over, and students dismissed, Karna walked towards the stream that flowed through the mountains. These mountains were bestowed with breath taking flora and fauna it had beautiful landscapes in every corner. The hot and humid summers were a little harsh sometimes. The humidity made it more challenging to live. The eastern ghats kissed the clear blue skies, and its top remained covered in the fog that would get accumulated on the highest peaks, often making it invisible.

Karna was bone weary by the time the day at the Gurukul had ended. After the prayers Parshuram had expressed his desire to have a nap near the stream. It had dense foliage, and hence it was less hot out there. Karna had willingly obliged. Parshuram slept with his head resting on the thigh of his disciple.

By the time it was nearly evening, and the sun has already reached to the west, Karna's feet had gone numb, but he did not move even a little, fearing to disturb his Guru's slumber. Karna looked at Parshuram's face and wondered why did this person hate the non-Brahmins. In the past years, he had come to rear deep respect for Parshuram. He had noticed how he was generous and kind. The older man was not even near to what the world or Kripa described him to be. Yet he had never dared to ask him that only doubt he had in mind, what if an out-cast came to him? He feared it would anger his Guru, and he was not ready to take the chance. Parshuram spoke of all the rules that any Kshatriya must follow as a king or even as a solder. He defined the cast system in the same manner Kripa did. Had everyone mistaken his vow to teach only Brahmins?

Karna often thought that Parshuram was much more than the world saw him be. They had built this perception about him that generations were growing up with. They characterized him through the secondary information the world had. He thought of the time when Kripa had said to him that one must never judge anyone without personally knowing them. And after whatever Karna came to know about Parshuram, he loved his Guru. He had a Gurukul and may time he had seen Parshuram offering a place to destitute and lesser fortunate of any caste, a place to live, and a home to call one's own. Many people in Mahendragiri owed everything they had to this older man. And these unfortunate ones were from all castes, yet he refused to teach all. Why? No one dared to ask. He gave various homes and huts to all those needy people, yet he lived in a small cave, sleeping on a hard rock platform lined with hay to be called a bed. Karna had once offered him a string cot that he made himself, Parshuram had accepted it, yet he never used it. He always said, "Karna, not every student will do this for me, so when you leave I will have no one to mend this if it ever breaks. Then going back to the hard rock will be more difficult for me. Let it be in this cave of mine as a memory of my student, not as a commodity I need." The initial disgust that Karna had for Parshuram had washed away. Amongst all the confusion, he knew one thing for sure that Parshuram loved him like a son.

Sometimes dread filled his heart thinking of how would Parshuram react if he came to know the deception Karna had carried for these many years. He sighed as he felt too exhausted, tired of the day's classes and hard work. A sudden strong urge to speak out the truth-filled his heart. Karna did not want to leave this place without admitting what he knew was the truth. If he did not speak out, he was sure that in the future he would never live at peace knowing well that he had cheated this man who had given him what no one else could; knowledge. He could not leave like a coward and what if Parshuram found out from someone else? He would be deeply hurt, and then no one would be able to handle his wrath.

Karna was so occupied in his thoughts that he did not notice the wasp entering the folds of his dhoti. He did feel the tickling like something was walking on his skin, but he ignored it. He had much more important things to think of. Suddenly deep pain shot through his thigh. The wasp had bitten him. Karna's jaw tightened as he suppressed a cry. The problem spread faster than he thought to become acute and making it difficult to breathe for him. The wasp was still digging into his skin, and then he felt something cool seep down his legs. He immediately knew it was blood. The wasp finally stopped and walked out, but Karna's thigh kept on bleeding. He bit his tongue to seize a moan escape his mouth. He struggled to remain still; his concern was that he did not want to disturb his teacher. Karna caught hold of the long strand to grass as his struggle and pain grew. The blood kept flowing and yet with every ounce of determination, he could muster he remained sitting in the same position.

However, his blood was still flowing, and then it went down to touch Parshurams shoulder. When the Brahmin felt the cold substance on his skin, he woke up, and almost instantly, he noticed Karna's flushed face and bleeding thigh.

Karna stood up with great labour. Finally, tears rolled down his eyes. Parshuram was just staring at Karna. Karna had expected some concern in his eyes, but what he saw was the realization. Really? But before Karna spoke, the older man spoke. His voice had gained a dangerous edge. He said, "Karna tell me the truth, who are you?"

At that moment, that question drained all the colour from Karna's face. He knew his deception had been discovered, and now it will be worse than ever to face Parshuram's wrath. "I...I am..." Karna only stammered, not being able to gather the courage to speak. His words were failing him; they refused to come out. He felt like choking himself to death.

"Karna you are not a Brahmin. I know it, I had always questioned it, yet I never asked you. I thought you are different, that's it. But this!

No, not at all. No man from the three casts can withstand so much pain and yet remain unmoved—only a Kshatriya. You are a Kshatriya. Yes, only the warrior clan, the Kshatriyas, can endure so much discomfort. This patience, endurance, and devotion are not a part of any other clan. You young scoundrel, you rascal, you deceived me into believing you are a Brahmin and never told me that you are a Kshatriya. I fought the Kshatriya's all my life, and now a Kshatriya decides to deceive me?" Parshuram spoke with his voice high.

Karna folded his hands and desperately spoke, "Guru... no yo... you are getting me wrong. I am not a Kshatriya, forgive me Dev, I am a Suta, a son of the charioteer." Karna spoke, weeping frantically.

"Throughout my childhood, I tried finding a Guru for myself, no one accepted me as their student because of my caste, and then I went to Aacharya Kripa. He told me to come to you. I swear I am not a Kshatriya."

Parshuram had calmed down a little after he heard Karna. This time he spoke in a gentler tone. "Karna, you are living a lie. No, you are not a Suta. Go find out your truth, you are a Kshatriya. And I know it when you find it you will see that I am right. Karna, why did you not tell me the truth. I would have indeed sent you to someone who could teach you. I do not teach the other castes because of my vow; I am not against them as I am sure you were told that I hate all others who are not Brahmins. That is not the case, I had a promise I had taken up years back in the heat of the moment, and so I kept it by teaching only Brahmins. You shouldn't have cheated and deceived me like this Karna. Karna, you have gained this knowledge by telling me a lie.

And do you not know that a dishonest person can never live with self-respect? Do you see how you are not able to look straight into my eyes today like any other day? Karna, I am not cursing you. Do not think what I am going to say is a curse; it is just the truth of life! Whatever you acquire in life by cheating and lying, will never help you. You will lose whatever you learn in the most crucial moment of life. This knowledge that you got by cheating me will be of no use in the most critical moment of life, you will forget it. Anything, be it wealth or knowledge when taken by deceiving someone is never useful. Karna, you brought this upon yourself. Leave Karna, go back to Hastinapur. This is ridiculous; I wanted you to thrive but… forget it. Follow your destiny, Karna, go away." A teardrop slipped from Parshuram's eyes as he watched his beloved student crying. Whatever he said, Parshuram knew it; he was not a Suta.

Karna spoke after a little while, "I am an idiot Guru, you told me to call you Guru and not Lord. But while following your order I forgot, you are the Sixth Vishnu. You are a part of that creator, God himself, and God does not discriminate. Fear is not at all good for the great Lord. I kept fearing your wrath and forgot that for you, all are equal and important. Forgive me; please do." Karna bowed his head lower, his face soaked with tears.

Parshuram walked past him, walking towards the Gurukul when Karna called him out. Parshuram stopped, when he turned around, he found Karna on his knees, his student bowed down his head, placing it on his feet. He then again came up and touched Parshuram's feet with his palms and said a mantra.

"Gurur Brahma, Gurur Vishnu.

Gurur Devo Maheshwarayah

Gurur Sakshat Param Brahma

Tasmay Shree Guruve Namah"

(Guru is verily the representative of Brahma, Vishnu, and Shiva. He creates, sustains knowledge, and destroys the weeds of ignorance. I salute such a Guru.)

"Aayushman bhava, Kirtiman bhava, my son. May your struggle, pain, achievements, failures, morals, and dutifulness be remembered by this world until eternity. May they learn from your life and your character! I am sure when people listen to your story, every teacher will wish for a student like you. I am glad I was your teacher."

Parshuram couldn't speak further. Tears were now streaming from his eyes. Without saying anything, he turned around and left. Karna stood there looking at the retreating old figure of his Guru. The man he had misunderstood and failed. Why did he not realize what he did today? Why couldn't he understand him the way he did today? He should have remembered who Parshuram was. He didn't, and here he was, contemplating his actions. He should have known. The wasp sting was long forgotten, the only part that ached now was his head and more than that his heart. Finally, after all these years, it was time to leave Mahendragiri and face the harsh reality of the city he had come from.

❖ ❖ ❖

20   Suyodhan to Duryodhan

Back in Hastinapur, the darkness was evident. This darkness was not only at night, but it was a darkness that was enveloping daylight as well. This symbolically was agitating the grand regent. He was on his seat, placed on the right side of the throne in the great court of Hastinapur. Vidur, the prime minister, was sitting on the left. The king, Dhritrashtra, was on his throne. The activities were on a full swing when one of the most hated men entered into the court. Bhishma's expression soured the moment he saw Shakuni. So much effort he had put in to throw him out of Hastinapur, yet he is here in front of them, back after his father's death. He was now the King of Gandhar Bhishma despised Shakuni from the core. He was much more dangerous than the most poisonous snake. He had poisoned the mind of Duryodhan, which was now beyond repair. What a lovely boy he the eldest Kaurav was. He was named Suyodhan; he lived up to the prefix "su" in his name which in Sanskrit was significant as it was an expression of something promising. He was understanding, well mannered, and respectful, always treating everyone with respect. But slowly he drifted into the company of his maternal uncle Shakuni. This company was more harmful than any weapon on earth. The kind and gentle boy who was loved by all grew up to be despised and hated by all. Bhishma had tried various means to bring him back into the company of people who would rear his passion for helping the needy and nurture his kindness yet the clutches of Shakuni were not that easy to be freed. It was impossible.

It was Drona now, the primary teacher of the Kauravas and Pandavas who first started calling him Duryodhan. Replacing the suffix "su" with inauspicious that was "dur". At first, Bhishma was enraged at Drona but soon realized that the "Suyodhan" he had admired had already died with time. Now this boy before him was becoming hopeless and the only thought in Bhishma's mind was how will he convince Dhritrashtra about how his son was no better enough to become the King. He had lost all his morals and principles. The problem was Suyodhan was not the only person Shakuni had poisoned. The other ninety-nine Kauravas were not far from influence and Dhritrashtra! He was unbelievably hopeless. If the king was physically disabled, he couldn't see it would have been a different case, but this man was mentally blind and useless. Anyone could easily influence him. He was the last person Bhishma wanted to talk to at any time.

It was Vidur's voice that brought Bhishma back to the present. He was addressing Shakuni and "trying" to be fair to him. Bhishma knew Vidur did not want to be acceptable to him, but there was no choice they had. Bhishma took a deep breath and added his consonance to Shakuni's father's death. Shakuni strides towards Bhishma, he spoke in his fox-like voice that could irritate the most patient of people.

"Oh! Thank you, Grand Regent, by the grace of your true war strength my father has finally descended to go to a more peaceful world."

Bhishma gritted his teeth, though he wanted to break this man's teeth then and there." Well, now that you are King, I hope you will take more care of your people than our people. By the way, you don't look too bad after your father's death as well. I hope he died a natural death or... you know what I mean. Right!"

Shakuni put up his sly smile and received a glare from Bhishma accompanied with a taunt. Now he was not a man to keep quiet, so obviously he spoke again in a lower voice. "Oh, do not think like that Dev. Yes, he did not listen to me, but I am not a murderer for a son. Yet let me tell you that I did lose him, but I still have him with me." Shakuni showed two dices to Bhishma. "These are made from the bones of my father's skeleton. He is with me all the time, you know. So, I have to look good. Right?"

Bhishma's face lost colour. No, he wasn't scared to see the dices made with the bones. He was shocked as to how much of a leer this man was! Who does that to his father's bones? God, this man was getting on his nerves. Bhishma's face was flooded with contempt and hatred. He was desperate to kick him out of the state and never let him return, but the manners of the state-bound him.

Shakuni walked towards an empty seat in the hall and took his place. Bhishma shook his head and muttered "Stud... idiot..."

Bhishma sat back when Drona entered the courtroom. He surveyed the entire room, and his face was filled with contempt when he saw Shakuni. It seemed that everyone who saw Shakuni could only hate him, and he did not seem to mind the fact either. Drona then looked at Dhritrashtra. This man was another pain. For him, the only thing that mattered, in the end, was his son Duryodhan. When it came to him, Dhritrashtra forgot all his duties. He did not think twice as to how his children were spoiled because of his ignorance and favouritism. Drona offered his salutations to the King and the Grand Regent Bhishma and then spoke.

"Maharaj, I have been teaching your sons and nephews for a long time, and after all these years of training, I have realized that they are all ready to graduate."

Dhritrastra's face lit up he smiled to himself and said to the guru "I am so happy Aacharya that my sons have finished with their education. I am sure my Duryodhan must be the best warrior amongst all of them. When will you let them come back to the Palace?"

"I think you forgot that you even have five nephews Dhritrastra, learn to remember that they are here. After all these years you should begin acknowledging the fact that the Kuru clan has 105 princes." Bhishma spoke with contempt for Dhritrastra's behaviour.

Drona ignored his comment; he knew there was no use speaking to this King. Having a physical disability is a different thing, but making it a mental one was a whole other thing. "I suggest organizing a ceremony, where the princes can prove their skills and that will also mean, the people of this state will also know who deserves to be the next king."

"What do you mean Dev? My eldest son will inherit this throne! Is there even a question about that?" Dhritarashtra eagerly said.

"The most deserving becomes King Dhritarashtra. How can you think that there is no question about it? The person who is best suited for this post must be the one having it. This throne is not your property but your responsibility. Don't forget how Lord Parshuram had killed all those who tried to make the kingdom their property. If you don't want to meet a similar fate, remain just. The graduation contest will happen and that's it." Bhishma did not notice Vidur walking to stand next to him. Vidur had placed his palm on Bhishma's shoulder so that he calms down. Slowly it was becoming difficult for Bhishma to hold back his anger and irritation. He was so done with the line of stupid scions in the family.

As Bhishma's voice had gained an edge a while ago, no one dared to speak. Even the devious Shakuni was quiet. Vidur was sure that that fox of a human must be plotting ways to kill the sons of Pandu. Drona sighed and spoke, breaking the uncomfortable silence that had enveloped the hall. "So... I fix the graduation to be held after ten days. Please do get the Kridangan ready for the event."

Drona did not want to stand there anymore. He had already sensed Bhishma's frustration; he could feel him. Everyone was feeling the same these days. All of their patience was slowly melting away. No one was happy with what the kingdom was going through.

The court was dismissed after Drona left, and then Bhishma just stormed out followed by Vidur who knew Bhishma was bit by bit building this silent anger in his heart.

When Bhishma reached his office room and muttered under his breath "This freaking Kul has inheritors which are worse than animals." Bhishma's voice became loud when Vidur entered the room. It's easier to speak out when someone is listening! "Idiots, I swear Vidur, that leech of a man, Shakuni will someday destroy this house. He is already stuck to Hastinapur, sucking all good senses like a leech sucks the blood from the human body. And Dhritarashtra, he is a freaking body ache. That man will someday give me a mental breakdown. And his stupid son, why couldn't he remain the way he was as a child and look for some good friends instead of that poisonous Ashwatthama and his brother Dussasan? I would have made him king in one way or the other if he hadn't begun walking on the wrong path. Plotting to kill his cousin and finding ways to cheat, oh! what is happening in this damn palace." Bhishma stopped now, panting. His growing age was not helping him either.

After some time, he finally said in a low voice, hardly audible "Now it's no use, Duryodhan has walked a long way, he can never come back to what he was. I just hope he gets the least one person in his life who has a little sense of Dharma. At least it will help him remain sane with all the junk Shakuni filled up in his mind."

Vidur saw how helpless Bhishma was. He just was losing control over his own family. The younger generation was becoming a bigger problem to handle.

❖ ❖ ❖

21   The Warrior Rises

The city of Hastinapur was ready for the most significant event. Eight years of training were to be tested today at the stadium. A hundred sons of the King and the five sons of Pandu would show to the world their skills and how much they had grown under the watchful eyes of Guru Drona. The passing out ceremony of the princes of Kuru clan had been organized in one of the Kridangans of Hastinapur big enough to accommodate the entire population of the city. Every citizen had come to the contest that would prove the might of the princes and also determine the best warrior. Even though all were allowed entry, the seating arrangement had been designated according to the caste. The people were still treated; there was no change in the city after all these years. Among all the kings who couldn't think beyond the confines of the deteriorated caste system which lost all its meaning and became a total reverse from what it meant in the Vedas, there were only some who recognized talent and acknowledged it. It was midnight when Vidur was summoned to the quarters of the Grand Regent "Vidur I fear tomorrow's contest. You know how the cousins do not get along very well. I fear the contest will take the form of a war between brothers and the world will come to know about the rivalry between them. The other states will surely try to use it against Hastinapur." Bhishma kept his eyes transfixed on the dark sky laced with stars.

"I agree, but this ceremony has been a part of the state's rule for decades now, and we cannot delay or cancel it either. The least we can ever do is make some rules that will bar the Princes go against each other and let this remain a contest and not make it a war." Vidur waited for Bhishma to answer.

"And what do you think we can do? Dhritarashtra is eager to prove to the world that his son is the best, and to do so he can do anything. Shakuni is after the Kuru clan and will try to use all means to provoke his nephews against Pandavs. And Pandavs are not better at this as well. I am sure if anything happens, they would not even try to resist their anger." Bhishma spoke while he turned towards Vidur.

"Sir, as I said earlier, we can at least try. Before the contest begins, you can outline a few rules so that they remember their limits and act accordingly. And we can make sure that the princes do not meet anyone before the contest." Vidur stopped himself from taking Shakuni's name.

Bhishma still understood what Vidur meant by "anyone,". "Kunti had come to me today! She said she did not want her sons to take part in the contest." Bhishma said.

"Is she sure she wants the same! Here in this palace, we cannot trust anyone. It is more like a political arena than a home anymore." Vidur spoke, gazing at the shining moon. The peace that surrounded the city outside the window was misleading and suddenly sent chills down his spine.

"She feels that people will think her sons are trying to become heir to the throne. She thinks everyone will take it as a plot against the succession."

Bhishma's voice disturbed Vidur's musing. He glanced towards the old man and back at the night sky "Sir if we consider the technicalities then we must remember that Yudhistir is the eldest amongst all the brothers. He is the rightful ascendent of the throne. Also, he has grown up to be a fine warrior and a well-principled person. He does not utter a single lie even in the worst-case and lives up to the persona of a crown prince. So, considering the Vedas and the laws to political science, Yudhistir is the rightful crown prince! Yet I do not think Dhritrastra will anyway agree to this."

Bhishma chuckled, "If a person refuses to acknowledge the presence of the sun, it does not mean the sun is not at all there Vidur! That fool of a king is too much of a part to even consider the fact that his son has lost his best and has become an evil man like his maternal uncle. But what is right has to be considered and followed!"

Vidur was brought back to the present as Arjun was shooting arrows at Duryodhan. He made sure it did not hurt Duryodhan at all. Vidur knew how Arjun was Drona's favourite student, he did have the skills, yet Vidur despised the favouritism that followed behind. A teacher must remember that a teacher destroys his self-esteem unknowingly when he or she starts focusing or someone more. There was no doubt that Arjun was unparalleled until now, but this created a sense of hatred amongst the other students, and that was not acceptable.

Drona was now in the arena proclaiming to the world about how he had created the best warrior of all times, Arjuna. Vidur noticed Dhritrastra's face held a sore expression, Vidur shook his head. This man was unbelievable. Just then an arrow came from somewhere and freed Duryodhan who was pinned to the ground with the tons of arrows that had chained him without hurting him even a little. The second time arrows went straight and fell on Bhishmas, Drona's, Kripa's, and on Vidur's feet. It was a symbol of respect shown by a warrior, the difficult archer's salute. When the third time arrows did not come at all Drona's angry voice boomed "Who the hell dared to shoot an arrow without permission. Come forth, idiot. Vidur was looking around fearfully as the security was his responsibility when he saw Kripa smile to himself. Like he knew who it was. Vidur ordered the guards to search through when a voice laced with a warrior's roar and a gentlemans grace-filled the Kridangan. The entire stadium went silent.

"Whenever someone shouts amidst mountains, the voice for sure echos. The sound does not wait for someone's orders and permission to be reflected, Acharya! You proclaimed that your student is the best and also challenged all the archers of the world. So here I am accepting your challenge!" Everyone was now looking towards the source of the voice. A young man walked from the front gate and came out in front of the crowd.

So, this was not an attack, Vidur sighed in relief. Yet he was surprised to see that someone was ready to accept Drona's challenge to fight Arjun. "Either he is mad or living in some kind of dream!" thought Vidur. Kripa, who was sitting next to him, spoke "Vidur, this man is neither mad nor is he living a dream. He is the best."

Vidur was not surprised, Kripa was a very observant man, and he could see right through anyone. "I cannot see right through anyone Vidur; you know everyone must be thinking the same thing. Often people who go against the flow are considered mad," said Kripa with his mischievous grin. Vidur admired Kripa, but at times he also felt irritated as to how weird he was.

Vidur turned his attention back to the young man standing before him. He was handsome; he looked like a rising sun; that face was so radiant. He stood there like a God. He looked so attractive that the harsh khadi that he wore looked a misfit. Many young women gazed at him with lust and love; the stadium was still very silent. No one spoke.

Drona was the one who began, "Who are you, young man? And do you know who are you challenging?"

"I know it very well whom I am challenging Acharya! He is Arjun, the Prince of the Kuru clan and your favourite disciple. And I think I am confident that I can defeat him now and right here in front of you!" the young man said.

"What is your caste? Would you bother to tell us?" An old Brahmin spoke from behind Drona.

"You are not supposed to do so, Pandit Ji! You cannot insult a warrior by asking him about his caste," said Drona to the Brahmin who looked down at his feet.

"I do not fear to tell my caste, Acharya! I do not think it is an insult to speak what caste and Gotra I belong to. I am Dev Bhishma's charioteer's son. I am the son of Radha and Adhirath." The entire crowd gasped. They were all shocked as to how a Suta dared to challenge the elites.

"How dare you, idiot? You came here to challenge the Kshatriyas. You..." the same pandit said while standing behind Drona.

"I know you, aren't you the same boy who had come to me to learn the art of Archery?" asked Drona frowning as he recalled the day a young boy had come to his house years ago, and he had turned him away.

"No Aacharya, the boy who had come to you with folded hands begging for knowledge had died years ago on the same day when you refused knowledge to him. Your knowledge was confined to Kshatriya's only so how could I be taught, right? The person you see today is not even near to what you saw years ago!" answered the young warrior, pain visible in his eyes. Drona steered his gaze; he could not face him suddenly. He had this strong urge to hide his face somewhere when his eyes met Arjun's who was looking at his Guru with a questioning look. But before anyone else could say anything, the caste people began shouting.

"Go away, Suta. Go away.

Go away, Suta. Go away."

The man who was so confident some time ago was now looking all around him. His caste men were also against him, shouting with the others. Disbelief filled his heart; the confident young warrior had tears filling his eyes. Vidur was observing him, and then the crowd. "These are people we want to help and bring up their place in society, and here they are not even ready to support their caste men. Idiots…" Vidur said in disbelief to Kripa.

Kripa just shook his head and said, "You can't help people who do not want to help themselves Vidur. Cooldown and watch let's see what happens to the only person who is trying to help himself." But when they turned their gaze back, they saw something else happening.

Suyodhan or Duryodhan, the eldest Kaurav had grasped the young warrior's wrist. Both of them smiled at each other. Suyodhan's entry into the feud had silenced the crowd back again. He then spoke in a calm and clear voice addressing the people "Do you not feel ashamed insulting a warrior in this manner? The origin of rivers and warriors can never be defined. What does it matter if he is a Suta, he is talented, and hence you should learn to recognize it? And why are you quiet, Arjun? Are you afraid that you will lose in the hands of someone much better than you in archery?" Suyodhan turned to Drona and said, "You just said guru that asking a warrior his caste is an insult then tell your beloved caste men to let Arjuna fight this young man. And as much as I remember when Ravan and Asura had called for war Ram, a Kshatriya had fought. So, when the seventh Vishnu did not discriminate thinking Ravan was an Asura he was a Brahmin son of sage Pulasthya as much as I remember, then who are we to discriminate? Instead of hiding behind stupid beliefs, Arjun should fight like a warrior; you claim him to be!"

The pandit now looked up and spoke in a loud voice, "There was a difference Suyodhan Ravan was a King, and Ram was also already declared the King of Ayodhya. That challenge was of a King."

"OK! so you say that anyone who is a king can challenge a Prince?" Suyodhan questioned.

"Yes, a King can challenge a Prince." The pandit said scornfully yet suspiciously.

"Fine then, I the Crown Prince of Hastinapur declares this young warrior a King. I Suyodhan crown him the King! Listen to all the citizens of Hastinapur; this man is a proof and example of the fact that talent knows no caste. There are people in our society who do not want to overcome the filthy rules of caste and harm their positions. Far away towards the east of this country lies the kingdom of Anga which was won over by the Grand Regent. That kingdom has no king! So from this day, I announce you to be the King of Anga Pradesh."

"I do not want a kingdom, Prince. I do not need one; my only motive to come here was that I could prove my talent and my knowledge would be recognized. You do not need to do this!" the young man countered Suyodhan.

"You have questioned the entire Kshatriya clan, so you must get a chance to prove your talents and the only way that can be done is if you become King. Hence, I am giving you the kingdom and a chance to prove who you are." Suyodhan said.

"Stop! Suyodhan you are not supposed to........" Bhishma began, but before he could finish, Dhritrastra jumped in between and started.

"I am happy to hear what Suyodhan said. I agree that he has the talent, and hence he must get the chance. So now I Dhritrastra the king of Hastinapur announce this young warrior to be the King of Anga. he from now will rule Anga Pradesh." Dhritarashtra spoke. And then a loud cheer erupted in the crowd as everyone said in a chorus.

"Anga raj Karna ki jai! Anga raj Karna ki Jai!"

The young warrior who was unrecognized till now was now a King. The people who were not ready to acknowledge his presence were now shouting his name happily. Tears of happiness slipped from his eyes. The young warrior was now Anga raj Karna and not just Vasusena Karna. All because of this one man is standing before him, Suyodhan. Karna went near Suyodhan and said in a husky tone, "Prince, today you have given me what I did not ever think of. I came here to prove my talent, but you gave me a chance to not only prove it but to live it for my entire life. I came here a Suta; you made me a King. I, at this moment, promise my ability, my talent, my wealth, my sincerity, and prosperity to you. I promise my intelligence to you and pledge to always be there for you whenever you call!"

"I do not need all of that Karna; I just want your friendship. Come." Suyodhan said and hugged Karna. This was the beginning of a friendship that would last a lifetime. Vidur kept silent while all of this and noticed Shakuni give a sly smile to Suyodhan. Though Vidur knew that Suyodhan was a man who did not believe much in the caste boundaries, he also knew that Shakuni had made him a poisonous snake. Vidur felt scared, not for himself, but the man just now made a king. He feared that in the dirty game of politics that was coming soon would harm Karna the most.

"Go fight Arjun now and prove your talent friend!" said Suyodhan to Karna. A warrior had risen as the sun rises from the east; this man had come up as bright as that sun.

22   Arjun and Karna

The stadium was now bursting with cries and shouts of the conservatives. They were all contemplating the fact that the King also supported the prince. Bhishma stood silent. He was already stopped in between his tracks and defied by Dhritarashtra. The only thing that mattered to Bhishma now was "Karna". "Will this man become a victim or remain the person he is today?"

Vidur, on the other hand, was examining Kripa's face. Kripa was sulking. This man who should have been the happiest of all is here sad for the coronation of his student. Why? Who would ask and earn the Brahmin's wrath, which was already not in an excellent mood! Vidur was still suspicious of the look on Shakuni's and Suyodhan's face. Every time he thought about it, he got chills in the entire body. Meanwhile, on one side of the Stadium, Kunti was watching the event keenly. Gandhari accompanied her, Dushala, the sister of the Kauravas and Supriya, the princess of Amravati.

Inside the stadium stood the two warriors facing each other; the mid-afternoon sun was getting harsher and more challenging to handle. Yet the newly assigned King of Anga was looking straight towards the sun, much to everyone's surprise. He folded his hands towards the sun, looking directly at it, and then did his Pranam. He then spoke loudly "I the student of Lord Parshuram and Guru Kripa, the son of Radha and Adhirath, Vasusen Karna challenge you for a duel, Arjun."

Arjun accepted the challenge by bowing his head in front of his

Guru, Drona. But Drona stood transfixed in his position with a stricken face. For the first time, he did not acknowledge the salutations of his favourite Arjun. His eyes were on Karna, and his bow. At first, Drona thought Karna was bluffing about being the student of Parshuram, but when he saw the Bow. The Vijya bow of Parshuram, now his heart felt weak. He had vowed that he would make Arjun the best archer in the world, but his Guru Parshuram had chosen Karna, and he knew that the sixth Vishnu would never give up his mighty Vijya to some random person. He did impress Parshuram, but he knew he was not good enough for the Vijya bow yet if Karna was given the bow, he must be the best. Karna was for God's sake precious; Drona's heart was racing as though it would jump out of his rib cage and say hello to everyone. He was pulled out of the shock when he heard Arjun call out his name two to three times. It felt like his voice came from miles away. Drona said nothing; he just pulled up his hand and blessed Arjun. Now that he knew his student was not no more, the best. Drona's instinct told him, "I have chosen Arjun, but my Guru chose Karna. Arjun is good, but no doubt Karna is the best. He just is the best!"

The duel began with Arjun shooting the first arrow which was countered by Karna skilfully. Arjun started to shoot a trail of arrows with his mantras and opposing that Karna shot an arrow towards the sky instead. That arrow went up to form a protective shield around himself. The protection shone like a fireball, blinding most standing nearby.

The next arrow went out from Karna's bow. The missile was not of much power, yet it was unknown to Arjun. A black plume of smoke was discharged from the arrow, and it went straight to envelop Arjun. Drona's eyes widened. The arrow shot was an ancient technique of Arura warship. Drona never gave it to Arjun, nor did he teach him about it, because he did not know it. Parsuram never taught all the students to use those deadly weapons. Parshuram had said to Drona, "You should never teach everything to everyone. The mind of a person defines the knowledge he is capable of gaining. If you hand a missile to a child, he will surely end up killing hundreds."

Parshuram did not even find Drona worthy of those mantras. Drona was ready to die with a heart attack now. This student whom he had tried to make the best was not no more, the best. In a group of hundred fools, he might be, but this one new warrior who came up out of the blue was, at last, the best.

Whereas Arjun was struggling in the smoke, he had never known about such a missile. He cursed under his breath. He had to hit several arrows, after which he finally was free, and the smoke was gone, but yes it did leave him breathing heavily and coughing. His face went red because of the fits of coughing, as he angrily looked at Karna. His confidence was becoming a little weaker. To come out of the smoke itself, Arjun had taken a long time. The sun was now nearing the western sky. The night ready to cover the day. Arjun shot an arrow towards Karna while he was distracted. His anger was taking its toll. He was furious at the man standing before him and also at his Guru, who had said that he was the best. But now that he stood before Karna, he felt small, Karna towered over most of the Kuru princes except Bhim and Duryodhan who looked mighty all.

Karna noticed the arrow very near to him and hence did not have the time to react therefore out of reflex, he stood still and let his breastplate appear on his body. That thankfully happened on time, so when the arrow hit Karna, it just collided on the shining golden armour and broke into pieces. Karna pulled another hand to shoot, but only then the sun went down on the western horizon signifying the end of the day. Karna stopped and shot the arrow towards the ground. An arrow, when pulled on the shaft, cannot go back into someone's quiver. Arjun smirked and said, "So this is the limit of your warship qualities, Anga Raj?" He pressed the title, making it sarcastic so he could hurt Karna.

Karna was angry, but he composed himself and said, "I think you were too busy learning to shoot arrows Arjun that you forgot listening to your Guru. I am sure he told you that after the sun sets you are not allowed to use your weapons in a duel or a war. It's against the war rules, am I not right Aacharya Drona?" Karna spoke in an equally sarcastic tone, making Arjun angrier. Even though the result never came up for the ordinary people who had begun leaving the stadium, the men who called themselves great warriors knew who was the better archer.

Arjun left in a fit of rage; he had so many questions for his beloved Guru. Caste men felt angrier at the fact that the Suta was trained by the greatest warriors of their caste. Suyodhan and Shakuni were indeed happy as they got someone who could fight the Pandavs and was much better than all the warriors.

Radha and Adhirath left the stadium with all others, Adhirath feared the time he would have to face Bhishma. Yet a slight commotion was heard from where the queen was sitting. Even Karna's attention was drawn towards the origin of the racket. In the balcony, Kunti had fainted. Her last words before passing out were "My Son! My Son!". The princess of Amravati and Dusshala were holding the queen, not letting her fall to the ground. Her maids helped her leave the arena. The princesses followed by Gandhari.

"Why did Kunti faint?" Bhishma and Vidur spoke in a union. The two of them looked at each other, and their eyes widened.

The rumour of Kunti having a child before marriage had not failed to spread. It was strong enough to find its way to Bhishma's and Vidur's ears. They thought for a moment, and then Vidur said: "She passed out after Karna's breastplate appeared, she said My Son before fainting."

Bhishma's face lost all its colour. The logic Vidur presented was not baseless. That is what happened. But why did she not speak? Ah, something was missing, something not adding up well. Wasn't Karna Radha and Adhirath's son yes, he was, of course, he was.

Bhishma brushed away the thoughts and ignored his thoughts.

But Vidur was not that easy to forget. This man had the brains that did not forget till he got hold of what he had called into his mind.

Just then Kripa walked up to Karna. Karna instantly bowed down before him. Kripa was beaming; this was his student, yet there was a hint of sadness in his eyes. Karna was not a person who would ignore it. So, he did what everyone does, he asked.

"Guru, are you not happy that I achieved what everyone could never think of?"

Kripa smiled, sadness still visible on his face," Karna, I am proud that I taught you. Today, when I saw you at the stadium, I was thrilled. You looked every inch a Kshatriya! If you did not disclose your actual caste, no one would know." He sighed and continued, "You worshipped your Karma and found your God in Kshatriya dharma, you are now much better than all the warriors here. But Karna remember, I told you once, nothing comes for free? Son this kingdom and position you got today came up to you from Suyodhan. He said he wants nothing but your friendship, but no Karna this position will cost you more than anything in life. You promised him to be there for him always, be aware then; he has Shakuni by his side! That man is toxic; you will soon realize the cost you will have the pay for this kingdom."

Karna did realize Kripa's concern, but he did not feel Suyodhan was a wrong person. He had his share of pain. All taunted him for being a blind man's son. He was never given the attention that any child received from his mother. Karna brushed away the doubts emerging in his mind after conversing with Kripa. Karna was happy that at last, he got a respectful place based on his merit. He was delighted that now he will be able to give his parents and brothers and his wife a better life. Karna left the stadium alone and walked towards the humble home of Adhirath. He had to meet his parents and tell them about his success.

The day had ended, and so had Karna's life ended. The next day was to bring a new life, a new beginning, and a new responsibility. Soon he was going to live a better experience of respect and have a position that he had achieved based on his talent and hard work. Little did he know that his struggle was beginning now. The difficulties were to come up from now.

"Not all the glitter you see in the palaces is always Gold, Karna. It's dark in there, really very dark." were Kripa's last words to Karna before parting ways in the stadium.

23   Bhishma and Vidhur

Karna climbed the stairs of the beautiful palace of Hastinapur as the night descended. It was dark all around, but the castle was illuminated with thousands of earthen lamps celebrating the coming of their prices. Dhritarashtra had ordered all to organize a dinner party for all the family members. It was evident that he did not like it that Pandavs were also a part of his so-called "family". For him, his family started and ended with his sons, himself, and his wife. Shakuni was like a gift of Gandhar he lived in Gandhar for one month or so and then he came back to Hastinapur.

Karna could hear the musicians playing instruments and singing in the silence of the night. The happy songs were beautiful to hear, but something inside of him was not pleased. He stopped at one of the entrances and thought about the happenings of the day. In one single day, his entire life had changed. He was now the king of Anga, but that post ended up taking away his family from him. For years now, the entire family of Karna had moved to Hastinapur, leaving Champanagri behind. When he went back to the house where they now lived in Hastinapur after the event at the stadium had ended, he was happy. His heart yearned to tell all of them that now they will live a better life in a palace. But what happened in the house was not what he had thought. When he entered the home, he saw all of his brothers having a silent chat. His mother was sitting near the kitchen, and tears were streaming down her face, Varushali was helping Radha, and Adhirath was sitting alone deep in thought. Shom was the first to notice Karna. He stood up and walked towards Karna and hugged him. "So finally, you decided to come back to this home, brother! When are you becoming a legit king, though?"

Karna heard the sarcasm dripping from Shom's voice which he ignored. He just silently walked towards Radha and sat next to her. Varushali moved when Karna took his seat. He did not say anything for some time, though. He just sat there searching for words; what he thought would be easy was now so difficult. Suddenly the eight years of distance had dug a deep hole in their relationship. Karna's family was standing on a cliff, and he was standing on an opposite one without a bridge to connect them. Suddenly, there was an uneasiness descending between him and his family. The years away had left him with no words; no thoughts and emotions were far not being found. It was ugly, not at all nice.

Karna struggled for some more time and spoke, "Mata, I am now the King of Anga, Prince Suyodhan has given me the kingdom, and we are now friends. Mata, I want you, father, Varushali, my brothers, to come along with me to the palace of Anga and live there with me. I want you all to have all the comfort that you deserve. Please let us go there. Come along with me."

Radha turned towards Karna, caressed her son's face. He had grown into a fine young man, too beautiful to be true. For years he was away from her, after some time she wiped her tears and said in a low, shaky voice, "Karna, son you remained away from all of us for so long! But that distance never felt too much; you were there somewhere in our mind always. You were my Radhye. The quiet and silent Radhye. But today, Karna! Today you seem so distant. This distance is mental; it is sudden and unbelievable. You know it feels like you are someone else. It is just so sudden and so not true! Karna, the King of Anga, is not my son; he is just any other ruler, far away beyond our reach and unapproachable."

"No mata, I am still here, your son, Radhe! Why do you think I am far away from you, or unapproachable? I am still the same Vasusen you called your son!"

"No Karna, I might not be educated, but I have known life. Remember you had told me the story of Ram years ago? You might have missed, but do you know what I noticed? I noticed that Ram became unapproachable to his family, a distant man far away from everyone when he became King. Karna, you might think that you are the same man, but no son, you can never be the same the moment you become King. When the Lord himself couldn't change his fate and his situation as a King, how do you think you or anyone else could?" Radha spoke her tears began flowing again.

"Karna, what your mother wants to say is, we cannot come along with you to that palace. And one day you will realize why! Karna goto perform your duties as the King. Follow your Dharma, but remember everything is not what it looks like inside the confines of that palace. There are deep cracks within, invisible and dark. You will soon know the reality, and then you will realize what you have landed yourself into! Karna go and do what you have promised; this humble home will always wait for you; the doors will always remain open for you. We will keep this home full of Dharma for you Karna so that when reality becomes unbearable, you will have a peaceful place to come back to." Adirath said to Karna with a small smile.

Karna's eyes were full of tears now; he was contemplating the fact that he had to go there alone, without the people he had spent his childhood with. Without the people he called family, he felt empty within.

"Karna, I know you are not happy with the fact that we will not see your Rajya Abhishek, nor will we see you become king! But Karna remembers you achieved that place with your talent and your merit, but Karna I, your father am a common charioteer. When you become king, you will see dignitaries coming into your court; even Pitamah Bhishma will be there, do you think me or your family will ever feel at ease there amongst all those around? Karna some things should remain the way they are! Don't be sad, we will come to see you around, but we cannot live there forever with you. That is how it is meant to be Karna." Adhirath tried explaining and then asked if Varushali would like to go along with Karna.

"I do not want to go to the palace, father. I have lived here all my life now; this is my society and my family. I will love to stay back here. This is what is best for me." Varushali gave Karna a small smile. She knew he would understand.

Karna sighed deeply and stood up. He knew there was no use saying anything now that everyone had made up their mind. He did see that they were all speaking what was best for all of them, but his heartfelt weak, his mind did register his family's thoughts, but the heart ached.

He wiped his tears and touched his parent's feet to take their blessings. He smiled at Varushali and then hugged his brothers. Karna after which walked away to the river bank where the royal attendant sent by Suyodhan was waiting for him with silks and ornaments, a crown, and a chariot.

Now, standing on that entrance, he felt a knot in his heart. He knew, once he ascended the leftover palace steps, there will be no turning back. With a heavy heart, he climbed up the steps. "Didn't I always want the respect that I have gained? Did I not want my Talent to be recognized? Then why is this feeling wrong? Why is this so difficult for me? Why am I doubting every step that I am taking?" His trance was broken when the steps ended, and he saw Kunti standing near the entrance as though she had been waiting. Her eyes were shining the moment she saw him. Unknowingly tears escaped their eyes; both were crying. Why? They did not know. Karna felt drawn towards the widowed queen. She stood there eagerly waiting for him to come near her. An affectionate smile on her lips made Karna feel happy.

While walking towards her he saw a large brass pot with water in it, kept beneath the front dome of the palace. Fresh lotus flowers had been placed in the water to beautify the area. Karna couldn't help stop his urge to pick one up, and he took a lotus out of the pot. He walked towards Kunti, he bent down and placed the full-bloomed lotus near Kunti's feet. Kunti flinched a little but stood still. She tried speaking, but her words were caught in her throat. Only she knew how she wanted to embrace Karna and cry her heart out. Her throat was now hurting because of the tears she was controlling with so much effort. Karna stood up; his eyes were red from tears; he refused to let go. He took a deep breath and said, "Maharahi, the first time you came to Hastinapur, I had a strong urge to welcome you with lotuses being showered on you. And I did it! You were thrilled; I had seen it in your eyes that day. Now that I have come here to this palace for the first time, I felt the same urge to offer this flower to you. I hope you accept it."

"Karna, I am not worthy of this respect that you have given me son! One must be worthy of having this flower placed in their feet! I am not; I simply am no....." Kunti couldn't complete as the memory of her pushing away the basket with Karna in the river came back. What a grave sin she had committed!

"A mother is as respectable as God himself, Maharani. When you came to Hastinapur, I had silently hoped that you would help me gain an education. As a child, I had seriously accepted the fact that the king and queen are equivalent to one's parents. But you left soon after; I was internally hurt that my secret hope and desire will be heard by none. Though I achieved the respect, I had so wished for, yet I still respect you. You were the first queen of Hastinapur when I had come here. You will always have that respect and that place in the hearts of all the people." Karna said in his soft voice as if he instinctively was trying to stop Kunti from shedding tears.

"I am flawed Karna! I have done something that no woman can ever think of. And I am sure when you come to know the truth, all this respect you talk about will fade away."

Karna smiled, this queen, who was known for her beauty, and her determination to leave everything for her husband was crying because she feels one day his respect for her will fade away! Karna was surprised his heart ached for her. He did know the rumours about her, but yet he never judged her. His heart did not allow him to do so. "Maharani, that respect will never fade away. I can promise you that! And who is not flawed? Everyone has their flaws if we start concentrating on how bad a person is then we will never see how good they are!"

Kunti just looked at Karna straight into his eyes. He was telling the truth, every word he said was genuine, she knew it. The queen might not know, but the mother knew it. She went down and picked up the flower; a small smile made its way on her face. She suddenly embraced Karna, he went stiff for a moment, but after that, he relaxed.

Karna there at that moment for once felt all his worries fade away. There was so much affection in Kunti's embrace. This time he did not stop his tears; he let them flow. All his doubts were far away from him; the confidence he lacked some time ago was back with just one embrace.

Kunti pulled back and spoke ones again. "Karna, you are here for the first-time son, be aware of all the steps you take. These palace walls are gigantic, but the people here have a heart smaller than a rat hole. Karna behind these walls there are only two shades in people, either they are black or white. Grey shades are seldom found. Extremes live here; you never know who is who. You are too good at heart. People might try to influence you to do things that are against Dharma, but please listen to your soul. Never let yourself commit a crime that you will not be able to forgive. You get me, right?"

Karna was so confused as to why was Kunti so concerned for him. She feared for him like he was her son like she was the one who gave birth to him. But he was well aware that she was right; she had lived all her life in those palaces and knew what people are like. He had heard the same advice from Kripa and Adhirath as well.

"Karna, these people can be serious vexations for your mind, heart, and soul! Just try to remain unmoved from the path of Dharma. Poison tends to mix with everything well, but yet it does not leave its true nature! Yet it only kills Karna." Kunti stopped. She was sure that he must have understood what she wanted to tell him.

"I will try my best to keep all you said in mind, Maharani!" Karna said in a soft voice.

After giving Karna another affectionate nod, Kunti turned around and walked away. Karna watched her turn left, and her figure faded away. After she was gone, Karna also stepped inside the palace. He was guided by one of the guards to Suyodhan's chamber.

What Karna did not notice were two figures standing hidden behind one of the pillars. They had been watching from far away, listening to what the queen was talking to Karna about. The guards did not question the two men, who would dare to ask the Grand Regent and the Prime minister.

Right then if someone saw the two men, they would laugh as to how they stood there with shocked eyes which were ready to pop out of their sockets and lips parted in disbelief. Bhishma was the first one to compose himself, Vidur followed. The two men were just too shocked to speak, yet Vidur spoke. "Yes, Pitamah, the rumours about Kunti's firstborn are indeed true! The way Kunti has been behaving speaks the truth. That affection can only be of a mother. Did you see how she carried away the flower-like it was the most precious object she ever received."

"Still Vidur, keep an eye on Kunti and her maid, the one who came with her from her maternal home. I want solid proof. And if this is true, the rightful successor of this throne is neither Yudhistir nor Suyodhan. It is Karna! It is him, Vidur. By merit and by age as well. He is the eldest of all Kuru Princes, and he is the best among all! Now I recall, Adhirath had once told me that Karna was adopted. Karna is not Adhirath's biological son. I knew I was missing something, this was a memory that I hadn't paid much attention too."

Bhishma was thrilled; he did want Karna to be king. In the back of his mind, he was now praying that Karna is the eldest son of Kunti. That was the simplest way to end the possibility of a dangerous family feud in the future. But Kunti! She was not ready to speak the truth! And no one else, not even the Grand Regent could tell this to anyone if the mother was not prepared to disclose the fact. He had to remain silent until Kunti decides to break her silence, which he knew would take a long time to happen. The two men remained silent after that and directly walked to the hall where the royal dinner was to be held.

❖ ❖ ❖

24   The Palace of Death

Since the day Karna entered Suyodhan's chamber, he was welcomed like a friend, an equal. Ashwatthama, the son of Guru Drona, had become another new friend for Karna. Karna had also gone to Anga Pradesh; it was a beautiful little state, a part of the gigantic northern plains of Bharat, its land was fertile and irrigated by the tributaries of Ganga.

His coronation was held in the palace of Anga with much pomp and show with alms were distributed to all. The Brahmins were at first not very happy to see Karna ascend the throne, yet when they began the proceeding of the court, they were impressed by the new king. They closely observed how he functioned his manners and his way to deal with matters related to the state. He would speak about Dharma with ease and also worked accordingly. Slowly, the kingdom he ruled was becoming a beautiful mix of equality and prosperity. He tried everything he could to induce the sense of indiscriminate nature in the people he was heading over. He knew one thing that his sole purpose was to serve the people who accepted him. For a considerable amount of time, he was hated by many in the kingdom, especially the elites. For them, it was a matter of their long history of hierarchy rules, and that was the only way they knew how to function. The man had reduced himself into a slave, a slave of old wrong interpretations of Vedas and they were trying to resist the impact of the new liberal ruler they got. You can never resist what is right for a long time, the farther you push it away, the closer it comes to you.

The king impacts his people a lot. The leader not only leads the city, but he also makes an impression in the minds of the people, and that is what makes him a good leader. Karna had a profound impact on his people. He bowed down to the Brahmins and Pandits; he gave the Kshatriya ministers and other men with posts immense respect; he provided the Vaishya's and the Shudras rights that safeguarded their interests and prevented discrimination. Slowly the Kingdom had come up to love their new King. The impact he made was a matter of discussion on the evening meetings of people around the city. Though most never admitted his good nature, he was not resisted at all. When one makes an effort, it can never go unnoticed. Karna had been too busy with his work that he did not go back to see his parents in Hastinapur and Suyodhan his friend.

The only visitor of the palace of Anga was Ashwatthama, the only son of Dronacharya and Kripi. Karna was intrigued as to how this friendship took shape. He had met Ashwatthama on the night of the feast after the graduation ceremony, Ashwatthama's father's disdain for Karna was unpleasant as his undying affection for his sishya (disciple) Arjun. Ashwatthama did not follow his father's ideas about everything around him. The hatred Drona reared in his heart was equal to the friendship Ashwatthama pledged to Karna. Drona's distrust for Karna went a long way to the time when he had refused Karna of the knowledge he was capable of having. He felt that Karna would somehow poison the lad, and he will drift away from his family. Little did Drona know that his partiality with Arjun had taken away his son from him. Ashwatthama would often joke saying "My old man, seriously does not like you, Karna!" The two would laugh together about how Drona spared murderous looks to Karna at the dinner party. Karna remembered how Ashwatthama was seated next to the seat of Drona, glaring at Arjun and then back at his father.

A few months back Karna had received news about the war with Panchal, where the Guru had asked the Pandavas to defeat Drupad, the king of Panchal, and bring him on his foot crawling like a worm. And the Pandavas had given in to his orders. Karna was shocked at the news; he looked at Ashwatthama with wide-open eyes. "Hey, why are you giving me that look? I am not accountable for my old man's deeds and misdeeds. It's not my fault that his ego is bigger than his appetite!"

Karna had burst out laughing at his last sentence. He knew the story behind the rivalry between Drupad and Drona. Drona had been insulted by Drupad in his court about thirteen to fourteen years ago. That man was taking revenge for an event that took place more than a decade ago. Seriously, his ego was huge. The matter could have been resolved by talking with each other, but no. He would not agree and were Pandvas fools to agree to such a stupid thing, Karna shook his head in disbelief and then let it go, anyway his opinion would not matter to the Guru nor anyone else.

Karna reached Hastinapur in the evening. When he came there, he found out that Yudhistir was announced the crown prince, and he was leaving Hastinapur for some time to go to the small village of Varnavarta. They had been invited there for a stay at the newly built palace.

Karna was surprised as to why were the Pandavas invited instead of any of the Kauravas. On inquiring about Suyodhan, Karna was taken to the basement of the main palace of Hastinapur. The room of the Basement looked unused, and hardly anyone visited the place. "Why would he come here?" Karna thought.

When he entered the room, he saw a model of a beautiful palace in there. And he saw Dussashan the second Kaurava, Suyodhan, and Shakuni standing around it. Suyodhan saw Karna, and his face brightened, he looked visibly happy as he pulled him in a hug. But Karna's attention was on the modal and how Shakuni was smiling looking at it. And when they were done exchanging talks about the new kingship and the crowning of Yudhistir Karna questioned Suyodhan.

Dussashan was the person who answered instead. "This is a palace modal Anga raj. This is the exact look of the palace of Varnavarta. The place where Pandav's are going."

Karna noticed the colour of the modal and touched it. The smell of the substance told him that it was lac. But usually, models of the palaces were never made out of lace; they were built of clay and soil. It was unusual to use lac. Before Karna could question further, Dussashen spoke.

"The name of the palace of Varnavart is Lakshagriha! The palace of lacquer. It is a beautiful palace with a secret hidden in its wall." An evil smile was now playing on his face, similar to Shakuni's.

Karna then realized what secret he was talking about. It was sure that no one knew about the substance with which the palace was made of. Lacquer was a highly flammable material that could catch fire within seconds. One spark and the entire castle would be in flames. The palace was built with orders from evil Shakuni. It was a plot to kill the Pandavas along with their mother, Kunti. Purochan the architect who was also a close associate of the king of Gandhar had built the palace in the forest of Varnavart. The house was a death trap since lacquer was highly flammable. The plot was such that no one ever would suspect any foul play. Lacquer was a substance used to protect and decorate almost on any kind of surface even or otherwise. The presence of Lacquer on the walls was unusual, but it was gaining importance amongst architects, and it would never be questioned by anyone even if they notice it. Eventually, everyone would think it was an accident, and Pandavas would forever be forgotten.

Karna was shocked to see how devious Shakuni could be and how much influence he had over his nephews. Karna wanted to warn Kunti about what was about to happen with them in Varnavart and stop them from leaving, and of course, Shakuni sensed it. After which he pressurized him to keep mum, reminding him of his promise to Suyodhan to remain loyal to him forever. Karna was bound by his commitment and felt trapped in this hideous game that the Gandhar's King was playing.

25   Karna's Dilema

The Kuru's had gathered on the verandah of the Palace. They were all ready to bid farewell to the Pandavs and their mother. Karna waited far away near a pillar, his heart was racing, and he did not feel at peace at all. His body was tensed, and his entire existence felt numb. He had never in his whole life felt so unsure and so confused. He wanted to tell Kunti right there, but he couldn't. His mind told him to keep quiet, and his heart asked him to speak up. He became restless with each passing moment. At one point he wanted to leave, but he couldn't arouse suspicion as well.

Karna was distraught, and his withdrawn behaviour today was noticed by Vidur. By now, his suspicion was proved, and he was now sure that Karna was indeed the eldest Pandav. When his spies came up to him with the news, he had rushed to Bhishma and informed him of it. Bhishma was happy yet not glad because till Kunti did not reveal the fact, there was no way out. Vidur sensed something wrong. Karna's restlessness could mean a lot. His spies told him that he had seen the King of Anga go to the Basement the night before, and that was something unusual.

Kunti bid farewell to all and then walked towards Karna. Many had noticed this pattern as to how Kunti never ignored or refused to acknowledge Karna. She might sometimes miss Suyodhan or Dussashan or the other Kauravas, but never did she forget Karna. For those who did not know the truth, it was like Karna was the son Kunti never had but wished to have. The Bheem, Nakul, Sehdev and Arjun did not seem to like this much but kept quiet as Yudhistir the eldest Pandava would say that Kunti had every right to talk to anyone she wanted to."Anga Raj might be with the Kaurava's no one could overlook the fact that he is a great warrior. And as a warrior, one must respect the other warrior before them."

When Kunti went to Karna, he remained grave and touched her feet to get her blessings. When he stood up, Kunti placed her palm on his cheeks and said, "Keertiman Bhava, son! May God bless you with name and fame. Karna may Dharma reside in your heart always and forever. Son Adharna is a corrosive that can corrode gold as well. Let not Adharma harm your soul. This is the blessings I have for you."

Karna this time couldn't hold back tears. His eyes were not helping him. He let the tears flow down his cheeks and gave Kunti a sad smile. He did not speak because he knew, if he did, he would tell her everything, and that would not be great for the Kuru prince. Kunti thought he would speak for some time, but he didn't. He just folded his hands and nodded, tears still flowing down his cheeks.

Kunti turned around and descended the steps of the palace. When the chariot of the Pandavas left, and all the others had entered the palace, Karna saw Bhishma and Vidur waiting outside looking at the leaving chariots. Karna did not speak anything and wanted to leave the place as soon as possible. But Vidur stopped him. He said in a gentle tone to Karna "Anga Raj, are you tensed about something? Your face is soaked with tears! You do not seem at peace, as always."

"Mahamantri Ji, some situations are just out of one's control. And when you know what is happening is not great, you tend to lose all the peace you have at heart."

Karna was about to enter the palace gate, but he stopped. He thought for a while and turned back to find Vidur still looking at him. This man was the only person who could help him, he thought.

Karna was hesitant at first. He walked back to Vidur and said again "Mahamantri Ji, when you watch the random statues of a palace fall and break into pieces it does not hurt, but when the statue kept in the Garbagriha is shattered into pieces, one does feel fear and pain enveloping one's heart."

The moment he spoke, Karna turned around and left the verandah, taking large steps, consciously trying to avoid any more questioning. Bhishma had not heard the conversation but Vidur was trying to understand the message Karna was trying to give him through his words. There was something that was hidden in his words, but what he had to find out because this had to be something severe.

26   I Hope You Win!

A messenger had come from Varnavarta after six months of the departure of the Pandavas, who informed Karna about the death of Pandavas and their mother Kunti. It was announced in the royal court of the King of Anga. He was having a discussion with his ministers about some serious issued concerning the state's agricultural taxes. When a guard informed him about the messenger who had come with a piece of news related to the Pandavas, he had immediately sent for the messenger. Karna's heart was pounding, fearing the worst. He was anxious; he was not sure if Vidur did understand the riddle he had spoken to him. Karna was fearful about what he would hear now after six months of peaceful silence.

The messenger entered the court. He said, "Anga Raj, I have been sent by Gandhar Raj, Shakuni to inform you that the palace of Varnavarta suffered an accidental fire and the five Pandava's and their mother Queen Kunti were burnt alive inside it while they were sleeping......"

The man kept on speaking the details, but Karna had stopped listening. His eyes were full of tears blinding his vision. He felt a deep hatred for Shakuni in that one moment, so much that he could have killed that man if he was to stand in front of him. How could someone plot such a murder so cruel? Burning people alive! Ugh! just so inhumane was that. And he felt miserable and hated himself for what happened. He knew it all, yet he couldn't stop it.

Karna did not like the way Drona groomed the Pandav's. He hated the fact that they grew up to be such discriminating men. Trained with the degraded points of Veda's which were not true, but Karna honoured them as warriors. Arjun was his sworn enemy, the man who said to be the best because he was born in a better place than him, but Karna did not deny the fact that he was good at the art. Not the best, but better than all in Aryavarta. Karna could go against his enemies but never be cruel to them. And that is how it should be; enmity does not mean cruelty. And the death the Pandavas had died made him feel worst. If it were a war, he would never hold back, pulling up arms against them, but this death was a murder. There is a difference between dying in a fight and being murdered. Indeed, the Gandhar King was a cold-blooded murderer. Karna felt a deep pain in his heart. More for Kunti than her five sons. No one deserves such a cruel death, no one!

The messenger was now standing before the King uneasily, waiting to get dismissed. All the ministers eyed the archer on the throne, and his sad, stricken face hidden by none. Before anyone could question him, Karna stood up and left the room, slamming the door shut with a bang. None in the court spoke. They had never seen the king in such a state of mind. The calmness he had was all gone.

An invitation for the swayamvar had come to Karna after a few years after the Varnavarta incident. Karna did try to forget it, but his mind was not ready to listen to him. When Karna got the invitation for the swayamvar, he was a little hesitant. Karna was unsure if he actually should go to Panchal and participate in the event. His doubts were washed away when he received a letter from Suyodhan who asked him to participate and accompany him to the swayamvar without fail.

Karna had left Anga and met Suyodhan, who was accompanied by Ashwatthama, Dussashan, and Shakuni. His expression instantly soured when he saw the Gandhar King. All of them met on their way to Panchal. Suyodhan and Ashwatthama were confident that Karna would be the one chosen. He was a bit embarrassed after as the teasing that continued all along the way was quite enthralling. Karna did not feel very good about the entire event. He felt uneasy as they entered the boundaries of Panchal. It was already evening, and the event had to take place the next day. He couldn't understand what that feeling was all about. His mind got diverted when they reached the main entrance of the palace. The Panchal king was waiting with the Crown Prince on the main entrance to greet all the guests. Karna looked at Drupad; this man was the same person who had failed because of his arrogance years back. Yet he did not let things change; he held his head high, the arrogance and pride still not worn out. He wore his pride as any other jewellery.

Ashwatthama whispered so only Karna could hear him "Some things never change........ Never did my father change neither did this man. No doubt they were once best friends. Laws of attraction failed here."

Karna suppressed his laughter and folded his hands as they reached the place where the Crown Prince had been standing. Drishtadyumn was a young man, the elder brother of Draupadi. He was the only son of Drupad. He embraced Karna and said, "I know you are the best archer of this country. And I am sure you don't have much competition here Anga Raj." he gave a warm smile to Karna and went forward welcoming other princes and kings.

All the guests were shown their rooms as they would stay there for one night. Karna and Suyodhan had adjacent rooms, but Suyodhan retired to his own assigned chamber. Everyone was already tired of the long journey. Karna had built this habit of going to the garden when he was at Anga every evening. He would spend some time in the gardens before he went to sleep. When the evening descended deeper, he became restless and decided to go to the adjacent park in the palace of Panchal.

Karna was strolling in the garden looking at the sky filled with stars wearing a simple white dhoti and a soft white silk shawl. There was no one in the garden at that time. People would go to the park reserved for royals during the day, but he had no choice. His days were busy, and he had a packed schedule. Sometimes he would even skip lunch because there was too much work. The evenings were the only times when he had time to breathe, not literally but mentally yes, this was the only time he had. And these were the times when he felt the loneliest. He had no family to come back to after the day's work, no one around in the palace waiting for him to talk. He missed the company of his brother Shom, who was in Hastinapur, doing his job as a good son. Suyodhan was a rare company, he was usually in Hastinapur itself, and he was unable to visit frequently. Ashwatthama was the only visitor he usually had. Still, he had to leave early every time because of his matters with his father and the wealth his father had suddenly acquired after the war with Panchal. Varushali could be a wife, but what would he tell her? She did not care for matters that he sometimes needed advice for, which could only come from a constant companion. She loved him, and he knew it, but she could never give him the friendship he or anyone would need from a wife. She was the mother of her children, but they shared nothing in common—no interests, no topics, neither ideas.

Karna was immersed in thoughts when he felt someone standing behind him. He placed his hand on the knife that hung on his waist and turned around. Karna stood still as he looked intently, his face expressionless and calm. He detected the flush on the girl's dark-skinned face: her heart had picked up the pace. She stood there looking at him with her large, doe shaped eyes. She was tall, her head reaching his shoulder. She looked like the forms of Adi Shakti with her lean but well-structured physique. She wore a yellow coloured dhoti and a cream-coloured single cloth blouse. Her angavastra draped over her left shoulder and the other end pinned around her right hand.

Karna felt a strange restlessness in his heart, a peculiar feeling that did not let him stray away his eyes, from her face. Her long jet-black hair was open; it reminded him of the flowing river. It made her look all the more beautiful.

The way she looked at Karna, it was clear that her feelings were not significantly different. Her brown eyes just did not leave his black ones.

"Princess Draupadi!" came a loud voice of a woman. Her humble attire suggested that she might be a maid. "It is time for you to go back to your chamber, you must go to the Shiv Temple tomorrow early morning, you better leave or else Shikhandi will keep on sending maids to call you back."

The maid then, eyes Karna, she bowed down before him with folded hands and introduced the princess to Karna. "Princess he is the King of Anga, Maharaj Karna. He is one of the suitors at the swayamvar."

Karna smiled slightly. Draupadi folded her hands in a namaste. Karna did the same as he noticed how her beautiful face was not only beautiful but held the same pride as her father, Drupad. Her high cheekbones radiated her intelligence; she had a small sharp nose; her lips were neither full nor thin; her eyes showed her confidence. Her firm, sharp brows were in perfect curves, and her entire aura was as bright as the fire, from which she lept out. This woman was flawlessly beautiful and beautifully sculpted.

"All the best Anga Raj, I have heard of your courage and your skills. I hope you succeed in hitting the target tomorrow." Draupadi's voice seemed to have come from a faraway land. It was simply inaudible Karna stood there as if carved from stone. Even Draupadi looked lost. She had to be dragged from the garden by her maid. Karna still could not compose himself. He was so enchanted. He lifted his gaze from the retreating figure of the princess and turned around to leave the garden himself.

He felt light-headed because of the rush of emotions that he just felt. Suddenly he collided with a figure who was as tall as himself, Karna was surprised. He looked up and saw Ashwatthama standing before him with a childlike smile on his face. He was excited and happy and thrilled after witnessing the event before him.

Karna did understand the look on Ashwatthama's face. He just shook his head and left the place his friend followed behind and kept smiling. He was ready to get him married there and then.

27   Draupadi's Swayamvar

The swayamvar of Draupadi was held in the open arena instead of the royal court. This was because the onset of spring made the open sky look beautiful, and the trees that lined the outer circle of the arena were full of new leaves that gave everything a fresh look. The entire auditorium decorated beautifully, and it looked even more beautiful with the different colours all around. The arena was like an open stadium built of stone and mortar. It was a circular building with a hollow centre which made it look more like a stadium. The King of Panchal sat on his throne with Dristadyumna on his right and his daughter to his left. There was one more person whom Shakuni recognized first; Krishna, the king of Dwarka. The Yadava leader was known for his witty nature and his brilliant mind. He was a much more dangerous person than Shakuni, just that he was like the protagonist, if Shakuni was the antagonist. He had gained fame because of his various adventures and his might, with which he brought life to the celestial city of Dwarka. No ruler in the Aryavarta had the strength to fight Krishna, because everyone knew whoever tried was bound to fail. The man had a mind where he played the most devastating games. He was terrific at politics; it was like it ran in his blood like plasma.

Karna also knew how influential Krishna was and how he was known for his ideas about Dharma. He did admire the mind that man had and keenly wished to meet him once in life.

Ashwatthama had been teasing him since the time they got into the arena. Karna glanced towards Draupadi, who had suddenly lost the smile she had when she came into the hall. She was looking down on her toe and sat there grim and with a sad little face. Karna was agitated as to why did the colour of the princesses' face drain out? What was wrong? He wished she looked at him once more with the same smile as the previous evening.

The contest began in earnest. The first few kings and princes were bluffing about the simplicity of the task we're now returning with a hurt expression. Suddenly everyone understood the difficulty of the job. The bow was heavy, and when most lifted it, they disturbed the pot of water kept there, and the reflection of the fish was not visible anymore to them. By the time the water became still even the time was up. Many were now sulking and were contemplating coming to the contest in the first place.

Karna's turn came after about a dozen people had come back, failing miserably. Karna's attention still fixed on the person whose one glance made his heart go spinning around. But she never looked at him. Karna pushed away from the longing lover and brought back the warrior in him and moved towards the bow. He had already judged the technicalities of the bow before he reached it. Karna lifted it without a single ripple in the water. He strung the bow back again, fixing the fault it had. Karna then looked at the revolving silverfish, placed right above the brass Parat. He finally judged the speed and took a position holding the bow in the correct angle. The group of kings waited anxiously for what that happened next. Karna strung the bow, and after raising it he positioned the arrow on the bowstring. His eyes did not leave the reflection of the fish in the water below.

Not even for a split second could anything break his concentration. He shot the arrow and the moment the arrow left the bow he heard a familiar voice say, "I will not marry a Suta."

Karna's ear could not deceive him; it was Draupadi. He could say it without even looking at him. The arrow hit the target. The clang of the arrow was audible in the pin-drop silence of the arena. Karna's brain did not function at first. He just could not register what the princess had just said. But when he did, he felt his legs turn into jelly. Karna looked at Draupadi, fury burning his heart.

"How could you do this, Princess? How dare you insult a warrior!" Suyodhan's strong voice filled the arena. Dristadyumna stood up, his face flushed with shame. He was glaring at his sister; he never expected this woman to do such a thing.

"Draupadi we had invited Anga Raj here, you cannot insult him like that!" Dristadyumna spoke with gritted teeth. He was not at all happy with what his sister had just done.

Karna stood silently there; his friends were the ones fighting for him. He stood silent; he waited for the princess to look straight at him once. "Just once Princess, say that what you said was not true. Didn't you wish me luck yesterday with the hope that I win in the swayamvar?" he wanted to shout at Draupadi.

Just then, Draupadi lifted her head to look at Karna. Her eyes were teary, and her face had lost its colour. When the tears escaped her eyes, he saw through them; deep sadness was what he could see there in those beautiful eyes which had once captured his heart. Her sorrow was more profound than the grief he was feeling then. That moment he realized he had bitterly lost this game. He had lost the contest after winning it. Krishna sat next to her with a grim face. He did not look at Karna, not even for once, nor did he participate in the swayamvar. While his friends were trying to reason with the Panchala king, Karna kept quiet.

"What the hell are you doing, speak something, Karna!" Suyodhan spoke with fury evident in his voice.

"What do I say Suyodhan?" he shook his head. "It is hopeless to fight people who do not want to listen and cannot stand for themselves. But yes, I do want you to remember princess; to be dishonoured is to die.

One day you will know." Karna addressed Draupadi and stormed out of the arena. Everyone stood there silently, watching the warrior leave with his anger burning his heart. What none noticed was Draupadi's grief and Krishna's departure from the arena.

Karna stood on the river bank outside the city of Panchal alone. For a usual passer-by, he would look like a calm nobleman taking a stroll. But a closer look could speak the inner fury and turmoil his heart was going through. When he left the palace arena, he had sped past the busy roads of Panchal. He did not stop until he reached the secluded area. Some of his frustration was also vented out on the horses pulling the chariot. His chariot was dangerously fast, and it was a miracle that no one got trampled below it. He saw the place empty and pulled the reins urgently and stopped the chariot. He reached down and cursed under his breath. No one could explain the anger and hatred welling up in his heart. After a long time, Karna heard someone play the flute. He cursed under his breath and turned around. When he saw the person in front of him, his curse died on his lips. It was the king of Dwarka, Krishna. The music filled the surroundings and Karna felt peace. The Yadava leader's fame about playing the instrument was not wrong at all. Krishna stopped playing after a few minutes. By now Karna's anger had subsided a little, but the hatred hadn't.

"Do you see the river flowing behind you, Anga Raj?" Krishna spoke, his charismatic smile still present on his face. Karna did not say anything. Was that even a question!

"When the river flows down the mountains, it faces a lot of barriers. Those barriers try to stop it. Hundreds of times the river is barred, yet it finds its way back to the ocean. That is where the river belongs. No barriers, not even mountains, can ever stop its flow."

"I do not understand Madhav! What are you talking about?" the question escaped Karna's mouth before he could even think about

Krishna's statement. He did not have the state of mind to think at that moment.

"Some things are just not meant to be Karna; that is what I am talking about. The future of a human being does not take shape in the manner he plans to. It just is dependent upon one's actions in the present day. But some things are not determined by Karma, it's just destiny. Something that's meant to happen. Like the barriers are strong yet it cannot stop the flowing river because it is sure that one day that river will meet its ending or so to say its beginning; the ocean." Karna smiled as he explained his point patiently to the Karna.

"But what have I done to deserve the insult I have gotten since childhood? It cannot have 'meant to happen' Madhav! And what happened today was not justice at all. The princess....." before Karna could complete Krishna cut him mid-sentence.

"Karna you have done nothing wrong to be insulted the way you have always been. But still Karna some things happen in life because of the Karma other people decide to perform. Some things are mere effects of other people's Karma. You cannot blame yourself for everything that happens to you! And stop doing it to yourself, Karna." Krishna was speaking in a low voice now.

"So, you say, all that I face is because others decide to follow the wrong path? Madhav that is pure injustice. Why will my life be so challenging just because others are mindlessly stupid in life?" Karna's rage was back again. His voice was rising as he spoke the last line.

"Karna does it not work like that? Your Karma affects people around you so their Karma will affect you as well. Karna, why do you not see the luck you had in life, why do you always focus on the darkness you faced? OK! look at it like this." Krishna smiled again, "You have struggles in life, but why don't you see how strong you have become? Look at yourself; you are a self-made man, Karna. You have become what you are because you were good enough for it. Now think about it, do people matter?"

"I..... Madhav I am....." Karna was looking for an excellent point to counter Krishna yet he couldn't. This man was too good with words.

"Karna you have this challenging life because you were strong enough to live it. And you know the world needs examples." Krishna spoke, Karna noticed his eyes were dancing with some hidden mischief. Krishna patted Karna's back and turned around to leave. When he reached his horse, the Yadava leader turned around "You are a strong man Karna. Why don't you start distributing alms to the underprivileged? You will find happiness in it."

Krishna had left. Karna was now suddenly not feeling any anger in him; it was just hatred that was left. Contempt for the Princess. Never had anything hurt him more. She did not have any right to do this to him, insult his talent, his credibility so profoundly that it caused a scar in his heart. It was already afternoon when he heard his friends calling out his name, searching for him. He sighed, trying to exhale the anger that was flickering within as he recalled the events.

28   The Return of Pandavas

Hastinapur was full of festivities. The entire city was well decorated to celebrate the coronation of the crown prince as the king, though the crown prince was not Yudhistir but Suyodhan. Since the Pandavs were all dead at Varnavarta, it was now inevitable that Suyodhan would be the next king. The nights were spent in merriment and the days were full of ritualistic pujas. Today was the last day of the celebration as Suyodhan would be crowned the king of Hastinapur from then on. Dhritarashtra's happiness knew no bounds. He was the one person who was unable to contain his smile whenever the Pandav's death was spoken about. No one failed to notice.

Karna was seated in one corner next to Ashwatthama, watching the rituals followed for the coronation, but he was filled with doubts. No, he was happy for his friend, but he somehow felt that the Pandavas were not dead. He had gotten news from Panchal that a Brahmin had won the contest and married Draupadi. But the match was not at all easy; he had this slight doubt that Brahmin was not a commoner. He had succeeded, but other than him only Arjun could do the same. Karna wanted to speak up, but he had no right to question the state matters of Hastinapur.

He was still trying to decide whether his doubts were correct or not when Bhishma entered the court with his bow and stopped the rituals that were in full swing. He angrily glared at Dhritrastra "With whose permission did you decide to crown Suyodhan? Have you forgotten that you must inform me about any decision you take regarding the state matters?"

"I do not think he needs to……" Shakuni started but seeing Bhishma glare at him dangerously he stopped.

"I think you should learn to shut up Gandhar Raj! This is a matter concerning the Kuru state, and you are no one to intervene. Bhishma was too angry to think before he could speak. "Dhritarashtra, you cannot crown Suyodhan because the elder Crown Prince of this state is still alive. He is not dead." Bhishma gave Shakuni a winning smile.

Everyone was shocked, Suyodhan, Dussasashans, and Shakuni's face lost all colour. They were staring at Bhishma. Their plan had failed miserably, and this was a disaster for them. Karna, on the other hand, took a deep breath, a happy smile appearing on his face which no one notices. He was finally relieved that he had at least tried to undo the wrong his friend was going to do under his uncle's influence. He realized that Vidur had understood; his intelligence had not failed him.

The Pandavas entered the royal court of Hastinapur dressed in their silks. Karna noticed Bheem's murderously glancing towards Shakuni. Now, this was one place where he agrees with the Pandavas. Both of their loathing for Shakuni was similar and maybe equal. No one saw Bheem's glares, though. They were all just looking at Yudhistir. This man was a potential threat to Suyodhan, and he was back. "Bheem is a lucky man," Karna said softly to Ashwatthama, who smiled in return. "This man is the only one here who does not care about Dharma, Karma. For him, food is love, and his brother's and mother's orders are Dharma." Karna smiled after speaking.

"I think we need to be serious Karna!" Ashwatthama says smiling towards Karna. "This is a serious situation, I guess. Though look at Shakuni, see how much he hates Pandavas. Every time he tries to kill them, they come back again. He must be frustrated. And this time they came with a bonus. A wife!" Ashwatthama was smiling while he looked straight towards Shakuni. When he did not get any answer from Karna, he turned to look at him and found his face sad, and his eyes were on Draupadi. She was staring back at Karna, her eyes downcast and glistering with unshed tears.

Ashwatthama was confused as to why this woman even choose not to marry Karna if she was so sad about it. Damn, she agreed to marry five men but refused a chance of a happy life that only Karna would have given her.

They both looked away when the court heard Bhishma's loud voice. He was unhappy with the face that Pandavas has married the same woman. He was arguing with his family members as to why did this happen. It was Kunti's words that had led to this situation. When he Arjun had told her that he received the biggest daan of his lifetime Kunti was busy with her puja and had said "Whatever you got, divide it into five parts. All of your brothers share the daan." Little did she know that they were talking about Draupadi's Kanya Daan and not a mere object. Because of this, the five brothers had to marry Draupadi. Karna looked at Kunti, "How could she do this. Divide a human between five people. Share a wife!" he was shocked to hear what Kunti had narrated. He looked back at Draupadi, who stood behind her husbands. He now knew why her eyes looked so sad. She landed in a situation where everyone treated her like a mere object. Karna did feel sorry for this woman. A woman born out of the fire, a princess, was now reduced to a mere object. But suddenly her words returned to him, and his heart dripped with rage and anger took over his pity. He looked away from Draupadi. That anger against the person you love comes out in the form of what people call hatred. Ashwatthama was the only person who had noticed what was happening between Karna and Draupadi. "You only hate the person you once loved!" he whispered so that no one could hear him.

While in the background, a decision came that the kingdom

would be divided between the Pandavas and Kauravas. The Pandavas were to leave for Khandavprasta as that was the only part of the state Suyodhan agreed to give away to his cousins. The land was barren in Khandavprast, and it was said to be cursed. Yudhistir not ready to argue anymore had accepted the part of the kingdom and decided to leave as soon as possible.

29 Supriya's Swayamvar

onths had passed since the Pandavas had left for Khandavprast. Shakuni was again back to his planning and plotting. He was becoming more dangerous day by day. These hateful ideas were filling up Suyodhans brain. Every time Shakuni tried to poison Suyodhan, Karna tried and told him the right path to becoming a better person. He tried to wash away the venom that was slowly rotting the leftover goodness in Suyodhan. Karna tried every way to speak reason, but it was difficult to influence him. The evil that had affected him since childhood was so strong that Karna's talks of righteousness were hardly working. But he never stopped, he knew that giving up would mean pushing him towards drudgery. He frequented his visits to Hastinapur as well; he was not sure of what Shakuni was capable of doing. He tried by all means to stop Suyodhan from paving his path to death. On one such trip to Hastinapur, he received an invitation to a swayamvar. It was the swayamvar of the princess of Pukeya Supriya, a close friend of Bhanumati, Suyodhan's wife. Bhanumati was a loveable woman; she was like the sister Karna never had. She would tease him whenever he came to the palace. For her, Karna was an elder brother nothing more nothing less. She respected him and revered him. Since she had come to Hastinapur, she called Karna Dada, and Karna called her Kumari. For her, Karna was not her husbands' friend, nor the great warrior. He was a brother whom she said anything and at any time because he did listen. Karna did not mind her teasing him, ever.

Karna was not pleased to go to the swayamvar. He had not forgotten the embarrassment he faced at Draupadi's swayamvar. Karna was not at all ready for another such situation. Karna was explaining why he was not prepared to take part in the swayamvar when Bhanumati had barged into the room without any announcement and had confronted Karna. "Can you tell me why you are not going to my friends, Swayamvar?" Bhanumati's voice was angry while she was standing before Karna with her hand folded against her chest. She was looking at Karna with a wave of mocking anger in her eyes. Karna and Suyodhan burst out laughing at the act that she was trying to put up.

Bhanumati did not look pleased with this, and she again spoke, this time, her face did show some hints of anger. "I am no cracking some kind of joke here, why are the two of you laughing?" She was irritated by the childlike treatment she got around these two friends.

"Kumari, your angry face does not do much justice with the word angry", that's why we are laughing. And I do not want to go to the swayamvar. Why are you so eager to send me to Amravati?" Karna tried suppressing his smile. She looked like a little child who did not get her toys.

"Because she wants you married to her best friend Supriya and bring her nearer to where she lives." Suyodhan comment brought a smile on Bhanumati's face.

"Yes, I want you to get married to my friend who is just so amazing." She spoke with her voice full of love as she thought about her friend. Karna shook his head.

"And Kumari, why do you think she will choose me instead of a Kshatriya prince or a king?" Karna questioned with his face grim.

"Because she loves you...." Bhanumati spoke so fast that the two men understood not even half of what she said. Bhanumati said their confused expression and said again, "Dada, you just go there you will know why she will choose you. Think this to be my wedding gift."

"And how many times will you take wedding gifts from me Kumari?" Karna asked Bhanumati, who looked at Karna with a happy smile. Whenever she wanted him to do something, she would ask it as a wedding gift.

"Karna, she asks me for wedding gifts every time she wants something. I have lost count of how many wedding gifts she has taken from me." Suyodhan laughed as he told Karna about Bhanumati's only way to make people listen to her. She had a baby face which could not do much in the anger department, it instead made her look cute, and people would often start laughing instead of being scared. When she realized the two men in the room were not going to listen, she made a sad face and looked at Karna.

"OK! Fine, stop being so dramatic! I will go." Karna was sure that if she begins crying, it would be difficult to stop her.

Suyodhan just laughed, seeing how Bhanumati could easily convince his friend. These two together were some real entertainment package. No one could say even for once that they were not brother-sister by blood.

Even though Karna agreed to go to the swayamvar because of Bhanumati's emotional drama, he did not feel nice sitting in the beautifully designed hall of Amravati. When he came to Amravati, his friends Suyodhan and Ashwatthama accompanied him there. The three had travelled on a slow pace, having fun, joking around, racing on horses, and teasing each other. Suyodhan had sensed Karna's discomfort when they joked about the swayamvar and hence dropped the topic there and then. After about a week and a half, they reached their destination.

Bhanumati had accompanied them, but her cavalcade had left early as she wanted to reach as fast as she could to her friend. Karna was surprised because Bhanumati was so happy to see him accompany the others for the swayamvar. She had been speaking at length as to how her friend was a loveable woman, and her intelligence was unparallelled. While Bhanumati was continuously talking, she told him how Supriya had different names. She even recited them -Chandravali, Padmavati, and many more to which Karna did not pay much attention. He was so done with her chattering about the same topic for so long on the first day.

"So, for how long can a woman talk about the very same topic, with the same person Bhanumati?" Ashwatthama had said to which everyone laughed and Bhanumati frowned.

"You are bad, Ashwatthama...." She had said to him before she stopped talking.

Suyodhan had smiled lovingly at his innocent, lovely wife. Everyone knew that he loved Bhanumati. With her presence in his life, he had forgotten the scar of his previous love Subhadra.

"So, the evil crown prince is a love-stricken husband, huh Suyodhan" Ashwatthama commented, which made Suyodhan look away and go crimson red. Everyone laughed at this except Suyodhan, he had glared at Ashwatthama. Ashwatthama was like the comedian of the group. They were coming up with comments and taunts that made everyone laugh. The next day Bhanumati's group had picked pace, and she had reached early while the three friends took their own time.

Nobles from all over the country attended the swayamvar of the princess of Amravati. The Pandavas had also visited the kingdom. Karna saw Krishna with his elder brother Balram as well as Dristadyumna. When his eyes met Karna's, an apologetic look filled his face, and he mouthed a sorry. Karna smiled when he saw this. They did not meet each other, though. Eager spectators had also visited the hall other than the royal suitors. Karna wanted to be far away from this madness and festivities. He knew like all others that this swayamvar was a show, all knew that the princess would choose one of the Pandav's. He tried to stop the next memory that flooded his mind as the day of Draupadi's swayamvar haunted him again.

Karna was thrust into the present once more with the ringing of bells, the sound of trumpets and beating of drums filled the room. A grand escort of maids and dancing girls entered the hall with flowers showered on the ground. When not one inch of land was left without flower petals, the princess Supriya entered the Grand Hall. The entire hall fell silent when they saw her coming in. She was beautiful, exotic, and innocent. He had a small smile plastered on her face while she walked into the hall. She looked straight at her father, who admired his daughter. She was wearing wedding silks. She wore a dhoti of deep turmeric coloured silks with a red angavastra and adorned jewellery made of the most beautiful rubies and pure gold. She was as far as the colour of milk. Her lips were covered with a little beet extract, and the kajal enhanced her pretty eyes.

She went straight to her father and stood next to him. "Bhanumati had not lied about her looks," Suyodhan said to Karna, to which he just nodded. "I am thankful O great princess, warriors, and king for your arrival in my kingdom for this swayamvar," The voice of King Veerbhadra came from where he was sitting. "There is no competition here because I believe that a contest destroys the entire meaning of a swayamvar. A Swayamvar is organised so that the princess has the right to choose her groom. A great warrior need not be a good husband. So as you know, I have not put forth any condition here in this swayamvar. My daughter will be wedded to the man she chooses today." The king lovingly looked back at his daughter and said, "Proceed daughter! Think before you make your choice."

The princess walked forward as she clasped the garland given to her by the maids. She, at one point, felt uneasy as everyone looked at her with a curious look on their faces. Supriya slowly walked forward, and a collective gasp came in the hall as she passed the Pandavs and kept walking towards the end of the hall. She kept walking straight with slow steps. She stopped when she reached the place where Ashwatthama, Karna, and Suyodhan were sitting. Everyone was trying to guess what was happening. He turned to her left and saw the three friends sitting in one line. Supriya took two steps forward and was standing straight in front of Karna. Karna was shocked as to why she was there in front of him. She kept standing there with her eyes glued to her toe. Karna slowly stood up as the princess did not move from the place. He was amazed and shocked as to what she was doing. That moment she lifted her head and looked straight at him; their eyes met. She raised the garland of rose and mogra, and he lowered his head instinctively, too shocked to react. She placed the garland around his neck, and a genuine smile made its way to her face.

There was silence in the entire hall for some time when the whole crowd began their collective disagreement of the marriage, as this was not a welcomed match. "A Suta and a Kshatriya princess, this is the worst thing to witness." said one king.

"Are you trying to say that we are incapable and he is better than us?" another one shouted.

"Just because you are blue-blooded kings and princes, you do not become the best," Krishna's voice silenced everyone. "If you feel you are as capable, then why do you need to compare yourself? The swayamvar rules are that the bride-to-be has the right to choose whom she marries. The princess has chosen the King of Anga, and you have to respect her decision. It is her swayamvar, not yours. She will choose whom she wants to marry and not you! If others were to choose, her parents could do it instead of giving her the freedom to choose her groom in a swayamvar. Accept her wish and let the wedding proceed. Please don't make me question the fact that you all are respectable kings. And for the social status, did you forget that many brahmin women in our Shastras have married Kshatriya princes? Did you forget social hierarchy then?" Krishna's speech ended, and that was the end of the argument. Who would take up the rivalry with this man? Most people unanimously feared him.

The crowd went silent, and the marriage rituals began in full swing. Suyodhan, Ashwatthama, and Karna gave a chirping Bhanumati a "Now we know what was the talk was all about!" look.

"Karna!" Suyodhan gave a soft laugh, he stepped forward and embraced his friend. Karna remained calm, and his mind was preoccupied.

"Well, she will be an amazing new Bhabi!" Ashwatthama commented with a smile on his face. Karna frowned, seeing the enthusiasm in his friend's voice.

"I guess we will have a nice home in Anga. Will you invite us Karna; for family dinners now?" Suyodhan said winking.

"Let's go where we have been invited right now, later we will surely discuss who will get an invitation to come to Anga," Karna said his eyes cold yet the sarcasm evident in his voice, replying to his friend's one-liners.

"Correct!" said Ashwatthama, still laughing, "Of course we need to act mature! Stoic, calm, composed, according to dharma, controlled! Oh, I guess I have forgotten some words. What say, Karna? Mind reminding me?"

Karna's eyes narrowed in warning. He aimed a punch on the mischievous Brahmins face, but Ashwatthama ducked and began laughing. They all went to the temple where the wedding was arranged.

Bhanumati ignored them as she was pleased and sat beside Supriya, guiding her throughout the ceremony.

❈ ❈ ❈

30   Supriya – The Bride

Karna had gained a reputation as a philanthropist. He would give away alms to everyone approaching him for them. He never had anyone turned down from his door. Conservatives loathed the structural setup of Anga, but the liberals admired it. His popularity as a warrior and as a king grew as the years passed. It's known that he would take good care of his family by providing them with whatever they needed. But never too much, he did not consider wealth important. His sons were living with Varushali and his parents until they were old enough to start gaining an education. These talks had not escaped the house of King Vahusha. And secondly, his daughter had once seen Karna in the Kridangan years back and had fallen in love with him.

The marriage ceremony was grand and beautiful, fit for a princess. Bhanumati was on cloud nine; her joy knew no bounds. Everyone noticed it. Suyodhan had continuously teased Karna as to how he was dragged into the marriage without even understanding the motive. The two women told every single thing to each other. This was a matter of talk for both the girls and so Bhanumati had promised Supriya that she would bring Karna to the swayamvar "I will drag him here if he does not come." Bhanumati had repeated the lines before Karna that were earlier said to Supriya. Karna did not say much during the wedding. He was confused as to why did the princess choose him instead of any other Kshatriya prince.

"So, my dear friend Karna, would you like to have some tips as to what you should speak to the princess when you go inside the bridal room?" Suyodhan said, suppressing his laughter. He and Ashwatthama had caught Karna outside the room. They wanted some entertainment before the night ended, so who was the victim, of course, the man for whom it was "d-day".

"Yes, Karna ask us, we will teach you!" Ashwatthama joined Suyodhan.

"You know what? You both are rascals!" Karna said, trying to sound angry, but he couldn't. The two looked amusing at this point. "But Ashwatthama, aren't you supposed to be meditating now as your father had asked you? And Suyodhan, don't you have a wife to go to?"

"No, we are free! You know, outside the state we are pretty jobless!" The two said in unison and then let out a loud chuckle.

Karna wanted to bang his head on the pillar next to him. These two were not people who let go quickly. They would irritate the hell out of Karna before letting him leave. He was thinking about ways to free himself from them. Not that he was excited about his new wife, he just did not have any energy left to be irritated by the two men.

"Well Karna, what do you think? Should we ask her to come out and we can help you, narrate your antiques to her? The love at first sight at Kampilya the capital of Panchal and how you wanted to get one single glance of the princess before shooting the fish's eye and the heartbroken king wandering near the riverbank, the day she ditched you. Oh! how could we forget the "I hope you win Anga Raj" ...." Ashwatthama was listing out events to list to his newlywed.

"Oh! That is an amazing idea, Ashwatthama. Let's go tell Bhanumati to call for Supriya. Or you will call her Anga Raj?" as Suyodhan was speaking, Karna was ready to shove the two on the floor and begin pummeling them. But before the next comment came from Ashwatthama, Bhanumati came into Karna's rescue and pulled the two together, finally leaving Karna to himself.

Karna smiled to himself. "These idiots are the best of friends, but can be an as big ass as they look sometimes."

Karna entered to find his uncertain bride gazing at him with wide-open eyes. They were seriously strangers, did not know each other. Karna stood quietly at a distance, stiff and cold. They were together by marriage, yet there was an uncertainty. After a moment passed, Karna finally decided to walk towards her. He stopped and sat on a couch in the room. Supriya was sitting on the bed with her veil pulled down. She looked at him through the cover and a smile crept on her face.

Karna's face remained cold and expressionless. "Why did you choose me?" was the only question that came out. That's not what you do to your wife. Karna just couldn't stop thinking about it, and he had been disturbed the whole time because of this question. He wanted the answer there and then.

Supriya was just watching Karna. She did not speak. She had wished this forever, him before her as her husband. "Why did you marry me, princess?" came his question again as she removed her gaze. She was surprised, no doubt. His voice had become sharp and edgy.

"I am sure all around you must have thoroughly enlightened you as to how marrying me will be a sin for you. Then why did you marry me?" Karna spoke again after he did not get his reply.

"You sound like I am a defaulter ready to be punished in a court." Supriya's soft, sweet voice came to him like a fresh breeze. He was surprised but contained it as he realized he had been questioning her like some criminal ready to be sentenced.

"Why did you marry me, Supriya?" His voice was softer this time, but determined.

"Because I have loved you since the day, I saw you in the Kridangan of Hastinapur. I have loved you since then, I have dreamed of this marriage for all these years waiting for you, Karna!" Karna was surprised. He had never heard Varushali take his name. He had told her to, but she never did. Karna, at last, had finally given up. Supriya without hesitation call him with his name. He loved how it sounded from her lips.

"Karna, I have loved you throughout, this marriage might just be a duty for you, but for me, it is the most sacred thing ever. I am aware of all that will happen after this marriage. I know for you I might be a nobody till today but......."

"But you married me. After knowing all of that, you still chose me. You went against society, your family, the did not even fear the consequences." As he said it, he suddenly felt a deep respect for this woman. She had forsaken every bit of her existence to have him in her life. She had given up all her ties to pave her path towards her true love. "Was love so strong that she could sacrifice everything for that one feeling?" Karna wondered.

Yet he did not let the admiration he felt for her suddenly waver his thoughts. He persisted, "Still, you should have chosen something easier. My life is just not well deserved for a princess."

"And why do you think I want an easy life? I do not mind living in the smallest hut as long as you are there. I do not mind walking barefoot as long as you are by my side. I do not mind all the difficulties as long as you are with me." Supriya said as she stood up from her place to sit in front of him on the sofa.

When she came closer, Karna noticed her beauty. He looked at her innocent face, those eyes full of determination and truth. Eyes are the mirror of a human body. It reflects everything. There he saw love, deep love something very sacred and clean. Pure and confident. She knew what she was doing, Supriya had not done this just because she was head over heels for Karna but because she had accepted all that he had in life. She had taken all his faults and all his difficulties. She had already welcomed him into her world, the world he had never known the world he never had; and that world was built with the bricks of love, sacrifice, and reverence.

"Still Supriya, how will you live with a Suta? Will you ever find the heart the respect me or accept my family?" Karna questioned her.

"Karna! Respect is the first pillar of love. I could have never loved you if I did not respect you! And I respect you for everything you are I have all these years respected your giving nature. I have respected that very soul residing within you. And that is why I love you! It's simple; whatever you are today it's because you dared to do all that others couldn't. You had the courage, and so you did it. Your generosity is your wealth, and your goodness is your strength. I do not need anything more. Talking about your family, I will love them, I am sure." Supriya flashed a bright smile to Karna. He remained silent; admiring the determination, she had within her.

"Any more questions Maharaj?" Supriya's suppressed her smile. She had folded her hands and was looking at him keenly. His cold eyes warmed seeing her that way. "No one more left." She smiled as he spoke.

"You know I did not visit swayamvars after Draupadi's so why did your father send me an invitation." At Draupadi's swayamvar Karna had lost not only his self-respect but also his son Sudhama. He was killed in the scuffle after he had left the place. When he had come to know of the little boy's death, his heart had never left the guilt. He felt immensely saddened. He blamed himself and the princess for all he had gone through that time. Supriya knew the details through Bhanumati. She had felt immense pain for the man she loved to have faced such a tremendous problem and insult even though he was worthy of respect and love.

"Because you left me no option! I had to get married, and the man couldn't be anyone other than the love of my life. And that was you, Karna. So, I gave my father some serious strain as I convinced him to send the invitation and I also took a promise from Bhanumati that she will drag you here if you refuse to come." Supriya spoke as though she had learned the entire paragraph beforehand as a student does.

Karna felt his anger subsiding, under her pure innocence. He felt a strange emotion surge through his veins that made him nervous but gave pleasure as well. The beautiful woman with her great patience was slowly calming him down. A softer unknown feeling was now replacing the inner turmoil. This woman had gone against the entire society for him, to have his affection and to be with him. This woman had fought desperately with her parents and her family as well just for him, was her love so deep?

This was the kind of woman he would choose as a bride if he were given a choice. Karna would do anything for that smile she had on her face. He had seen how she looked so weak when she was being insulted in the court. It tore him apart and his heartfelt sad as he had seen a single tear escape her eyes. Now sitting here, he felt terrible that he was the reason she was insulted in the hall.

He was a compassionate man; he soon realized that in the future, there would be times that she would go through similar situations and all because of him. Their marriage was of great social contrast, yet he wanted her beside him. He found a friend in his new bride.

"By the way, I must say you were daring enough to go against everyone, just to marry me. You must be a strong-minded princess, that you did not listen to all the advice you received free of cost from all around you. Instead of all the other Kshatriya's, you chose a Sutputra- an outsider." Karna said to Supriya.

"Why do you say that Karna? Don't you think you are worthy of the respect you get?" Supriya's voice was laced with a bit of sadness. Karna felt it, and it stirred something deep within his heart.

He was reminded of something his friend, Suyodhan, had told him when he had found him on the banks of the river after the swayamvar at Panchal. He had said "Karna, you know one must fall in love with someone who makes you love yourself as well. Fall for someone who reminds you of how worthy you are and how much respect you deserve. Draupadi was not that woman at all. And it's good that this did not happen!"

This moment he realized Suyodhan was right, Draupadi was not that woman because that girl was now sitting here before him. Her words were soul awakening, that reminded him of his worth, reminded him that he had reached where he was with his hard work and his merit. She looked like a beautiful angel right out of the kingdom of Indra; it was a lovely coincidence that the realm of Gods was called Amravati and Supriya was also the princess of Amravati a small kingdom in southern India. His eyes caressed her beautiful moon-shaped face that radiated like the moon shining outside in the sky. No doubt, she was called Chandravali. He basked in her love that was like a soft, gentle breeze on a summer day. So, reliving and so important. His soul was relaxing in her presence. A smile made its way on Karna's face as the happiness of having her and finding her filled his heart. He finally found the companion he had always missed.

❖ ❖ ❖

31 Khandavprast or Indraprast?

A year passed after the stormy swayamvar. The couple went to Hastinapur first, to meet Karna's parents. Karna did notice the unhappiness Shom felt. He did not like a woman who was not one of them to come one day and become his sister-in-law. For him, she was the outsider Kshatriya princess and a threat to Varushali. But what surprised Karna's family was the earnest words Supriya spoke, her down-to-earth behaviour and her respect for all members of the family. She had gone to say sorry to Varushali for becoming the second woman in her marriage. And what was a bigger surprise was that the two women bonded together like they were long-lost friends meeting after years of separation.

The days they spent at Hastinapur were of merriment and happiness. Suyodhan had invited them to a feast one day. Supriya had made it clear to Karna that she did not like Suyodhan much. She was not against him because he was a Kaurava, and she had this blind faith that Pandavas were only right, but she was rational and knew that he only spelt danger for their home. He was good as a friend, but as a person, he did commit deeds that were not at all acceptable.

Karna did not do much to change her ideas; she was independent to think and have her conceptions about people. He had gone back to Anga with Supriya after two weeks, and there Karna had already ordered the maids to get ready for her Grihpravesh. He tried all means to make her feel welcome in her new home. When they had reached Anga, he said to her "Supriya this might not be as lavish as your home back in Amravati, but this is where I live, and I hope you like the palace!"

"I love this! Not because this is a palace Arya, but because it will be our home. You are giving me this palace, and I will give you a home in Anga." Supriya had smiled and relieved all of Karna's worries.

The time he spent with his new bride was beautiful for him, and he cherished it. The connection they had was not of lust but friendship. She was a dependable mate whom he told anything and everything. Every evening when he came back to the palace from a routine round around the state, he found himself unconsciously walking towards Supriyas quarters. He would speak to her about topics he never thought he could talk to his mother or Varushali. The connection with Varushali was more because of the sense of duty. She was his wife, the mother to his children; it was his duty to look after her and take care of her. He was fond of her but did not surely love her. He did his duty as a husband there; they were husband and wife nothing more than that.

Whereas, Supriya was different, different from all the women he had known in his life. They would discuss political matters, matters concerning the state as well as scriptures. With her, he was able to be venerable and weak, bossy and controlling, meek and silent all at once. She made him laugh, gave him a reason to come back to his house, and which he now called home. She gave him the friendship he wished, the companionship he desired, and the peace he craved for.

She soothed him and fascinated him; he admired her. Their connection had developed on love and admiration and not lust; it was just beyond. She was his pole stare, guiding him, advising him, telling him the truth without hesitation.

She removed the logic he looked for in everything and added the magic of life in him. The pain he kept his heart trapped in was painful; she freed him. Helped him move towards spiritual freedom, of mind, soul, and spirit. She made him believe in him more and more, and that was when he realized that he had found love in life. He found the girl he would respect forever and love deeply until eternity.

Karna was waiting to welcome his child to come. His happiness knew no bounds when he came to know that Supriya was pregnant. He had received the invitation for the Rajasyu Yagya in Khandavprast renamed as Inraprast.

Suyodhan had also written to him asking him and Supriya to join everyone at Indraprastha. He couldn't say no to his friend, and hence the two of them reached the palace of Indraprastha. They were welcomed by the Pandava's, Kunti and Draupadi. Karna looked cold and indifferent when he came across Draupadi. He remained impassive, but Supriya knew the calmer he looked, the deeper the turmoil within. She did not say anything. Karna's face brightened when he saw Kunti. He smiled and bowed down to touch her feet. She was surprised to see the connection the two had. He was one of the enemies of Pandava's yet Kunti became elated like he was one of his sons. She did not know. No one knew.

Bhanumati arrived after them with Suyodhan and Ashwathama and the other Kaurava's. Bhishma, Dronacharya, Kripa, Vidur were all present as well, Karna sat with Ashwatthama and Suyodhan. Supriya was with Bhanumati. The two best friends were having a great time chatting with her and sharing her experiences in her new home. But when she looked at the place where the Yagya was happening, he saw Draupadi and Yudhistir sitting, performing the puja. But Draupadi was distracted. She was like her mind was somewhere else. She was looking at someone. Her eyes showed tenderness and love. Deep love, she knew the look, for a man it might not be essential but a woman knows. Supriya followed her eyes and found her looking at Karna her breath caught, and she stopped breathing for some time. She loved him; there was sadness in her eyes. A sadness that one feels when you lose something. The pain of losing the most valuable, the regret of rejection. Did Draupadi not want to say no to Karna? Was she pressurized to speak no to marry him? Supriya felt a knot in her stomach.

Karna remained oblivious and unknown about Draupadi. He did not mind her being in there and maintained a distance from the princess now a queen.

The same day the guests had left the palace, but the family had stayed. The Pandavas had requested them all to stay. It was a surprise when Yudhistir had personally come to ask Karna to stop him from leaving. He had insisted for a long time, and at last, Karna had to give in even though he was not so sure if it was a good idea but turning Yudhistir down would be rude.

The next morning, Supriya was with the other woman in the palace. Kunti was incredibly fussy about her. She was extra affectionate to Supriya. Being the woman that she was Supriya asked Kunti when they sat together alone.

"You are Karna's wife, Supriya! And Karna is like my son." Kunti had answered, smiling to her. Supriya found it strange, though. She had informed Karna about it at night, but he just said that Kunti had always been like this. He had ever asked himself the same question but never got the answer. "I have first time come to know that; she feels I am like her son." He had said the previous night.

Kunti, Gandhari, Subhadra and Bhanumati was sitting together in one of the living areas of the Palace. The palace was in itself, magnificent and strange. It wasn't what it looked. What looked like water was hard granite, and what looked like granite was actually water. It was delusional. Anyone could get confused and make a mistake here if not guided.

Suyodhan and Shakuni were exceptionally disturbed. They were simply jealous, they had given the Pandava's a barren land, and they got this palace better than the one in Hastinapur built. Karna was there with them, but the palace was of no appeal to him. He did not want wealth; it was just not what he needed or wished. Yudhistir and Draupadi were showing around the palace to Duryodhan and Karna. Karna remained next to Suyodhan not even glancing at Draupadi, but it was not the same with the queen. She would steal glances and look at Karna with longing evident in her eyes. He could feel her eyes on himself, yet he did not turn to look back. He did not dare to do so. He knew the haunting memories of the insult, and his son's death would flood him once again. She kept talking to Suyodhan and sometimes to Yudhistir. At one point in time, Arjun and Karna were also having a conversation; if someone looked at the two men, then they would not even make out that they were sworn, enemies.

Karna watched Draupadi icily who walked towards the courtyard across the rippling the water and asked all to follow her. But Suyodhan being who he was said: "I will rather walk on the granite." Before Karna could stop him, Suyodhan walked straight towards the granite floor, which was again an illusion. It was actually water.

Suddenly as the woman was talking, they heard a splash. Someone had fallen in the water, mistaking it to be granite. They all turned around to find Karna helping his friend Suyodhan come out of the pool of water. He was inside the pot of water; the pool was waist-deep. He was dishevelled and soaked in water. Everyone around suppressed their laugh.

Just then all heard laughter ringing in the room. It was Draupadi! in between the laughter she said "Blind son of a Blind Father!" she still did not stop even after that. They were all stunned by Draupadi's deed.

How could she insult her guest like that? Karna had already pulled Suyodhan out of the pool and held his hand so that he did not do something stupid in his rage. He was so angry that Suyodhan, if not held him back, would have slapped Draupadi right on her face. Suyodhan went white with fury, his entire body shivering with the rage that was rising within his heart. Yudhistir was apologizing for what just happened. His face was pale; he looked disturbed.

Suyodhan freed himself from Karna's grip and left the place with a loud, angry cry. Karna watched the retreating figure of his friend. "I hope this does not turn out to become disastrous. The situation does not look at all pleasant." Karna said to the now unhappy Yudhistir who was glaring towards his wife. Karna left the hall following Suyodhan; he spared a last glance at Draupadi who was still smiling. He shook his head in disbelief, "This woman has still not understood the gravity of this situation!"

32 Supriya and Karna

*I*n the east wing of the palace of Hastinapur, a man was sitting alone with the chausar spread on the table. He held the set of dice in his hand. His eyes are deep with mirth and anger. His gaze fixed on the table before him.

He sat in darkness, a faint light filling the room. It was a single Mashal that spread its light. Karna entered the room and tried to see who it was. His face was not visible to him.

"Who are you?" Karna asked alarmed.

"I....... I am the destruction of Hastinapur. I am the death of this entire kingdom." the person spoke in a deep voice.

"Why are you going........"

"You will see it, Karna, you will see it yourself. once you reach Hastinapur, you will see." He began laughing, his loud laugh irritating Karna he wanted to run away from the darkroom. The man stopped laughing, his voice was deep, almost inaudible, he whispered "Twelve", and the dice spun on the floor, it hit each other, reversed the direction of the spin, and then came to rest. Both had a six on them—an exact twelve.

Karna looked at in horror; suddenly he saw flames erupting behind the man. The fire was slowly engulfing the entire room, Karna's forehead was covered in sweat. He struggled to get out of the room trying to open every door and window in the room. He failed, he desperately banged the door, but the smoke blurred his eyes. He fell to the ground unconscious still trying to open his eyes.

He failed! Every time he tried, he failed.

And then with great labour, he finally woke up, with a cry. He looked around, Nothing! He turned around to see Supriya next to him, looking at him with deep concentration. She had woken up after hearing his loud cry. Her face was pale and her eyebrows drawn together in a frown.

"What did you see? What dream?" Supriya said in a whisper.

"I saw a pair of dice being spun. The fire burning the entire place, I was stuck in the room, unable to get out, I struggled and still, I couldn't. I was just stuck there in that fire. It was a strange dream..." Karna said resting his head on the back of the bead. It was midnight, the room was dark, a single earthen lamp sat on the table beside the bed. It was Amavasya hence the entire sky was dark. The night was silent, and the room even more silent. Supriya placed her head on Karna's shoulder. Her gentle touch relaxed his restless mind.

"I have a gut feeling that the insult Suyodhan faced in Indraprast will lead to something devastating. What happened was not good at all." Karna says in a barely audible voice. If the night was not that silent Supriya would need to strain to hear him speak.

"You know Suyodhan is not in his right state of mind. He is a man taken over by jealousy and anger, both dangerous feelings that are the beginning of signs of downfall. He will lead you to a no-man's-land one day. Why don't you...?"

"I will not leave my friend Supriya." He spoke coldly, "I know he has his faults, but he has been a loyal friend, I cannot leave him. And the dream, forget it. I might be because I was stressed about the event in Indraprastha. That's it. Come on now go back to sleep." Karna brushed away his thoughts and tried to pacify Supriya. But she was not a person to easily let go of.

"Karna you are not looking at the other side of the picture. The dream might not be important but the truth anyways is undeniable. Suyodhan is dangerous. He just is." Supriya tried to reason with Karna.

He gave her a wary look and out of nowhere kissed her on the lips. She whimpered as he pulled away. "Sleep Supriya," He said in a serious tone. The discussion just ended there; he knew what she was saying was right but he was indebted to Suyodhan. Even if he left him for good, he would not be able to repay him for what he had done for him. Supriya frowned again and left the topic, she knew it was useless to discuss the same topic with Karna.

33   The Roll of Dice

Karna was having a hard time placating Suyodhan, he was infuriated as the mocking laughter of Draupadi and her remark kept ringing in his ears. Draupadi scratched and ripped opened the barriers Karna had tried building against Suyodhan's jealousy and anger. Suyodhan was thirsty for revenge- he was so raged that he was ready for anything that he could. Karna was aware that secret meetings were being held between the Kauravas and their uncle the vicious Shakuni. Karna was always kept away from those meetings. One day when he entered the room where Suyodhan was with his brother and uncle, they all fell silent, an uneasy silence that was. Karna could sense something wrong. He could smell something fishy. A plot being designed, and he knew Pandavas would be the one this trap was being designed for. He visibly could not do anything, what can one expect him to do? Get detectives after the Kurus, he would never be forgiven if someone found out. He was at last considered a Suta.

Karna was growing restless, he knew Suyodhan was the kind of person who would confront, shout, demean, insult if he was angry. But this time he was doing nothing. He was keeping quiet, and that meant danger was approaching. "Why can't he confront his cousins and end the feud?" he one day asked Ashwatthama. The deceit and subterfuge were not understandable.

After the incident at Indraprast, there had been various arguments between Karna and Supriya. This woman who had become his most precious possession in such a short time had been enraged every time he decided to go to Hastinapur. Every time she would warn him of Suyodhan. He was the external factor of their arguments. It felt like he was seeing a fear in her eyes every time he looked at her. He could sense something very wrong with her. She had been moody and her anger easily sprouted up at little things. He always succeeded in pacifying her yet her sullenness did not decrease.

He looked at her sleeping form next to him. Her face looked pale due to the stress of maternity. Her eyes were swollen and puffy, she had been crying when he had come to their room. It did not surprise him though after she was pregnant her head was all over and she would cry for little things. He was looking at her intently, he smiled thinking how she had cried like a child when he came in and asked her the reason for her tears. She cooled down when he embraced her and eventually fallen asleep in his arms.

A knock on the door brought a frown on his face. It was night time so the soft knock sounded loud enough to wake up anyone. He rushed to open the door fearing it would disturb Supriya's sleep. But when he went out, he found a messenger with a letter from Suyodhan which asked him to come immediately to Hastinapur. He was at first confused, but he had to go he thought it might be urgent that he was asked for. Karna came back to the bed and placed a soft kiss on Supriya's forehead. She was a light sleeper, and the kiss stirred her from her sleep. He smiled when he saw her open her eyes. She looked at him with a questioning look on her face.

"I need to leave for Hastinapur right away. Suyodhan has called for me. So I will leave right away." Karna said to her. but the moment Supriya heard it, she sat up straight.

"Why does he call you now Karna? I have a very bad feeling about this." Supriya was agitated she did not want him to leave.

"I have to go Supriya and I cannot delay. So, you take the rest you need and let me go. And yes, just because you don't like Suyodhan you should not suspect every move he makes." Karna said in a flat tone.

"I? You are talking about me, Karna? No one likes your alliance with Suyodhan, Radha Ma, Adhirath baba, Varushali, your brother Shom, no one likes it. You are the only ones who are not seeing what everyone can. He is not a good company Karna. Don't go!" there was a plea in her voice. Karna had never seen Supriya so desperately stopping him. He brushed it away and refused to listen.

Supriya stood looking down at her toe at the main door of their house. She was visibly sad but Karna could do nothing but leave. He climbed the chariot, and it raced towards the exit of the palace. He turned back once and saw Supriya still standing there amidst the swaying curtains. When he straightened up again a bone wracking shiver gripped him. Darkness! Profound Darkness lay before him. He wanted to shut the ominous hooting of an owl in the silent surrounding. His chariot was moving into the deep darkness laying forth him.

Karna looked around at the gathering of noblemen in the hall of Hastinapur. He was again sitting next to Ashwatthama. The gambling game was in full swing before him. When he reached the city, he was told about the dice game Suyodhan had invited his cousins the Pandavas for. He sensed something wrong and immediately asked Suyodhan. "Suyodhan I hope you know what you are doing! Do not lead yourself to something that can harm you and your entire city."

Suyodhan had smiled uneasily, Karna was sure that Shakuni had devised something dangerous. He now looked at Yudhistir who caught his amulet nervously. He had heard that Yudhistir was a skilled player in the game of dice but he was playing against Shakuni. That man had used loaded dice. Shakuni would call out the numbers and it showed the numbers he wanted. Karna watched in disbelief as the eldest Pandav was losing badly. Shakuni had laid the plot well. Yudhistir slowly lost his kingdom, his wealth, his power, and his brothers as well as himself.

This was the last chance he had to win everything back. He watched Yudhistir take a deep breath and then he spoke the unthinkable.

"I put my wife at stake!" The entire hall goes entirely silent. Karna was shocked beyond extent. For a moment he could not function, Yudhistir had staked Draupadi. How could he stake his wife in a gamble?

"Fools, Idiots! Are you serious?" spoke Kripa he was watching but no longer could control himself.

Shakuni spun the dice and muttered twelve, and the two dices showed six, a perfect twelve! Yudhistir lost, once again. He lost Draupadi. Smiles vanished from Arjun, Bheem, Nakul, and Sehdev's faces. They were all dead silent. An evil smile appeared on the faces of Dussashan and Shakuni. Suyodhan looked at his cousins triumphantly.

Shakuni smiled at his victory, "So now the Pandava's are your slaves dear nephew. You can do whatever you want to with them!"

Suyodhan laughed in merriment, "Oh! yes, uncle. Sure, but since they are my slaves now, are they not untouchables? Because as much as I remember the slaves are treated this way, right?"

"Of Course! Now we will need to clean the place they sit on with cow dung and sprinkle Ganga Jal there. Too much work." Taunts came up to the room without a pause. The elders quietly sat there watching.

Suyodhan stood up and spoke "So now that you have lost your wife, the queen of Indraprastha and the princess of Panchal will become a slave. Go get her here into the hall."

"Stop Duryodhan! In the first place, Yudhistir did not have the right to stake Draupadi, when he lost himself, he lost his right over Draupadi. Hence, he did not........" Vidur stood up to speak.

"But if he had the right to stake and lose his brothers, then staking Draupadi was dharma." Shakuni cut in.

Suyodhan smiled wickedly and called for Dussashan "Go get her here. And if she does not come on her own bring her here, pulling her via her hair. Remember she is a slave."

The entire hall went silent as Dussashan left the room. Karna kept mum, not even a word coming out of his mouth.

34   Vastraharan

The silence of the hall was broken with the loud cry of the Panchal princess. The entire hall looked at the entrance in horror. A woman was pushed inside the hall, she was wearing a single saree. She was on her mensuration days. The woman wore a single saree only when they were on their menstruation. She was fallen on the ground. Dussashan walked inside after a moment, he grasped her hair from behind and dragged her towards the centre of the hall. Still, no one spoke. They watched Draupadi barely covered, hair unbound, saree stained, and torn at some places pushed to the floor of the hall.

Karna sat on his seat quietly, a thunderstorm raging in his heart. The words Draupadi spoke were coming back to him.

Dussashan left her in the centre. She stood up slowly and looked straight at the king sitting on his throne. He sat there smiling. She turned around to look at every person, sitting there like mute spectators and bystanders. They spoke nothing at the insult visibly coming upon the daughter-in-law of the Kuru clan. A mocking smile made way on Draupadi's face. She snorted "So none of you is ready to speak up? And you say you are following the dharma? Very good, great men! Very good! Your promises and your stupid vows are much more important than a woman's honour?"

"Stop your banter slave, stop speaking!" Dussashan shouted.

"You stop wanker. You stop! You speak about a slave's boundaries and you have broken your boundaries. You stop speaking and You," Draupadi pointed towards Bhishma, Vidur, and Drona "You: men you bluff about being followers of Dharma speak and answer me dam it!" Draupadi was crying, her anguish flowing from her eyes. The ever-disobedient Dussashan had entered into her room as she sat in the innermost quarter of her room with a blood-stained saree. She was at first startled by his audacity and then when she protested, he had grabbed her by her hair and dragged her into the hall. She struggled to get away, but she was nothing before Dussashan's force. The women of the palace hid in the shadows too scared to help Draupadi. Even after listening to her, they maintained a stony silence. They remained unmoved. They just stupidly hung their head in shame "For God's sake speak! No wait, you men have lost all your shame to even think of God, you do not deserve to even think about God! So now for the sake of the dharma that you so to say follow stop this from happening!"

Suyodhan laughed, he could never stand her haughtiness spoke in a voice laced with hatred "Why do you not stop speaking, Slave girl? You are now are the slave." He added extra pressure on the word slave "Now that your useless husbands have staked you and lost you along with whatever they had. So now come to me share my bed. Sit on my thigh."

He sat on the chair behind and exposed his left thigh and mocked Draupadi. His face had a lascivious look on his face. Draupadi's anger sprouted, she was filled with disgust looking at Suyodhan's vulgarity. "And this was the man I was waiting to say sorry to for what happened in Indraprast the other day!" Draupadi thought her anger rising slowly. She was disgusted that all were still quiet and watching the open display of shamelessness.

Suyodhan did not stop even after what he did, he went further "Go Dussashan strip this slave naked along with her husbands." The people looked in shock. The Pandavas followed Suyodhan's order but

Draupadi wailed in anger. Her patience was slowly giving way. After hearing what Suyodhan said none of the elders spoke. They were silent because according to then "No Rule was Broken". And Dhritarashtra that unbelievable man was smiling indifferently, for him his sons could never be wrong. He was enjoying the mockery of the family of his younger brother Pandu. At one point he had said to Draupadi "Follow the instructions of your master. You are a slave now Draupadi!"

"You excuse of a human being!" Draupadi cried "You are not only physically blind. You are internally blind as well. I know now, why a blind man is not allowed to have the throne. You men are a shame to humanity."

"How dare you? Go Dussashan strip her naked." Suyodhan's voice came in. Before Dussashan could proceed Vikarna the youngest son of Dhritarashtra said "Don't bother. I know you are angry about the incident in Indraprast and you have already stripped the Pandavas of their honour but stripping a woman is a whole different case. You have disrobed the Pandavas, you have taken away their weapons. There is nothing more insulting for a warrior than giving up his weapons. But do not strip Draupadi, she is the honour of Kurus. You will only lead yourself towards destruction!"

"Are you serious Vikarna? Have you decided to side with the sons of Pandu instead of your brothers?" Dussashan said.

"But...." Vikarna tried to reason. He was cut off by Karna. Expressing the hurt and bitterness spurned by a woman he had once loved; Karna spoke the most heinous words of his life.

"Leave it Vikarna. If Suyodhan has control over the Pandavas and their possession, then they also own Draupadi their wife. She became the slave of Kauravas the moment she was lost in gambling. And you say that she is the daughter-in-law of Kurus? A woman does not become the epitome of purity just because she wears the tiara and the vermicelli. She has married five men and so that is the proof that she is nothing, nothing more than a whore." Draupadi looked at Karna with pure contempt and disgust. He wanted her to beg for help but she did not, he only saw disgust in her eyes and that made him all the angrier...."Let her be stripped here in this hall. Let her be disrobed. Her husbands are like seeds removed from the kernel and her soul now looks for new husbands. She is at the mercy of the Kuru princes, her husbands pawned her, she is nothing but a harlot. She had insulted warriors at Indraprast and she does not deserve respect. Even the clothes they are wearing belong to Suyodhan. Just seize them." Karna stopped as he spat venom.

Draupadi chuckled and said "Warrior! Oh, Anga Raj? You call everyone here warriors? This hall has nothing but a gang of rascals. If even one was a warrior, then you would now be standing in the battlefield fairly deciding the result. All of you here are sitting watching and persuading a woman to be stripped and you freaking call yourselves warriors! Must say you are living in a delusion!

"You say you all are followers of Dharma?" Draupadi examined every ones face in the hall. "Then tell me which Dharma allows a woman to be stripped in a hall full of men. Do you call yourselves men? You all are much worse than animals! You people are the ones whom we call the extra weight on this earth. Bloody rascals you all are." Every word Draupadi spoke rung through the hall in the silence.

Suyodhan even instigated the other four brothers to go against their brother and save Draupadi but none did, they chose their brother instead of the honour of their wife. "Certainly, blood is thicker Pandav's. Well done! You have shown the world today that men can never make their wives their priority. She is just a woman at last. Right?"

Dussashan moved towards Draupadi and snatched her saree and started to unwrap it. A woman was being stripped in public- amidst the greatest warriors and learned men of the era- yet everyone kept quiet. No-one stopped the atrocity. Draupadi realized that she was alone. Alone in the entire world, no one to help her. So, what she was the princess of Panchal, the daughter of Drupad, and the sister of Dristaduymna. So, what, she was the daughter-in-law of Kuru clan. or the wife of the Pandavas, the feared warriors. She was, at last, a woman, born to be pawned and suppressed. Born a woman she was meant to just live with the worst pain any human can suffer.

At last, she was a Woman!

At last, she turned towards God, her only defence, her only safety, the only one who would not fear the superficial boundaries of Dharma. The one who would embrace her and give her the safety no human was ready to provide.

"Krishna! Krishna! Krishna!.......Krishna!" Draupadi exclaimed in between sobs. Her pain was evident on her beautiful face which was now bruised. Blood was flowing from her forehead. Her lips had suffered and blood was oozing out. Her hair dishevelled and tangled. Black marks on her arms, blood was coming out of her limbs which had a deep cut on it. And yet the men were silent.

The Kauravas were laughing at the crime that was committed in front of the others hung their heads not ready to witness the outcome of their silence and shameful logic of the following dharma.

Karna was still burning in anger, Draupadi's words "I will not marry a Suta" echoed in his ears but then something happened. Like magic was happening. Dussashan was pulling Draupadi's saree from the left and from her right yards of saree would get extended. The never-ending saree kept on extending. Dussashan pulled yards and yards of the saree she wore and yet it did not end.

Right there in that one moment, Draupadi opened her eyes. Karna's eyes met hers, and he suddenly imagined the unthinkable. In his mind, he saw his wife, his beloved Supriya being stripped naked. Draupadi's cries of help became Supriya's cry for Karna. That moment his anger went away and guilt, unending guilt made its way in his heart.

There at that moment, he lost everything, his morality, his kindness, his dharma, his logic, his self-respect everything. There in that hall, it was not Draupadi who was stripped; it was the unrealistic cloak of dharma that men wore was stripped open. Karna felt his legs becoming weak, and it gave up. He fell back on his chair. A single teardrop slipped his eyes as he watched Draupadi, her eyes closing again. Had he just imagined her opening them? When he had seen into those eyes' years back in the garden of Panchal, he had seen endless love in them. Today he saw only contempt, rage, and anger burning in those doe eyes. They were as red as burning fire; he was burning in the fire of her insult that he had done to her.

Karna was in a frenzy of hate at that moment. His anger, the insult that he had suffered had taken over him, and he spoke those shameful words shamelessly. Karna had called her a whore and a harlot! His heart burned as he recalled what he had said.

There was a thin line between love and hate. It did not take much time for love to become hate and hate to become love. He had once loved this same woman. He had once fallen for her beautiful eyes. No! That could not be love. If it were, he would have saved her from the Kauravas instead of helping them reason their deed. If it were to be love, he would have never wanted her to beg for his help. He would have run to her and covered her injured body. He did none, but he knew he had passionately loved her once. Was his love so shallow that he let this happen to her and did it to her?

Hadn't he said to this same princess "To be dishonoured is to die?" And still, he had dishonoured her; he had contributed in this collective madness of revenge and deceit. He had been a part of this crime, the worst of all he could not even leave Suyodhan after this. "Suyodhan, not Dronaacharya was right he must be called Duryodhan, yes that is what he is good for." He thought as tears were streaming down his face.

He was brought back from his trace when a collective gasp erupted from the room. He looked up and saw Draupadi standing with her hand folded, her eyes closed, and her body straight in prayer. Dussashan had fallen on the ground sweating profoundly, a massive pile of saree lay on the floor. The sun hid in shame, nature was itself felt ashamed that day, the sky was dark, and it looked like it was already night in the afternoon itself. Mother nature cried painful tears every time Dussashan had yanked Draupadi's saree; it cried every time a woman was being insulted. Every bit of nature had called when the woman was shedding tears and dying as she was dishonoured. The several reams of fabric that were pulled off Draupadi lay on the ground, but she was still covered. When no one had heard this woman's pleas when no one had stood up to speak, Krishna stood up. The eighth Vishnu stood up to save the honour of a helpless woman that day defying logic, time, space, shastras, and the so-called dharma that the Kauravas had manipulated to drag a woman to this state of insult and brokenness.

Karna looked sadly, Vishnu had sided Draupadi and was now standing with her. Vishnu stood up when human beings stood immobile like a statue watching a woman's helplessness. Did they all forget that a woman's revenge is more fearful than anything the world can ever see? If she is the one to bestow life, she could destroy everything when she became bloodthirsty?

Karna watched in disbelief, as Draupadi slowly opened her eyes, his face soaked with tears. But not Draupadi's! All her tears were gone. Her eyes were wide open; bloodshot and fierce. The daughter of fire was burning like the forest fire. Untamed and unleashed. And finally, this fire was going to burn down everyone who had brought her to this state, the fire she was burning in would kill all who had murdered her very soul.

Karna thought about his dream again, the rolling of the dice, the darkness the sealed doors, and the fire. Every single thing was the symbolism of this heinous crime. The crime he was the part!

He watched as the nurturing Gauri in Draupadi had died and the Kali; the fierce goddess, the untamed goddess, had risen.

35 Draupadi's Vengeance

Gandhari and Kunti entered the court where they had stripped Draupadi. Gandhari and Kunti had gone out to the temple, feeding urchins and had returned to hear the horrifying news of how Draupadi was dragged inside the hall. They ran towards the hall and saw, Panchali standing still like a statue and the men around staring silently. Shakuni was smiling, and Suyodhan stood there, surprised.

Kunti proceeded towards her, but Draupadi stooped her. She stood there, her eyes blazing, flashing fire. "I from today am nobody's daughter, I am not anyone's wife nor do I belong to a clan or Gotra. I give up everyone related to me. I give up everything that was a part of me. From this moment on, I am just death! The death that will consume each one of you who have done this to me, your death is my dharma, and ensuring your destruction will be my Karma."

Dhritarashtra finally stood up but what he spoke was unbelievable still. "Forgive everyone, Draupadi! Don't make this an issue. I will compensate, I will grant you a boon. Ask whatever you want."

Draupadi's face remained void of any expression. Her voice remained even and calm as she spoke every word. "Give my husbands their freedom!" she stated flatly.

"I agree with you; I free the Pandavas. I give you my word." Dhritarashtra spoke, panic visible in his tone.

"I am not giving them freedom, father; I will not. If they want freedom, then they have to live in exile for twelve years and one year in hiding. So they will live in exile for thirteen years with no claim to property and wealth." Suyodhan said, he still did not have any regret about what he did.

"I do not need a boon to gain what is rightfully ours. That can come back with the might Pandavas have." Draupadi said pointing towards her husbands. "But they need their freedom to do so. Hence, I asked for their freedom. Now listen to me "great men", I shall never forgive the Kauravas or anyone of you for what has been done to me. I shall not tie my hair until I wash it with Dussashan's blood. I will ensure that none of the Kaurava's remains alive when the war happens. May the world despise me or blame me forever, but I will make war inevitable. I will do whatever I can to bring the war to your doorsteps, King Dhritarashtra. Live a happy life till you can see happiness, but the day we come back, your misfortune will stand knocking on your door."

Outside in the city, dogs wailed, donkeys brayed, cats whimpered, goats were bleating, and cows mooed loudly—misfortune creeping into the city of Hastinapur.

"You have achieved what no woman could ever Panchali!" Karna who had earlier flung terrible words at Draupadi said with his head bent low. He did not dare to face that woman ever again. "You have rescued your husbands from drowning in the terrible sea of misfortune, even when you stand here drowning in your misfortune. Your courage is unparalleled."

"You call it courage Anga Raj? I call it helplessness. I am helpless; this is the only way I can survive this life. But remember my words Anga Raj, you will die with nothing left in your soul. The respect and good Karma you take pride in will all go in vain. You will die a beggar from the soul." She spat angrily.

Karna spoke nothing, "I deserve the death she has cursed me. I deserve it." He thought and tears streamed down his face. He couldn't even face his reflection in the mirror how would he face the world?

Draupadi cursed each person their death and did what you can expect only from a woman hurt and pained. Everyone rightly deserved every lash of her anger. She mockingly bowed towards the elders and said "Sorry, I forgot to pay my respects when I had entered the room. I bow to all the elders and superiors. You know I had been dragged here and not given a chance to do so earlier as I was being stripped naked by your prince." her statement was dripping with sarcasm.

Draupadi then straightened up, turned around, held her head high, and left the hall. Even though her honour was in shambles and her life was a mess, she did not let anyone bring down her pride. Her pride was precious, she could not let that fall, her honour might be gone for the world, but till her last breath, she would not let the world make her look down and nor would she allow her tormentors to hold their head high.

Later in the confines of Suyodhan's room, Shakuni, Suyodhan, Ashwatthama, Dussashan, and Karna sat together. The other four were happily talking about how the Pandavas had been humiliated. They were celebrating the ruin of Draupadi, the once prideful princess of Panchal. Karna sat silent like someone had extracted his life out of his body. He was numb, shocked beyond words. Every time Karna replayed the scene of the hall, he only felt contempt for himself. The more he thought of the words he had spoken to Draupadi, the more he hated himself. He wanted to leave, Suyodhan, his friendship, Anga everything forever but he was caught in by the promise he had made to Syodhan. He said to himself this man does not deserve it. Drona was right the suffix 'Dur' suites him more.

Being in the same room with them was suffocating, and if he did not, he would surely kill one of them. Their laughter was piercing and making him want to hit his head on the wall and die. What had he done? "How would I absolve myself? How would I be able to live with this guilt?" Karna thought.

"By the way, did you hear what she said to Karna? He would die a beggar from the soul!" Shakuni said, and everyone laughed. Karna's anger knew no bounds. He stood up and lashed out on him.

"Gandhar Raj! Don't you dare to speak about that again or joke about it? It is none of your concern whether she curses me or blesses me. You have no right to interfere." Karna was serious. He felt that whatever happened in the sabha was something very personal something that was in between Draupadi and him. It was something very much exclusive, nothing that can be insulted or demeaned by the world. That one moment of anger had ended everything, the sting of the insult he had been holding had vanished away. There was no rancour, no fury there was nothing left. He never understood which feeling made him speak the most terrible words to Panchali; was it passionate hatred or painful love?

In his anger, he further remained silent and left the room where everyone fell silent after his outburst. They were all confused at his reaction. No one ever imagined what he was going through. He walked straight towards the exit of the palace. Remaining in the court of Hastinapur was becoming an uphill task for him. He felt trapped; he was becoming weak. The sense of duty he once felt towards his friend Suyodhan was not slipping down his throat like venom. It was killing him bit by bit. The friendship he had cherished had now lost its respect. He had no respect left for himself how would he ever respect his friends anymore. He was indebted to Suyodhan, and he had to endure living by his side.

Karna was nearly at the end of the corridor; he saw Draupadi walking in the opposite direction. He stopped dead in his track. He couldn't move, his legs froze, and his eyes went down, gazing his toe. Draupadi stopped in front of him. She hadn't dressed her wounds, nor did she change her saree. She still had her hair open and no churamani on her head. The blood on her face had dried, and her wounds had become black. Her face soaked with dry tears, but she looked determined. Her face flushed a fierce determination. He recalled her exiting the hall, even in the moment of extreme humiliation, she gathered her courage to strike back the people who caused her so much embarrassment and who had brutally tortured her. Even in her worst state, she dared to speak for herself. She had stood up without wasting time on tears of pain and regret. The princess who had leapt out of fire and was named Yagyaseni was ready to burn the entire Kuru clan in the fire of her revenge. He slowly walked towards Draupadi with his hands folded. He gathered all his courage and looked up at her. The harsh, angry lines on her face relaxed and a new tenderness.

"Your anger is justified. I do not know why I did that, but I was taken over by anger, my rationality had forsaken me, and I had become blind with rage. I spoke words that no woman should be told, yes Panchali your curse will come true one day. I will die the death you have cursed me. I.....can just...."

"I am more hurt than angry with your words Anga Raj! You were known for your goodness, your kindness, your generosity, and your righteousness. And honestly speaking, I expected you to come to my rescue. Even though I knew you hated me for what I did to you, I felt that you would speak up against the misdeed. My husbands had gotten me into that situation in the first place. I knew that they would not help me neither would the Grand Regent or Dronaacharya. Guru Kripa had been already opposing the entire game since the beginning as I heard he had tried but failed. But your reaction was the counter-attack of what I did to you. I do not blame you for that either; I had wronged you. I have reaped what I had sown. I had dishonoured you in front of everyone, and today I have been dishonoured in front of everyone. You were right; to be dishonoured is equivalent to death. Draupadi had died today in that hall. But there is a difference; there is a difference in the insult we faced. And that difference will make all the difference in future events."

"I know Panchali what it feels like to be dishonoured. You feel ashamed, humiliated, and sullied. But your insult was different, and that difference will yield the worst fruits in the future. Yes, you dishonoured me, you insulted me, but what I did to you was not justified. I have wronged you; I mocked your sacrifice. You had no choice but to follow Polygamy. Your curse will come true, one day it will. Justice will be served." Karna broke into sobs. His tears were that of anguish and remorse.

"No one can never measure the severity of a crime. The course of justice is subtle. Even the wisest men fail to serve the course of justice. I will have those burning in the fire of my insult." She took a deep breath and said "I forgive you for what you said to me Anga Raj! I had once made you feel shamed and sullied, and today your words did the same to me as well. And for that, I forgive you! Love knows how to ignore the most heinous crime. I forgive you, sincerely saying.

And this is the last time we are meeting because next time there will be a war and then I will not be able to restrain anyone. It is inevitable. You will not leave Kauravas, and I will not forget my insult."

Karna looked at the woman standing in front of him; she forgave him! How was she able to absolve him after those words, those shameful words that he had said to her. She was justifying and condoning her behaviour! He could not believe what he heard her say. She was ready to forgive her oppressor! He knew she was well aware that she had wished him luck, and she also knew that she was aware of his capabilities. But still, she had insisted on rejecting him, for his low birth, dishonouring him. He wondered what this woman was about; anger, revenge, pride, or just sheer arrogance. And did she just say "Love knows how to forgive...!"

Karna was still wondering while Draupadi turned around and left the palace. She had once turned back to look at the palace, the tenderness now gone and anger flashing on her face. She was the daughter of Agni, the fire god. She was born with the motive to take revenge. She would live with the fire burning within her and make others live through it too. But who was to blame her, how could anyone expect her to keep quiet and not hit back? She had been wounded. A wounded tigress becomes much more dangerous. She won't sit licking her wounds like a dog; she was the wild and untamed. She was ready to pay any price to seek revenge.

Before leaving to Indraprast alone, she said out loud so Hastinapur could know and remember this till she was back "You saw the moment of my weakness, now I will show you the strength of my vengeance." Karna kept gazing at the princess of Panchal on the chariot holding its reins and leading it alone. People of the city stood at the pavements looking at the queen, leaving fear gripping their hearts. She looked determined even in her moment of weakness. Karna could only regret what he had done for his entire life. He had no choice, what had to happen was irreversible, and now there was no turning back. It was the beginning of doom.

❖ ❖ ❖

36   Karna's Guilt

Karna did not dare to go to his parents in Hastinapur; he did not dare to do so, nor did he have the courage to go back to Anga and face Supriya. He felt that his existence was a lie, forever. That one moment of sheer madness had forsaken him of the self-respect Karna lived with. His heart felt weak as he walked towards the house. He did not find Supriya standing on the entrance as she always did in the past. His heart sank as he thought about her knowing everything that happened at the court.

When he entered the main hall, he found his entire family waiting in the room for him. Supriya stood in one corner, with her eyes swollen. He instantly knew what must have happened. They all knew about the incident in Hastinapur. He silently examined everyone. Shom his brother, the one person who worshipped him like some deity was scrutinizing him with his gaze. He looked aggrieved, beyond words. He could not handle that at all. He had always seen respect and love in his family's eyes for him; this change was not at all, helping him overcome his guilt and anguish. No one spoke, an uneasy silence filled the room. Supriya snorted and walked towards him. Her eyes boring holes in his body. Karna knew it was going to be more difficult than facing Draupadi. He did not look into her eyes. Karna knew if he did, he would surely see contempt in Supriya's eyes. He loved her too much ever to watch her hate him.

"Would you be gracious enough to spell out all that you have done

Karna? Any justification of what you have done?" Karna could hear the hidden anger in Supriya's soft voice.

"I have nothing to say Supriya. I cannot justify anything that happened in the court." He spoke with his head, downcast.

"What do you mean you cannot justify? You have done something so disgraceful, and you say you do not have an explanation to give? How could you do that?" Shoma's voice was loud and angry. Karna's answer had added fuel to his anger. "If you cannot justify this brother then seriously your entire life, you have been living a lie. I now doubt whether the righteousness that you lived with was true or living with that idiot Duryodhan you lost it!" For the first time, Shom had raised his voice on his elder brother. Karna did not mind though, "I deserve every bit of their anger." he thought. Karna did not speak at all.

"Karna you once said to me that you hate Draupadi for what she did at her swayamvar. It that hate the reason you did this horrible thing to her?" Supriya still spoke in a very soft tone. She was trying her best not to yell at Karna. She wanted to, though, only she knew how she had been controlling her anger.

"Oh, please Bhabi, that is not a justification. Even if dada hated Draupadi, he could not say what he did. Just because she was married to more than four men, she was nothing but a "whore"! Just because she was inflicted with such a dreadful destiny to be married to the five Pandavas, she was nothing more than a "Harlot"!" Shom was yelling; he had lost his patience. He hated the fact that Karna was friends with Duryodhan. He passionately hated their friendship. He was one of those who had warned him millions of times about Duryodhan.

"You are right Shom." Supriya said "you are right! So Karna how do you feel after what you did. Happy? did the sense of Accomplishment fill your heart?" Tears rolled down her eyes. She was done with her patience and softness. "Have you seen Karna, what have you become? For god's sake, can you now see what have you landed yourself into?" she raised her voice a little. "You are walking towards your doom Karna why can you not for once see it? How could you, you out of all the people behave so shamefully? Did watching Draupadi crying for help, her sorrow and her being stripped and insulted make you merry at heart? Did her pain make you happy?"

Karna said nothing still, his eyes downcast. He just kept listening to words Supriya and Shom poured over him.

"I am talking to you, Karna. Speak to me and answer me!" She was shivering with anger now. "Karna did you just notice that it was not the Pandavs who lost their possessions or Draupadi who lost her honour, it was you who lost your soul! You know, my father would tell me that when a person killed his body it's called "dehhatya". There only your body dies. But when a person murders his soul, it is called "atmahatya". I never understood the difference, but thanks to you Karna, you have explained it to me today. The moment those shameful words escaped your mouth, you killed your soul. You committed suicide Karna, in that hall it was you killed that very soul that tells you the difference between right and wrong, you murdered your entire existence." Supriya broke down. She lost all the courage she had. Varushali, Radha, and Adhirath kept crying. They had no words left.

"Jeshta, you struggled your entire life to attain the respect you deserved. You struggled each day to have your skill honoured. You had suffered the worst insults in life. You knew how it feels every time you are insulted. They why did you for once not think about how that woman would feel. Instead of saving her from the disrobing, you made her suffer the ignominy that you knew hurts. You called her a woman available for all! Not done, not done at all, Brother!"

Karna knew all of what the two were saying; he also knew that they were right. Yet he did not have answers. The last words Shom spoke was what Karna had been wondering all this time. Even he did not know what took over him. Karna should have saved her; he knew how it would feel. How could he become so cruel that he did not even think that he had suffered similarly? You can never predict what turn life would take. When doom awaits a person, even God cannot help him. Karna was fated to be doomed the day he had promised his life and friendship to Duryodhan.

"Why couldn't you forgive her? Why could you not let the anger that had been buried deep in your heart leave you? You would have been happier and would have done what was right. A man guided by anger, in the end, paves his path towards destruction. You have done the same." Supriya's words triggered something within him. Shom left the room, he did despise Draupadi for her arrogance, but he never wished something like this for her. Not even for your worst enemy would someone wish such a fate. The others also left, leaving a sobbing Supriya and a transfixed Karna in the room.

Karna took a deep breath as tears streamed down his eyes. He could no longer hold back; he needed to get rid of those tears he had been controlling all this while. He sank on his knees and began crying. The two sat there crying out their pain and anguish tears streaming down their faces copiously. No, restrain, no self-control, and no holding back.

After what felt an eternity Supriya heard Karna speak "Supriya you are right. I should have forgiven Draupadi. I should have let my soul free and let the anger vanish from it. But I couldn't, I do not know why. I had loved her for once and sought her. But she insulted me, and that love turned into anger. The other day, after the events at the hall, I met Draupadi. She was bruised and hurt. Yet in her extreme pain, she said she forgave me. I had seen an unusual tenderness in her eyes. I know now that it was love and longing. She said to me "Love can forgive the most heinous crime." And then she said she forgave me. Now when I think of what she said, I can only wonder, I can only wonder how! How? Could she do it so quickly? Was her love so large heartened that she was ready to forgive the most gruesome words I spoke to her? And was mine so shallow that I could not even think about forgiving her all these years?" Finally! Finally, he had admitted his love for Draupadi to Supriya. He had said what he had hidden for all these years.

"Supriya, after all these years I have hated her, but now I doubt it. I was not brave enough to forgive. I did not dare to forgive. All these years I have denied this but today I cannot. Ignoring the obvious is called foolishness. I have been so foolish that I never accepted my faults. I might be the best warrior, but I failed to gather the courage even to forgive Draupadi. This sorrow of being a tormentor stirs a broken piece of my heart that is now hurting my entire body. It's physically painful now Supriya. I just feel so so helpless."

Supriya's tears died down as he laid down every mask that he carried for all those years. He laid down his defences that he had built around himself. She was that one person whom he could show his weakness and venerability. She was his saviour and his sanctuary. She was his only safety the person who could accept his flaws.

"Karna!" she wiped her face and went close to him. She knew he was equally broken; his own words were haunting him. Supriya knew he needed her support. "It's not you; it is not her; it's just the situation that went wrong. You were the wrong person in the wrong place. Do you say your love was shallow? No, it cannot be Karna. You knew love, that's why you were scared of it, but still, you gave it a chance. Yet again, you dared to love. And that is what matters. And you want to know where you went wrong? I'll tell you. You couldn't forgive. That is where you went miserably wrong."

Karna embraced Supriya, and he was home. She was his home. The woman who could help him absolve. She was the person who had made him love himself- and that reminded him that she was the only person who could help him, take him out of the hell to which he had pushed himself. He cried there in her arms, shedding all the pain that was hurting him.

After a long time, Karna said "Supriya will you give me a second chance? Will you ever forgive me even if you don't forget?"

"Oh! Second chance? No, I'll give you a million chances. Because you matter to me more than the world does." Supriya said as the day descended into the darkness of the night.

37   Karna's Promise and Curse

Months passed in the blink after Karna confessed his weaknesses to Supriya. Since that day, she witnessed Karna change. He became even more distant and even more detached.

Supriya always noticed that even though Karna had a family that loved him dearly, he was distant and withdrawn. I was like he was looking for something; he was always in search of something. Even Karna did not know what but it was like he wanted to find himself; he was agitated continuously about looking for a purpose. He looked all calm and composed on the exterior but within he was fighting with the contrast of nature.

Supriya gave birth to her child while the sun was rising in the east. The sky was full of varying colours of the rising sun. The spectrum of the sky was spitting out into numerous colours telling of the beginning of a new day. Karna had been on a battlefield when his son was born. The baby was plump and round with crimson red cheeks and a natural pout on his lips. He had visibly large eyes like his mother but had the depth of his father's eyes. He was as fair as his mother was, and he was adorable. No tantrums came in with him; he was a happy baby with an "I will not trouble you" nature.

Supriya was filled with happiness as she looked at her beautiful son sleeping in her lap. Before Karna came to Anga to see his son, someone unexpected came with Bhanumati. Supriya was not surprised by Bhanumati's arrival, as she was her best friend; she was the first person she expected to see. Radha and Adhirath had already arrived a few days back with Varushali, Shom, and Karna's other kids. They were elated to see the little boy.

Kunti had arrived with Bhanumati. Bhanumati had become a lot quieter after the dice game event in Hastinapur. She was visibly not happy about what had happened. The chirpy and happy friend Supriya knew, was not there anymore. Kunti's arrival was more of a surprise to everyone. Pandavas had left for exile while she stayed back at Hastinapur. She lived with Vidur and his wife. She had refused to leave saying she would remain in Hastinapur to remind Dhritrastra that one day the Pandavas would come back to get what rightfully was theirs.

"He is just like, his father!" Kunti said one day after the baby's birth. Just then Karna had entered the room "No, Maharani, he will not be like me. Let him have a better role model and certainly, I am not that role modal any child needs." Supriya had noticed something in Kunti that Karna had missed in the happiness of having his son in his arms. It was like she was speaking about something that they did not know. She had something in her eyes when she looked at Karna happily cradling the baby in his arms. A softness and affectionate look filled her eyes then. Supriya brushed it away from her mind thinking it to be the same unusual affection she has for Karna. Karna was not aware of it, though. He was elated when he saw Kunti in Anga though. For a few days that that Kunti was there in Anga Karna was in a better mood than ever. Supriya thought it to be the happiness of seeing his new baby cooing and tugging on him, but she noticed that the indulgence slowly faded after she left. Karna himself wondered why he felt that way, but he couldn't put the finger on it.

There was an unusual line that had was drawn between his family and himself. They slowly forgot his mistake, but Karna himself did not heal, nor was he ready to forget. His conscience reminded him of the pain Draupadi felt because of him and the pain his family felt afterwards.

When he had met Bhanumati after the incident, she had a shadow cast under her eyes. It was like she knew what the future holds for him. She knew what it might bring upon her husband and her loved ones. Every person he was related to had been withdrawing to their cocoon waiting sadly for the next event. Gloom had made its way to the deepest corner of Hastinapur and Anga. It was almost suffocating for everyone now. The birth of his child was one good event that had happened to him recently. He was winning battles after battles for Duryodhan- yes, he no longer called his friend Suyodhan. Respect was long gone away. Wars were not something that can make anyone happy. Thousands die as gloom filled the cities. Was there not enough misery in their own home with which they had to deal? It was like everyone had turned a blind eye at the approaching war, yet the thought of it would creep in and traumatize all.

The little child was named Vrishaketu. The first part of his name was that of Karna's one of many titles that he was given. The word Vrisha meant righteous; someone engaged in a long penance and someone kind even to enemies. The people of Anga often called him Vrisha. And the second part of the name the word Ketu in Sanskrit represented the spiritual process of evolution or the refinement of materialization to spirit. Supriya had decided the title when she came to know that she was pregnant. She knew that she wanted her son to have his father's name with him always, and she wished to induce those qualities into him as he grows up. Arya Varta believed that the name of a person greatly influences his or her nature. When she had proposed the name after the horoscope reading and the little puja at the palace temple Karna had noticed the use of his name there and was quite uncertain about it.

In the beautiful garden of the palace of Anga, the next day Karna questioned her. "Why did you use my name in his Supriya? I told you I do not want him to be like me!"

"But I want him to be like his father, Karna!" Supriya said with a smile on her face.

"But I am not..."

"O my God! will you stop saying that Karna? You don't know what an amazing person you are. You are a righteous man and a kind human being. You are loyal. You love your family and are you speak the truth without fear." Supriya said dramatically.

He smiled at her annoyance and teased her "But you never said how well I keep my promises Supriya!" He knew she would snap the moment he says that.

"Ya, sure! You also keep your promises "good man". Even if they are miserably wrong and given to wankers like Duryodhan." She rolled her eyes as she stood Duryodhan's name. He knew well that she did not like him much, though.

"Well, Duryodhan is a good friend Supriya!"

"And a terrible brother. I think he finds his entertainment in agitating his cousins. Point to be noted, Bhanumati must be having a tough time dealing with his hatred towards Pandavas." She spoke as she watched her little child sleep in the crib placed nearby.

"Well, if you say so tell me........do you feel the same with me Supriya? Do you also have a tough time in this marriage?" Karna's face was serious now.

"Karna, you know what it is not easy to be a wife. Never was it easy for me, nor Bhanumati, Maharani Kunti, and Gandhari, or Draupadi or Queen mother Satyavati or in that case even for Ganga? We all are married to such complicated men that we do not need anything else to complicate our lives. Do you think it is easy for us to see you men fighting each other for nothing?"

"Nothing! Supriya it is Nothing!" Karna argued.

"Really! What was wrong in sharing the kingdom with the Pandavas Karna? Duryodhan could not even do that much? And don't tell me this is about something else. The inevitable war is born from the womb of jealousy and hatred that Duryodhan had been nurturing in his poisoned mind for years!" Supriya stopped to pat her son's back as he was beginning to wake up. When she saw him drift into sleep, she continued.

"Karna, I know Duryodhan is a fierce warrior, he is an amazing friend to you, he loves his family and his wife a lot. He knows that he will be the king one day, but he is a fool. He is full of anger and hatred. His uncle poisons him, and frankly speaking, anyone can easily influence him. He does not have it in him to share and coexist peacefully. And he is arrogant and ruthless all bad traits for a king. Think about it Karna, a man who can trick his cousins and takes away their wealth and kingdom, a man who can strip a woman off her clothes in a hall, can any woman ever feel secure in his reign? And after what he had done to Draupadi the entire Hastinapur has gone against him. Even you know well that how everything will end Karna. Why do you not just leave and for once break your promise? Karna Duryodhan is so confident in the war because you are beside him. If you leave, the entire country will be able to withdraw from the upcoming war." Supriya knew he would not leave, but she feared to lose him. Even though he was a formidable warrior, she could not deny the fact that he was on Duryodhan's side.

"Supriya, I will not break my promise at any cost. And you fear the death that awaits me? Supriya I am bound to die, if not in the war then somewhere else. I am cursed Supriya." Karna watched Supriya's face change expression. The calmness was fading, and alarm flooded her face. Karna continued ignoring her reaction. "I was cursed by my guru Parshuram that I will forget what I learned from him in the most crucial moment of my life. He felt I was a Kshatriya and not a Suta.

While coming back from Mahendragiri to Hastinapur, I had been practising shabdabhedi baan. I hit the target as I heard the water rippling, thinking it was some deer drinking water. It was a cow instead of a deer. The poor cow died and then the Brahmin who owned it had come there, when he saw his cow dead, he cursed me a similar death. He said I would die as helplessly as the cow had some time ago." Karna did not want to stop. He had never shared these incidents with anyone ever. He tried to speak out everything that he had hidden in the depths of his heart for years now.

"Once I was coming back from Hastinapur to Anga when I saw a little girl crying. She had dropped her milk on the ground. I felt sorry for her, so I took a handful of soil, and I pressed it to extract back the fallen milk. I handed the girl the bowl of milk, and she went away happily. But then I heard a painful cry of a woman. I turned back and saw Budevi standing there. I was about to bow down to her, but she began speaking before I could do so. She said that the way I extracted the milk from the soil and pained her, similarly one day she will trap the wheel of my chariot into her depth and not let it leave it until I fall in pain. She left after that. Also, you already know about Draupadi's curse." Karna took a deep breath as he recalled the events from the past.

"So Supriya I am already cursed, I have to die one day. I am already dead, maybe not literally, but my destiny has that in store for me. So if I die one day, I want to die a death where no one can question my honour and by righteousness. I will fulfil my promise no matter what comes."

He watched Supriya keenly; she sat there still. A strand of hair was fluttering near her face in the soft breeze of the spring. She did not even blink her eyes for a moment. He knew she was scared, fear had gripped her heart, and she was trying to calculate and register everything he had said to her.

"You are scared?" Karna asked her softly.

"Fear is undoing for a warrior's wife, Karna!" She closed her eyes for some time and deeply inhaled. She went closer to Karna and softly placed her head on his shoulder. Instinctively his hands wrapped her into a hug. She curled up in his arms and instantly felt at peace. She knew well that her days with him were just a few, and she wanted to live peacefully with him every day every second. He knew she would never stop fighting him about Duryodhan. And he knew he would never leave his friend's side. This disagreement was never going to end.

"Are you not weary, arguing with me about the same thing from these many years?" Karna said a smile in his voice.

"No, I will keep arguing about it till you listen to me. And since I know you will never listen to me, so you will have to listen to the same reasoning for your entire life."

"Correction; I have to handle your reasoning for whatever life is left for me!" Karna said and felt her body stiffen in his arms. They stayed there for some more time watching their little Vrishaketu sleep in the crib.

38　Pandavas Rescue Kauravas

While Karna returned from one more war after he had been victorious, he walked in the palace of Hastinapur. He was instantly informed that Duryodhan had asked him to meet in the forest of Kamyaka. He was told that the prince wanted to count the number of cows they have. Karna thought it to be some kind of joke at first, but soon his doubt was cleared as he was told that he had to leave instantly. Ashwatthama had to accompany him, Duryodhan, Dussashan, and Shakuni had already left with others.

"I am sure this is Shakuni's plan Ashwatthama," Karna remarked plainly.

"Of course, it is. I think the Gandhar King wants to become a cowherd now!" Ashwatthama said flatly. "And nurture cows to get rid of all his sins. I am sure he has committed many." This time Ashwatthams laughed at his joke.

"It was not that funny Ashwatthama! A lot of our population depends on livestock. Hence counting livestock is common." Karna said. "Well, in this case, I know what Shakuni is trying to do. He is going there to make fun of the Pandavas. Didn't you hear what Sage Maitreya had said last time he had come? Pandava's are living in the Kamyaka forest right now."

"Oh! Unspoken intentions, I see! Well, you and Shakuni understand each other very well though." Ashwattham was trying to tease Karna, but he was in no mood to indulge in rants. Karna did not answer back, and his friend understood the silence. Karna was exhausted. He had not slept for two nights; the wars were taking a lot out of him. He knew that something would indeed happen between the cousins. Whenever they come face to face, some argument or fight is bound to happen. He sighed, preparing himself for the family drama that was likely to happen. He could not understand why Duryodhan could not stay at peace sometimes. Being with the Kaurava's was becoming mentally and physically exhausting for him.

Karna and Ashwatthama reached the Kamyaka forest after continuously travelling for two days. Duryodhan and his group had also called the same morning. "Hush! we did not miss any drama." Ashwatthama chuckled.

"Unbelievable you are sometimes Ashwatthama." Karna glared at his friend.

The Kaurava's had set up their tents on the boundaries of the Kamkaya forest. They were purposely making a lot of noise there, cooking food, and playing music, making it impossible for Pandavas to ignore the commotion in the usually silent forest.

It was Bhim who came to inspect the cause of the noise which had left furious as he understood the motive of the Kauravas. Suddenly the noise stopped in the tens, Karna looked around confused as he was alone in his little tent. He picked up his bow and left the tent. The moment he entered Duryodhan's tent, he was pushed forward from behind and tied around with a rope. He saw his friends held captive and then noticed the Gandharvas who had captured them. Karna tried to struggle and free himself, but the Gandharva's threatened to kill Duryodhan. Karna stopped the moment he felt that Duryodhan's life was in danger.

A loud call was heard outside the tent. Karna instantly recognized it to be Bhim's voice. He was challenging the Gandharva's for a duel. A few went out to fight the Pandavas, but after a little skirmish, the

Gandhrva's left allowing the Pandavas to free the Kauravas.

The Kaurava's left from the Kanyaka forest shamed as they were freed by the cousins they had once cheated and brought misfortune. Karna felt even more humiliated as it was Arjun and Bhim who released the Kauravas instead of him. Arjun's presence was even more humiliating because they were sworn enemies and Arjun defeated the Gandharvas who had also captured him. Finally, after this incident, Duryodhan decided to leave the Pandava's alone for the rest of the years. He said, "We can look for them in the thirteenth year so that we can force them to live in a much longer exile later."

✳ ✳ ✳

39   In Search of Pandavas

"Do you still love Draupadi?" Supriya had asked Karna after Jaydrath had returned with his head shaven with only five tufts of hair on his head. He had tried abducting Draupadi while the Pandavas were living in Kamkaya forests. The Pandavas had arrived on time and after that Jaydrath was no match to them. He learned a great lesson, and he had returned humiliated. Jaydrath was Duryodhan's brother-in-law. The entire incident had created another call for war amongst the Kauravas.

"No Supriya. Not anymore." Karna remarked flatly with no emotion showing on his face. "I did love her.....once in the past. But that love faded long back. It was shallow, and it had no honest base, I guess. The day she insulted me, I had only anger left within me, it left my heart after the incident at the game of dice. The fact is that the anger had come up that day, and words I spoke to her are now troubling me instead. I should have known it will happen, but then I did not realize anything. I was blinded."

"She forgave you, Karna. She still loves you!" Supriya was troubled when she mentioned Draupadi, but the flatness in Karna's tone relaxed her anxiety.

"Supriya that is none of my concern anymore. Even I have forgotten the event that took place in her swayamvar. And you know what, when two people forgive each other there is nothing left in between them. Because then they become strangers for life. Now, I think me and

Panchali both are strangers nothing more. She is married, and I respect her as someone elses, wife. Yes, I do sometimes think that why did she choose such a life. But then what can ever change destiny. Do you call her forgiveness love? I call it courage. At first, even I thought that she loved me and she said it even though not directly but it was direct enough to be understood. Yet Supriya I say that she was courageous. I admire her for that; not everyone can accept their faults and gather the courage to forgive someone who wronged them. She did it, and that is what I admire. Her courage to strike back. Love no, not anymore. Admiration yes. She deserves to gain admiration for her strength and courage."

Karna loved the fact that he was able to talk about Draupadi to Supriya without any emotion or hesitation. He was happy that he had overcome the anger that once was burning him into ashes. And after thirteen years the rage suspended and the war inevitable, Karna watched the man standing in the court of Hastinapur. He was a detective, part of the search party Duryodhan had created to find the Pandavas while they live in hiding. There were just a few days left for Duryodhan to look for then as the moment the thirteenth year would end the time for war would come dangerously near and he was not ready to share his kingdom with his cousins.

The search party had no legit news of the Pandavas. But some shocking news had come to them.

Keechak, who was the brother of Queen Sudeshna of the kingdom of Matsya, had been killed by some random cook called Ballav. The messenger said that the queen had asked her hairdresser Shairendri to go to his brother, for a night. Kichak was an oaf with wandering eyes. He found the queen's new maid and had shamelessly asked her to send her maid to his room one night.

The queen could not say no to her brother, and so she pressurized Shairandri to go to her brother. Later that night Kichak had been crushed in a bear grip. He was drunk; hence the opponent was stronger and quickly broke his bones, smashed his flesh, and left him with a cracked skull.

Duryodhan exclaimed the moment the messenger stopped "We have found the Pandava's" he said "Kichak was one of the strongest wrestlers, and if someone crushed him and left him nothing more than a bundle of flesh and bones, it can only be bhim. Only he can kill Kichak!"

"We will attack Matsya and send the Pandava's back to living in exile," Dussashan said.

It was challenging to reach Matsya soon enough, so Duryodhan asked Susarma the king of Trigarta to attack the southern frontiers of Matsya. The army of Duryodhan attacked the northern boundaries as only a few soldiers and women were left in the city. Uttar, the young son of King Virat. When he came out, it was rather funny for the Kauravas. The charioteer was a eunuch, and the warrior was a young boy. The Kaurava's laughed, and Uttar shook in terror as he saw the great warriors on the battlefield. Bhishma, Drona, Duryodhan, Karna, and many others intimidated the young bow.

Speaking brave words does not make one brave. The young boy trembled with fear as he eyed the warriors. He was ready to run from the battlefield, but his charioteer tucked the reins and changed the direction of the chariot. The chariot vanished out of sight, confusing everyone.

After some time they saw the chariot returning. This time the eunuch was the warrior, and the boy was the charioteer. The Kaurava's laughed, but Karna stood still in his chariot. He eyed the eunuch and then noticed the bow in his hand. He looked at it keenly and recognized it to be the Gandiva. He knew Arjun had attained the Gandiva from Shiva.

"This is no eunuch Duryodhan; he is Arjun. I am sure that is Arjun. Look at his bow" Karna said loud enough for all the warriors to hear.

"So, we have forced them to come out. Now they are discovered, and so they will be sent to another long exile." Duryodhan said glee hidden in his words.

"Do not be sure Duryodhan, the Pandav's are no fools. They will not show up without thinking about exile." Karna was sure the exile period must be over as Arjun decided to come out in the open with his weapons. Duryodhan was however still happy within, Karna eyed him and shook his head. Estimating your enemy to be a fool is the biggest mistake one can make. Duryodhan was making a mistake; only Karna knew how he wished to knock some sense in his friend.

Before anyone could do anything in the Kaurava army, Arjun shot three arrows. Two landed on Drona's and Bhishma's feet as reverence, and the third was some missile that put the entire army of the Kaurava's to sleep.

❉ ❉ ❉

40　　The Peace Treaty

The Kauravas had come back to Hastinapur humiliated. The angavastras of the warriors had been taken away. The thirteen years had been over, and the Pandavas had come back openly before everyone. They had sent a peace emissary to Hastinapur, but Duryodhan had refused to give them their kingdom.

Karna did want to speak, but he had boundaries set. He could advise Duryodhan, his friend, but he had no right to speak in between the family matters of Hastinapur. Karna kept quiet as Duryodhan was adamant. One evening it was informed that Krishna would be coming to Hastinapur carrying a peace treaty.

The city was ready for Krishna's arrival. Duryodhan had organized a lavish lunch party for his welcome and a grand room for Krishna to rest in. But all was in vain as Krishna entered the city but did not reside in the royal palace nor did he eat food cooked in the palace kitchens. He willingly chose to stay at Vidur's home who did not eat the food of the castle himself. He and his family ate what they grew in their backyard. When asked, Krishna said he would eat in the palace only when the treaty was finalized the next day.

It was not long before the night was spent and the day came in. Krishna entered the court of justice with the treaty. Karna was also present. When Krishna finally met the king, he was not happy. Things were not at all pleasant in the court.

"Duryodhan, you had promised that you would return Indraprast to Pandavas when they come back after the humiliating exile of thirteen years. Now it's time that you do what you had promised." Krishna said coolly.

"No need Vasudev; I am running Indraprast well. The people have forgotten the Pandav's, and so no one needs them back." Duryodhan answered arrogantly.

"I do not need to hear all that Duryodhan. It does not matter if people have forgotten then or not. What matters is that you have to fulfil your promise and give back what is rightfully theirs."

"No, I will not do that."

Krishan took a deep breath and said "Fine then! If you do not agree to give them Indraprast at least give them five villages that they can govern and live in. They would not ask for anything more."

"No" was the reply that came from Duryodhan. "I will not even spare them land as big as a needlepoint. That's it!"

"OK! Anga Raj will you please explain to your friend what is the very basis of Dharma?" Krishna said slyly.

"Promise. A promise is the basis of dharma. If taken back the other pillars of Dharma collapse." Karna said with an even voice.

"Now that you have given up your promise and destroyed the very basis of Dharma and hence you made yourself unfit to rule. A king who cannot fulfil his promise is unfit to have the throne. You hence will be destroyed Duryodhan." Krishna got up to leave the palace, but Duryodhan's voice boomed in the silent hall.

"How Dare you! You cowherd, how dare you threaten me!" shouted Duryodhan getting up from his seat. "You dared to do this so now I will make sure you do not leave the palace and live in one of the dark cells of Hastinapur all your life."

Krishna stood there smiling, without a trace of fear on his face. Duryodhan was further infuriated, and he lashed out "You maverick, you think I will spare you that you are smiling. I am not going to let you go without punishment. Guards seize that man and bring me the chains. I will myself have him tied and will take him to the cell."

The guards stood uneasily, holding their swords against Krishna. They were unsure of their movements as one of them brought an iron chain, as ordered by Duryodhan.

"Stop this madness Duryodhan. Are you thinking about what you are doing? You are trying to imprison Vishnu himself! Don't be stupid; stop it." Karna shouted as he watched Duryodhan take the chains in his hand. Duryodhan ignored what Karna was saying, and he did the unthinkable.

"Are you sure you want to imprison me Duryodhan?" Asked Krishna with a smile on his face.

"Yes! You will be imprisoned." Duryodhana stated.

Suddenly the entire court was filled with blinding light. Krishna appeared with thousands of heads, that represented his thousands of forms. The whole universe within him. He was beyond the seas and skies. The various forms were showing the beginning of the universe to its end; it was like the most beautiful thing anyone could see.

After a long time, Krishan came back to his usual form. The smile back on his face. He had a warning in his eyes for the Kurus. "This will be the end of Duryodhan. Now you lost your last chance to save yourself. I will take your leave, and I announce the beginning of the war. Now either you live, or you die. And this war will be like no other, and brothers will fight each other to take each other's life, death will spread its wings and misery will envelop the whole of Arya Varta. Your bad luck starts today Duryodhan."

Krishan left after declaring war, the bliss of witnessing Vishnu himself died down as the fear of the terrible fate filled the air with gloom and despair. Everyone in the hall fell silent as they recalled the terrible words Krishna had uttered. Karna quietly left the hall to meet Krishna for one last time. He wanted to save his friend for one. Karna knew that Duryodhan couldn't win the war having Krishna against him. Least he would survive but winning the war was impossible.

41   Krishna and Karna

Karna stopped Krishna as he was ready to leave the palace of Hastinapur on his chariot that waited on the gate. Karna went to him with folded hands, Krishna just smiled again and asked him to accompany him on his chariot. Karna climbed the chariot and sat next to Krishna silently. The two did not talk while the charioteer drove towards the exit of the city.

"Take us to the river bank…" Krishan ordered his charioteer. Karna did not speak as he feared to question Krishna. The image of Krishna had not left Karna's mind. He still remembered the beauty of the form of Vishnu that he had shown in the hall.

When the chariot came to a halt, the two men got down. Krishna asked his charioteer to get him some water. When he was going to get it from the river, Krishna stopped him and asked him to get it from the city. Karna and the charioteer both looked at him confused, but no one said anything. The charioteer left, and Krishna turned to Karna "Karna do you know that you are siding with the ones who are wrong. Duryodhan's death is inevitable. His victory is impossible."

"I know!" was what Karna managed to say.

"Even I know that you know. I am asking you, why are you with them when you have realized that Duryodhan is committing Adharma and he is clinging to other's wealth in an unrighteous manner?" Krishna said to Karna in a soft tone."You know it right, Duryodhan is fighting this war just because he has you by his side? He will rethink this war if you do not fight for him in the war. Your ability is what he thinks is his capability."

"Keshav, I know all of this already. I cannot leave him; I'm here to ask you to find a way that can bring this disastrous war to an end. Is there no way you can do it?" Karna almost pleaded.

"I already told you! Your ability is his capability. He thinks he can defeat the Pandavas because you are with him. You leave him, and you will see how he instantly forgets the war. And even if he does not, he has to die; Dharma had left him Karna, and he as abandoned Dharma as well. Now you see, I do not have a choice but to declare war.

You can stop this war, Karna if you want to. If you listen to what I say you might be the one person to stop this war."

"But I already refused! What now, Keshav?"

"What if I say you are not a Suta but the son of a Kshatriya? What if I tell you to have a celestial father and a mother who is a queen?" Krishna spoke in a grave tone. Karna was at a loss of words. He wanted to laugh out loud; he felt it was some kind of joke, but he respected Krishna, and he had no intention to offend the Yadav leader.

"Karna you are the adopted child of Radha and Adhirath. They found you in a floating basket on the riverbank in Champanagri. You are the son of.....," Krishna paused to watch Karna's reaction. "You are the son of Lord Surya and Queen Kunti."

That moment, that very moment Karna's world came crashing down. Judging the look on Krishna's face, he could say that this was no joke. His heart was filled with disbelief, for his entire life, he had lived a lie. Forever he had struggled to gain a respectable place amongst the Kshatriya's even though he was one of them. He had been fighting with the people who taunted him and pushed him away because for them and himself; he was a Suta. Suddenly he felt anger shoot through his veins; his parents had lied to him; they never informed him of what was the most significant truth of his life. He felt betrayed and broken.

"You live as a Suta Karna; you support the Kauravas, each moment of your life you spend fighting the Pandavas." Krishna kept on speaking "You never had your mother's love, no one ever found out the truth, nor did you reside with your family ever. You were not at fault when you faced every insult in life. The pain and struggle were all part of your destiny. Since you know now, who you are and where you belong, come along with me to your family. Accompany me and take what is rightfully yours. Come with me to your brothers, to your mother."

Brother's!

Karna's breath hitched, Arjun was his brother, his younger brother. He still remembered the day he had to see the young Pandavas with Kunti. The sudden love that had filled his heart had overwhelmed him. Was that connection of blood? His greatest rival was his brother, his younger brother. The man who married Kunti; Pandu, was his father. He was the eldest Pandav!

"Karna you are powerful, intelligent, and a follower of Dharma! You are the best amongst all the Kurus. Come back to your brothers; they would be thrilled to make you king; they would happily serve you for their entire life. Oh! What a sight it will be Karna! There will be happiness all around; the world will recognize you for who you are. Think about how happy your mother will be when you return to her.

"The war will never happen, Duryodhan will himself bow down and accept you, the world will head towards a peaceful future. I will give all that is rightfully yours Karna, the throne, the crown, respect, honour, name everything will be given back to you just do me a favour; help me stop this war."

Karna just watched Krishna. This man was one person whom he believed to be true to all. Karna knew everything he was saying must be right, and he would do anything to stop this war. A pleasant image of the happy family he would have filled his heart with joy and bliss. His brothers, his mother everything would be perfect. The endless search of his identity would be over. He finally would be able to justify why he was different from all the others, why he had dreamed of being an archer instead of a simple charioteer. His kavach and kundal was no mystery. He had for many years struggled to understand why were his interests and manners different from those other kids he lived around, that search had dragged him away from his family. He was detached and distant because of that one question that had made his way into his brain when he was only a little child. The frustration of being rejected all the time just because he was a Suta had made him withdraw himself from everyone around him, his wives, children, father, mother everyone.

The distressed image of his friend popped up in front of his eyes, from the back of his mind. The fallen and failed friend's image pulled him away from his little moment of Happiness. He soon realized that he was not free to do what Karna had asked him. He was a Kunteya, son of Kunti. The woman Karna deeply respected. He knew now why she was so affectionate towards him, why she warned him all the time about the danger of being in the palace, why she loved him so much. She was his mother! The affection he had for Kunti was nothing less; he loved her, yet anger made its way into his heart. Tears filled his eyes, and his soul felt deceived. Karna took a deep breath as he realized that Krishna was waiting to hear from him.

"Keshav, I am thankful that you told me all of this; you spoke the truth that my mother did not tell me ever. But I wonder what kind of a mother is she that after giving birth to a child she left him to die, she abandoned the child she had carried for nine months without a second thought? Is she less than a monster that she left the child she had born for so long in her womb?

I do not want to know about her; she left me. She killed me the day she abandoned me. Was her heart made of stone? Was the society much more important than the child she gave birth to herself? While she had been watching me from afar, struggling to live, what she watched me being insulted by all, did her heart not feel the pain? Was I such a shame to her that she could not even spare a bit of kindness upon her firstborn? Never did I ever have a love of a mother, and instead I received the curse because she made a mistake, she made a foolish mistake in life!"

Karna was so drained of energy that he went down on both his knees and sat there. His feet were weak and wobbling. Bet he wanted to speak, he was tired of holding back everything and every time. Whether it was anger or pain, he was tired of carrying the burden of the mistakes people around him make. He had done it long enough now; his life was in itself a mistake, a mistake his mother had made as a girl. He had been living the curse of Kunti's fault. Yet his heart ached that she never helped him, nor did she ever try telling him the truth when she knew that he was her son, all along. He would have been happy if she acknowledges the fact to him, there was no need to tell it to the world, at least she should have told him! He had dreamed every night of the scene where a woman pushed the basket with the baby into the flowing water, never did he think how painful it would be to know that he had suffered the fate of being rejected and thrown away.

"Keshav, Queen Kunti pushed me away because she feared what the society would think of her character because I was a curse to her. Does she not know that the curse that she pushed away years ago, the curse that she had been running away from all her life is still in me. I am still her firstborn, cursed child. I am still the sin that she committed before marriage. Nothing has changed!" Karna spoke with much malice in his tone, Krishna did not expect it from Karna. "Can you tell me why she suddenly feels that she should come clean before all? What did change all of a sudden that she is ready to speak the truth? Let me tell you; she is doing this not because she wants me to be happy but because she wants the Pandav's to win this war. Keshav today I have become an archer, I have become the king of Anga, yet there was a time when this society made fun of my dreams, they showered comments that tore my heart. I was a pun for those around me. In those worst years of my life, it was Radha Mata who comforted me with her love and affection. Throughout my life, she was the only mother I have known! She nurtured me, cared for me, she was the one who cried for me when I left the house. The mother who gave birth left me to die, but the mother who adopted me gave me a new life."

"Keshav, I was nothing for the society, when I had come to participate in the graduation contest, no one accepted me for my talent. The Pandavas never stood up for me! It was Duryodhan. He was the one who gave me the respect that I deserved; he made me a king based on merit and talent. People say that he did it because he needed me against Arjun, yet Keshav, he was the man who sheltered me. Even though he helped me because he had his hidden motives, still that man is the reason I stand here as King. The social respect I struggled for is all given to me by Duryodhan. He has been more than a friend to me; he has been a brother to me. The passionate hate that he felt was reserved for the Pandava's; he has been a genuine friend to me all these years."

Karna was sure about his last lines a person cannot feign affection, love, and friendship. He had seen his friend. He had heard Bhishma saying once "Duryodhan's friendship to Karna is the one good thing left in him." Duryodhan had always stood up for him, whatever be the circumstances.

"You are right; all his expectations are directed towards me. And think about it Keshav, the man who gave me his friendship, and respect, he trusts me more than anyone else, how can I break that trust? He is pinning his hopes upon me; I cannot betray him not that the war is just about to begin. If I leave him now, I will also be called a sissy.

If I leave now, why will the world believe me that I am the son of

Queen Kunti? Why will the society, accept me? The Pandava's would forever be loathed for the world would think that they were not good enough to fight so they chose the easy way and called me their brother. If I leave everyone will believe that I was greedy and I had befriended Duryodhan for becoming king. My life-long struggle for respect and recognition will all go in vain. People would never believe Queen Kunti at this point, and my friendship, charity, effort, pain, hard work will all go in vain."

"Karna I can make sure the world believes!" Krishna said.

"You cannot make people believe. Belief comes naturally; it is the voice of the soul. We have come a long way Keshav! I have come a long way. From here, there is no turning back. There is no returning. I am thankful that you spoke the truth about my birth, but I have to be with my friend. You warned Duryodhan because he did not fulfil his promise, so how can you expect me not to fulfil my promise to Duryodhan? No Keshav, I will not do that, I will not betray him."

"So, you want this war to happen Karna?"

"I do not want this war to happen, it will only mean destruction, but I also do not want any wrong to happen with the people of this country. This war will ensure a better future for our country, let it happen. This is the end of all misfortune the world has been suffering for decades, Keshav." Karna said as he composed himself. He stood up to face Krishna who was standing at a distance.

"Keshav, Pandava's deserve what is rightfully theirs. And the Kaurava's deserve the fate they brought upon themselves. I am unfortunate enough to fight against my brothers but is this war not being fought between relatives? I will fight every day to make sure Duryodhan wins, which is far from happening, so why stress about something that will happen. And when you know, it will happen! It is a lost war for the Kaurava's; they lost the day Draupadi was stripped. It just has to happen now. But I will fight with all my might; I will do all I can to have victory walk towards the Kauravas."

"Why are you fighting if you know what is bound to happen, you have a chance to save your life." Krishna was trying his best to convince Karna; he was visibly failing. Karna smiled and said.

"A warrior never thinks of life Keshav! A Kshatriya lives to die! I have lived with bravery; I will die with courage. A warrior's death is better than a tainted King's life. I will be proud to die a warrior's death, fighting till the last moment." A small smile made way on Karna's face. "I never wanted kingship or wealth, I have forever lived wanting respect that a warrior deserves, and till my last breath, I will do the same. If wealth mattered to me, I was capable of conquering states for myself. I wouldn't give it to Duryodhan." Krishna watched Karna for a few moments, tears threatening to fall from his eyes. The man before him had impressed him; admiration flooded Krishna's eyes. Krishna smiled at his conviction and his friendship.

"Veer! I am sure no one ever had a friend like you. Your friendship is the most beautiful possession a person can have. Duryodhan is a lucky man! You are not only Duryodhan's prized possession but also a boon to humanity. They will learn from you, Karna! They will learn a lot from you and your life!" Krishna said, with his eyes glittering with pride.

"Can you do me a favour Keshav?" Karna asked the Yadava leader.

"Anything for you, Karna!"

"Do not tell my brothers about me. Yudhistir will give up war if you tell him. Pandava's would never get their rightful place." Karna felt blood rush to his face when he addressed the Pandava's like his brothers. That was how it should have been, but it never happened, nor would it ever happen.

Krishna nodded; he knew he had to do it for this person standing before him. A life-long struggle had been involved in the making of this man. He deserved respect, and he earned it. Karna folded his hands before Krishna and left the place silently. Krishna watched Karna go; his head held high and back straight. Yet only Karna knew about the storm raging in his heart. He had finally found out who he was, why was he different, why did he never fit in, but it was too late. There was always a "but" in his life, never did anything come to him quickly; nothing was easy. This would not be easy as well, but he had to do it like he always did.

He had to rise from the ashes of broken dreams to fulfil his promises. It was not his choice; it was his fate.

42   Daan Veer

Karna returned to Anga for a few days. He wanted to see his wife and son once before the war broke out. Few days were left, before the beginning of the war. The entire palace of Hastinapur was busy preparing for the war with the Pandavas. Karna and his elder sons were all fighting for the Kauravas. He watched Varushali struggling to let go of her sons, but she had no choice. Vrishaketu was too young to fight, though Karna was training him for quite some time now. Still, he was just a twelve-year-old boy. When he had come to the palace in Anga, he found Supriya standing on the entrance waiting for him like she always did.

The usual sparkle of her face was all lost; they looked sad. She had not aged a bit over the years. She looked as lovely as the day Karna married her but when he returned that day, he saw a dramatic change in her. She suddenly looked tired and sad. Her smile was sad. Of Course, he knew the reason but did not speak of it. Now it was the same everywhere. Duryodhan had refused to listen to anyone. He was adamant. So, everyone stopped talking and go ready to fight the war. The day the country was dreading was coming nearer. Sleep had deprived most people. A day later, Radha, Adhirath, Shom, and Varushali went to the palace. His sons lived in Anga anyway for years now. Supriya insisted on having food together. She and Varushali made sure that everyone ate together, As a Family!

When asked the reason she had said "There are few days left Karna, in these few days let us be a family and live together. It will not happen afterwards." Even though she did not say it directly, but her hoarse voice said it all. Everyone was putting a brave front, yet everyone was fearful. The people of Anga had come to love their King in all those years. The people watched his chariot with longing and fear evident in their eyes. In those last few days, Karna went to every part of his city thanking his people for accepting him as their king. Most would break down while he spoke to them.

After he returned to Hastinapur, he went to the river bank once again to pray. The rain made the soil soft and moist. It had showered all night. He had a visitor before he came to pray in the early hours. It was Lord Surya, his father. He had warned him if Indra. After his puja to Lord Surya, he gave away alms. The last Brahmin was the one he was expecting to see. He looked somewhat different. He was unusually tall and had a well-defined torso. If not for the beard and moustache he would no doubt look like some god. He was dressed in a saffron-coloured dhoti and the same colour angavastra. Karna instantly knew who that man was.

Indra!

"I have come to you to ask for alms, Anga Raj..." Indra said oblivious to the fact that he was discovered.

"Sure, accept the gold and the grains sir," Karna said, aware that Indra had not come to him for gold and grains. Indra tensed; he was there for something else. He looked around nervously and then said: "I do not want gold and grains Anga Raj."

Karna smirked. The man slowly came to the point. "Then what do you want me to give you Dev?"

"I want your breastplate and earnings. They are divine right?"

Indra said, thinking he had not been discovered. Karna smiled, finally the truth! Indra looked at him curiously as he felt that he would have to leave without having what he wanted.

"Yes, they are celestial, Indra Dev. May I know why do you need these?" Indra's face went white. He was clearly caught. So, he decided to answer his question.

"The Kauravas need to be punished for the sins they have committed Karna. They were given chances and a lot of opportunities to amend their mistakes, but they never considered it an option ever. They are seriously a threat to society. The people who can take pride in disrobing their sister-in-law can never be good rulers. The people of the kingdom will always follow the example of their king and Duryodhan certainly in a lot of fields is not a good example.

Now that the war is happening, they must be conquered, and we must establish a new way of governance. But you Karna, you are the one person who is the shield for the Kauravas. Your Kavach and Kundals will only serve as a safety for not only you but the entire Kaurav Army."

"So that is why you want my Kavach and Kundals?" Karna shook his head.

"Karna you have promised that you will not let anyone leave empty-handed from your doorstep. The Kavach and Kundals are like your second skin. And it will be painful for you to take them out. So, I give you an option. If you promise me to not participate in the war, then you will not need to give away your armour. Now the choice is yours."

"You think you have given me a choice Dev? Even you know well that I will not betray my friend, so I do not have an option but to give you my armour and earrings." Indra had already planned this. He knew that Karna would not give up his dharma, and in the end, he will have to give away his armour. Indra was sure that Karna would not compromise and hence he would finally get what he had come for. "And will you not tell me that you fear that I might kill your son Arjun who is also my brother. You fear that if I have the Kavach and Kundals, then Arjun would not be able to kill me, and the war would not end anytime soon?" Indra went pale. What he said earlier was the partial truth. Yes, he did want to save his son; he did want to protect Arjun. Karna just shook his head and chuckled.

He then pulled out a knife hanging on his waist and removed the shawl that covered his upper body. The armour appeared magically on his body, as the sun came up in the eastern horizon, the armour sparkled and reflected a gradient light around. The reflecting light was blinding. Karna reached for the kavach and began ripping it out of his chest. The pain was unbearable; he was trembling. A layer of his skin came out along with the armour. The shining armour was slowly being ripped out by Karna, he screamed in pain. From head to toe, he felt like he was struck by lightning. More than the simple problem, it was like a burning sensation that shot through his entire body.

When he finally took out his armour and handed it to Indra, his entire torso was covered with blood. The blood was flowing uncontrollably and sliding down his chest in drops leaving a trail of blood all along. His white dhoti was soaking the flowing blood as it slowly started becoming red around his waist.

Karna ripped out the earrings similarly and gave it away. Indra stood there; his jaw dropped as he witnessed the sight before him. He watched in disbelief as the knife fell off Karna's hands. He had come to a man with a straight back and a strong aura around him, but now he was seeing a man reclining and sweat dripping from his forehead. He was trembling in pain, his eyes which were earlier alert now looked tired and weak. Slowly it was becoming difficult for Karna to stand on his legs. Indra's tears welled up as he watched the man before him.

Under the face of a strong man and a brave warrior, lived a king with a radiant soul.

Beautifully perfect and perfectly flawed!

"Karna I have taken away your safety, your prized possession. It will be a grave sin on my part as I have deprived a warrior of his safety. I cannot make up for this." Indra said, looking towards Karna's armour and earrings which were now in his hands. "But I will surely give you something in return."

"There is nothing that one can get in return for a charity Dev. I gave you my armour because I had promised never to let anyone return disappointed if they come to me seeking for charity. I fulfilled my promise nothing more." Karna said, and he groaned in pain.

"No doubt you are the son of Surya, a Suryavanshi. It runs in your blood to fulfil your promises. You have done your dharma, and for being true to your dharma Karna I grant you my Indrastra. One of the most powerful weapons amongst the Devi astras." Indra was determined to make up for what he had taken. Little did Indra know that he had taken away the only safety Karna had? He had ripped him off the last piece of protection that could save Karna; an Indrastra would do nothing for him. It was like compensating gold with grass.

"You would forever be called Daanveer Karna. All will remember your sacrifice to fulfil your promise." Indra said.

Karna let out a painful chuckle and nodded his head. He did take the weapon, but he knew it was nothing when compared to the armour and the earrings he had since when he was born. Indra left, and Karna began walking towards his chariot.

The fragrance!

The first rain of the season brought about the sweet fragrance in the air. The sweet-smelling flowers diffused their smell in the surrounding. The soil was moist, and it felt soft. The sun had risen in the eastern horizon, long back but looked dull. The small drops of rainwater that rested upon the leaves sparkled a few moments ago in the blazing sun, but now we're left lifeless and still. The sun was gone. The day looked grey; the sun peeped from behind the clouds. The lustre and grandeur were all lost. The river flowed swiftly, making its way and breaking the silence of the quiet morning. It was melancholy that enveloped the bank of the flowing river. The breeze cool and soft provided peace in the ever-growing heat of the surrounding.

A man at a distance struggled to stand straight without any support. He could barely walk. He dragged himself towards his chariot. With all the fragrance infused around him, he could get a pungent smell.

Blood!

It was an unmistakable smell. It was all over his body his chest was ripped out of the skin. Blood dripping from his earlobes, his naked chest covered with blood and a nerve wreaking pain left him shivering. The soft muslin, his white dhoti was slowly turning red soaking all the blood that slowly moved down his body. Tall and well built, a man with broad shoulders was right there in a state of immense pain and…

"Water, water, wat…"

He could utter no more! His words sunk before it could escape his lips. He shivered because of pain. This pain was ripping out all the energy that was left in his body. He was in desperate need of water!

He kept walking, back to his chariot. Slowly trying to maintain his balance, he took the help of the Ashoka tree within reach.

It was becoming difficult now.

Fall!

He fell on his knees, trying to remain steady while resting his weight on his knees. His head burrowed down. Eyes full of water, he looked at the soil. With one of the fingers, he digs out the ground which quickly came out. After staring at it for a long time, his eyes went blurred, unable to see anything around him.

He collapsed, falling on the ground, unconscious and murmuring the words "Water...". Darkness took over him.

* * *

43   Nakul and Sehdev

Karna had felt himself being lifted from the ground; he was semi-conscious. He could hear someone calling out his name, but he felt like it came from some distant land. After that, he only could feel the pain that was making him weaker. His breath was laboured and heavy. His torso felt numb except the occasional pain that made shivers run through his body because of medicines applied on his wound. He wanted so inconvenient that he wanted to be left alone without the medicines. He was willing to do anything to open his eyes. He couldn't. It was like living in a dream and not being able to wake up. He felt as though his death was near.

Karna was struggling to open his eyes when a pain shot through his entire body. It was nerve-wracking. It was like a burning sensation. Even though the sensation was only on his chest and back, he could feel the pain throughout his body. He groaned and let out a painful cry. Slowly the burning sensation soothed, and the pain slowly went away. The occasional shivers that passed through his bones ended, and then he felt at peace. His wound on his chest, back, and earlobes did not pain as much. He had been sweating because of the pain that was all over his body now died down. He felt better and slowly opened his eyes. At first, he was confused, looking at the two men standing on before him. They looked at him intently, and their eyes were like searching for something in his. He frowned; his brows drawn together. Karna looked around and saw Kunti, Radha, and Adhirath as well. He then again turned to look at the two handsome men before him. No, he was not dreaming; it was Nakul and Sehdev standing before him. Karna struggled to sit up straight.

The charioteers had brought a fallen Karna back to a tent on the outskirts of Hastinapur. The tents were prepared for those fighting the war. When Kunti had heard of what Indra had done, she had pleaded before Nakul and Sehdev to help, Karna. They were adamant at first, but the shocked Arjun had insisted saying, "A warrior like Anga Raj must receive a death worthy for a warrior. He has become an epitome of sacrifice by giving up his armour and earrings today, it's your duty to save him."

Nakul and Sehdev had agreed to what Arjun had said. They were reluctant at first as they were angry about how Karna had insulted Draupadi, but they did what was told when they saw Karna in immense pain. The twins were the sons of Ashwini Kumara. The god of medicine, associated with the dawn. Nakul and Sehdev were born like other Pandavas using the celestial mantra given to Kunti by Durvasa. Kunti taught the mantra to Madri, Pandu's second wife, and then the twins were conceived.

Nakul and Sehdev straightened when they saw Karna had recovered from the pain. The concern in their eyes suddenly replaced by anger, as they glared at Karna. Kunti sighed in relief as tears flowed from their eyes.

"Thank you, Nakul, Sehdev. For coming here and healing my wounds." Karna said softly he knew they hated him. The twins looked at each other but and spoke softly.

"We came here because you deserve an honourable death of a warrior but do not think that we will not fight against you on the battlefield."

"I do not expect you not to fight me, but still thank you for coming even though I am your sworn enemy." Kunti cringed, hearing the last few words her heart fluttered with fear. Nakul and Sehdev nodded and turned towards Kunti.

"Let's go Ma. Back to the Pandava camp. You are not safe with the Kauravas."

"I will not Nakul, Hastinapur is the place where I belong. I am bound to remain here with Gandhari didi and Maharaj Dhritarashtra. Don't worry about my safety." Kunti knew where her boundaries were.

"But..." Sehdev intervened.

"I promise you to keep mata safe. Whatever may come, I will make sure that no one ever harms Mata Kunti." Kunti looked at Karna, love evident in her eyes. Nakul and Sehdev did not protest this time they were assured. This man who could risk his life to fulfil his promise would fulfil his promise to keep Kunti safe as well. They were surprised themselves, but there was so much sincerity in Karna's voice that they took his words right away. They were sure that he would honour his promise.

Karna watched the twins leave the tent. Radha placed her hand on Karna's shoulder and smiled. She was visibly happy that he was okay now. What she did not see was the affection in Karna's eyes for his brothers. Adhirath did see it, and then he understood whose son Karna war. It was none other than Kunti. He looked back and forth, watching Karna and Kunti. He understood why she had so been so adamant about calling Nakul and Sehdev to save Karna's life.

The war was to begin in a few days, and it scared Adhirath when he thought about Karna fighting his brothers.

❖ ❖ ❖

44 Bhishma and Karna

The war of Kurukshetra had begun and the tenth day of the action marked the fall of Bhishma, the great son of Ganga. Bhishma had put down his weapons when Shikhandi, elder brother of Draupadi had come in front of him. It was said that Shikhandi was Amba in disguise who and vowed to be the death of Bhishma. Shikhandi was born a woman but had attained manhood from a yaksha. There was a constant debate about whether she was a man or a woman. In the end, what mattered is opinion and perspective.

For Arjun Shikhandi was a man, and for Bhishma, she was a woman. Bhishma laid down his arms when Shikhandi came in view of Arjun's chariot. The moment that happened, Arjun shot Bhishma, and the shower of hundreds of arrows had Bhishma pinned on the earth. Bhishma had a boon that he would die when he decides to. So, by pinning Bhishma on the bed of arrows, he was made incapable of fighting.

The fall of Bhishma was a significant loss for the Pandavas, and his death was a blow to Duryodhana. But for Karna, it was the beginning of the war. Before the first day of the action, while the Kauravas were plotting their strategy, Bhishma had entered the tent and said suddenly, "I will not fight the war if Karna takes part in the war."

Duryodhan looked at the older man in disbelief as Karna was his strength, but Bhishma was also an asset to the Kauravas. Both the warriors were essential to the Kauravas.

"But why do you say that, Pita mah?" Duryodhan sweetly said as he could not risk losing temper at that moment.

"He is a Suta, and I do not want a low cast charioteer to fight alongside me in the war. Choose now Duryodhan, who do you want, me or Karna." Karna was furious when he heard Bhishmas words, but he could say nothing to the Grand Regent. And Karna knew how important it was for the Kaurava's to have him. His leaving Kauravas would make matters worse for them.

Duryodhan looked at Karna unhappily but chose to keep Bhishma. Karna was angry with the fact that Bhishma could do this to him and insult a warrior. It was a sin to ask a warrior his cast. It was considered an insult to the same. Karna hung his head as he was reminded of Kunti. He wanted to shout out to the world that he was a Surya Putra and not a Suta Putra, that he was born a Kshatriya. He couldn't though, so he said nothing instead went red with the anger burning him within.

"You can fight when I fall." Bhishma had said and left the place. Karna felt humiliated, yet he spoke nothing. There was now a new relationship he had with Bhishma if he was the son of Kunti. He did not have a choice but to keep quiet.

Now that on the tenth day that Bhishma had fallen and could not fight, Karna's time to enter the battlefield came. The eleventh day was his beginning. Drona was chosen as the new commander as he was the older adult and the guru of Kauravas and Karna's anger towards Bhishma subsided, Karna decided to meet Bhishma before he entered the battleground.

Karna walked at night towards the banks of Ganga where Bhishma lay on the bed of arrows. As Karna neared Bhishma, his eyes were filled with tears. He recalled their first meet. Bhishma had stood tall and strong with all his handsomeness. Those were the times when no one could ever imagine him here in such a state of helplessness, unable to move and in immense pain. The Grand Regent had fallen. It was not only the end of his struggle against the evils lurking in the Kuru's but also the end of a lifelong legacy of strength and truth.

Karna stood silently near Bhishma's feet and watched the meditating older man. His life was not easy, as well. Since the day he vowed to remain celibate and serve the Kuru clan he had witnessed the fall and rise of generations. He had seen the useless men who could not even think of helping the people. He had seen the struggle of kingship, so he remained away from the throne even though he was better than everyone else.

Bhishma sensed someone's presence in the silent bank and opened his eyes. Karna folded his hands to greet him. His words were hoarse and shaky.

"I am going to join the war tomorrow Grand Regent. I had come to seek your blessings. Even though I know you despise me and hate my mere presence in Hastinapur still I respect you for the person, you are. I hope you will bless me at least today." Karna's voice went raspy as he spoke the true feelings of his heart.

Bhishma let out a painful chuckle and said, "You are a fool, Karna! You never understood what I was trying to do. You simply concluded, and that is not good Kunti Putra." Karna at first thought he heard it wrong but then realized it was Bhishma's words. He knew his secret! Bhishma did notice Karna's baffled expression in the dim lights of the lanterns burning around.

"Yes, Karna I know your secret. I know that you are Kunti's son. And I have known this for years. Why do you think I have been trying to keep you away from the war and Hastinapur for so long? It is not because I despise you or hate you, son! I have done this because I have sympathy for you. I wanted to keep you away from all the political upheavals that were taking place in the city. Though I failed to do so still, I tried to protect you."

"Why did you never tell me the truth?"

"How could I, Karna? It was a personal matter; it was between a son and his mother. I cannot disclose the truth, I did not have the right to, but since you know the truth now, I decided to tell you my reasons." After a small silence between the two men, Bhishma said "Karna I should have accepted you a Kshatriya in the Kridangan at least. It would be easier for you."

"I was bound to suffer Pita Mah; no one could help me. My fate was to live like an outcast and suffer the insult of society. The society was living with a distorted rule that destroyed the culture we had." Karna sighed.

"Karna people who know dharma harm society more than those who do not know it. Our ignorance is the cause of this war. The Caste system that was meant to provide people with identity without discrimination through their job and Karma became a way to discriminate against the lesser fortunate in our country. And since people like me who had power decided to go with the flow and ignored everything, we ended up leading the society into this war." Bhishma's tears flowed as he recalled events from the past. Karna nodded. "Karna can you not back out of this war? It will end if you leave." there was a plea in Bhishma's voice. Karna's heart was crushed as he heard Bhishma's tone. The man who had been the one ordering things was pleading today. He was laying there with nothing but the pain of watching his own family fight each other. He was lying there broken and crushed. The family had failed him, miserably failed him.

"I cannot; I have promised Duryodhan. I cannot leave him now. He had sheltered me once, and I cannot abandon him when he needs me today."

"I knew you would say this Karna. You have decided your faith just by being with the wrong people. I wish things were different. You know when you mix brass with gold; the gold loses its colour the brass does not. You were born a divine child, you are the son of Lord Surya, but the greater the birth, the more painful is the death. You were the eldest Pandava; you could have had a beautiful future only if you were the right man on the right side instead of the right man on the wrong side. You being with Duryodhan has made your life a nightmare. Duryodhan remained the impure brass but the gold you were changed its colour. You lost yourself, your true self."

Karna remained quiet. He had nothing to protest about. For how long would he ignore the truth? Ignoring reality does not make you an optimist; it makes you a fool.

"Hmm..." Karna hummed as he tried to control his tears. "I know Pita Mah. I Know. I have been a fool. I wish we had acted the day the dice game was happening. Things would be different. No one is to be blamed for this war other than you, me, and Guru Drona. We should have acted when we had time, we did not, and hence we are suffering today. We do not have the right to complain."

"Yes, we do not have the right to complain." Bhishma sighed, his breath shaky. "Well, Karna, it is just useless to discuss it now. But Karna I cannot bless you to come back victorious, both of us know what the future holds. Other than that, what blessing do you want?"

"Pita Mah, we are fighting a war that we have already lost. I cannot ask you to bless me with victory, anyway. I have been struggling to gain respect in society throughout my life. Bless me that after my death, my name is taken with respect. Just that, nothing else." Karna smiled a little.

"Karna, respect can only be attained by being true to be your Karma and being honest to your dharma. Blessings can only bring you wealth and power but not respect. Karna when you go to fight the war, do it for victory. Even if you know, all this is just stupid that the Kauravas fancy still be honest to your dharma, like you have been till today. All those high ideals that you live with must remain with you every second. Do not fight to kill, fight to win. You can kill by cheating someone as well, but you cannot win by cheating, and you will gain respect in society."

Karna nodded in agreement. Those words spoken by Bhishma were more than enough for him. Karna respected Bhishma even though he had been insulted by him numerous times. Those were forgiven the moment he came to know it was all because he was trying to save him, to protect him.

"Karna.," Bhishma called out as he turned to leave. Karna stopped and looked back at Bhishma.

"Ashaya ye dasaste dashah sarvalokasya

 Asha yesham dasi tesam dasayate lokah.

People who are servants of desires are also servants of the world.

For those who desire is the servant, the whole world also serves them.

I hope you remember this always."

Karna was confused as to why Bhishma said it to him, but he returned the smile the older adult was giving him and left the place after touching his feet. The next day was the beginning of the war for him.

❖ ❖ ❖

45   Kunti and Karna

As dawn broke the sun slowly came up in the east. The riverbank was scattered with the first rays of the sun falling on the earth's surface. The soft breeze on the banks of the flowing river would fill anyone with merry thoughts and peace on a summer day. Yet one unhappy soul stood there praying to Lord Surya; today, it was more like completing a ritual. To pray you need a peaceful mind, but his mind was not at rest. Karna stood on the bank alone, few helpers from the palace stood at a distance carrying jewels and gold coins. Some were with food grains for charity. Karna would give away all of those items to the needy who approached him in the morning. He was a well-known philanthropist amongst the people of the people and the royals as well. For the helpers, it was like any other day, yet you could not say the same for the King of Anga. A storm was raging within his cool and calm exterior. He was standing there in his white dhoti and a white shawl on his shoulder. His kundals were no more shining with the morning sun.

People who came for a daan were standing at a distance waiting for the warrior to finish his puja. He would every day distribute alms himself to the needy. Little urchins stood there happily waiting for the king to come and give them food. Karna loved those kids, the little ones had a lisp, and they sounded cute when they spoke. Those little ones reminded Karna of Vrishaketu when he was little and spoke his gibberish whenever he returned home after wars. Vrishaketu had now grown up into a young boy of twelve.

Karna was taking longer today; his prayers did not end, so the kids began chattering. He was lost in thoughts as he watched the Sun coming up slowly. Krishna's words were still ringing in his mind. It was like things were becoming complicated, he felt like he was drowning, and no one was helping him come up. He felt helpless. The chatter of the little ones brought him out, of his trace, and he walked towards them. The kids went quiet when he saw the warrior's pain and severe expression. Now, this was new; all had seen him a lot of times, he always came to them with a smile on his face, he had troubles, but he always comes up to them happily.

The older men and women also noticed the change, but no one dared to ask. He kept on distributing the alms without saying a word. After everyone left, he called out "Is there anyone else who is here to accept the alms?"

When there was no reply to his question, he dismissed the men and stood there alone for some more time. He was trying to calm down. At first, he was trying to forget everything that was told to him by Krishna and Bhishma, but he realized that trying to ignore a problem does not make anything easy, it just becomes bizarre. When he had questioned his parents about his birth; Radha completely broke down. She feared to lose him. Adhirath kept quiet, but Shom and his brothers were shocked. When he said his mother crying, he realized that there was no doubt about what Krishna had told him. He was indeed adopted. "I have heard that Krishna also has two mothers, Arya! Devki gave birth to him, but Yashoda nurtured him. Why do you feel betrayed? I am sure Queen Kunti has loved you a lot, throughout." Varushali had said to a grieving Karna.

"I am here to beg for something, Karna. Will you give it to me?" Karna heard someone speak; he instantly recognized the voice. It unmistakeably belonged to Kunti.

He turned around, and how right he was, indeed Kunti stood

there. Kunti looked at Karna for some time. His eyes were swollen, his face soaked with dry tears and the hidden anguish that flashed in his eyes were all scary for Kunti. She looked distorted. Karna had spent the entire night on the river bank trying to make sense of the situation that he had landed himself into.

"After gathering a lot of courage, I have come to you Karna," she spoke slowly. Shame evident on her face. When he did not know the truth, it was easier; she could caress his face and look at him straight into the eyes. But now that he knew what their relationship was, it was difficult even to look at him leave alone talk to him.

"I am surprised; it took you so much time to gather courage Maharahi!" Karna's taunt made Kunti look at him.

"Karna I know you are hurt, but you are my son. I have loved you always. You are my firstborn. You made me a mother; I was the scared son. I was scared to tell society." Kunti took a step forward and cupped his face with both her palms.

"I was not your firstborn; I was a mistake—a curse to you. You left me, that is the proof." the tears he thought were over again filled his eyes. He let them flow. Whom would he hide it from? His mother, yes she left him but still, she was his mother.

"Karna even if I accepted you, taking any insult upon myself, how could I forsake my father's image? I had no other choice! I did not know what would be the result of my mistake; I was young to understand the consequences."

"Consequences mother? I am the result of your mistake; my life is the consequence of your mistake. My suffering is the result of your mistake. I am going to fight a war against my brothers is the result of your mistake. My brothers with whom I share my blood, hate me, and take me as their enemy is the result of your mistake." Karna's words were dripping with accusations. "Do you see the consequences of your mistake? You make me feel that I am nothing more than a mistake for you. An illegitimate child."

"Karna, a child, can never be illegitimate, it's the parents who are. Karna, you might think that I never loved you, but I know how much you mean to me. Since I pushed you away, I have never lived in peace. In a garden, there are hundreds of flowers, every person who goes to it has his favourite. But for the gardener every flower is precious, every flower comes from the seed he plants."

"The flower that you say you love today has grown from the seed you refused to grow and accept Maharani." Karna stepped back. "Why did you come here, Maharani? To ask me not to fight the war? Or to tell me how I am with the wrong people? If it's that, then let me tell you that I am not doing that. I am bound to be with Duryodhan. He is wrong, yet he was the only one who helped him in my darkest days when my mother refused to come to help me, even though she watched me struggling."

"Karna after so long you finally know who you are, who your brothers are. Why do you want to lose everything again?"

"Because I have reached a place in life where losing people makes me happier than being with people. And Maharani, I have never left people; they left me. You get it, right?" Karna was done with living a lie for so long now. He was tired of people trying to fool him, insult him, and leaving him.

"Can you not forgive your mother, Karna? Can you not do this little thing for me?" Kunti said in a broken voice.

"I have no right to forgive you because I do not have the right to be angry. You killed me the day you chose society over your son!" This is what hurt him the most; she had chosen herself, her pride, society and her father over him, always.

"Karna the world would loath you if I accepted you then. They would insult you!"

"So, was I not insulted when you left me?" Karna spoke loudly, irritated. Did she not know how he was rejected, dishonoured, and insulted all the time? "Maharani, do you understand the difference? I was insulted, even though I was talented. You were my mother. If you were there, it would never be as bad as it was like this. I did not fit in; do you not see that? I never fit in with the children in Champanagri! I was friendless and alone. As a child, I watched the other children indulging in play; I felt out of place. It was frustrating; do you get it?

Sometimes what you need is that one person, someone who slaps the truth on your face and makes you believe that even the worst of you will replace by something better. Someone who persuades you on days when you cannot even be proud of yourself. And throughout my childhood, I never had that one person because I was different for people around me!"

Kunti was crying, she knew it was hard for him, but she never knew how bad it was. He had suffered because of her fault. She wanted to justify, but again his question "Was society more important than your son?" reminded her of those times when he was fighting the same society to be recognized. She lost him the day she chose society over her son. No explanation could undo the pain he went through. How could she be so stupid? She never had the love of a mother, and she did the same to Karna. The experience of not having the motherly affection had always pained her, yet she did the same to her son. She pushed him away. He had the right to call her his mother, and she deprived him of it, forcing him out to a life where he was all alone struggling to become someone. He had a family, yet he was alone.

"You were happy Maharani, in your la-la-land where you had everything a doting husband, five sons to love you unconditionally. You would not understand the meaning of being alone, would you? Not only that, do you know how it feels to work throughout your life to achieve something and to have your hard work and talent met with hesitation! I know what it means to prove my intellect and talent each day and later to be seen as an object unworthy of respect."

"Karna, I made one wrong choice, and because of that we ended up here, can you please make one right choice and change everything?" Kunti was slowly losing the courage that she had gathered to come to Karna.

"One wrong choice? You had so many chances mother every time you saw me, you had the choice to speak the truth. But you chose not to. Did you not think then how your choices could change the entire scenario? How I wish you made this choice earlier Maharani; things would have been different today. But you have come now when a promise bounds me. And I will not break the promise. I would rather die than break a promise and be called an Adharmi for ever."

"But Duryodhan is wrong he will lead you to a painful ending, Karna. I do not want to see you die!" Everyone knew what the end was, leaving Duryodhan, his hate, anger, and arrogance had taken over his entire being to understand the evident truth.

Karna let out a painful chuckle. His eyes were now red, and his face redder. Someone who knew their relation would easily recognize the similarity Karna and Kunti had in their usual ways. "I was killed the day you pushed me away from yourself. I was just lucky that the basket you had placed me in did not drown. Unfortunately, I survived. If it did drown, I would never be here, that would have been easier for you, I think."

"Karna!" Kunti harshly said, not at all liking the fact that he thought she would want him dead. Almost immediately, her anger subsided and pain filled her heart. She knew he was hurt, and she had hurt him more than anyone. "Karna, I know you are angry. I have not been just with you. I never spoke up for you, nor did you ever have the love that you deserved from me, but you cannot say what you just did. For any woman, her firstborn is the most precious for her; I am not different. To whatever extent you deny it, I know how much you mean to me. I have lived each day longing to talk to my son, Karna! Why can you not try? The pain will heal!"

"It is easier to heal when you are separated from those causing it. I cannot separate myself from anyone who had caused the pain in my life. I will not heal Maharani; there is no time left; the war is here." Karna scoffed. Hearing him, Kunti knew his conviction was unmovable. He would never come back. She had lost him the day she left him. There was nothing that she could do now, in this game of life, she miserably failed.

"I am sorry Karna, for all the darkness you lived in because of me," Kunti spoke softly, Karna heard her. He smiled in between his tears. Blood took over the anger, and the anger subsided as he saw his mother slouching before him crying for being forgiven. Yes, he was angry with what she did, but he nevertheless loved her. At last, blood is a strong connection. You can never hate your mother forever, anyways. How could Karna hate his mother forever?

"I am not sad about the darkness I lived in! That darkness made me the person I had the potential to become." He took a deep breath and placed his hands on Kunti's shoulders. He looked at her straight in the eyes "I cannot handle the pain for my entire life for temporary happiness Maharani. Being with you and the Pandava's would be the best thing I will have, but at what cost? I have to give up my dharma to attain that happiness. I carry my Dharma with pride and not my pride with dharna! It is my only safety. Fulfilling my dharma has coasted me people, relationships, family, material things, happiness, self-respect, and truth. I chose that dharma over everything that came my way. After giving up so much for Dharma, I will not choose to forsake it."

"I get it, Karna! I will say no more. Now that you have made your choice, can I ask you a question?" Karna nodded.

"Do you hate your brothers so much that they still are your

enemies?" Karna was not prepared for this question, though. He thought for a while and then spoke.

"There's a saying in Anga; a brother's words are as piercing as the heat of Magh. They are my brothers; we have the same blood running in our veins. Every time they taunted me, it was more painful than the taunts of society. I think I somehow expected them to be better than all the others when it came to matters related to caste inequality. When they were the ones insulting me, it felt like someone was stabbing me, it was painful. Surprisingly, all the anger went away the moment I realized they are my brothers, my siblings."

"But the war..." Kunti intervened.

"You wanted something from me in charity, right? So, I will not let you leave empty-handed. Never have I ever turned down anyone who came to me asking for something, how can I let my mother who gave birth to me go away empty-handed? Maharani, I promise you I will not raise weapons against your four sons. My competition will only be with Arjun. Either he will kill me or the other way round, you will always be called the mother of five Pandava's. I had vowed to kill Arjun, and he promised to kill me. One of us would survive the war. If he dies, I will be your fifth Pandav.

I said this to Keshav; I am saying it to you too, don't tell the Pandavs that I am your son and their brother. They would give up war and remain deprived forever. I do not want that for them. And don't stress about me, if I have endured everything in the past, then this too shall pass. I am used to living in pain." His last sentence broke her heart. His life was written with the ink that was suffering and pain. Kunti looked at her son; he was the most confusing person she had known. She searched his face to find if she could at least understand him a little.

"Let us say our goodbyes, we both have hurt enough to heal in this lifetime, "Karna muttered. Kunti sighed deeply and embraced her son. This time he reciprocated, "Maa..." the word just escaped his lips as tears streamed down his face. The peace that he felt there was unparalleled. They cried uncontrollably in each other's arms for some time. He pulled away and touched her feet.

"Aayushman bhava..." were the only words she could say. She had heard him call her mother. That one moment was enough for her to last a lifetime. Her sons called her Maa always but hearing it from Karna was precious. Even if she went deaf now, she would not regret it. She did not want to hear anything more. Before she could say more, Karna stood up and left the river bank taking long strides towards the chariot waiting for him at a distance. He did not know how long would he be able to remain composed if he stayed there with Kunti for longer.

Karna noticed a trend in his life. The larger the things were, the eviler they ended up. Whether it was people, palaces, mountains, emotions, or fear; a fear had coasted him his entire life. He could not risk a sentiment that could cost him his dharma. Kunti was his mother, he had seen the love in her eyes, yet he could not stop himself from accusing her. All those years of frustration had filled him with an unknown pain. He never knew that he was capable of such extreme emotions. Once he was blaming her for his problem, and the next second he was longing for her affection. It was no use anymore; the war was here. Karna had realized that even if Kunti kept him, chose him over society and her father; he would anyhow live with a stigma attached to his name. As a result of that realization, he had softened. He realized that he would anyway feel the stings of pain and insult, yet a mother is a mother.

Time gives people everything needed to heal. And he did not have time.

* * *

46   Mahabharat

The dark clouds of the great war shadowed the entire country. It was as devastating as Krishna had predicted it to be. The cruel war was engulfing the country slowly. Thousands were dying each day. On the first day, Karna had received the news of Karna's death. He blamed himself for the end of his brother. Then Vikarna died in the hands of Bhima. Karna was astonished when he heard that Bhima had cried bitterly before killing his cousin. It was said that Vikarna was Bhima's favourite cousin, perhaps the only Kaurava the bulky Bhima loved and adored. Then the tenth day marked the death of the fall of Bhishma. All were shocked as the world knew that Bhishma was a great archer and him being pinned to the ground with hundreds of arrows was a massive blow for the Kauravas. But there was no time to cry over death and loss.

"The Grand Regent was the strongest shield that could ensure the victory of Kauravas." Karna had tried to reason with the now fuming Duryodhan who was accusing the old sire of being bias and helping the Pandavas.

"You never respected him, at least respect his sacrifice Duryodhan!" Karna was trying all to remain patient, but Shakuni was still instigating the prince. He was irritated when Shakuni said "I think even you are with the Pandava's Anga Raj! The way you take sides and preach all day in front of Duryodhan."

"Have you ever met a headache of a human being?" Karna said softly in disbelief to which Ashwatthama chuckled. "Well, Gandhar Raj

Mitram Dharne Niyojayet. I hope your disastrous brain that is capable of plotting can understand that? May you explain it?"

"Yes, I know the meaning!" Shakuni sneered "It means one must guide his friend to follow dharma!"

"Ya, so I am doing the same." Karna glared at Shakuni and turned to look at Duryodhan. "Listen, I know you will not back out of this war. And you will give me all random explanations as to why, and I am done listening to those. I just want to tell you that the Grand Regent is your great grand uncle. He has done everything that was a part of his dharma. At least respect it, at least stop insulting his loyalty and his dedicated service to the Kurus." Karna left the tent as he was losing his patience. Ashwatthama had followed him.

"Are you sure you are the same, Karna?" Ashwatthama asked Karna once they were out of earshot. His eyes were dancing. " I mean the cool, calm, controlled, any word I forgot you could add in your brain OK! So, the man whose speech was always measured is now blunt, so are you sure you are the same?"

"Shut up!" was all Karna said and left him behind. He heard Ashwatthama chuckle.

Now that Karna was on the battlefield, seeing his brothers in front of him, made him feel useless. "This is a lost cause for me." He spoke to himself and chuckled dryly. Yet his charioteer King Shalya who was the uncle of Nakula and Sehdev said: "Yes, Karna this is a lost cause for all Kaurava's as you all are going to die in the hands of my nephews."

King Shalya was tricked into coming to the Kauravas. Since he was a Kshatriya and could not break his vow to be with the Kauravas, he had to be there with them. Duryodhan wanted to insult Shalya, so what he did was unthinkable. He made a warrior a charioteer. Shalya was ordered to become Karna's charioteer. That time he had vowed to demotivate Karna as much as possible so get back at Duryodhan. Karna knew since the beginning that it was a bad idea to have Shalya with him, but no one listened to him. He ended up giving up as no one in the Kaurava's camp was ready even to hear.

Of Course, Shalya did not know why Karna had said those words, so Karna did was what his only option was; quietly ignore.

The fight on the eleventh day was directed by Drona the new commander-in-chief. He had vowed to kill Yudhistir, but the third Pandava, Arjun fiercely protecting his brother ended up doing no damage to the Pandavas. Karna was on a different part of the Battlefield where he was fighting Nakul. The latter was a sword fighter, and hence the two men fought on the ground, leaving their chariots. After a struggle of almost half a day, Karna defeated Nakul before sunset but did not kill him. Karna's sword was on Nakul's neck, and the Pandava was looking straight at Karna, no fear in his eyes even though Karna could quickly kill him. When Karna did not harm him, Nakul stood confused the sword still placed on his neck.

"Why are you not killing me Anga Raj? You have the choice to!" Nakul asked desperately; he was confused about seeing Karna's behaviour. He hated him for what Karna did at the dice game but could not deny that he was a fierce warrior. Such action was surprising for him.

"You are years younger to me Nakul. And you bless those younger than yourself." Karna did not know what else to say he did not have a choice. That was the lamest excuse he had ever made, even worse than the excuses made to save himself from his father's scoldings. He turned around and left. The sun had set, and the war had stopped.

Nakul stood there watching Karna's chariot leave. His eyebrows were drawn, and he stood there confused. He was troubled deep within, and it was not because Karna left him but because he noticed something in Karna's eyes.

"Affection!" came a voice from behind Nakul. It was his twin Sehdev he was at a distance defending himself. He had noticed everything.

"But why?" Nakul was so confused. "And do you know what was his excuse not to kill me? He said "You are years younger to me Nakul. And you bless those younger than yourself." There was something amiss about him today. He was not the same man who had come to the Kridangan years back."

Sehdev, the quietest of all Pandavas, stood there in the slowly emptying battlefield with his twin Nakul. He was a man who paid attention a lot. He was quiet and observant. A scene flashed before him from years ago. He recalled the boy who had touched Kunti's feet when they had for the first time come to Hastinapur. Those eyes, he still remembered more because it was similar to his brother Arjun's and stepmother Kunti's eyes. He said nothing then. But now standing there he noticed the Karna had the same looks; like Kunti's and Arjun's. What caught his attention was that Karna's eyes flashed the same affection for a second that he had seen in that boy's eyes years back.

The twins left the place long after Karna was gone. They did not speak about the incident to anyone. Yet Sehdev's mind was cluttered. So was Karna's in the Kaurava camp. He kept replaying the event of that day.

"I shouldn't try to lie. I am bad at it." Thought Karna recalling his own words to Nakul. "So, lame!" He muttered to himself. He wanted to laugh out thinking about the excuse he made. Just that he couldn't lie, he never did. Whenever he tried to, he did something stupid, similar to what he did with Nakul.

❊ ❊ ❊

47   Abhimanyu

The twelfth day of the war brought more pain for the Kauravas as the gentle son of Duryodhan who was so unlike his father was killed by Abhimanyu, the sixteen-year-old son of Arjun and Subhadra. Lakshmana was the son of Duryodhan. The prince was more of a saint than a prince. He was a gentle boy the same age as Abhimanyu. Even as a child, he indulged himself in games that did not have many players. He would play alone most of the tome. It was Vrishaketu, Karna's youngest son he sometimes played with when he was young. The little prince would come running into the palace of Anga to see the small Vrishaketu. Karna had seen the little boy grow. Bhanumati tried all means to keep him away from Shakuni, and that was the reason she would send her young son to Anga for days so that he remains away from the clutched of the nasty Shakuni.

Duryodhan had been inconsolable with grief seeing his son dead, and he did what Shakuni filled into his brain again, device a plan to kill Abhimanyu. What shocked Karna was that Dronaacharya was the one to device the plan. He offered the formation of the Chakravyuh. It was a formation used in wars where the soldiers created a pattern depicting the wheel of the chariot. No one amongst the Pandava's other than Arjun knew the technique to enter the Chakravyuh. Krishna, Arjun, Balram, Karna and Krishna's son Pradyumna were the only warriors who had attained the knowledge and skill to penetrate the labyrinth of the Chakravyuh.

Karna tried to protest, but Drona said "You are bound to do what I order Karna. I am the commander-in-chief." Karna did not say anything after that. He had to listen to Drona, whatever happened.

The thirteenth day began, and the formation was made. Abhimanyu entered as Arjun was on the other end of the battleground. Abhimanyu knew how to enter the Chakravyuh but did not know how to get out of it. The sixteen-year-old boldly agreed to join the formation, unaware of what lay inside. Karna watched in dismay standing on his chariot. He wanted to stop him from coming in but couldn't. As Abhimanyu got in, he was surrounded by bloodthirsty men who had lost all sanity.

Abhimanyu was stuck in between six warriors- Dronacharya, Kripacharya, Ashwatthama, Brihatbala, Kirtivarma, and Karna.

Kirtivarma, the Bhoj King, was the teacher of Abhimanyu and the cousin of Krishna but he could not forgive the boy for killing his son during the war. He was ready to do anything to exact his revenge on the boy.

Drona ordered Karna to cut the reins of Abhimanyu's horses, forcing the lad on the ground. Abhimanyu was attacked from the back after this everything was mayhem. War kills but this war was turning warriors into heinous lads, bloodthirsty and ruthless. Abhimanyu's bow was broken and his horses as well as charioteer killed, he stood alone defenceless surrounded by the Kauravas. He then picked up a sword and a shield from his chariot. Drona broke his sword and Karna his shield.

He was stabbed with daggers, blood flowing from his wounds. The backstab had harmed him dramatically, cracking his spine. He still stood up with whatever might he had he pulled himself up on his feet and took up a chariot wheel, as his weapon and he whirled it like Vishnu's Sudarshana warding off the arrows being shot. With most of his energy drained, the wheel fell from his hand, and he fell on his knees. Dussashan came from behind and hit Abhimanyu on his shoulder, his bone cracked, and he let out a cry of pain. Karna stood there numb as he heard Abhimanyu's painful cry. His nephew was mercilessly killed before him, and he could do nothing but be a part of the horrific murder. The Kauravas were repeatedly hitting Abhimanyu. He saw Kirtivarma a part of the group hitting the boy unarmed and weak.

"Guru Drona you cannot torture a warrior like that. He fought the battle; you disarmed him. Kill him! For God's sake, kill him! He is in so much pain. Give him the honourable death of a warrior; what you are allowing is cold blooded murder." Karna shouted towards the unaffected Dronaacharya."Guru Kripa, at least you say something." Only Karna knew how much he hated his teacher right now for being quiet at the horrific sight.

Duryodhan came in and hit the boy on the head with his mace. Abhimanyu held his head for a moment as blood oozed out, his skull cracked. He still pushed himself up; he did not lose his courage. "I have vowed to fight until my last breath, and I will do it." He thundered for all to hear. He was panting blood flowing from his nose; he was struggling to keep his eyes open. He was stumbling, yet trying all means to fight as per his vow. The sixteen-year-old did not let a single tear fall from his eyes. His limbs broken, there was no intact bone left in his body. The handsome son of Arjun rised every time he fell. It was unbearable to see him that way. There was nothing left in him, his blood drained, even if he survived, which was impossible he would suffer all his life, and if he remained alive in the chakravyuh, he would not be spared.

Karna took a deep breath and pulled out his sword. He descended from his chariot and walked to Abhimanyu and pulled him into a hug. The boy smiled, trying to mock the warrior before him, but when he was pulled into a hug, he rested his head on Karna's chest. The tears that Karna had restrained flowed instantly when the sixteen-year-old exhaled, his breath more like a painful sigh. Abhimanyu looked up at Karna's tears and smiled again. "Will you free me of this, Anga raj?" The words that came out of Abhimanyu's mouth almost in a whisper broke

Karna's heart it shattered him. The young boy did not plead even in his most challenging time. Even suffering could not harm his bravery.

"I am your uncle Abhimanyu. I am the eldest Pandav. I am sorry for all that you had to go through, even though I was here. I am sorry for not saving you." Karna whispered back. The sixteen-year-old did not smile this time; he looked into Karna's eyes and said: "Free me then, Kaka."

Karna felt a stab in his heart. His hands shivered as he raised his sword. He did not want to do so; his heart ached for the boy. This was not how he was supposed to be treated. He had an entire life to live yet destiny had landed him here, amidst the most heinous of warriors who swore by their bravery and acted like mere Melech murderers. That day they had lost all their wits and Kshatriya dharma. All rules were broken; all morality put at stake.

"You are the true Martyr of this war son. I....I.." Karna stammered. His tears knew no bounds. He had never felt his helpless and weak before. Today he was unsure of his on Kshatriya dharma, the same dharma he had lived for all his life. He struggled for respect from society, where he was not able to respect himself anymore. "Abhimanyu, Arjun nor I could ever do what you have done today. None of us would be given the respect of the best warrior in the Kurukshetra. You deserve it, and you will have it." With this Karna stabbed Abhimanyu, freeing him of the pain he was going through. The sword went right through his skin, cutting through his stomach. The young lad inhaled sharply, his breath was caught within, he coughed out blood, and the next moment Karna knew was that his body lay lifeless in his arms. The Kaurava's began a victory dance around his body, while Karna held on to the boy, unknowingly trying to protect him from them all. He was scared that they would torture his dead body as well if he left it.

"Here goes one more warrior of the Pandavas. We did it." Came a voice that angered Karna. It flared him up more because it was Kripa's voice.

"I do not believe how can you all celebrate after this shameful act of yours," Karna shouted angrily looking directly at Kripa. Kripa turned away and began talking to Drona. It was Yuyutsu the son of Dhritarashtra from a concubine who eventually called to stop the shameful victory dance. The murder was not an act to be celebrated.

"He deserves his justice, and I deserve the death Arjun would bring upon me…" Karna whispered and left Abhimanyu's body after the Kaurava's had left. He made sure no one from the Kaurava camp even tried to touch his lifeless nephew. After the Pandavas took the body along, Karna left as well. He remained at a distance till Abhimanyu's body remained there guarding it. Karna's eyes were vacant, and his face drained. He felt dead on the inside. There are times when you cannot understand what you think not can to put it into words. That is what was happening to him. When the plan was devised to kill Abhimanyu, he never thought he would be in such a mess. He never believed that Brahmin's like Drona and Kripa who preach about Dharma each day would be OK doing such a sinful act. He was left in disbelief seeing Kripa quiet, the man who preached how Kshatriya's were losing their minds and were ending up being nothing more than bloody madmen was quiet when all the rules at that moment were being broken.

He knew he would pay for his sin; he knew the time was drawing near. "A little more suffering Karna, a little more suffering." He muttered to himself in the confines of his little tent.

48   Drona's Death

On the fourteenth day of the war, Karna entered the battlefield with only one motive that was to lead Kaurava's to victory. Every time he was filled with doubt, he would recall Bhishma's words to him. "Fight only for victory, not to kill." Every time he recalled Bhishma, he remembered the concern he had heard in his voice that night. Each time he thought of Bhishma his heart filled with an unknown happiness which he felt did not exist in him, that the Grand Regent had tried his best to protect him for so long.

With the same thought, Karna had entered the tent of Duryodhan for planning the strategies now what he called devious plots, the night of Abhimanyu's death. He had had a heated argument with Kripa; his guru. The same guru he once worshipped, the guru who had laid the foundation of his journey. The man he revered and respected. Sometimes it felt like it was him against the entire society. He was not only fighting against his brothers but also himself and the people who were his friends.

Kripa had taunted Karna for not being able to kill even a single Pandava when Karna had proclaimed that he would kill Arjun. Kripa had said "You can only bluff Karna if you could kill Arjun you would at least kill one of the Pandavas to date. But the fact is that you did not, and here you say you will kill Arjun. Karna your ability is nothing because you only know how to build mountains in your imagination but are useless on the battlefield. I think you are just not loyal enough towards the Kaurava army Karna. You do not deserve to be here."

Karna was aggrieved and appalled with Kripa. His anger sprouted, he felt he would go insane if he kept quiet now. All his life, he kept silent holding back his rage; every time he was insulted, now he did not have the patience left. He was done listening forever now. How could anyone question his loyalty? He had forsaken his chance, his only chance to live a happy life for a promise made to Duryodhan. He had decided to go against his brothers, his blood, his mother to fulfil that promise. He had accepted death just to remain loyal to his friend. Was that not enough? Even after these many years, his loyalty needed proof?

"Says the man who forsakes his dharma today in the battlefield, Acharya! You question my loyalty and my ability; please take the pain to explain how able you are! Because how you kept quiet when that poor Abimanyu was murdered, did make me question your ability and your preachings. You were the one who said to me that nothing could be more critical than dharma. So, if I can recall you were the one who told me that a Brahmin's Dharma is to knock in some brain into those who need it truly. Sadly, you forgot your dharma today on the battlefield, and so you lost the right to preach about loyalty and dharma.

I know that I have done my duty, fulfilling my oath each day. I have marched into the battlefield for victory. The only strength and ability I have is of truth and duty. Old man! If I say that I will do all I can to kill Arjun and defeat him, I do not understand what your problem is! If I am saying that I will do my best to bring victory to the Kaurava's I will do it." Kripa kept quiet after Karna's outburst. He had never seen his student like this ever. The cold and calm Karna was losing his cool as the war was proceeding. Karna had left the tent after he had spoken. Drona's presence was not helpful, as well. The only thought that came to Karna when he saw Drona was of Abhimanyu's dead body the blood-soaked body that had taken his last breath in his arms.

The fourteenth day was scary. Impassioned with anger and revenge, Arjun was on a killing spree. He had killed lakhs of warriors single-handedly. He had vowed to kill Jaydrath on that day. He was unstoppable that day. A wounded father had come to take revenge for his son's death. And true to his words, Jaydrath had been killed. On the same day as Jaydrath had, one more hero had been killed by Karna.

It was Gatotkatch, the son of Bhima and his wife Hidimba was from the Rakshas family. Gatotkatch was a demon as well but a brave and righteous one. He was the master of illusory craft and weapons. He could grow his size as desired and defeat thousands and lakhs in one go. When he entered the battle, he fought with all his courage and destroyed a considerable amount of the Kaurava army. He had a fierce duel with Karna. He wreaked terrible havoc in the Kaurava army. It was Duryodhan who pleaded Karna to use the Indrastra on Ghatotkatch. Karna had reserved the Indrastra that was given to him by Lord Indra after he donated his Kavach and Kundals. Karna stood there not wanting to use the Devi weapon. Karna noticed how the army was slowly losing control over the war, and Ghatotkatch was becoming a threat. Karna pulled up the missile and aimed it towards Ghatotkatch. "Why is it that every time I have to kill one of my nephews?" thought Karna, and he shot the arrow towards the warrior son of Bhim.

"This weapon was for Arjun, but the unfortunate son of Bhim had to face the wrath of the missile," Karna whispered sadly. At the end of the fourteenth day, Karna could not decide whether he was sad that he lost the weapon he had saved only for Arjun or that it had killed his nephew.

The fifteenth day of the war was the ultimate breach of rules. Karna had counted the number of ruled broken from both sides in the war. It aggrieved him, yet he said nothing because his subconscious told him that the entire war started based on deception. There was no moral basis of the war; how could it be fought with righteousness? There was no such rule that had not been forsaken in the war. Everyone was fighting to kill and seek revenge. Men who once were the epitome of dharma had lost all their self-respect and dignity while fighting the war. Karna understood one thing as he noticed each warrior from the Kaurava Army die that how every bit of the action was just stupidity. The battle was mass destruction born from the womb of a weak mind which had fallen prey to a devious plot.

The fifteenth day was the day Dorna was killed; it was a breach of trust and betrayal. Drona was fighting that day to kill. Karna could see how the old guru of the Pandavas was hungry for a kill that day. Each arrow he shot killed someone or the other. He looked invincible that day. It was sure that till Drona was fighting with his bow, no one would be able to kill the man. So, the most superficial way was to use his weakness against him- his son Ashwatthama.

Karna noticed that an elephant named Ashtwatthama had been killed in the Kaurava Army. Karna noticed the shift that happened in the Pandava army as well. Bhima took Yudhistir's place while fighting him. The time of the sun to set was nearing, and hence the day was about to end. Karna was engrossed in fighting Bhim who was overpowering him that day.

Bhima noticed that Karna was defending more and attacking less. His arrows did not prove to be fatal for him. He was a little confused with what he was seeing.

Whereas Karna was trying all means not to kill Bhim, he had promised Kunti, and he would do anything to uphold his vow. Karna was continuously defending when the news of Drona's death came to him. Bhima stopped fighting him as the conch was blown signalling the end of the war for that day.

It was later that Karna was informed about what had happened on the battlefield that day. Karna was told by one of the Kaurava's that "Guru Drona was beginning to become a threat to the Pandava army.

Then Krishna came up with a plan to kill Dronaacharya. An elephant in the Kaurava whose name was Ashwatthama was killed, and then a cry was raised amongst the soldiers that Ashwatthama was dead. When the guru heard the words, he turned to Yudhistir who happened to be there around. Then the righteous son of Dharma spoke the first-ever lie of his life which was half lie and half-truth."

"Is it true that Ashwatthama is killed?" Drona had asked in a shaking voice, to which Yudhistir replied in his usual calm demur.

"Ashwatthama Hatha." he murmured the last part *"iti narova Kunjarova."* Yudhistir had said to Drona. Yudhistir had said "Yes Ashwatthama is dead." then he mumbled, "I don't know if it's a man or an elephant."

A shaken Drona did not hear the undertone and lost all will power to fight. He was unconscionable with sorrow and pain. His son was his most important possession. He had loved his son dearly, and the words he heard were enough to have him give up his weapons. Drona surrendered his will to fight, and when he was defenceless, Dristaduymna, the brother of Draupadi went to Drona and beheaded him. The head was separated from his body in one stroke. Yet another rule of war flouted the end of Drona marked a significant end for the Kaurava army. Now the only hope of the Kaurava's was Karna, who was made the commander-in-chief for the coming days of the war.

Karna bowed to the lifeless body of the Guru who had once rejected him as a student. There was no emotion in his eyes. Karna watched Drona's body and said "What goes around, comes around. He had killed Abhimanyu with the same deception; it is not surprising that he was also killed with deception. He had ignited the fire, and the same fire had burned him today. He was killed, there was betrayal involved but how can we forget that this same man had ordered Abhimanyu to be backstabbed and be murdered while he lay venerable, he smiled victoriously. All our deeds come back to us; it's better to die than live a lie; we all have been all these years. At least we will find peace in the shadow of death because this life will never be peaceful. The lie and duplicity that we have been living with will all come back one day."

Duryodhan glared at his friend; he knew that Karna was trying to point out his deeds. Karna himself turned as he felt Duryodhan throwing daggers his way, but there is nothing he feared anymore. This was the end, "There is nothing to fear now!" he said to himself.

49   Pride of Arjun

Karna headed the sixteenth day of the war. There were few prominent warriors left in the Kaurava side, yet Duryodhan was not ready to listen to the words people around him. The tension between Karna and Kripa did not ease, though. Karna was still angry about how Kripa had questioned his loyalty. Karna led the army with all his might and made sure that none of the warriors was killed as the loss would result in the further downfall of the Kaurava side. He knew that he would not be able to win, but he fought for victory like a stubborn child. Karna might not win, but he would defend his army, who believed him. He had ignored all the Pandavas each time they came face to face on the battlefield or just defended himself. Sehdev, the youngest Pandav, was the most suspicious about Karna's movements as he had always observed what kind of a warrior this man was. Karna was more of an aggressive fighter; he was never defensive. Every story he heard about Karna spoke of his fierce fights. People described him as invincible when he was with his bow and arrow on the battlefield. He would not have believed the stories if he had not witnessed how Karna fought with the other warriors on the Pandava side. Yet the moment he had a Pandava facing him, he became defensive.

Karna would purposely ignore those areas where the Pandavas were. He had a promise to keep, yet he had not yet faced Arjun on the battlefield. He was waiting for the day, eagerly. After the war, Karna sat alone on the edge of the Kaurava camp. He watched the dark moonless sky. The night was unusually silent and deep. As the night was growing more profound and the sun had already dipped into a pail of cold water, the pole star was visible—the only star shining alone in the dark, clear sky. The star stood at the same point as always above the horizon- night and day, all year long. Karna watched the single star shining in the sky all alone. He felt his heart clench in pain thinking of loneliness.

"Only the one who has felt the pain of being alone can know how it feels to be alone!" Karna heard someone speak behind him. And that someone was undoubtedly his teacher Kripa. Karna then heard footsteps coming closer to him. He did not turn around. He stood there, stoic and expressionless. "So what do you feel about my statement Karna?" Kripa questioned softly. He knew his student could never be angry for long.

"Aacharya! I wonder why you are asking me this question now after all these years." Karna said flatly.

"Oh, you don't Karna!? So, tell me how has your life been to date, alone, and distant." Kripa said.

Karna felt a lump form in his throat hearing what Kripa said. He spoke after a minute's silence. "I was not alone Guru; I have a family and..."

"Do not fool me, Karna, I am your Guru. I know you! Well. You had a family, children, friends everyone yet you were all alone throughout your life. You had everyone, yet you had no one." Kripa was right, Karna had his family yet he never had it. He had remained distant and withdrawn throughout.

"I... I was searching for something. It was like an eternal search for an identity that I knew never existed, but I kept looking for it. And in the end, I did find what I had been looking for, it was like the most beautiful feeling to know who I am and yet it came to me when I had lost everything in that search. I was running behind an illusion, something that my heart knew was there, but my mind did not agree. I was always so confused that I lost my self in that search." Karna stopped to take a deep breath. "I know what I am saying does not make sense to you Aacharya but believe me it was true. I just do not know how to explain it. Aacharya, it was just one of those things called the voice of my subconscious mind, which said that I am not what I am told, there is something that I cannot find. I kept on looking, and I got entangled into the most difficult knots of politics and a promise. I was intertwined and shackled. Those knots became tighter and more difficult to open. And when I finally reached the end of my unconscious search, and a ray of hope flickered from somewhere, I found myself stuck in a deep frustrating prison of my own choices. I was so much involved in the knot of my promises and choices that coming out of it was not possible. They say that when a door closes another opens, but where I was standing the open door was useless. It was all meaningless. My entire life felt like a joke." Karna said whatever he had felt all this time.

"Remember I once told you years back that nothing comes for free? This is what I meant Karna. Do you see now how that one title took away everything from you? Do you see now how that one promise made you a handicap? Your choices were right just that there were made with the wrong people and all in wrong places." Kripa whispered only for Karna to hear.

"But I was following my Dharma Aacharya. I did what I was supposed to do." Karna argued.

"Karna, dharma does not always lead one on the path of happiness. Sometimes it is possible to be unhappy even when you have followed your dharma. It is not easy-to-understand Dharma Karna! Many talk about it, but not everyone can understand it."

"So how can we understand Dharma?" Karna was tired of this never-ending debate of knowing Dharma and understanding it.

"Respect comes with Dharma," Kripa said.

Karna chuckled hearing Kripa. "Really? So how do you explain my situation? I have been insulted since I was a kid Aacharya. And for no reason!" Karna scoffed. Kripa took a deep breath.

"Dam your case is confusing, Karna." Kripa laughed, followed by Karna.

"Yes, I was born special," Karna said sarcastically.

"Were you though! I mean not every other child is born with a breastplate and earrings as a part of his body. I wonder how your mother reacted when she saw an armour appear on your chest out of the blue. She must be terrified." Kripa joked trying to loosen the tension, but Karna's face became grim. The hint of a smile that had appeared vanished in moments from his pupil's face.

"Yes Aacharya, my mother was terrified not because of the armour but because of me. She was terrified when I was born. I would be the first child whose birth was a disaster for a mother." Kripa noticed Karna's shaking voice. He knew it was not a joke; he was serious. But he also knew how secretive and reserved Karna was. He would die but not disclose his secrets.

Kripa decided to move on and leave the topic of his birth there. He's supposed to be joking ended up digging a deeply rooted wound in Karna's heart.

"Don't you think the night is unusually silent?" Kripa was trying to change the topic now.

"Yes! It is silent. It feels like death stands nearby." Both men remained silent for some time after which Karna decided to break the silence. "I feel I will soon get my liberation, Aacharya."

For the first time in him like Kripa felt like someone had stabbed him. Though he never said it, Karna was the most loved pupil he ever had. Kripa had taught many, including the Pandavas and the Kaurava's but Karna was his best student. Quick to learn, he was passionate to know new things and learn. He loved knowledge. Maybe because he had seen the worst side of humans along with their best, he had seen the poor suffering and the rich thriving. Without realizing he had understood humanity better than anyone else. Maybe he faulted in understanding dharma yet he dared to be humane. He had struggled all his life, and however, he did not let cruelty touch his heart. He had lost his soul to the wrong man, yet he never allowed the venomous men around to taint his soul.

"What a person he is!" Kripa thought. No this was the kind of student every teacher would wish for. He made his flaws look perfect. Kripa felt proud to have taught him. He had tried to question his loyalty so he could at least find that secret Karna was hiding yet this man was so stubborn that he did not let out a word. No! Kripa did not want him to die. Men like Karna are few and rare to find. It pained him that there was no way he could save his dear student.

"Karna have you accepted defeat?" Kripa said after a long time.

"No! Never. I will fight till my last breath but not accept defeat Aacharya. I have just accepted the truth; death. I know what lies in the end, and I have accepted that. It is funny, but I don't fear death anymore." Karna said with a smile. "Anyways, our body dies, not our soul. This is what you said Aacharya. Now I understand it even better."

Kripa's eyes moistened, seeing Karna's genuine smile and the depth in his eyes. So sincere, his words were that Kripa felt sad. Karna saw his Guru's uneasiness. He did not say anything; he deeply sighed and turned back towards the pole stare that was still there in the sky in the same place. Karna smiled, looking at it. He wanted to remain there the whole night and watch the sun coming up as dawn would break, beginning a new day.

"Are you sure you can kill him?" someone whispered.

"Yes, I can! Why can't I? I think I am better than him." The answer came.

"Shut up! What you call confidence is overconfidence. Do not even think him to be that easy to kill!" The first voice said again a little agitated.

"You do not believe in me? You are my friend!"

"I believe in you, but I also know the truth! He is amazing with the bow and arrow. You cannot kill him until he has his bow with him!"

It was Krishna speaking to Arjun in the night, in his tent. Krishna had noticed Arjun's overconfidence and wanted him to realize the facts.

"He is not just anyone Arjun! It is Karna! It will be most difficult to defeat." Krishna was worried. It showed in his voice.

"He must be having his weakness! Like his sons!" Arjun said.

"No, he is not a man who would be weak because of emotions. I have seen it myself. He is not that easy of a shell to crack. I tried once, and I failed. His belief in dharma is unbreakable, and his belief gives him dignity. And a man with dignity can never break easily." Krishna said, recalling the time when he tried to bribe Karna with the truth about his family!

"Then... now what?" Arjun said softly.

"The biggest mistake of a man's life is his biggest weakness!" Krishna said quoting the line his elder brother Balram had said to him once.

"That mistake can be the words he spoke in the court for Draupadi! Or that he stabbed Abhimanyu." Arjun suggested and searched in Karna's face for the answer. Krishna shook his head; he was thinking deeply. Since Draupadi had forgiven Karna, means that was not his weakness. Also, Karna stabbed Abhimanyu to free him from the torture that the Kauravas were making him go through. That was not at all a disadvantage. Then what? Krishna was now frustrated.

"Dam! this man had done no such crime that I can use against him! There

has to be something right." Krishna thought. Krishna wanted that weak point.

"He is the Parshuram's student and..." Arjun was saying something but was interrupted by Krishna.

"Yes! Exactly, he is Parshuram's student. How can I forget that? The curse, Of Course, the curse is his weakness." Krishna chuckled, and Arjun stood confused. He did not know what Krishna was talking about. He sighed and left the tent after some time. He had to defeat his greatest rival, anyhow.

✣ ✣ ✣

50 The Sun Sets

Karna began his day with the same ritual that he had followed all his life. He performed his puja and paid his salutations to Lord Surya, who was his father. The surrounding looked unusually dull, and the sun was lacking its heat and shine. Karna looked straight at the sun as always and recited his mantras. The seventeenth day of the war was to begin, and Karna was sure that this was the day he would face Arjun in the battle. Even if Krishna found ways not to make them fight like the other days, he would make sure to make the face-off inevitable. He also gave away alms; he did not miss this ritual any day. He had vowed to donate and give away his wealth in charity until he took his last breath and he was keeping his vow.

The previous night he did not sleep at all, he watched the lonely pole star shining in the sky and after that the sun coming up slowly up the horizon scattering its light all around the world signifying the beginning of a new day. As the sun came up slowly, Karna watched the sky change its colour; from purple to a lighter shade of blue. He smiled as the clouds formed different shapes up there around in the blue sky. The night before Kripa had left him alone to think, and he was happy to be left alone once in life.

He felt like he was filled with an unknown feeling of ecstasy. Last night had realized where he went wrong in life. That one night of silent thoughtfulness had given him liberation. He felt free from everything that had once bothered him so deeply.

Karna realized that he was angry; he was mad with himself, the people who were near him, his life, his mother, and his brothers. And staying mad with people who had perfect lives was the only way he knew how to cope up with the pain of his own not so ideal lives. Repressing misery and keeping it at bay was the only way he could get hold of the rage he felt inside. He realized how his anger was futile. He had a beautiful family to be with, yet he kept searching in vacuum the unreasonable identity of his life. How stupid he had been! And now what would it all matter? The throne, the respect, the struggle. Once he is dead, everything would end up being nothing. Death did not have dignity or honour. There was just a corpse left, a corpse that would be burned down into ashes and combine in the same soil the same Pancha tattva we are all born from. The endless cycle of life will begin again; the soul will find a new body, again, and again, a story of life will start. Was the anger of any purpose? No, it just gave him pure misery. He kept fighting himself and his people. Would it not be more comfortable all this while if he dared to forgive each person who wronged him? Life would be so much simpler than what it had been!

As the night had passed, the ground below him crumbled and so did the wall of hatred he had built around him. The memories of misery he carried turned into dust, and then he felt like he was floating on the surface of the water. So light, so free and so peaceful. Surrounded by nothingness, devoid of all colours, pitch black; he was breathing. Then like the sun comes up at dawn from the womb of darkness, filling light around, realization dawned, gradually slowly and softly wit crept into his heart, releasing him from a chain. The chain of sorrow and walking him towards the light of happiness like a mother walks her child, softly holding him.

"I am alone! But this aloneness is blissful. I am free! But this freedom is not scary. I can forgive you! This forgiveness is peaceful." was his heart's cry. That moment he heard no sound, just his heart spoke. "I am free, and this is what I have been wanting." The void he is in becomes so ecstatic. He knew he was one day going to sink to his demise. So be it, for there is peace after the struggle like there is rain after a thunder.

Was accepting death not bravery, it is! Because the freedom from fear of death is the true bravery of all times. When we stop fearing death, we reach into the supreme state of bliss, where there is nothing left other than peace. Our heart, body, soul, mind, every cell is clenched. This is the level of spirituality the yogis want to reach where your soul becomes a part of the Parmatama. You become Mrityunjay and Shiva. You become everything, and Everything is in you. Karna had reached that level of supreme bliss. There was nothing left, no anger; no want nothing. Just a duty to fulfil and then everything would end. And this end would be much more beautiful than his entire life.

Karna smiled, this smile was real, genuine, and for the first time, his happiness showed in his eyes. He walked away from the river bank and entered the battlefield on his chariot looking as handsome as ever; he stood tall on his chariot as the war began with the conch blown and the two parties clashing the seventeenth time on the field of Kurukshetra. This was the beginning of the most unforgettable day of the war of Kurukshetra. This was the day the last barrier had to fall off. Karna knew this was the last day he was going to live! Shalya was so confused to see the mostly sullen Karna smiling like a maniac behind him like Karna was ready to fight, Shalya was also as always prepared to demoralize Karna.

Shalya hated Karna so profoundly that he was ready to kill him anytime, but he could not help but admire him at times. He hated to admit it, yet he did respect him. Duryodhan had come to see his friend and said that he wanted to see his friend victorious.

"If I kill him, I lose, and if he kills me, then you lose Duryodhan." Duryodhan was confused hearing Karna but did not react. Karna was so different today that Duryodhan felt like he was almost meeting a stranger. He had never seen his friend so satisfied before. His smile was also different. Karna knew the outcome; he was doing his duty. He was fighting to win, but internally he had already gained the victory, and that victory was more beautiful than any other. Karna knew that on that fateful day, he was walking towards his death. He had his celestial bow in his hand, the Vijaya, given to him by his guru. He thought of the time when he had given up his kavach and kundal. Indra felt he could make up with an Indrastra, but he did not realize that when your head is cut, you do not cry for your hair. He had lost his defence that day and today was the day he would die.

He had done a brilliant organization of his army that day. His last war had to have Karna's touch, which meant perfection. The fury of war was real, and Karna knew this fight was unto death. Karna watched his sons, Satyasen, Sushama, and Vrishasena die in the hands of the Pandava side warriors. But today nothing could check his might. He passionately fought. He gave in everything that day, all the hard work and years he had spent to become the warrior he was today. He used all that he had in him. Witnessing the death of a child is the worst thing any parent would have to suffer in life, yet Karna stood unmoved, this was the day of the final trial, the trial of Dharma. Nothing could make him contemplate today.

Karna alone fought with hundreds. The army of the Pandavas was of not match to Karna. He overpowered them like clouds are removed during a stormy day! Yudhistir was the first one to face Karna that day. They had a fierce battle, and at the end of the duel, Yudhistir's chariot was smashed and his bow broken. Karna defeated Satyaki and others who came to help the Pandava. One arrow pierced Yudhistir's armour as well, yet it just wounded him; it was not fatal at all. When Yudhistir stood helpless and defenceless before Karna, Karna said "You are a noble Kshatriya, but a brahmin at heart. Do not challenge those better than you are. This Sutaputra has defeated you today even though you thought that it was impossible."

Karna then turned and left Yudhistir alone. Those words meant nothing for Karna. Those were just an excuse to leave Yudhistir and fulfil his promise to his mother. Unlike last time, he did not want to make a lame excuse. Bu Bhima did not know that and charged on Karna, he injured Karna so bad that the pain was on its extreme to be handled, yet he stood up.

"Crying over pain is an undoing of a Kshatriya..." Karna said to himself and stood up. He tried to take up his bow, but the pain was still making him shiver. The most surprising thing happened then. The King of Madra who hated Karna with his absolute power of existence turned the chariot in a new direction as he saw Arjun's chariot approaching. Karna was surprised and could not help but ask him Why?

"You are a brave warrior Karna, A generous man, brave, and a hero. I am so impressed with you that I cannot let you die in this state. Gear up and fight, like you always do." Shalya spoke. He had realized that no one on the battlefield would equal this man's qualities. He had been arrogant all this while but not anymore. He was himself a great warrior and knew the skills of Bhishma and Drona yet he could say not that he had seen a much better man who had outgrown the two best warriors of the land- Karna. When Karna gained his composure, Shalya took Karna towards Arjun upon his orders. On their way, Karna was stopped by Bhima and Satyaki. Karna soon got them out of his way and killed Dristadyumna's son. Yet again, Karna was trapped. This time by five warriors, Dristatyumna, Shikhandi, Janmajaye, Yudhamanyu, and Uttamaujas. Duussashan was trying to help Karna, but Bhima killed him as he had vowed. Bhima finally killed Dussashan who had pulled Draupadi by her hair years back. Karna was sickened as he watched Bhima kill Dussashan being killed mercilessly but had the man not done a heinous deed by touching a woman without her consent.

When Karna finally defeated the five men surrounding him, he faced Arjun. Many were holding their breathe as a shiver passed every warrior's body. The two greatest living warriors of the time were facing each other. On one side was Arjun and the other side was Karna and Death standing in between them. The face-off began- first there were just simple arrows, and then a divine weapon. Agni astra's to Varuna Astra's were shot from both sides neutralizing the effect. When the duel reached a deadly pitch, Karna called Takshak the naga to induce his powers in his arrow and aimed at Arjun's neck. Krishna saw this and hit Arjun's chariot, making it sink six inches lower in the ground. And hence the arrow by Karna hit Arjun's crown making it fall on the ground and also cutting off the flag of Arjun's chariot. This made Arjun rethink "Who is the better archer? Me or him?"

Arjun was able to create a force that pushed Karna's chariot hundred yards away and Karna's arrow was able to move Arjun's chariot barely ten yards away to which Arjun smiled. Krishna chided Arjun for his overconfidence. "Parth, remember you are pushing away his chariot with only him and Shalya on it. But if he can push away the chariot upon which Narayan stands that shows his brilliance. His chariot is surely easier to push away."

Krishna knew it would be impossible to kill Karna that quickly and hence he changed the direction of his chariot and went towards the emptier section of the battleground. Karna's chariot fallowed, but before it could move forward, the wheel of the chariot got stuck in a small ditch full of mud. No divine weapon could be used twice. Hence the Indrastra which was used on Ghatotkatch could not be evoked again. Karna was left with no Astra to protect himself. The Brahmastra was too dangerous, and he had promised to use it wisely. He stood utterly venerable. He had to take the wheel of the chariot out now, it was necessary. He continued fighting, still able to stop Arjun. He did not need Devi weapons to fight. He was capable of doing so without those weapons as well.

Karna realized that the wheel of his chariot was going down, and it needed to come out fast. Karna put down his bow and stepped down the chariot. He asked time to take out the wheel of the chariot from Arjun, but Krishna scoffed and said: "You were the one who stabbed Abhimanyu to death and so you have no right to talk about the righteousness of a warrior."

"I did it to free him of the pain and torture that the others were giving him. He was in immense pain, and I could not see him that way. He was struggling; every bit of his body was bleeding Vasudev. I did it to save him of that pain." Karna reasoned impatiently. Krishna's words hurt Karna deeply; he knew that his words were valid somehow. Then he could have refused to be there and tried to stop Drona, but he did not, not because he lacked the knowledge of right or wrong but because he was blindly following his dharma.

"No, you do not deserve to be given any time," Arjun shouted from behind Krishna, his eyes glistered with tears for his dead son. Karna recalled the time when he had returned his arrow as the sun had set before it reached Arjun. He did not want the world to say then that a Suta had killed a kshatriya by deceit, but today it would happen but in reverse. Arjun was going to kill Karna with treachery!

Karna ignored the two men and struggled with the wheels of his chariot that was deep in the ground. Arjun shot an arrow towards him, and Karna straightened to retaliate. He tried to evoke a weapon to counter Arjun, but he suddenly froze. He could not recite a single mantra, not even the Brahmastra's mantra. The arrow shot by Arjun missed him, but he realized what was happening. He recalled the words of Parshuram. "You will forget this knowledge when you need it the most." Was what the guru had said. Fate had started its game. It had started working against Karna. Then when he looked at his chariot wheel deep in the mud ditch, he recalled Bhumi Devi's curse. "I will one day hold back the wheel of your chariot. It will be your last day, living. The wheel would be stuck in the ground."

He stood there helpless, defenceless and lost. Just the way the brahmin had once said to him "You will also die helplessly." Every curse was being fulfilled. "Shoot him, this is the only chance to kill him, or else you will never be able to defeat him Arjun." Said Krishna to Arjun. "Victory is impossible for the Kauravas, but this man can defend the Kauravas alone for a long time. If not today then never."

"I am capable enough to fight!" Arjun said panicking.

"You can fight, but the truth is you cannot trounce him. You cannot ignore the fact that if you had it, you would have defeated him by now. But you could not! So, do it. Hence, if not now, never!" Krishna reasoned with Arjun to make him face the truth.

Arjun shot the Vayu Astra towards Karna. Karna smiled and watched the approaching missile towards him. He straightened up, his head held high, and his heart determined. The arrow pierced his armour straight on his chest, ripping through Karna's rib cage. Blood gushed out of his mouth and the wound as well. Karna fell on his knees, his head still high and a smile on his face. Even in his last moment, he did not lose his splendour. He looked towards the west at the setting sun and folded his shivering hands. He absorbed the last rays of the setting sun; his face glowed a strange light illuminated from within, his soul was glowing with the happiness of liberation. The unbearable pain that was blazing through his chest was making him shiver, yet he did not let even one teardrop fall from his eyes. He was smiling like he had achieved his ultimate freedom and his peace: the sun had set early that day, morning for the fall of the greatest warrior. Every single person from the Kaurava to the Pandava army stopped the moment Karna's body fell to the ground. Kunti mourned far away in the camp for her eldest son, the son she never acknowledged. The son, whom she never called her own. She sat there, weeping alone in the tent.

Karna's snuffled, he did not die instantly. Everyone watched the fallen man, but no one noticed Krishna slip out of the scene. Arjun's eyes were full of tears, and his guilt took over his body.

"Yatkarma Kritva kuruvech Karishyamshrachev lajjati.

tajgyayam Vidyusha Sarvam Tamasam Gunalakshnam"

If the conscience feels guilty about an act, the act is a sin (of Tamas quality)" These words told to Arjun by Drona crept into his mind. He realized what a sin he had committed. He watched Karna struggling to breathe. He then saw an old Brahmin walking towards Karna's body. It was unusual to see a Brahmin at a battlefield at that time of the day. He stopped near Karna's body and said "Oh! Daan Veer Karna, now in your last moments, I have come to you, will you give me something in charity?" The Brahmin said with folded hands.

Karna looked up at the man standing before him; a gasp escaped his mouth as he struggled to speak. He said "Brahman Dev, I do not have any material good to give today. But I will not turn you away, I have promised not to let anyone leave empty-handed." He was struggling to speak. The pain was evident in his voice. "Dev today I give all my virtue and good deeds that I have done all my life. All the fruit of my good deed to date is all yours! This is the only thing I have been left with to give you. Accept it and bless me." Karna said to the old brahmin.

A teardrop fell from Arjun's eyes, as he witnessed the epitome of keeping once promise before him. Karna's body was weak, in this last moment of his life he had nothing to leave this earth with but the virtue he had gathered and lived with all his life yet he gave it away without a second thought. The pain in his throat increased as he saw the mighty warrior struggle. His state made one thing clear that Arjun was not the most excellent archer in this world. Because if he were one, he would not need to kill Karna with deceit. The debate the society was going through for so long was finally over. The best archer lay on the ground struggling with his breadth. The brahmin shifted his form, and Krishna stood before Karna with folded hands, tears streaming down his eyes.

"You passed this ultimate test as well Karna. Amongst all the men present here, you are the true Kshatriya, a true Surya Vanshi!" Krishna said in a teary voice.

Everyone looked straight at Krishna, "Was Karna not a Suta Putra? Why is he referring him to be a Surya Vanshi?" murmurers erupted amongst all the people in the battleground. They all looked at each other, trying to get the missing piece of the puzzle. That was when they heard a woman call out Karna's name. Arjun turned to see Kunti running towards Karna. The Pandavas descended from their chariots and watched their mother run to Karna and place his head on her lap. Everyone stood surprised as to what was happening. Draupadi stood at a distance she had followed Kunti to the battlefield. Karna smiled and relaxed, with his head on his mothers' lap.

Soon Radha, Adhirath, Supriya, and little Vrishaketu came there as well. The old charioteer and his wife broke down at the sight of their son. A crying Supriya held little Vrishaketu close to her; the boy had tears in his eyes, seeing his father in such a state of pain. The same father whom he had seen standing tall and proud was laying flat on the ground in pain, blood streaming from his body.

"Even the thought of this is scary mother, but tell me why are you here for him?" Arjun said with his heart fluttering with fear of what his mother would tell.

"He is your elder brother son. He is the eldest Pandava. My firstborn son, the son whom I have made to suffer all his life because I was foolish." Kunti said sobbing. She recited the story of how, in her childish curiosity, she had used Rishi Durvasa's mantra and conceived Karna. Arjun fell weak on his knees next to Karna's body. His tears knew no bounds. "He promised me that with or without Arjun, I will always be called the mother of the five Pandavas," Kunti said.

Yudhistir and Nakul recalled Karna's words. Now they knew what those words meant. His threats were just hollow words, safety for his brothers. "Means he knew that he is out elder brother?" Yudhistir could not help but question even though it was all clear. The Pandavas sat there weak and broken. Arjun was dying internally. He had first killed Bhishma, his great grand uncle, then be a part of Drona's death, his teachers' death, and then Karna; his elder brother. Arjun wanted to make seance of the war he was fighting but all in vain. Victory would quickly come to the Pandava's now that Karna was going to die, but would that victory be of use that had come stained with their own brother's blood? What would be that victory when it will kill them each moment, it will just be a reminder that they had murdered their elder brother, who is considered equivalent to the father? The Pandavas recalled each time Karna had spared their life.

"God! Mother, what have you done? A sin is kept hidden, not something sacred. You kept him hidden all along even though he deserved the respect of being your son. He was the most Virtuous son any mother could ask for, mother! Why did you keep this truth a secret?" Yudhistir cried in pain "Oh! From today, may no woman be able to keep any secrets in life! May no woman hide anything." He cursed.

"Why did you not tell us, mother?" Bhima thundered, anger raging in his heart as he recalled how he had hurt his brother the same day.

"Wou...Would you fight me then, Bhim?" were the words Karna uttered. His breathing heavy.

"No! Why would we fight our brother?" Sehdev said in between sobs.

"So, there would be no dharma! If..."Karna stopped as pain made him shiver again. "If you would not fight, there would be no Dharma established in Arya Varta! And that would be much worse than my death Sehdev." Karna said to his younger brother.

Karna turned towards Draupadi who stood at a distance watching Karna in pain, her eyes were glassy and pain was evident there. "Panchali, I have washed the stains of insult I caused you that day in the court, with my death, and by blood." Tears streamed down from her eyes. A woman can get over a man but not the feelings that she once cherished for him.

"Arjun will you promise me to train Vrishaketu yourself and make him a formidable archer?" Karna asked a sobbing Arjun who nodded in agreement.

"I will brother, will make him the best, like his father!" Arjun replied.

"And Madhav, will you do me a favour?" Karna asked Krishna, who was standing near his foot. Krishna smiled.

"I want you to light my funeral pyre. That's it!" Krishna nodded and agreed to Karna's wish. Karna then glanced towards his old parents and his wife and child. Varushali was nowhere to be seen; she had shut herself from the entire world so that she could find a little courage to live. Supriya looked into Karna's eyes, and for the first time, tears flowed from their eyes. Supriya smiled to him, she had prepared herself to remain strong, but the emotional trauma that she felt that moment was enough to prove all the courage futile. Mental and Physical healing takes time. Your imagination can never help you prepare to face emotional trauma. It can just give you a little assurance but never the courage.

His little son came to his father and sat down; his eyes glistered with tears. "I love you father! I will miss you." The boy's voice sent a sudden wave of guilt amongst the Pandavas. He was weak at that moment, but a proud son. Karna caressed the face of his only surviving son and tears rolled down his face.

"I have to go now!" Karna's words were shaky, and Supriya fell on the ground. When he said those words before she knew he would come back. But this time he was going, leaving forever. There was no coming back after this. This was the end, the final journey.

For the first time, the Pandavas touched their brother's feet. Karna blessed them for the first and the last time ever. He closed his eyes, and with one sharp breath, he left this body behind. His soul left the body and then walked to his final journey.

The man who never lived in peace died in peace. Knowing well that he was doomed, he entered the battlefield. Fought for victory and never for revenge, met his tragic end, unarmed, the wheel of his chariot stuck in the earth. Perhaps the only man who was fighting to fulfil his dharma, maybe not from the side of Dharma but yes for dharma. His only reason to fight that mindless war was to seek the respect that he so well deserved. He could have easily chosen the easier path, but he did not. Not even Narayan could waver on his will and his promise.

He died with grace and dignity. He was the quintessential common man, who fought against, prejudice, cast system, injustice; seeking recognition for talent and respect. He was a rishi since birth, and his entire life was a saga of penance and austerity. No words could wash away the gloom that enveloped the Pandavas and Kauravas.

The man who was born with the rising sun died with the setting sun. The sun had set symbolizing the end of the most beautiful story of one man's struggle against every wrong that the world had been doing.

❋ ❋ ❋

Epilogue; The Funeral

The pyre was made on the banks of the river. The funeral preparations were made by Pandava's alone. When the ceremonies were over, Krishna lit the pyre, according to Karna's wish. The woman watched from far away as the pyre went ablaze. Duryodhan was crying frantically. The man who did not cry even upon the death of Bhishma and Drona was crying. Perhaps Karna was the only person other than his brothers, wife, and children, Duryodhan loved dearly. He was more than just a friend to him; he was the only person who opposed him and tried showing him reason every time he was doing something wrong—when he heard the story of Karna's birth he cried more.

"Why did you not speak before, Maharani? He was the rightful heir of the Kuru throne!" Duryodhan cried before Kunti. "I would have happily made him king if you spoke. He was more than just a friend to me; he was my brother. Like the other Pandavas, he was my cousin. Wasn't he? Then why? I would never let him fight his brothers, at least I would never do that to Karna. He was dearer to me than my life." Kunti cried more hearing those words. Her sons were beyond angry with her. She wanted to talk to them, but they were not ready yet.

Supriya watched the sorrow on the Pandava's face. The pain was genuine. Arjun sood frozen gazing into space, he seemed to have aged dramatically. The once-formidable warrior stood alone at a distance silent. His eyes lacked the usual twinkle and mischief; it was sad and dull. The tears had dried down, and the emptiness of his soul was visible.

Supriya wondered what he might be going through. Two brothers who were the most bitter rivals all their lives. They were fighting against each other every day, and suddenly they came to know that they were living with the same blood in their veins. She thought of the similarity between Karna and Arjun. Both were the bravest warriors the world had; both had a passion for archery; both had the same dream, to become the best warriors. How amazing it would be if the two would have been together instead of being against each other. The world would have sworn in the name of the two warrior brothers. Arjun sat near the pyre the entire night. When the flame's died down, Arjun stood up and gathered the ashes himself in a Kalash. He did it so lovingly that anyone would see the affection in just the way he looked at his brother's ashes.

It was funny that not at his birth but during his death, Karna was recognized as a Pandava. He gained the legitimacy that was rightfully his. The funeral was done in solemn grandness, fit for a Pandava. He finally gained the respect that he had been fighting for all his life. He had yet attained what he deserved. Everything that he desired came to him after death; recognition, respect, the real family, and the love of his brothers.

Arjun walked towards Vrishaketu and put his arm around his shoulder. Vrishaketu looked at his uncle and noticed the familiarity of the features his uncle shared with his father. Arjun hugged the boy and said "You are like my Abhimanyu to me Vrishaketu. I will teach you myself and make you the person my brother wanted you to become." Arjun's voice shook when he said the words "My brother". It reminded him of Karna's smile when he had shot the arrow, the lump in his throat became more and more painful.

For the first time, neither the Pandava's nor the Kaurava's were looking forward to the war. It was like suddenly everything made no sense the entire war felt useless to both the parties. They had both lost with the death of Karna. One had lost a friend, and the other lost a brother. The man who belonged nowhere was the man who belonged to both the sides.

"What was started has to end!" Krishna said, and the eighteenth day of the war happened. The Pandavas won and the Kaurava's were vanquished. Yudhistir became the King, who hesitated to sit on the throne where Karna should have been sitting. Arjun trained Vrishaketu, afterwards to become as formidable as his father, becoming the last mortal to gain the knowledge of the Devi weapons. The knowledge of those deadly weapons died with Vrishaketu.

Supriya forgave Arjun; she could not stain the memory of the man she loved so much with anger and rancour. She went back to Amravati, spending her days in the quiet hills of her birthplace. She lived with the memory of Karna every day of her life. Like Karna, she accepted her fate but not losing her dignity even for a bit. Varushali had committed Sati willingly, not wanting to live after the death of her sons and her husband.

"Not every woman is a Kshatrani Supriya. You, Draupadi, Maharani Kunti, and Gandhari grew up, with the mindset to live with pain and endure it whatever may come, we were not. We never knew this side of pain and the fearful face of war. You all grew up sending your father's and brothers to war. We did not!" Varushali had said to Supriya before her death.

Karna was the only man who had never succumbed to Krishna's evident charm. He had remained strong and kept his self-belief intact even though he stood against Narayan himself. His self-belief came from his unending dignity. His sense of duty and his strong will power. His whole life was an example for generations to come.

The most beautiful lives have the most painful journeys. Karna's was one of those journeys. The world watched the man become a warrior, but not many saw the thorns he was walking on with each day. And thus, the flawed man perfectly became the hero of an endless saga of sacrifice, promise-keeping, and loyalty. The most loved man of the story of Mahabharat. The man who did not inherit respect but earned it.

He was the Flawed Good Man!

* * *

www.ingramcontent.com/pod-product-compliance
Lightning Source LLC
Chambersburg PA
CBHW020122180726
47992CB00020B/1511